"Emma ... brings ... S ... Are The ... puzzle ... es and losses, tr ... an, the Fair Maid of Kent. An impressively researched and realistically rendered novel."

—Karen Harper, *New York Times* bestselling author of *The First Princess of Wales*

"*A Triple Knot* is a superbly written, evocative tale of Joan of Kent that captivated me from the first page and held me until the very end. With a deft eye for detail and a wonderfully authentic evocation of time and place, Campion has delivered what is certain to become a classic."

—Diane Haeger, author of *The Secret Bride: In the Court of Henry VIII*

"In this meticulously researched, richly detailed, and empathetic novel, Emma Campion skillfully brings to life the enchanting Joan, Fair Maid of Kent and First Princess of Wales, who was described by the chronicler Jean Froissart as 'the most beautiful woman in all the realm of England, and the most loving.' With a bigamous union bracketed by two secret marriages—one to the Black Prince—she makes fascinating reading for anyone interested in the glittering court of Edward III, where intrigue and danger walk hand in hand with royalty and love."

—Sandra Worth, author of *The King's Daughter: A Novel of the First Tudor Queen*

"Emma Campion's portrayal of Joan of Kent is exquisite. *A Triple Knot* dazzled, packed with all the romance and intrigue of Plantagenet England. Vivid, well researched, and beautifully written, Campion's Joan of Kent is a worthy heroine and one you will never forget."

—Ella March Chase, author of *The Virgin Queen's Daughter* and *The Queen's Dwarf*

"With grace, accuracy, and authenticity, Emma Campion brings Joan of Kent and her world to vivid, captivating life in *A Triple Knot*. Campion's fourteenth century is as detailed, gorgeous, and fascinating as a *millefleur* tapestry—her history is immaculate, her characters convincing, and Joan, who is sometimes glossed over in the history books as the Fair Maid of Kent and little more, is complex yet sympathetic as Campion clarifies all the questions that historians might raise about this enigmatic woman. This exciting, compelling historical novel immerses the reader until the very last sentence. I loved *A Triple Knot* and I look forward to more from Emma Campion!"

—Susan Fraser King, author of *Lady Macbeth* and *Queen Hereafter*

"*A Triple Knot* is the story of a steadfast love pitted against the cold, political maneuverings of fourteenth-century Plantagenet royals. Set amid the hardships and uncertainties of the Hundred Years' War, Emma Campion's portrayal of Joan of Kent and of the men who seek to claim her is masterful, sweeping us into a high medieval world that is both gracious and grim. Brilliantly imagined, this is a complex and ravishing blend of history, intrigue, scandal, and romance."

—Patricia Bracewell, author of *Shadow on the Crown*

"Emma Campion's Joan of Kent is a remarkable creation. She springs off the page, completely alive, growing in stature and confidence as her young years pass, steadfast in her love in spite of all adversities. Compassionate, loving, she moves with grace and splendor throughout. *A Triple Knot* is a brilliant, tender portrait of a passionate woman in dangerous times."

—Chris Nickson, author of the Richard Nottingham novels

A Triple Knot

A NOVEL

Emma Campion

B \ D \ W \ Y
Broadway Books
New York

Published in the United States by Broadway Books, an imprint of the Crown Publishing Group, a division of Random House LLC, a Penguin Random House Company, New York.

www.crownpublishing.com

Broadway Books and its logo, B \ D \ W \ Y, are trademarks of Random House LLC.

Library of Congress Cataloging-in-Publication Data
Campion, Emma.
    A triple knot / Emma Campion.
        pages cm
    I. Title.
    PS3568.O198T75 2014
    813'.54—dc23
    2013050619

ISBN 978-0-307-58929-3
eBook ISBN 978-0-307-58930-9

Printed in the United States of America

Cover design: Najeebah Al-Ghadban
Cover photograph: Malgorzata Maj/Arcangel Images

10 9 8 7 6 5 4 3 2 1

First Edition

For Anthony Goodman,
Professor Emeritus of Medieval and Renaissance
History at the University of Edinburgh,
a brilliant scholar and my dear friend.

Dramatis Personae

English Royal Family:

Edward II, king of England, son of Edward I and his first wife, Eleanor of Castile

Isabella of France—Edward II's queen (after his death, the dowager queen Isabella)

Edward III—king of England, son of Edward II and Isabella of France

Philippa of Hainault—Edward III's queen; daughter of William, Count of Hainault, and Jeanne de Valois; sister of Philip of Valois, king of France

Half brothers of Edward II:

Thomas of Brotherton, Earl of Norfolk, son of Edward I and his second wife, Margaret of France

Edmund of Woodstock, Earl of Kent, son of Edward I and Margaret of France

Margaret Wake—Duchess of Kent, Edmund's wife/widow

The Children of Edward and Philippa:

Edward of Woodstock (Ned)—Prince of Wales and Aquitaine

Isabella of Woodstock (Bella)

Joan of Scotland

Lionel of Antwerp—Earl of Ulster, then Duke of Clarence

John of Gaunt—Earl of Richmond, then Duke of Lancaster

Edmund of Langley—Earl of Cambridge, then Duke of York

Mary—died of plague

Margaret—died of plague

Thomas of Woodstock—Earl of Buckingham

(plus three who died in infancy)

The Children of Margaret and Edmund:

Edmund—died of fever within a year of his father's execution

Joan—the Fair Maid of Kent

John—Earl of Kent

A Triple Knot

Woodstock Palace
NOVEMBER 1338

Joan's father, Edmund, Earl of Kent, was beheaded when she was not yet four years old. Yet even after eight years, she had only to close her eyes to remember how it felt to rest her head against his chest as he walked her back and forth, singing of fair maidens and valiant knights, her young bones resonating with his clear tenor. No nightmare could steal up on her when in his arms, no shadow creature dare approach. His warmth melted all pain. Her most precious possession was his drawing of a white hart seated on a lawn, a crown for a collar attached to a chain that pooled in the grass beneath. He'd had it embroidered on his cloaks and jackets—white hart, deep green lawn, and gold crown and chain. All long gone.

Joan had found the drawing at the bottom of an old chest the previous spring. When she showed it to her cousin Ned, he confided that his grandam, the dowager queen Isabella, crossed herself whenever a white hart was mentioned in ballad or romance, a reminder of her part in Edmund's murder. She'd done nothing to stop the Earl of March, her lover and partner in rebellion, from beheading Joan's father for his loyalty to her husband, the king. Joan hated her for it.

Unfortunately, Joan and the dowager queen were bound to each other. To atone for his uncle's unwarranted execution, the present King Edward, Isabella's son, had taken responsibility for Edmund's widow, Margaret, and her children, making them part of Queen Philippa's household. A cruel charity for which Joan was no more grateful than was her mother.

So, through the summer and into the autumn Joan had bent to her work, embroidering the white hart emblem while keeping in her mind the charms of protection she'd learned from her nurse, Efa, and then, in secret, stitching the square onto a large banner, whispering a spell of power.

Now she and Ned watched from behind a screen as Isabella and her ladies spilled into the great hall, taking their seats in a circle at the south end, where there was morning light for their needlework.

Look up, Joan whispered, as if Lady Isabella might hear her. *In the rafters just there. See how the morning sun lights up the white silk and the gold thread. Feel the power of my father's blood that flows in me and my brother.*

But the dowager queen had her head down, fussing with her embroidery frame, fingering the threads in her basket, choosing a color. At last, as she waited for her servant to thread her embroidery needle, Isabella sat back to survey the hall.

Yes, Grandam, up! Ned whispered, crouched beside Joan. Though three years younger, he was taller than she, and considered himself her champion. Even against his grandmother. *Look up! Aha!*

Isabella's full lips parted, dark blue eyes widened, ivory skin blanched to a deathly pallor. "Who dares hang that abomination in this hall?" she hissed. The jet beads on her black velvet mourning flashed as she reared up, a thundercloud charged with lightning, stabbing at the air with a bejeweled finger, pointing to Joan's banner.

His daughter dares, Joan whispered, and shushed Ned as he started to laugh.

Oh, it was worth all her hard work to see that look of rage

on Isabella's face. But why must her mother choose that moment to enter the hall?

Countess Margaret believed the invitation to celebrate Martinmas at Woodstock was meant as a peace offering, and though she could never forgive what Isabella had done, she thought it best for Joan and her brother that they accept with grace. King Edward, Queen Philippa, and the two princesses were in the Low Countries, the eight-year-old Prince Edward, Ned, left behind as titular Keeper of the Realm, but the boy answered to his grandam, the dowager queen. Best to keep in her good graces at the moment.

Now Joan cringed to see her mother's expression of dismay as she, too, stared at the banner, then looked around, searching for her daughter.

Time to run, Ned whispered. *You first*.

Joan backed away from the screen, then turned to dash out the garden door. Outside, her puppy greeted her with his terrier's high-pitched bark. She had forgotten him in the excitement. "Bruno, stay!" she ordered pointlessly as she hitched up her skirts and took off running through the garden and into the woods, dodging branches and jumping over exposed roots. Bruno was in hot pursuit, but with his short legs he fell behind, his barks growing fainter as Joan ran.

Halfway down Ned passed her, laughing, flying like the wind on his long legs. "Grandam knows it was you!"

"Who else would it be?"

Ned waited for her beneath the great oak, their special place, taking her hands as she arrived and spinning her round and round until he had no more breath and they both slumped to the ground, leaning back against the wide trunk.

It was here, three years ago, that he had found her, crumpled on the ground in pain, her ankle so swollen that her soft boots were cutting into her skin. She'd run out of the hall in a temper, disgusted by her mother's passive acceptance of the dowager queen's condescension, determined to run away from court and never return. An exposed root had caught her foot, twisting her ankle as she pitched forward. By the time she reached the oak, she could only hop on her good foot. Climbing back up the hill to the palace was impossible. Ned had stayed with her as night fell, covering her with his padded jacket, shooing away the night creatures, sharing some dried apples meant for his horse, telling her tales of how she would be his queen one day, the most beautiful and powerful woman in the realm. They had been good friends ever since, delighting in elaborate japes and escapades, fierce in defending each other.

Now he was grinning ear to ear as he caught his breath. "That was better than Will's sword belt falling off in the mock tournament! Or the bees in Roger's helmet!"

"This was no jape but a reminder," Joan said. "Your grandam must never be allowed to forget what she did to my father." Her head pounding from the run, she leaned back against him, smelling his boy scent—sweat, earth, animals.

He sat up abruptly, jarring her so that she bit her tongue. "Ouch!"

"Shh! Someone's coming."

She heard it now, leaves rustling and twigs snapping. Someone followed their path, quick but light. They both stood, ready to run. But it was just little Bruno who burst from the brush, barking triumphantly, his tail wagging wildly as he rushed up to claw at Joan's skirts, then at Ned's leggings.

"Cursed cur!" Ned scowled and kicked the puppy. "He peed on my shoe."

Joan scooped Bruno up and held him close, letting him lick her face. "He's excited. He loves a good run."

Ned sat back down, still frowning, pulling off his shoe and reaching for the hem of Joan's gown to clean it.

She plucked her skirt out of his hand. "No! And don't pout.

You remind me of your grandam when you pout. Let me enjoy my victory for a while. Mother will sour things soon enough.".

As if she'd conjured her, Joan heard Countess Margaret far away, calling her name. Let her worry. She was consorting with the enemy. Joan looked at the still grumbling Ned—at such moments she disliked him as well. He, too, was the enemy. The whole royal family. They'd not even tried to save her father.

Hugging Bruno close, she started down the slope in the direction of the village. Ned might do as he pleased. She had just stepped out of the woodland path onto the village track when he caught up with her.

"Look." He pointed. "On the church porch."

It was a young couple in their best clothes, turning to each other to clasp hands, an older couple holding flowers and murmuring encouragement.

"Bran and Tam are finally exchanging vows!" Joan was fond of the two villagers, who worked in the palace kitchen on state occasions, good-naturedly looking the other way when the children helped themselves. "He must have had a good harvest."

They crept to the side of the church and peeked round the corner. As the man began to speak, Ned turned to Joan, taking her hand and echoing Bran's vow in his high voice, changing only the names, "I, Edward of Woodstock, will take you, Joan of Kent, as my wife." As Tam began, he whispered, "Now say your part."

Joan shook her head. "Vows are not a jape, Ned, and our parents will never agree." Besides, she was almost as good as betrothed to Sir Edward Montagu, a handsome man she liked very well, the youngest brother of her mother's lover. Bruno had been Sir Edward's pre-betrothal gift to her.

"Say it." Ned squeezed her hand too hard, and she saw the temper in his eyes. In such moods, he could forget his affection for her.

Rather than risk his lashing out she bowed her head, crossed her fingers on both hands, and rushed through the words, "I, Joan of Kent, will take you, Edward of Woodstock, as my husband."

"Now kiss me."

Bruno wriggled out of her grasp. She pecked Ned's cheek.

"We are now betrothed, and you cannot accept another gift like Bruno."

"I have him. I don't need another dog."

Ned gloated. "Grandam will be furious when I tell her you're my betrothed. It's better than your banner. Joan of Kent, Queen of England. Hah!"

He would make a mess of it. "No! You must promise me you'll say nothing to Lady Isabella. Nothing. Or she'll punish Mother." Joan knew that vows taken on a church porch might bind commoners, but not the son and cousin of the king, not Plantagenets. Even so, Ned's taunt would give the dowager queen an excuse to do something unpleasant. Or to make certain her son the king refused Edward Montagu in favor of a husband who would take Joan far away from home. Isabella hated the Montagus even more than she did Joan's mother. "Promise."

Ned made a face, but muttered, "I promise."

Joan went off after the scampering terrier.

Late in the afternoon the cousins walked back hand in hand, Bruno leading the way. At the bottom of the garden, they came upon a group of young boys from Ned's household.

One of them stood with head bowed, hands tied behind his back, wearing the white hart banner as a tabard. Joan halted, transfixed in outrage.

"Here stands before you Edmund, Earl of Kent, traitor to the crown!" another boy called out.

"My father was no traitor! Isabella and Mortimer were the

traitors!" Joan snapped, running forward to tear the banner off the boy. "How did you get this?"

"The dowager queen had it thrown out onto the midden, where a traitor's banner belongs," said the one who had spoken.

Ned reared back and punched him in the nose, then pushed the other three to the ground. "My uncle was no traitor. Apologize to Lady Joan!" His voice might be that of an eight-year-old boy, high-pitched, ill suited to such declarations, but as that of the future king it held power over the boys. They mumbled their apologies to Joan.

Ned handed her the banner. "Keep this as a reminder of our troth."

She recoiled. "It's a reminder of my father." Though it was now tattered and stained, a muddy footprint dulling the colors, she clutched it to her heart and turned away, stumbling on through the garden, blinking back tears as she slipped into the palace and prepared to face her mother.

COUNTESS MARGARET PACED HER BEDCHAMBER, SO ANGRY THAT her voice was like a growl. "Did I not teach you never to let her see your pain, daughter? Do you hear nothing I say? Where is your pride?"

"You'd let her forget him. I won't."

"As if reminding her might make her care? Teach her remorse? Pah! The prince put you up to this, didn't he? You are three years older than he is. Stand your ground! You're always the one punished, never him. And this time your own maidservant will suffer as well. Kit's confessed to bribing the servant to climb up there and switch the banners. I've sent her to the scullery. Mary will replace her as your maidservant."

"Mary the telltale tit?" Joan cried.

"Precisely. I will know what you do, to whom, and when."

Margaret took Joan by the shoulders and shook her. "How could you do this to me? Your safety is within reach. We need only the king's blessing on the betrothal."

"I cannot bear how she orders you about as if you're still in her household. She had Father beheaded!"

"And would have had me follow him to the block but for the child I carried in my womb. Mark me, we will both pay for this." Margaret left the room in a silken fury.

Joan pressed the banner to her heart and flung herself on the bed, cursing the boys who had ruined it. Not for a moment did she regret angering Isabella with the banner. She regretted only her mother's distress. She understood why Margaret so wanted her wed to a Montagu—Joan would be safe from the dowager queen's meddling in the bosom of the family Isabella so detested.

By the time her mother returned, Joan was ready to beg her forgiveness for jeopardizing her hard work.

Margaret hugged her daughter. "I understand how you feel about Isabella, my love. This banner—it is beautiful work. I shall clean it and mend it, then hang it in our hall." She kissed Joan's forehead.

"And Kit? Can I have her back?"

"No, Kit needs to learn her place." Margaret mimicked Joan's pout, but smiled to soften it. "Mary cannot be all bad. Bruno likes her."

It was true. He went to the maidservant as readily as he did to Joan, happy to be held by her. "All she knows how to do is gossip and find ways to avoid her duties."

"Her parents have been good and loyal servants. It is up to you to train her to be likewise."

A FEW DAYS AFTER MARTINMAS, JOAN WOKE SHIVERING. THE AL-cove in which she slept with her maidservant, Mary, was ice-cold.

"Bruno!" She sat up. "Where are you, my little hand warmer?" He was always there with her when she woke. But not this morning. "Bruno?" She flinched as her bare feet touched the wood floor. "Bruno!" Pulling on her fur-lined cloak, she padded out to the landing. Down below, Mary huddled with Ned and two of the kitchen servants.

"Have you seen Bruno?"

She saw it in their faces even before Ned stepped forward with the puppy, lying limp and lifeless in his arms.

"No!" she screamed, rushing down to them.

"We found him in the horse trough, my lady," said one of the servants. "In a bag weighted down with stones."

Joan sobbed as she took him. "Who did this? Who drowned my Bruno?" She turned on Mary. "How did he get out? Did you take him?"

"No, my lady."

Joan did not believe her.

"I'll give you another terrier," said Ned, pressing his forehead to her shoulder and trying to hug her.

She backed away from him. "I don't want another terrier. I want Bruno back!" Cradling the tiny lifeless form, she struggled back up to the solar and curled up against the wall by her bed, choking with tears, rocking Bruno and praying that he had not suffered.

She sensed her mother in the doorway before she spoke. "I heard what happened." Margaret crouched down to stroke Bruno between the ears. "Shall I have a servant dig a grave for him in the garden?" She kissed Joan's forehead.

"Not there. I'll find a place."

Joan emptied a little wooden coffer of the few toys she was not ready to give up. She wrapped Bruno in a length of soft wool and tucked him in, kissed his nose, closed the lid, her cheeks wet with tears. Her mother helped her carry him down to the chapel.

That is where Ned found her.

"I dug a hole for him out in the woods, beneath our tree."

It was a good burial place. Dressed warmly, they each took a handle and carried the little wooden coffin down through the woods to the great oak, where they buried him.

"I swear I had nothing to do with his drowning."

He'd guessed by her silence that she suspected him. Of course she did. He'd been jealous of Sir Edward Montagu, and Ned was one for a grudge. He and his grandam, the dowager queen Isabella, were Joan's only suspects. With Mary as helper.

"I don't want to talk about it now." Kneeling at the grave, she closed her eyes and imagined her father crouching beside her, his arm around her shoulders, protecting her.

Ned stamped his feet. "It's bitter cold."

"Go. I want to be alone with him."

Her mother had hot spiced wine and heated stones waiting when she returned.

"Can we dig him up and take him when we go home?"

"That depends on how long we are here. The dowager queen has not decided how long she will stay."

"I hate it that you do what she says. What if she was the one who ordered Bruno drowned?"

"Then we thank God that she did not do something worse."

"Like what?"

"I pray you never learn what that might be."

Joan blinked back tears. "Tomorrow I will talk to the servants. Someone must have seen or heard something."

"And what will you do with such knowledge? Could you hate Isabella any more than you do now? Would you believe it if fingers pointed to your precious Ned? I forbid you to pursue this. Bruno's drowning was a warning. It is time for you to grow up, stop all this nonsense about remembering your father. You've no idea—"

Joan dived beneath the covers and closed her eyes, letting her father's voice cradle her grief.

But he could not quell her fear—as heinous as was Bruno's murder, if this was Isabella's revenge she might not be finished with Joan, and even Edmund of Kent had been no match for the dowager queen.

2

Antwerp

Queen Philippa tossed aside her eldest child's letter. Such hateful words. Clearly, his tutor Burley had not seen it. Ned defying protocol was nothing new, but more disturbing when she and his father were not there in England to rein him in. They'd taken up temporary residence here in Antwerp while securing allies for an invasion of France. *Rest easy*, she coached herself. *He is shouting into the wind*. His beloved cousin Joan was even now on her way to Antwerp and a future far away from Ned. And he was powerless to stop it, his angry letter serving only to reinforce Philippa's confidence in the decision. In truth, though she missed Ned, she was grateful to be spared the witnessing of his tantrums. She would pray for Burley and the others in his household.

Philippa held out her arms to receive her infant son from his wet nurse, kissing Lionel's plump pink cheeks, drinking in his baby scent, stroking his feathery dark hair. He was his elder brother's opposite, dark where Ned was fair, compact rather than lanky, and so far docile and content. If there had been a time when her firstborn was docile and content, she had forgotten it. And yet one could not help but love him, such a beautiful child, so lively and quick. He had even proved graceful once his cousin Joan interested him in dance.

Joan. Philippa looked forward to the time, quite soon, when young Joan would cease to be a problem, and, with any luck, her mother as well. She felt no guilt in the matter. The girl had only her mother to blame. It was Countess Margaret who had soured Philippa on her children, Earl Edmund's children, whom she'd taken in as her own upon his death, in memory of their deep affection. Everything might have been quite different had he lived.

Indeed, the Earl of Kent's beheading a few weeks after Philippa's coronation had cast a pall over what should have been a time of celebration. She'd no doubt that her mother-in-law, the dowager queen Isabella, had arranged it so, to diminish Philippa's moment, loath to give up her crown to her son's wife.

Philippa had been fond of her husband's uncle. Edmund had escorted her at her coronation, his hand there to steady her when she hesitated, his words calming her, his confidence in her lending her strength. She'd known him since the time Queen Isabella had come to Hainault seeking the help of Philippa's father in her struggle against her husband and his favorites, the Despensers. Edmund had been kind to plump, plain Philippa even then, before anyone thought of her as Prince Edward's consort. In her eyes, Edmund of Kent was the quintessential royal—gallant, handsome, tactful. Neither of them had known that as he escorted her through the cheering crowds to Westminster he'd already been caught in the snare set by the rapacious Queen Isabella and her lover, Roger Mortimer, his arrest coming but days later. Philippa felt sick as she thought of his kindness, and his ignominious death.

Edmund was beheaded as a traitor for the crime of plotting to rescue his half brother, the deposed King Edward II. The Earl of Kent had believed a false rumor, spread by Mortimer's lackeys, that his half brother yet lived, that Edward had not died in prison as officially announced. Edmund believed he might yet save his brother's life, if not his crown, but he must act quickly, for Isabella and her lover would never rest easy while the king they had wrongfully deposed lived. So Edmund had written letters recruiting support for his plan to rescue Edward and remove him to the continent, where he might live out his days in spiritual retreat. And thus he'd fallen right into Mortimer's trap. The letters were intercepted, and Mortimer staged a sham trial, after which Edmund was dragged to the block.

Outraged that such a thing could happen to a member of the royal family, Philippa had rushed to her husband, begging him to intercede. But Edward, at that time king in name only, had been powerless to stop the sham trial, the execution, the gluttonous haste with which the two lovers had taken possession of all that had been Edmund's to reward themselves and their toadies. In the end, Edmund's death spurred Edward to rally his most trusted knights and bring down Mortimer, at last taking control of his kingdom. But, for Edmund and his family, Philippa's husband had found his courage too late.

In sympathy, Philippa and Edward had taken in Edmund's widow, Margaret, Countess of Kent, and her three young children, welcoming them to Windsor. How regal they had looked entering the castle gates—young Edmund and Joan on ponies, Countess Margaret on her fine filly, only the infant John riding in a cart with his nurse.

Philippa had mourned with Margaret at the sudden death from fever of her eldest son, Edmund, just weeks after joining her household. Doubly mourning, and with her other son, John, less than a year old, born but weeks after his father's execution, Margaret of Kent was a woman to be pitied.

But Philippa quickly learned that Margaret did not want her pity. The widow blamed all the royal family for her husband's execution. That she had drilled her five-year-old and her four-year-old to ride so proudly from the royal barge to Windsor Castle should have warned Philippa that Margaret meant to put on a show of strength.

"It was not enough to murder my husband—now you claim

my children as your wards? You rob me of authority over my babies and expect my gratitude?"

"It is for their protection," Philippa had explained.

"Protection from what? Their danger is from Isabella and her son, your husband. The two of them carry the mark of Cain."

"The mark of— Are you mad? Do you hear what you are saying? The king has taken you in—"

"Your husband is just as guilty as his mother in his uncle's murder. He stood back and did nothing."

"Mortimer "

"Edward was the *king*."

"It was not so simple as that, and you know it. He held no real power. Now he means to ensure that John and Joan have every privilege and marry well, with property."

"He can do that through me."

"The property was dispersed among his barons."

"How can he call himself king when he cowers before his barons?"

Philippa had given up the argument, telling Edward there was no reasoning with Margaret. "Let her retreat to one of her own residences with the children and sulk, I implore you, dear husband." Philippa had enough challenges with the dowager queen's dark presence; she did not need another bitter widow casting a cloud over her household.

But Edward's conscience dictated that Edmund and Margaret's surviving children be brought up in Philippa's household. And where her children were, so too, far too often for comfort, was Countess Margaret. Indeed, Edward provided her with a house in Westminster, close to the palace. Isabella referred to Margaret and her children as Edward's hair shirt. "What sort of king will you be if you fill up your court with the families of your enemies?" Isabella asked her son. "A martyr king?" Though Philippa rarely agreed with her mother-in-law, in this they were of one mind.

For seven years Philippa tolerated their presence, her patience tested not only by Margaret but also, of late, by her daughter, Joan, the subject of her son's angry letter. He claimed that Joan was his betrothed, that her place was by his side. At the age of eight, none of Philippa's brothers had cared a whit about girls. This was Joan's doing, no doubt peeved because Edward had rejected Montagu's bid for the girl's hand. She was of royal blood, of far more use to seal a foreign alliance. The girl was almost twelve years old. It was time to betroth her to someone who would take her far from the court. God willing, her mother would then withdraw to her estates and leave Philippa in peace.

And recently she'd seen her chance.

Edward had come storming into her chamber enraged. "The arrogance! He proposes a match between our Bella and his son!"

"Who, my love?"

"Bernardo Ezi, the Sire d'Albret."

"The Gascon. Yes, I have noticed how he struts. He enjoys knowing how much you need his men-at-arms to protect our lands in Gascony. But our eldest daughter?" Philippa saw the blue pulse in her husband's temple, a constant in those early days when they'd feared what the dowager queen Isabella and her lover, Mortimer, meant to do with him. They'd killed one king, what was another? Now Isabella wrecked her son's peace with her fierce ambition—that her son would win back the French throne, that her son, with her Capet blood in his veins, must once more wear the crown, not a Valois. "Bernardo Ezi knows he will not win a princess," Philippa assured her husband. "He is merely letting you know that he expects a prestigious match for his son. What of your cousin Joan? You told Sir Edward Montagu that you had a more strategic marriage in mind for her." She was pleased by how she'd managed to make it sound as if it were a sudden inspiration.

But Edward had hesitated, troubled. "Give my dear cousin over to a man I reject for my own child?"

"Because he is not worthy of a king's first daughter, Edward. But a cousin with little to offer but Plantagenet blood—it is a good compromise, I think."

"What of his dependence on alchemists, geomancers? Timeus the astrologer, who guides his every move?"

"Just because you put your trust in God and in your own deep wisdom, that does not mean another man is wrong to seek guidance in these esoteric practices, my love. Why, your own son has requested an astrologer for his household."

Edward pressed his temples. "God give me patience. This is Mother's doing. I've asked her not to lead Ned astray with her astral nonsense."

And Isabella does as she pleases, thought Philippa. "No matter what you think of Albret, you need him," she said.

"Albret will not bend unless he sees the advantage."

"Joan's Plantagenet beauty. She could be our Ned's twin. Albret must see her. And, as I've summoned some of my ladies to sail with your men-at-arms, it would be simple to include the girl."

Edward was softening, his shoulders easing. "Her mother won't like it."

"We do not need Countess Margaret to like it. The children are our wards. Of course, I will look after Joan as if she were my own daughter. I will assure Margaret of that."

Lionel began to squirm in Philippa's arms, pulling her back to the present, and she looked down at him. "Have I ignored you, my sweet? Forgive me. But it is a good plan, n'est-ce pas? The only flaw is that your grandam Isabella will think I am granting her request to exile young Joan for flying the white hart. On the contrary, I applaud the girl's boldness. Earl Edmund *should* be remembered. Oh, what I would give to have seen Isabella's face!" Philippa sighed as she felt a dampness. Time to hand Lionel back to the nurse.

3

The Channel
AUGUST 1339

The cog felt alive beneath her, its planks shifting, groaning as it rode the waves, its sails, open to embrace the wind, clapping, sighing, clapping, sighing. Joan clutched the rail for balance, so that she might gaze up into the dome of stars. Could God see her there, a speck on a speck floating in the vast, churning darkness? Would he notice if a wave reached over the rail and washed her out to sea?

Shivering as she thought about how far she was from all she'd ever known, Joan put her hands over the square of embroidery sewn into her bodice. Too stained to clean, too tattered to repair, the banner had been put in the rag pile after she cut out the emblem. Through the winter Joan and her mother had worked on another, hanging it in the hall of their home in Westminster on Easter morning. *You are ever with us, Father. Watch over me now. The dowager queen thinks to exile me. I pray you, make it not so.*

One of the crew approached, lantern held high. "Milady." He bobbed his head and walked on, maneuvering past the barrels and coils of rope lining the edge of the deck with a rolling gait that adjusted seamlessly to the pitching of the ship on the waves.

"They call them *sea* legs."

Joan turned too quickly toward the voice and lost hold of the rail.

Sir Thomas Holland steadied her. "And when they disembark they must readjust to their *land* legs." Two dimples formed on either side of his mouth when he smiled. It was too dim to see them now, but Joan had spent a great deal of the past week watching for them to appear. He was the captain of the guard escorting the queen's ladies to Antwerp, a knight of the king's household.

"Sea legs." She smiled back, grateful that he could not witness how she'd blushed at his touch.

"I imagine you came out here for some peace."

"I did, but from the sickness in the cabin, not from you, Sir Thomas." She'd spent hours working alongside Lady Angmar in the crowded space, holding the heads of the seasick women, passing the buckets of bile to the two maidservants still standing, disciplining her own stomach to ignore the stench.

"Then if I promise not to bore you with unnecessary chatter, might I have the pleasure of your company with a little wine, bread, some cheese?" He patted the pack slung over his shoulder.

She imagined he'd been ordered to watch over her, but no matter. "I would be grateful for a companion. And food." Though she'd used the excuse of a queasy stomach to escape into the fresh air, she was actually hungry. But even had she not been, she would have pretended interest, anything to claim the handsome knight's undivided attention.

He piled up sacks for their seats, just at the edge of the pool of light from a lantern, then extended a hand to assist her in settling down, all without a word, as he'd promised. They ate and drank in quiet companionship, the lantern's sway moving them in and out of shadow. He'd created a place of comfort in the darkness.

Restored, she broke the silence. "It's so peaceful, with all but some of the crew asleep."

"It is." He shifted to face her, and she felt herself blush yet again. "I was too hungry to settle," he said. "And you could not endure the cabin, eh?"

"It stinks in there. And Lady Angmar wanted me to watch over the others while she slept."

"So you escaped."

"I said I felt ill and needed air." She sighed. "Being the strong one can be a curse."

A particularly large wave set the lantern swaying wildly, and for a moment Sir Thomas's face was in the light. His dimples were showing. "Always providing support, never receiving it," he said.

"You, too?"

"How else would I know? Is this your first time away from your family?" She nodded. "You are very young."

"Lady Wake offered to escort me. I begged Mother to agree. Aunt Blanche would make it an adventure."

"And Countess Margaret balked at the thought of it."

She laughed. "Yes."

"Blanche of Lancaster is your aunt? You sound fond of her."

Lancaster. What had possessed her to mention that family? Joan could not think what to say. The Hollands had no love for the Lancasters, whose men-at-arms had murdered Thomas's father. Sir Robert Holland had been the Earl of Lancaster's most trusted vassal until he went over to King Edward II's side when the earl rebelled against his sovereign. The Lancasters put the blame for the earl's capture and execution on Sir Robert, calling him a traitor. To them, loyalty to one's immediate lord came before loyalty to one's king. Sir Robert had thought otherwise. Several years later, men who had served the earl attacked and beheaded Sir Robert. They'd gone unpunished.

"My father was falsely accused of treason and beheaded as

well," she said, crossing herself. "I am sorry I mentioned my aunt."

"You need not be. I have fought in the field alongside her brother the Earl of Derby and consider him an honorable comrade-in-arms. My father was under the protection of your uncle Norfolk, and it was Queen Isabella who saw to the welfare of my family after Father's death. So our stories are entwined, for better and for worse." He offered her the wineskin. She shook her head, already fighting sleep to spend more time with him. "You must have been but a baby when your father was executed," he said. "Yet I sense that you mourn him."

"I'm not so young as that." She hoped he did not see her so. "I remember being in his arms as he sang and paced. He had a beautiful voice, and his drawings are full of life." She described her father's sketch of the white hart he had taken as his personal emblem.

"And so now it is your personal emblem?"

She had not thought of that. "Yes, I think it is."

"Do you have more of his drawings?"

"Yes. Sketches of my mother when she was younger, trees, two knights jousting, people's faces."

"A treasure hoard."

"It is." She smiled to herself. "What was your father like?"

"Loud, funny, quick to anger but equally quick to forgive."

"You smile when you speak of him. He must have been a good father."

"He was seldom home. But, when he was, all the household went about their tasks in good cheer. What do you like about your aunt?"

"She encourages me to think for myself."

"Ah. I see why your mother might be wary of your spending too much time with her."

"Mother says that thinking for myself is what earned me this exile. I angered the dowager queen."

Without having planned it, she found herself telling him all about the banner into which she'd sewn charms of protection and power to taunt Lady Isabella. He laughed in all the right places.

"It speaks well of Prince Edward that he assisted you. He must be a good friend."

"Most of the time."

"I should think that act of rebellion was quite satisfying."

"For an afternoon. But it was not worth losing my puppy and being sent away." She chose not to mention that she'd lost a suitor as well.

"The dowager queen took away your dog?"

"Someone drowned Bruno a few days later. I don't know that it was done by her order, but who else would do such a thing?"

"That was a vile deed." He was quiet a moment. "Who taught you charms?"

"My nurse, Efa."

"She sounds a worthy traveling companion."

"Mother sent her away long ago. She said depending on charms weakened me."

"What do you think?"

"I think one can never have too much support."

They were quiet awhile, looking up at the stars.

"You called this an exile, but it might still prove an adventure," Thomas said.

"Mayhap." She tried to stifle a yawn, wanting more time with him, enjoying how he listened to her and took her seriously. But the wine had relaxed her too much.

"Will you rest out here on deck? It's rough, but better than the cabin. I'll watch over you."

"When will you sleep?"

"In the field, we learn to sleep lightly."

He offered his pack for a pillow, and, warmed by the wine

and his presence, she tumbled down into dreams. Sometime in the night a ship's cat curled up in her lap, its chin resting on the back of her hand, just like Bruno. She woke whispering his name, then ached to remember that it couldn't be him.

"Is the cat bothering you?" Sir Thomas sat just beyond reach, in the lantern light.

"No. He's nice. He just reminded me of my Bruno."

She stroked the cat's soft ears.

"A sip of brandywine to help you get back to sleep?"

She shook her head, finding all the comfort she could want in Sir Thomas's presence. She closed her eyes, conjuring his dimples and the cleft in his chin. The ship's motion rocked her back to sleep. She dreamed that she offered Sir Thomas her colors for a great tournament. He kissed her hand. And Ned . . .

Lady Angmar's shrill voice startled her awake. The deck was bathed with dawn light.

"Mother in heaven, Lady Joan is not in the cabin. No one has seen her. . . ."

"She is here, my lady. Her sickness eased quickly out here in the air, so I offered to watch over her as she slept on deck." Sir Thomas spoke softly from someplace very near.

"May God bless you." Lady Angmar crouched down beside Joan, giving her a gentle shake. "Land has been sighted, and the men-at-arms are stirring, Lady Joan. Come refresh yourself. I trust that, now we are close to land, you will not sicken in the cabin."

The cat arched its back, stretched, and slipped away. Rising with reluctance, Joan thanked Sir Thomas. "You are my champion," she whispered.

"It is my pleasure, my lady," he replied, with the soft laugh of a confidant.

Joan rushed through her grooming and instructed Mary to see to her things, then hurried back on deck, hoping she might exchange a few more words with Sir Thomas. She found him at the rail among those watching as the cog navigated the River Scheldt. She squeezed in beside him.

"Antwerp Castle," he said as they passed a high stone wall encompassing many grand buildings. "And the soaring tower belongs to the church of St. Michael's Abbey, which will be your home for a while." He pointed out a boat with King Edward's banner rowing out to an elegant ship at anchor.

"I don't recognize the ship's banner," said Joan.

"They are the arms of the Flemish city of Ghent. It is said that the Duke of Brabant has banned the city captain, Jacob Van Artevelde, from Antwerp. So when Van Artevelde has commerce here he conducts it on board his ship."

"What threat is a merchant to the duke?" Brabant held great power in the Low Countries. His eldest daughter was wed to Queen Philippa's brother, William, Count of Hainault.

"As the head of the captains of Ghent, he led an armed rebellion of the militias of his city, Bruges, and Ypres that wrested power from the Count of Flanders. Brabant takes no chances."

"And King Edward? What is his business with this dangerous rebel?"

"Van Artevelde holds the key to the men-at-arms and wealth of Flanders. A valuable ally against France."

"Is it right that King Edward should bow to the edict of the Duke of Brabant and row out to pay court to a commoner? How can a king so humbled think to win the crown of France?"

"It is unwise to speak so when you might be overheard, my lady," Thomas said quietly.

He was right, and, considering her father's end, she should have more care when voicing opinions that might be construed as treason. Nor should she put Sir Thomas at risk. They had much in common.

"Forgive me for presuming to advise you, my lady," Sir Thomas said, startling Joan from her uneasy thoughts.

"No, I thank you. These are treacherous times for us all. I must keep my own counsel."

"Or speak quietly and in private with friends."

"Such as you, Sir Thomas?" she asked boldly as the crew rushed about them, ready to drop anchor.

"I am honored that you count me your friend, my lady. I regret that for the nonce I must bid you adieu, but Her Grace's houschold is part of the king's while here, so I hope to have the pleasure of your company often before the campaign."

"May God guide you and watch over you, my champion."

Joan watched him join his squire, Hugh, a freckle-faced young man who glanced back at her with interest as he shouldered his pack and Thomas's, bowing to her with an embarrassed grin when he found her eyes on him. She smiled back, and prayed that he took good care of his lord in the battles ahead. She was already inordinately fond of Thomas.

4

Antwerp
AUGUST 1339

The king's men were lodging in Antwerp Castle, their numbers too great to inflict on abbey or town. As captain of the company escorting the queen's ladies, Thomas spent the better part of the day overseeing the movement of men and arms from dock to barracks. He found the townsfolk wary of the muster of English men-at-arms, requiring careful bartering for wagons and extra hands, and by the time he relaxed in the tavern outside the castle gate with some of his fellow captains who'd been longer in the town, he expected to hear much growling about skirmishes between the townsfolk and the soldiers. And so he did. And more. His fellow knights did not seem to like Jan, Duke of Brabant.

"We've been too long on our arses," said Guy, downing a tankard and shouting for more. "And we've not been paid, not in coin or booty, while the king barters with the duke, that treacherous knave."

"Brabant had the gall to hold the earls of Derby and Salisbury hostage until fully paid his bribe," said Piet.

England's potential allies demanded huge bribes for fighting against France, their neighbor and, in some cases, their liege lord.

"The royal family as well," said Roland. "Brabant's ships

were manned and ready to prevent the queen's departure while the king was in England insisting that Parliament bleed their countrymen to satisfy the duke's greed. Holding hostage our queen, sister to Brabant's own son-in-law! There is no honor here."

"And the planned campaign?" Thomas asked. "Will the duke at least have his army march with us then?"

"Hah! A token number, mayhap, but it's for us to prove to them our commitment and our strength."

"Sounds like we need to win a battle," said Thomas. He drained his tankard and held it out to the serving wench for more. He did not like the smell of this. Nor the bearing of the two knights in the livery of Brabant approaching their table, swearing loudly about the English who were drinking without paying. In the brawl that ensued, Thomas learned that his fellow captains were in good fighting form, besting the Brabanters. Throwing some coins on the table that he could ill afford, Thomas and his friends limped out into the night, seeking solace in a far inferior brew at the barracks.

Afterward, lying on a cot in a cold barracks room, he found himself thinking of the previous night, watching over Lady Joan. He loved her contradictions, the courtly courtesy and sense of privilege mixed with the passion and vulnerability of a child. *May she remain so uniquely herself as she matures*, he prayed. *May nothing daunt her*.

St. Michael's Abbey, Ghent

JOAN'S COMPANY OVERWHELMED THE HALL OF THE ABBEY'S GUEST-house, the servants and ladies jostling for space. But seven-year-old Princess Isabella was a blur of rose silk and purple ribbons as she dodged beneath elbows to push through the crowd, emerg-

ing with arms outstretched to embrace Joan. "I've waited weeks
for you! What kept you? You were to be here before my sister
departed." Her younger sister, also a Joan, had gone to Munich
for her betrothal to the son of Frederick, Duke of Austria. The
women with whom Joan had traveled from England were filling the gap in the queen's household left by the five-year-old
princess's entourage. "Were you attacked by pirates?"

Joan shook her head. "No pirates. Merely muddy roads and
our ship becalmed for days in the Ipswich harbor. I've missed
you, Bella."

The princess kissed Joan on each cheek, then hugged her
tight. "It is so *boring* here when there's no one to share it with."

Before Joan could catch her breath, Bella led her away to the
nursery to meet her infant brother, Prince Lionel.

"MARY, YOU'RE HURTING ME." JOAN GRABBED THE COMB FROM HER
maidservant's hands. With so little sleep, her patience was thin.
The infant Lionel had kept her awake with his shrieks, the wet
nurses and servants helpless in the face of regal colic. Mary had
dark shadows beneath her eyes as well, but that did not excuse
the pain she inflicted with a comb.

"Fetch my shoes," Joan commanded as she reached up to
comb her own hair.

Bella plucked the comb from Joan's hand and gave it to her
lady's maid. "Sandrine is gentle."

Joan sighed with relief after a few strokes. "What is the occasion of this dinner?"

"Nothing special. I suppose Father will announce that his
war council has agreed to his plan to march south into Cambrai,
crossing the border into France. You will meet Marguerite of
Brabant, the second daughter of the duke. If the pope agrees
to the betrothal, she'll be our next queen. But that's old news."

"Not to me. Ned is to be betrothed to Marguerite of Brabant?" Joan's heart skipped a beat. "Really?"

"I *know*. It should be you. But Father *needs* the duke. You
hadn't heard?"

"Does Ned know?"

"Mother has given Grandam the task of telling him."

Would he tell his grandmother of their vows? It would be
like him to taunt the hateful old queen. If so, Joan prayed the
dowager queen merely ruffled his hair and reminded him of
his duty to the realm rather than taking the betrothal seriously,
else Joan and her mother, perhaps even her brother, would pay
a heavy price. Ned gave little thought to how his speech affected
others.

"At first it was to be a double match," Bella was prattling,
too caught up in revealing the news to be bothered by Joan's
silence. "Ned and Marguerite, you and Marguerite's brother
Henri. But the duke thought one Plantagenet was enough. So
you are still available."

"Available. Like merchandise." Joan felt dizzy. "Is Marguerite pretty?"

"No. She has pretty hair. But her eyes and mouth are too
tiny for her round face, and she has too many chins." Bella dem-
onstrated by pulling in her chin until she coughed. Joan forced
a laugh. "My brother will not be pleased. Even so, if the pope
agrees to the union, Father will see that it is done." Bella sighed.
"Nothing will ever be the same with Ned and my sister married, and, if Mother has her way, you too."

"And you? To whom are you promised?"

"No one. I am to be held in reserve."

"Fortunate you. As long as you are small enough to sneak
about, you will remain the queen of rumor."

"But I'll have no one to share it with."

"I wish your mother had agreed to Sir Edward Montagu's

suit. I like him. He's handsome and loves to dance. I could have been happy with him, and I might have stayed at court with you."

"Mother had nothing to do with that. It was Father who put a stop to it. What would he gain in giving you to the Montagus? William Montagu is already his closest friend, and absolutely loyal."

So Bella did not know of her grandam's part in the decision.

Sandrine held up a mirror for Joan to see her work. Two braids entwined with gold thread and pearls held Joan's hair back from her face and looped round a gold circlet from which a small pearl pendant hung down her forehead.

"Oh! How lovely," Joan whispered, smiling sincerely for the first time that day. "Mary, I hope you were watching how Sandrine did this. Mary?" Her servant had fallen asleep on a stool by the door, Joan's shoes forgotten in her lap.

Sandrine fetched the shoes.

"Your mother might have sent you with some new gowns," Bella said. "That one's tight and a little short." She leaned close to whisper, "And why did she send you with Mumbling Mary? You need a lady's maid."

"She says that, as your mother ordered me here, she can pay for new gowns or a lady's maid." Joan resented her mother for it, and Bella for erasing the speck of confidence she had found in her reflection.

"Mother pay for it? She says Parliament has left us begging. Both crowns have been pawned to bribe our allies. You'll have nothing from her."

Perhaps Joan should be grateful. Her mother's meanness might keep suitors away. Except that the king was desperate.

Bella swept a bow and extended her hand. "Might I have the honor of escorting you to the great hall, Lady Joan?" she said in the lowest key she could manage.

Joan took Bella's hand and twirled her around, then, hand in hand, they hurried off.

A raucous swirl of color greeted them in the crowded hall. "We'll be able to see from atop a bench." Bella had a servant lift her up onto one near the door, then Joan. With much giggling, she pointed out the French fashion some of the young men were wearing—short jackets that revealed the shapes of their buttocks, ballock-knives hanging over their codpieces. "Lady Lucienne says if you've as yet no fortune, display the goods."

Lucienne, Lady Townley, was the liveliest of all the queen's ladies, a songbird among the crows. She was so out of place in the household that Joan's mother believed the aged and infirm Lord Townley must pay the queen handsomely to keep his wife in the thick of the action so that he might have peace on his northern estates. Bella, Ned, and Joan believed Lucienne was the queen's spy among her fellow courtiers, but so far she'd evaded their attempts to trap her. It was true that her husband denied her nothing—when she traveled, she required a large cart and a dozen packhorses to accommodate her wardrobe. What Joan and Bella liked best about her was her irreverent wit and her refusal to shelter them from the salacious goings-on at court.

Bella exclaimed over the prancing ponies and wondered how some of the younger women ever dared bend over, their bodices were laced so tight and cut so low. "There is Jan, Duke of Brabant." She pointed to a squarely built man in a calf-length houppelande of green brocade with deep blue trim, a peacock feather in his hat. "That is not a friendly but a cunning smile."

"I will remember that."

"And the young woman surrounded by Mother's ladies is Ned's future queen, Marguerite, daughter of the cunning peacock."

Ned's future queen had a plain, though pleasant, face, but in her bright yellow silk gown with slashed sleeves, revealing a deep green silk beneath, she seemed elegant, regal. "How old is she?"

"Sixteen. But look, follow her gaze."

It led back to a strikingly handsome man talking to Marguerite's father. Though his jacket was not cut so high as to be lewd, he wore it to such advantage that Joan felt herself blush to look on him, standing with chest thrown out, chin up, one leg slightly bent in front.

"The Gascon stallion," Bella whispered. "Can you blame Marguerite for adoring him?"

Dark hair, dark eyes, chiseled face, full lips, his garb sable velvet but for a crimson hat. "Who is he?"

"That, cousin, is Bernardo Ezi, Lord of Albret, a powerful Gascon. Another man Father needs on his side. He is said to have asked for *my* hand. For his son. But Father will not hear of it. I'm for someone grander. A pity. If his son is half as beautiful . . . Oh, look. There is someone far too skinny for the short fashion." Bella giggled.

Joan glanced at the young noble, whose leggings hung like empty sacks, but her eyes were drawn back to the Gascon stallion, then to a dark-haired, olive-skinned beauty in deep green silk slashed with cream and decorated with seed pearls headed in her direction.

"Lady Lucienne!" Joan called.

Perfuming the air with roses and spice, Lucienne bowed to Princess Isabella and whisked Joan away, keeping up a merry banter about the guests to put her at ease. She introduced her to German lords, dignitaries of Antwerp, Vilvoorde, and Brussels, as well as to one of Queen Philippa's brothers and an elderly aunt. Queen Philippa herself took over to introduce Joan to the duke, his sixteen-year-old daughter, and the Sire d'Albret before handing her back to Lucienne.

"Why was Her Grace so keen for me to meet the Gascon stallion?" Joan asked Lucienne.

Lucienne's laugh was wickedly throaty. "Never let Her Grace or the other ladies hear you refer to him that way. Is that all Princess Isabella told you of him? Not how important he is to His Grace in Gascony?"

"Yes, but what is that to me? Is he peddling an heir?" Joan pretended she did not know where this might be going, curious to hear Lucienne's take.

"Aren't they all? Or a blushing daughter. Faith, I know little of his family but that his wife, Lady Mathe, was disappointed to be married off to someone not remotely related to Philip of Valois, no matter how handsome. How cold-blooded she must be. He is beautiful, is he not? Like a god, so . . ." Lucienne's voice trailed off as Sir Thomas Holland entered the hall.

Joan's heart dropped to her stomach as she watched Lucienne watching Sir Thomas all the way to one of the lesser tables, where he joined his fellow knights in the king's guard. How could she hope to compete with the beautiful and experienced Lady Lucienne?

"Sir Thomas and I shared a pleasant meal on deck the last night aboard ship. After everyone slept," she said with more than a little venom.

Lucienne looked down at Joan as if she'd forgotten who she was. "Did you?" She wrinkled her nose. "How kind of him. You must remind him of his little sisters."

That jibe had certainly come back to prick her. "Do you know him well?"

A lusty laugh. "I know every part of him very well indeed. When my dear Townley breathes his last . . ." She wiggled her brows as she took Joan's hand. "But to the matter at hand. We must find your place at the high table."

All the fun had gone out of the day. "I was hoping to sit with Princess Isabella." To whom she could make her moan.

"Not today. Her Grace wishes you to sit between Marguerite of Brabant and—" Lucienne's violet eyes sparkled with glee as she mouthed *the Gascon stallion.*

"I would prefer Bella."

Ignoring the comment, Lucienne swept her over to the bench, ensuring that she had sufficient cushioning and instructing the servant to make certain that Joan had only watered wine. "For we do not want you to embarrass yourself adoring the Sire d'Albret," she whispered. And, with a throaty chuckle, she was gone.

Marguerite of Brabant slipped into place beside Joan. As the first course was served, the two exchanged pleasantries, then Marguerite turned to address the person on her other side.

"My lady, have you tasted the mead?"

Joan had not noticed the deep resonance of his voice when the queen introduced them. It was like a warm hand on her heart. She turned to the Sire d'Albret. "No. Mead is too strong for my liking."

"Too strong?" He reached beneath her hair, gently lifting it to the light, then arranging it on her shoulder, his hand brushing her neck. "You have the Plantagenet coloring and beauty, Lady Joan. Even young as you are, I see the woman who will be, a pearl beyond price." He proffered her his mazer, holding it close so that she smelled the honey. "A taste to bring a blush to your cheeks." He held it to her lips and tilted it. She sipped, feeling the heat.

He smiled, lines radiating from his eyes. "Ah, another course." He abruptly turned away, breaking the spell.

Joan had been holding her breath. Now, with the warmth of the mead coursing through her, she breathed deeply and stared down at her untouched food, her neck warm, her heart racing. She managed somehow to make idle conversation with Marguerite, though in her mind she was reliving how Albret had touched her hair, her neck, how strange he'd made her feel.

By the time the meat courses gave way to savories, even the watered wine was too much for Joan and she pushed her chair a little away from the table, preparing to withdraw with the excuse that it had been a long, tiring journey.

Only then did Albret turn back to her. "Rest well, my lady." He kissed the top of her hand, then turned it over, brushing her palm with his lips, her fingers perforce stroking his face.

"My lord," she breathed, withdrawing her hand, confused. Why was he behaving so with her? Did he mean to tease? Whispering her apologies to Marguerite, she fled the hall without a backward glance.

AT THE END OF THE FEAST, QUEEN PHILIPPA INVITED JAN, DUKE of Brabant, for a walk in the garden while the king engaged young Marguerite in his round of farewells. Philippa smiled to look on them—Edward so tall, so regal, leaning down to say something to make the young woman laugh. Marguerite's eyes sparkled, and she seemed to grow taller as she crossed the room on Edward's arm.

Philippa, too, had her hand through the arm of a man bent on charming her, but she knew that, unlike her husband's, the duke's good humor was a mask meant to shield him from scrutiny. Despite the proposed betrothal, Jan of Brabant could not yet be counted on to support Edward's cause when the time came. Until the pope gave his blessing to the marriage of Marguerite and young Edward, and the Parliament back home raised the additional funds needed to secure this man, he was easily wooed back to Philip of Valois's side, supporting him as the reigning and rightful king of France.

When they had passed through the yew hedge and were no longer in sight of the guesthouse, she turned to him.

"Is Lady Marguerite happy with the prospect of being the future queen of England and France?"

Jan continued to smile. "She will be when she ceases her worrying about how I shall manage without her. Marguerite was still young when her mother died. It forced her to mature too quickly, running the household and acting as my hostess.

In truth, I fear I kept her with me too long, out of selfishness. It is time she had her own household. At sixteen, my wife was already a mother. My daughter will do her duty, Your Grace, never doubt that."

Fortunate parent to be so certain of his child's obedience. Philippa's son was not so easily commanded.

"Soon your husband takes his men south, into France, challenging your uncle's right to the crown," he said. "It must be difficult for you. His Holiness and your own mother favor your uncle's claim over your husband's."

A fact of which Philippa was only too aware. Just that day she had received yet another letter from her mother, the dowager countess of Hainault, urging her to dissuade Edward from *coveting your uncle's crown*. Her mother reminded her that she was still in mourning for Philippa's father. *Would you add to my grief?* But Philippa was not moved by her mother's sudden affection for her brother Philip of Valois, remembering how often she'd supported her own husband against her brother's aggression.

"My husband's claim is far stronger than my uncle's. The dowager countess of Hainault will see that in the end."

The duke murmured his agreement, remarked on the rose garden, then slowed to examine an espaliered pear as he said, "Regarding Lady Joan, Albret would be grateful for the details of her birth."

"Her birth? She is the daughter of Edmund, Earl of Kent, son of the great King Edward, my husband's grandfather—"

"Forgive me for not being clear, Your Grace. He asks for the date, time, anything that might be of use to his astrologer. Bernardo consults Timeus on all important decisions."

"Why does he not ask this himself?"

Brabant shrugged. "My friend is a cautious man. He wishes to know more before approaching you. And he is—to be frank, though she is a lovely child, she looks a poor cousin, her ill-fitting gown, her lack of jewels." He shrugged. "And there is the manner of her father's death, executed as a traitor."

"My husband cleared him of all guilt years ago."

"Of course. But the memory lingers, a slight metallic taste in the mouth. You understand. A princess, now . . ."

"Out of the question. As for Lady Joan's wardrobe, she has just arrived—we've had no opportunity to freshen it. She is at a changeable age."

"My apologies. I pray you, do not tell my daughter that I have offended you in my role as go-between. Lord Bernardo is certain to think differently once Lady Joan is dressed according to her status. First impressions are, fortunately, quickly forgotten."

"Just so. What can you tell me of his son?"

"Arnaud Amanieu? He is of an age with Lady Joan and favors his father in appearance. He's had the finest tutors and already trains with his father's knights. He will inherit his father's extensive lands and power."

Philippa nodded. "I shall have my secretary gather the information."

Jan bowed to her. "I shall inform Bernardo."

They strolled back to the guesthouse, discussing the art of espalier.

As Joan neared the nursery, she bowed her head so that the guard at the door would not ask the cause of her distress. Within, it was blessedly quiet, even the wet nurses fast asleep. Joan woke one of Bella's maidservants to assist her in undressing.

"Are you ill, my lady? Shall I send for your Mary?"

Joan shook her head. "I just need rest."

As soon as her hair had been brushed out, she climbed into bed with a loud sigh to persuade the young woman to leave her in peace. Pulling the bedclothes up over her head, Joan drew

the white hart emblem from beneath her pillow and pressed it
to her still pounding heart. Her neck tingled where Albret had
touched her. Her stomach hurt to think of how he had held her
eyes, as if he exerted some power over her. *Watch over me, Father. Keep me safe*. It was the first time she'd been formally introduced to the royal guests at such a gathering. Bella was right.
Nothing would ever be the same.

When Ned married Marguerite, would they still be friends?
Joan had counted on his companionship for so long. Her
watcher, her protector, and sometimes her tormentor, her fellow dreamer. She need never explain why a piece of news held
import for her—he knew. He was always in her thoughts, even
when away. She and Bella hoarded stories to share with him,
saved found treasures to present to him when he returned. Always, he had returned. But now it was Joan who had gone away,
and she very likely would not return, would wed someone who
would take her far away. Ned would no longer know anything
of her life.

Remember your vow, Ned had said the night before she departed. He believed he could refuse Lady Marguerite. But, seeing how the Duke of Brabant strutted in the hall, sharing the
dais with King Edward as if he were his equal, his guards interspersed with the king's round the hall, Joan doubted that her
cousin would have any choice in the matter. His father would
not tolerate Brabant's arrogance unless he was desperate, and
Ned would be powerless against him, powerless and too proud
to let his father's mission fail.

Nor would Joan have a choice. Not that she'd ever wanted
to marry Ned. He was too changeable, and his parents tolerated her only because she was a Plantagenet—they did not like
her. Nor would she ever wish to be a queen. She yearned to
escape court. But Gascony was so far, and Albret frightened
her. She hoped she was not meant for the son of the Gascon
stallion. She shivered and pressed her eyes tight, conjuring her

father, praying that he watch over her. But it was Sir Thomas's dimples that her mind's eye summoned, and the cleft in his chin, how warm and safe she'd felt as he watched over her that last night on board ship. There wasn't a man at court who was immune to Lady Lucienne's charms. Why did she have to choose Thomas?

Bella woke Joan when she came to bed, kissing her on the cheek. "I'm sorry about Ned and Marguerite. I didn't think. Of course you didn't know. *He* doesn't yet know."

Joan rubbed her eyes and turned to look up at the princess, blinking. "It's not just Ned. I felt like the poor cousin in the hall compared with you, Lucienne, and Marguerite."

"The Sire d'Albret did not seem to mind." Bella propped herself up on one elbow. "What is he like?"

"Frightening." Joan described how he'd lifted her hair, touched her neck, held her hand as he kissed her palm so that her fingers brushed his face. How he held the mazer to her lips, how funny he made her feel.

Bella sighed. "Fortunate Joan."

"No! I wish Father were here to tell him to keep his hands off me and not do that with his eyes."

"I heard my parents arguing about the Gascon stallion and 'the match' after the guests left. Father said, 'You knew his nature when you proposed this.'" She imitated perfectly how his voice snapped when he was irritated. "'Better her than our Bella.' What do you think they meant by 'his nature'?"

Joan shrugged, though she guessed it had something to do with his effect on her. "Who do you think they meant by 'her'?"

"I think it's *you*. What if *you're* to marry his son?"

"I pray you are wrong."

"Why? His son might be as handsome. Ned will be so jealous!"

"He may never see him. I'll be whisked off to Gascony, never to return to England."

"I hadn't thought of that."

"Your mother wants Ned and me far apart, doesn't she?"

"She does, it's true, especially since Ned's letter. He was so angry when he learned you were to come here. She would not let me see it, but her ladies say she almost choked with rage upon reading it and quickly had it destroyed."

"I don't want to talk about this anymore," Joan whispered, and turned away, burying her head in a pillow.

5

When the river mists vaulted the abbey walls at dusk, Thomas understood why his fellow guards had lit a brazier. He'd laughed. In late summer? By the time he found the buttery door after his watch, his fingers were so stiff they did not want to bend round the latch. Cursing, he pulled off his gloves to rub his hands.

"Here," Lucienne whispered in his ear, reaching around him to push open the door. She kissed his neck.

How bold she was, how sure she would not be caught moving about the abbey guesthouse in her chemise, her hair unbound. Even with a cloak, it was daring, and exciting. He drew her into the storeroom, pulling her close, burying his face in her fragrant hair.

"I have missed you so!" she whispered, pushing away to shrug off her cloak, then guiding him down.

By the time they came apart he was naked and slick with sweat. As was she.

He opened a shutter of the lantern so that he might look on her. "How is it you grow more beautiful with each passing year?"

"Sweet Tom, close that and come back to me." She laid her

head on his chest. "Every day the war is closer. I want to savor what time we have before I am reduced to praying for your safe return."

"Lovely Lucienne." He stroked her thick, tangled hair, pushing away the unwelcome thought that she entertained others in the buttery—how else had she known they would be undisturbed? He was accustomed to sharing her; no one man enough to satisfy her. But he wondered whether he was still the one who had her heart.

"Have I a rival?" he asked.

Her laughter tickled the hairs on his chest. "Never so long as *I* have none," she said. "Have I?" She propped herself up on one elbow to look him in the eye. "I saw how you watched Lady Joan today."

Had he been so obvious? He'd wanted to knock that mazer from Albret's hands. How dare he? "She's young and far from home. Someone should warn her that Albret is called the Gascon stallion for a reason."

"It was my fault," said Lucienne. "Her Grace asked me to watch over her, but I had not anticipated his behavior. I will in the future."

"Good."

"You *are* interested in the girl. She told me you befriended her on the crossing."

"I merely offered her food, watched over her so she need not sleep in a fouled cabin. She's just a child."

"Not for long. She is at a dangerous age, Thomas, have a care. A man can overreach his place thinking he is helping." She sighed. "I am sorry I brought it up. Come, kiss me."

When she had gone, taking the lantern with her, he went to the kitchen for a bowl of ale, and managed not to spill it on the snoring servants as he picked his way among them to the door out into the night garden.

Above him the firmament was alight with stars and the breeze was cool and fresh, inviting him out past the tidy plots of kitchen herbs into the small orchard. He stood there awhile, letting the night sink into him. Climbing to the top of the wall overlooking the Scheldt, he found a perch from which he might stare out at the wide river as he drank. Lucienne was the perfect mistress for a knight bachelor with a long road of campaigns and tournaments ahead before he might have the means to support a household, and a wife. She asked nothing of him but sex and adoration, which he gave willingly. In his itinerant life she was his anchor, his touchstone, and he was grateful to her, and to her skill in making him feel that he was her only lover. Sated, he pulled up his hood and let sleep take him.

A guard woke him just before dawn. "You must leave before my relief comes, Sir Thomas. He makes a bloody fuss when he finds a sleeper on the wall." He held out a wineskin. "You'll have a woolly mouth. The brew here will do that." When Thomas hesitated, the guard assured him that it was watered down. "I carry nothing strong. Wouldn't want to fall off into the river on my watch."

After rinsing out his mouth, Thomas climbed down into the orchard, relieving himself against the wall. A bird sang out, just one trilled note, the first of the morning, signaling dawn. It took him back to such mornings at home, he and his brothers having slept out under the stars for no other reason than that they could, and he smiled at the memory as the warbler of dawn was joined by his fellows. Turning toward the abbey kitchen, he saw Lady Joan pacing back and forth beyond the trees. When her back was to him, he slipped past her and headed for the kitchen.

The cook, Piers, a burly lay brother, stood in the doorway watching the dawn as his minions bustled about behind him.

"Might I have some bread and cheese, a jug of ale?"

"If you'll share it with Lady Joan. Child's been out there wearing a path between the onions and the rosemary since before dawn. Been crying a bit as well. And cursing. She'd take naught from me, but if you offered company . . ."

By the time Thomas returned, laden with more food than he'd planned, she had vanished. He cursed the cook for taking so long.

"Sir Thomas?"

He'd walked right past where she sat on a bench beneath a rose arbor. He held out the bundle he'd brought from the kitchen. "Cheese, a meat pie, and a jug of cider. Will you join me?"

Her sad eyes belied her smile. Cook was right. She'd been crying, and now she just picked at the pie.

"How do you like the abbey?" he asked when the silence became burdensome.

She shrugged.

"You seem unhappy."

"I want everything back the way it was."

"Homesick?"

She shook her head. "It doesn't matter where I am. Everything's changed."

Growing pains.

"I must be going." She leaned toward him, tilting her head to one side for a brief moment as if noticing something. Was his breath so sour? he wondered. Then she kissed him on the cheek. "Thank you."

Before he could respond she was away, her long sleeves fluttering in the breeze as she flew down the garden paths and into the kitchen, almost knocking over the cook, who stepped aside just in time.

Thomas stretched out his legs and leaned over, sore from his sleep on the damp wall. But had he found his way back to his bed he would have missed Lady Joan in the garden, and that would have been a great loss.

"You cheered her, I see," said Piers as Thomas handed back the jug and the dishes.

"You're wrong there, but she ate a little, and that is something."

6

The gowns arrayed on Queen Philippa's bed would in any other circumstance entice her—bright Italian silks embroidered with gold and silver thread, decorated with pearls and gems— but this day they were the means to an end of more lasting satisfaction than new robes, one or more of them to be remade to fit Lady Joan. "Well?" Philippa turned to the girl whose inadequate and suddenly inappropriate wardrobe was the occasion for this display. "Have you chosen?"

"They are all so beautiful."

Upon hearing of the conversation with Brabant, Edward had pecked Philippa on the cheek. "Find something that shows my cousin to some advantage. Make her look like a princess. At present, she looks as if we can't afford to dress her."

Indeed, they could not. The crown of France was a bankrupting ambition for which Philippa cursed the dowager queen Isabella. "I shall find a way," she'd promised. And she had.

"Hold the blue dress up to Lady Joan," Philippa ordered a servant. "What think you?" she demanded of her ladies.

"Perfection!"

"It brings out the blue of her eyes."

"Red would give her some color. Her hair is so pale, her skin so white."

"Red is unseemly for such a young woman. We are not hawkers, shouting the virtues of our wares. Lady Lucienne? Which of your gowns do you think will best set off Joan's beauty?"

"I agree there is no need for a bold display, Your Grace. Were she in russet, with no ornamentation, she would still be a beauty. Of my gowns, the deep blue, I agree." Lucienne's silken tone contradicted the resentment in her eyes. Philippa had explained to her that Lady Joan must dazzle Bernardo Ezi, and one of her extravagant gowns was just the thing to show off the girl's blossoming attributes.

"As you wish, Your Grace. But, if it please you, the Sire d'Albret's reputation suggests that such encouragement might not lead to the outcome you desire. You want him interested in her for his son, not for himself."

Philippa valued Lucienne's opinion, encouraging her to speak freely when they spoke privately, but not when she contradicted Edward. "This is the king's wish. Our part is to ensure that Bernardo Ezi admires but does not touch." She held up a hand against Lucienne's protest. "He was bold on meeting her, but we are now forewarned." She pressed her stomach. "I would rest now." She was again with child. Too soon, her physician said. She could keep little down, and sleep eluded her in the long hours of the night.

Now she rubbed her stomach as she considered Lucienne's gowns. "The blue it is." Joan would need several, but this was a start. Ordering the servants to proceed, she settled on a high-backed chair beside the bed, motioning to her ladies to be seated near her so they might all watch the seamstresses at work.

Joan protested. "Your Grace, might I retire to my chamber for the fitting?"

"The nursery is already crowded, child. We're all women here, you've nothing we haven't seen." She tsked at the girl's obvious distress. "We've no time for tears, either."

"Could you not at least allow her to undress behind a screen, Your Grace?" Lady Angmar whispered. "Young girls are so easily embarrassed as their bodies begin to change."

"If you think it so necessary, arrange it. And have another brazier brought in to warm her."

Angmar rose to see to it.

Philippa sipped a soothing tisane while observing how Lucienne's gown hung on Joan's smaller frame, the low-cut bodice, weighted with pearls, dangling almost to her waist, the skirt pooling at her feet. Lucienne's lady's maid tugged at the top, demonstrating to the others the tucks to be taken, the modifications to be made.

"Remove the pearls before you do any cutting," Lucienne said.

"I'll see to it, my lady," said the maid.

When Philippa's view was blocked by a carved wooden screen, she turned to Lucienne to ask her maid's name.

"Felice, Your Grace."

"You will share Felice with Lady Joan. The girl needs more than a maidservant, and Bella's Sandrine is not nearly as skilled in such work."

"I can manage with only my maidservant for the day, Your Grace," said Lucienne.

"Not just for the day. Lady Joan has more need of Felice's skills in dressing than you do at present."

"As Your Grace wishes." Lucienne looked away, but Philippa had seen the murderous expression. Perhaps she'd gone too far, the maid as well as the gowns. It was unfortunate, but she must now stand her ground.

When the screen was moved aside so that Philippa might approve the work so far, she circled Joan, suggesting a lower waist to accentuate what little hips the girl had, and tight sleeves fastened with tiny silver buttons at the wrists. She indicated that they should use the buttons from one of Lucienne's other gowns.

"Taper the sleeves to points to show off her long fingers." Satisfied, she ordered them to finish the work in the chamber her ladies shared.

"I am to cross the corridor in such disarray?" Joan asked.

Felice showed the women how to temporarily adjust the gown so that Joan might be more at ease.

Philippa nodded to herself. "Felice will serve you well, Joan. Lucienne shall work with your maidservant, who will benefit from her instruction. You would not deny her that, would you?"

"Thank you, Your Grace." Joan lowered her eyes, but her voice and the stiffness of her minuscule bow suggested anger.

"Perverse child, we are making you beautiful."

As Philippa returned to her seat, Lady Angmar sighed.

"In a little while, go to her," said Philippa. "You seem to have a calming influence."

"She is but a child, Your Grace. Must you—"

"Yes, I must. You heard how she insulted the dowager queen. She must be tamed. And we must stop thinking of her as a child."

JOAN TURNED THIS WAY AND THAT, LOOKING AT HERSELF IN THE mirrors Felice and Sandrine held up for her. The eyes that gazed back at her were huge with fear. Her Grace meant her to look ripe for the marriage market, and she had succeeded. Nothing could make her intention clearer. Joan was glad when they helped her undress so that she could join Bella in bed. It was late, the work having continued through the day and into the evening, pausing only for meals.

"He won't be able to take his eyes off you," Bella whispered. "That's why you're afraid, isn't it? The Gascon stallion."

"He needed no such encouragement."

"I have good news. William Montagu returned today. Father will confide in him, he always does, and if Earl William sees cause for concern he'll say so, and he'll alert your mother, won't he? Are they not friends?"

Joan suspected that her mother's long affair with William Montagu, Earl of Salisbury, was not the secret the two lovers thought it was. As one of the king's most valued barons and his good friend, the earl often interceded on Margaret's behalf with the royal couple. Bella *would* notice, having a nose for gossip.

But would he intercede for Joan now that she was not to wed his brother?

She lay awake long after Bella was asleep, remembering how the heavy silk caressed her skin, how her body had tingled. Much like when the Sire d'Albret had kissed her palm. She shivered and turned onto her side, drawing her knees up together and calling on her father to watch over her. Tonight it was his kind face she saw, not Sir Thomas's. She would not be so silly with Thomas again. He had reeked of Lucienne's rose and spice scent that morning. And, in the gown fashioned from her rival's, Joan smelled like her as well. It was so unfair.

7

Lucienne turned from the other ladies as the king's household knights arrived, Sir Thomas Holland bringing up the rear. How handsome he was in the dark velvet ablaze with the king's arms, the three golden lions of England on a red field. She quickly stepped forward so that he would see her first.

"My lady," he folded the lean, muscular body she knew so well in a formal bow. "How beautiful you are." She liked that he looked her in the eye as he said so. But it was a fleeting triumph, someone just behind her now catching his attention. "Is that Lady Joan?" His eyes had not shone so for Lucienne.

She glanced over her shoulder. "Yes, your ungrateful little friend in *my* dress, cut down, taken in—ruined—on the queen's orders. Her Grace has given her my lady's maid as well. I am lady bountiful."

"Surely you will be rewarded for your largesse, Lucienne," he said with an affectionate smile.

She laughed, regretting having sounded so shrewish, and made him promise to dance with her. They were preparing to leave for a feast at the Duke of Brabant's, and he was said to have the best musicians in the city.

"I shall fight to claim your first dance, my lady." Thomas

kissed her hand and moved forward to bow to the pretty Plantagenet.

JOAN WATCHED WITH ENVY AS LADY LUCIENNE GREETED SIR
Thomas. How gracefully she moved, how easy she was with
him. She hated that, with every move, her own body heat
stirred the ghost of Lucienne's perfume in her gown. Perhaps
if she stood very still. But what about at the feast? What if they
danced?

"Lady Joan." With a flourish, Sir Thomas bowed to her,
then kissed her hand. "How you tricked me with your earlier
disguise. I thought you a mortal child, but you are an enchant-
ress come to steal my heart."

Oh, those dimples. "I promise to keep your heart safe, my
lord." She smiled and hoped she sounded lighthearted even as
her heart broke.

"By all that is holy, is this little Joan?" Earl William's voice
boomed, and Thomas was gone. Montagu turned his head to
study Joan out of his good eye. "Cursed Scots. A man wants
two eyes to admire such beauty." He'd been blind in his left eye
for more than a year, since a war hammer bashed in his helmet.
Even so, he was a commanding presence. "Such a gown! I fear
Her Grace is pushing you from the nest before you have the
strength to fly. I'd not thought our situation so desperate that
our children were put on such display." He sighed. "But then
you are a marriageable Plantagenet. Such a pity His Grace refused my brother as your husband." He tucked her hand round
his arm. "Let me escort you to the litters."

"My lord, I am comforted by your presence."

"Are you, now? Fretting about feasting at the ducal palace?
Do not worry. You are not intended for Brabant's son and heir,
you can be thankful for that."

"It must rankle, playing at courtesy with Duke Jan, the man who has held you hostage for the king's promises," she said.

"He has treated me with great courtesy. I've lived here comfortably, albeit not freely, and all in the service of my king." Montagu handed her into the waiting litter, bowing and kissing her hand, then backing away so that the curtains might be drawn. Nothing in his behavior suggested that he meant to rescue her.

By the time the litter stopped and a servant opened the curtains to proffer an arm for her support in stepping out, Joan felt hot and disheveled. Felice and Lady Lucienne took her in hand, straightening her gown and repinning her hair, even retucking the silk padding in her shoes, finishing just as Bella came rushing over.

"Come, let me introduce you to Henri of Brabant." Taking Joan's arm, she led her over to where the duke, his daughter, and a young man with a too large nose and knobby knees were greeting King Edward and Queen Philippa.

The queen looked Joan up and down, then nodded to the king and the duke with a satisfied sniff.

"My dear cousin." King Edward bowed over Joan's hand. "I cannot imagine the man who would not fall in love with you on sight. Am I right, Lord Henri?"

The young man smiled uncertainly.

"Will you take us to see the peacocks in the garden, Lord Henri?" Bella asked.

Looking relieved, he offered Joan one arm, Bella the other. "It will be my pleasure, Princess Isabella, Lady Joan."

"Now lift your chin and carry yourself with pride," the queen whispered as Joan brushed past her. "You are a Plantagenet."

Wending their way through the hall, Joan felt the prickle of eyes following her. But once in the garden young Lord Henri put her at ease. Hearing that Joan enjoyed hawking, he showed her the mews, going on at great length about a treatise on falconry that he was reading with his tutor. Having read much of it herself and shared it with Ned, Joan could appreciate his clear comprehension, and soon they were extending theory into their own experience, allowing Bella to join in. By the time Henri escorted them to the high table, Joan wondered whether Bella and the earl had been mistaken and she was being wooed by Henri of Brabant, he'd been so agreeable. No sooner had Joan been seated beside Lady Lucienne than the Sire d'Albret slipped into the seat on her left.

"I will leave you now, Lady Joan," Lord Henri said. "But I will return later to claim you for a dance, if you will."

"I would like that very much, Lord Henri."

When he was gone, she forced herself to look at the Gascon. "My lord Albret."

He bowed to her and greeted her courteously, but nothing more and, throughout the courses, behaved as she would expect of a lord much her senior humoring a young girl. Had her impression of his behavior two days ago been the product of her own exhaustion, the gossip she'd heard of him, the mead? She began to relax. To her right, Lady Lucienne pointed out the nobles Joan had met before, and many she had not, and commented on the elegance of the hall, the grace and ease with which young Lady Marguerite played the hostess.

"She is suited to be a queen," Joan said. "And her family will bring wealth and strong influence in this part of the world to King Edward and the prince."

Lucienne stared at Joan a little too long for her comfort. "Then it is not true that you hoped to wed Prince Edward?"

Joan felt herself blush. "Who said such a thing?"

A little laugh. "No doubt someone pointed out how like the two of you are, what pretty children you would have, and it grew from there. No one meant you harm." Lucienne quickly changed the subject, commenting on the fashions round the hall.

During the course of the afternoon, Joan danced with Lord Henri; King Edward himself, who made small talk with jovial good humor; the duke, who thanked her for helping Marguerite feel welcomed into the family; other nobles who bragged and flirted; Earl William, who was comforting in his familiarity. But her favorite partner by far was Sir Thomas, her least graceful dancing partner, but gallant with his compliments and free with amusing observations about their fellow dancers.

Only at the very end did the Sire d'Albret take her hand and lead her out to dance, saying little, as if concentrating on the music. Of all her partners, he was the master of the dance, letting the music move him rather than moving to the music. She found herself watching him, fascinated by the perfection of his features, the grace of his gestures, the warmth of his hands. Did he perhaps hold her hand too long in each round, or was it she who held his?

And then, as he escorted her toward the cluster of queen's ladies preparing to depart, he said, "I detect Lady Lucienne's intoxicating scent in your gown. Is that how you sought to ensnare me, my lady?"

"Ensnare *you*, my lord? I would never wear this gown again if I thought it might do so."

"Ah! There is the Plantagenet spirit. At last."

"Does arrogance pass for courtesy in Gascony?" They had reached the ladies. "Good day to you, my lord."

He reached out to touch her cheek, then kissed her on the forehead. "You are like a heady wine, little one, once you open and breathe. I shall remember that."

"My lord." Earl William stepped between them. "Have you a moment? I wanted to discuss with you a matter of some import."

Joan felt faint as she joined the ladies.

"I shall speak with Her Grace about his behavior, Joan," said a shocked Lady Clare.

When Bella fell into bed that night, she declared it a most splendid day. "I almost wish the duke had agreed to a double match. I like Lord Henri."

Joan concurred. "I like both Henri and Marguerite, though not their father." Once again, he had not given the king and queen the deference due them, seating himself on the same level as King Edward, his chair as grand and cushioned, his canopy as prominent, the arms of England and Brabant side by side. "I do not trust him."

"I don't like the peacock, either. Oh! I heard—is it true?—that Salisbury caught Albret kissing you and pulled him away? *Tell* me!"

"He just kissed me on the forehead. And Earl William did not pull him away, but stepped between us and asked to speak with him about some matter."

Bella sighed. "Still, he *kissed* you." Her voice was fading.

It wasn't the kiss but the hand on her cheek that had flustered Joan. She'd felt so vindicated by calling him out for his arrogance. And then he'd touched her like that and she felt helpless again. He knew Lucienne's scent. She wondered whether she trembled when he touched her, and whether she liked that—if what she was experiencing, these feelings that frightened her so, if this was how a woman felt with a man. If Thomas touched her so, would she like it? She thought she would. Very much.

8

Joan woke to the sound of women whispering, only Bella still curled up beside her. Pulling back the curtains, she discovered Sandrine, Felice, Mary, Lady Lucienne, and two of the queen's lady's maids sorting through her clothes.

"What are you doing?"

Mary dropped the gown she was holding up for one of the ladies. "My lady, they said the queen—"

"Her Grace says that, as none of these fit properly, we are to use the fabrics to create new gowns." Lucienne held up the deep blue silk and the rose taffeta to suggest the blending of the two—the rose as the bodice and sleeves, the blue as the skirt. "We're deciding what we can use, and then Lady Marguerite and Lord Henri are escorting us to the market to shop for decorations. We shall have such fun!"

Felice came over to plump up the pillows behind Joan and Bella, who sat up rubbing her eyes.

"You might have asked before you began," Joan said.

Bella elbowed her. "Why so glum? You were angry with Countess Margaret for refusing to make you new gowns. Now you'll have them."

Maybe Bella was right. Joan loved how she felt in the gown made from Lucienne's, and this one would not smell of roses and spice. Why would she resist such a gift? "I want the bodice fitted all the way to my hips."

Lucienne beamed. "Of course!"

The duke's children arrived with such an escort of guards that their company crowded the townsfolk out of the market as it entered and spread out among the stalls. The hawkers grew quiet, though not the musicians and performers, who followed in their wake. Joan would ever think of the Antwerp market filled with music and song, alive with puppet shows, jugglers, dancing bears, and performing monkeys. The merchants spread their wares before them, silks, velvets, the finest wools, a rainbow of gorgeous fabrics, ribbons, leathers soft and supple—some in strips to use for lacing, jewels, buttons, buckles. Lucienne and Felice took charge, draping the soft fabrics around Joan's shoulders, discussing colors, texture, carefully cool and straight-faced to give them the upper hand in bargaining with the merchants. Marguerite guided them to the stalls of the cloth merchants and jewelers her father favored, but that did not mean they would give the English visitors a fair price, nor did Lucienne and Felice expect it. That was part of the game for them, and they excelled at it: Lucienne charming the merchants, flattering them into competition; Felice standing firm, pointing out flaws, brighter colors in neighboring stalls, the telltale whiff of mold suggesting damp warehouses.

Their hosts made purchases as well. Marguerite presented Joan and Bella with strings of tiny silk flowers like the ones that bordered her surcoat; Henri gave each a marvelous plum pastry, his favorite. Joan and Bella fingered ribbons and buttons, jeweled mirrors and combs, even saddles and harnesses.

Joan was particularly taken with the harnesses at one stall, decorated with hundreds of tiny silver bells. With one in each hand, she was shaking them, comparing their tones, when she saw Bella's eyes go wide at something behind her.

"The higher pitch would startle most palfreys," said the Sire d'Albret as Joan turned to him. He took the hand in which she held the harness with the lower pitch. "If you would permit me, Lady Joan, I would make you a gift of this one in atonement for my behavior yesterday. I was jealous. You had eyes only for Lord Henri."

His banter unsettled Joan. "Did I?"

"Jealous of my brother?" Marguerite laughed. "You do so enjoy playing the heartsick knight, my lord. But have a care, you'll turn Henri's head. And you're confusing Lady Joan. She isn't accustomed to your teasing."

So it meant nothing. Now Joan felt foolish. Covering her embarrassment, she tried some banter. "Lord Henri is a gracious host and has the finest mews and a deep knowledge of falconry. I *am* quite taken with him."

Henri blushed, and so did Joan, as Lord Bernardo kissed her hand, the harness bells jingling merrily, his eyes crinkling in pleasure. She wished he would not do that. Even though she knew now that he was teasing, he had a disturbing effect on her. She forced a smile. "My lord, I accept your apology and your gift."

He bowed to her and snapped his fingers for his man to make the purchase, then proffered his arm to escort her back to Lucienne and Felice, who were arranging for the delivery of their purchases. Lord Bernardo—*do call me that, little one, it is my name*—left them at the end of the square, professing to remember the business that seeing her had quite put out of his head. She laughed at his exaggeration, blushed at yet another kiss of her hand, and tripped off with the others in such good humor that she teased Lord Henri about the smear of plum on his cheek and boldly asked if she might go hawking with him on the morrow.

The sun was low in the sky when they returned to the abbey,

but the air was still mild. As Henri and Marguerite were saying their farewells, a page appeared at Joan's elbow. Queen Philippa awaited her in the garden.

"Come, Joan, walk with me awhile." They strolled along the paths, Philippa pointing out to Joan the plants that were familiar from her childhood, sharing some fond memories of a gardener who had befriended her. But at last Philippa sank down on a bench, gesturing for Joan to stand before her so they were eye to eye. "I have heard about Bernardo Ezi's behavior at the duke's hall. Earl William and Lady Clare called it most inappropriate. Did he frighten you, Joan?"

"A little, Your Grace, and I was grateful knowing the earl watched out for me. But Lord Bernardo made his apologies today, buying me a beautiful harness with silver bells as a token of his respect."

"Lord Bernardo was at the market? Did you accept his gift?"

"I did, Your Grace. Lady Marguerite seemed to think I should."

"And you trust her judgment?"

"She and Henri laughed as if he teases them all the time. I thought perhaps I had misunderstood. Was it wrong? Should I have refused him?"

"No." The queen drew out the syllable, as if testing it, and then, more firmly, repeated it. "No. It was a graceful gesture on his part. I am glad of it." But she did not look so. She seemed uneasy, as if someone were not playing the game as expected. "He behaved appropriately?"

"No one protested when he twice kissed my hand."

The queen made a sound low in her throat. "How many times did he kiss Lady Marguerite's hand?"

Joan closed her eyes, retracing Albret's movements. "I'd not thought of that. He kept his distance from her, Your Grace."

The queen cocked an eyebrow but said nothing.

"Shall I return his gift?"

"Return it? No, child." Philippa took Joan's hands and looked into her eyes, not unkindly. "I heard that Lady Lucienne gave you an unpleasant surprise this morning. She should have consulted with you before touching your gowns, and I have told her so in no uncertain terms. But she meant well, and I do hope you will enjoy the new gowns." Her face had brightened. "You are maturing into a young woman of much grace earlier than either your mother or I anticipated. Edward will not have you looking like a poor cousin."

"I am grateful, Your Grace. Truly." Joan returned the queen's smile. "Would you like to see the pretty silk flower borders Lady Marguerite bought Bella and me?"

"I should indeed. Come. Let us go within."

As they retraced their steps to the guesthouse, Philippa interrupted Joan's account of the day with questions about the Brabant children and Albret. Were the children and the Gascon close? Intimate? Joan found the inquiry assuring. Philippa must have been concerned about Albret's behavior. She meant to watch over Joan.

For a fortnight Joan encountered Lord Bernardo almost daily. She observed Lady Marguerite dancing with him, blushing, teasing, approaching, retreating. Never did he touch her other than to take her hand in a dance or to assist her in some way. In all things quite chaste. Joan held back, allowing Bella and Marguerite to bask in his teasing attention, but he merely grew bolder, brushing her neck with his hand as he assisted her with a cloak, cupping his hands round hers when she passed something at the table, trailing his hand along her shoulders when moving past her seat. He was adept at this game, apparently convincing the king and queen that he was filling her head with stories of Gascony to interest her in his son. Or so said Lucienne. But to Joan he never mentioned Arnaud. What was his game? Joan complained to the queen, who suggested that she was misinterpreting his courtesy. But she promised to speak with him.

And all the while Joan watched Lucienne and Thomas, hating how easy they were together. But he had not forgotten her. Thrice Joan stole out to the garden in the early morning, hoping to see Sir Thomas, and twice she found him there, seemingly waiting for her on the bench they had shared that first morning, with a treat from the kitchen and weak cider or ale. He made her feel welcomed, cared for.

Both times she intended to ask him how to persuade Albret to keep his hands to himself. But both times she managed only to sit quietly beside him, resenting the scent that clung to him—roses and spice, Lucienne's scent. It confused her feelings for him, and she found herself embarrassed about burdening him with her problems, fearful lest she sound childish. Each time she regretted her hesitation. He meant to be her friend. Why else wait there, with food? Next time she would trust him.

THOMAS HAD ALMOST GIVEN UP WHEN LADY JOAN RAN OUT INTO the kitchen garden holding a short cloak over her head as a shield from the soft summer rain. With five days or so before he departed on a mission, he was anxious to talk to her about Lord Bernardo. Warn her.

"*Benedicite*, Lady Joan."

"Good morning, Sir Thomas. What have you there?"

"Still warm bread and soft cheese."

She inhaled deeply before spreading some of the cheese on a chunk of the bread and biting into it with relish. She laughed as she brushed the crumbs away and sipped some weak cider. "You must think me a savage, but I've not eaten since before nones yesterday."

"Savage? Never."

"I am glad to find you here again. I need your advice."

"Is this about the Sire d'Albret?"

She nodded as she chewed, then swallowed more cider. "Her Grace believes he woos me for his son. But he never speaks of him. In truth, he behaves as if——" She suddenly dropped her gaze. "You carry Lady Lucienne's scent, as you do whenever I find you here at this time."

He'd not thought of that. "What has that to do——"

"There is a connection. I pray you, be patient." She crooked one leg over the bench, carefully draping her skirts, so that she might look at him directly. "You are lovers, I know. Do you want to marry her?"

"She has a husband."

"If she were not married?" Her eyes demanded the truth.

He shook his head, as if that were less of a betrayal than the word "no."

"You would shun Lucienne because she has let other men make love to her?"

He bowed his head. "A man wants to trust that his children are his. I suppose that makes me a hypocrite."

"You and most men at court, I expect, including the Sire d'Albret. Why, then, if he means me for his son and heir, would he behave as if he has no respect for my honor, kissing my hand repeatedly, touching my neck, cupping my hand in his when he passes me something at the table?"

Thomas sat up straighter to ease the clench of his stomach. "The queen's ladies permit this?"

"They do."

He cursed beneath his breath. "Lady Lucienne promised to watch him more closely, to keep you safe. Has she not escorted you on these occasions?"

"She has, but——" Joan frowned. "You discussed this with her?"

He felt himself falling into trap after trap under the girl's close scrutiny. "I did not like how he behaved the day you were introduced."

A little smile, a blush.

"I will ask Lucienne to mention this to Her Grace."

"I have told Her Grace of his behavior," Joan said. "She promised to speak with him, but nothing has changed. I think she fears he will lose interest in the alliance. She still believes that's his intention."

Thomas bit back a second curse. "I will talk to Lucienne again. And, if you wish, I will instruct the men who stay behind when we ride south that they should keep their eyes on Albret when he is near you."

"You would do this for me? Even after I asked you about Lucienne?"

"Even so."

She leaned close, her breath sweet with cider, and pecked his cheek. "My champion. I will pray for you all the while you are away." She unwound her legs and rose.

Without thinking, he caught her hand. "You know where to knee him if need be?"

Her eyes widened as she blushed. "I do." She pressed his hand to her cheek. "You are my perfect knight."

And she was gone, leaving him with an unquiet heart. He cared for her far too much, this royal child.

How bold she had been! Joan's heart pounded as she rushed away from Thomas. He'd promised to protect her, and he'd held her hand!

But he'd not kissed her. Had she been Lucienne . . .

She slowed down as she reached the hall. Thomas and Lucienne had *discussed* her. Could Lucienne be right, that Joan reminded Thomas of his sisters? Was his attention no more than that? *Oh, please, God, let it be more.*

SEPTEMBER 1339

Her father's voice rose on the air, leading her deeper into the wood. Father! Wait! *she called. He gave no sign that he heard her, never faltering in his song. She pushed through a thicket of thorn bushes, the thorns catching at the wool of her gown, scratching her arms, her face. She caught a flash of white out of the corner of her eye, and suddenly she was through the thicket, stumbling into a glade wide enough that some light filtered through the trees in the center. There stood a hart, blood staining its white coat, dripping from something large caught on an antler. A low hum replaced her father's song. It seemed to come from the hart, beginning softly, gradually increasing in volume. Joan took a step toward it, then froze as an overwhelming sense of danger made her glance over her shoulder. Her heart pounded in her chest.* Where was her father? *She opened her mouth to call to him, but no sound came forth. The humming grew louder, louder. She took a few more steps toward the hart, trying to ignore the sense of something reaching out to her from behind. The mass on the antler seemed to move, as if pulsing in rhythm with the humming. A few more steps and she saw that it was a swarm of flies. The hart sensed her, turning to look at her. The flies rose up as the antler moved, allowing Joan to see what it was on which they fed. Her stomach turned. It was her father's head, horribly eaten. Joan screamed.* What is it, sweet Joan? *He was so close she felt his breath on the back of her neck. She screamed again—*

"My lady, Lady Joan, you are dreaming," one of the wet nurses whispered as she gently shook Joan.

She sat up, hugging herself to stop the shaking. "God be thanked."

Bella had a pillow atop her head, already back to sleep.

Felice had raised up on one elbow. "You were thrashing about and gasping as if you would scream, my lady. Should I send Mary for some wine to soothe you?"

Joan had already seen that her maid was not asleep at the

foot of the bed, as she should be. It did not matter. She could see a hint of dawn out the window. "There is no need. Go back to sleep."

When Felice's breath steadied, Joan rose and dressed, telling the wet nurses that she would be in the chapel. Her soft shoes whispered down the steps and across the tiles of the great hall. She slowed down as she walked through the kitchen, savoring the warmth and the ordinariness of the servants beginning their day, then wrapped her short cloak round her and stepped out into the garden. She meant to gather dew from the lady's mantle growing there, her nurse Efa's herbal spell to free one's soul from a frightening dream—a thimble's worth of dew, then thrice round a willow. There was a great old willow out beyond the fruit trees, so old that it had been there when the river wall was built and it curved around it, leaving just enough space for a slender person to pass between the wall and the trunk. She and Bella sometimes hid there to trade gossip. She picked a leaf from the bed of lady's mantle, tipping back her head to drink the sweet dew. Now for the willow. Removing her shoes so the dew damp grass would not ruin them, she tucked her front hem into her girdle and ran across the lawn to the dry ground beneath the ancient willow.

It was dark beneath its thick, hanging branches, and the bole so broad that someone might hide on the far side. Three grown men might just span the trunk with arms outstretched. She would not have dared make the circuit had this not been such a protected place, an abbey garden surrounded by high walls patrolled by the king's guard. Even so, she shivered as she moved into the absolute dark inside the hanging foliage between the trunk and the wall, feeling her way over the twisted roots, one hand on the rough trunk for balance, barely breathing. Coming round to the orchard side she found the rosy dawn replaced by a soft river mist, settling down over the fruit trees, chilling the air.

Taking a deep breath, Joan wrapped her cloak more tightly

about her and forced herself to begin the second circuit, telling herself that, now that she knew what to expect, it would not be so frightening. But the gloom had deepened and her heart pounded as she fought the memory of the dream, the hot breath on her neck. *Who had it been? No, do not think of it. This is a cure. It will take away all memory of the horror.* Her hand on the trunk, she focused on placing one foot in front of the other, whispering Hail Marys. The prayer was not part of Efa's cure, but it felt right.

Her teeth chattered as the cold spread upward from her chilled feet. *Holy Mary, Mother of God, I do not feel the cold, I do not feel the cold. My feet are warm. I am walking on sun-warmed sand.* Coming out again within view of the orchard, she was torn between pushing on for the third circuit, because to pause was to cool down even more, or to sit down on the grass and cover her feet until they warmed a little. She remembered Efa telling her that a counterspell, once begun, must not be abandoned or else the power of the original spell tripled.

She pushed on, back into the darkness, her feet so cold now that she had trouble feeling for her balance. But the dream had been so frightening, she must complete this counterspell or she would be afraid to sleep. She felt the wall beside her, the half-way mark. A shudder went through her, forcing her to pause and catch her breath. She felt a presence. Behind or ahead? Behind. She hurried forward, saying a prayer of thanks when, once more, she could see the orchard through the foliage. *Silly Joan, you frightened yourself.* But she had completed the spell. The dream was dead. Slipping down, she rested against the trunk, closing her eyes, catching her breath.

"What have we here? An orchard sprite?" Startled, Joan tried to rise, but Lord Bernardo put his hands on her shoulders as he crouched down, trapping her as he slipped a hand beneath her skirt to touch her bare feet. "Is she real? Ah, yes, I feel flesh. But so cold!" He rubbed a foot in his warm hands, the action pushing up her skirt and causing a strange sensation up her thighs. Her whole body flushed and tingled.

What was he doing? She pushed at his hand and pressed her legs together, trying to twist away. "Stop! Leave me alone!"

"Let me warm the other, my sweet." He kissed her forehead as he reached for the other foot, tucked farther under her.

"Don't touch me!" She shrieked, hoping someone would hear.

"My lord!" a man's voice called sharply.

God be thanked. Thomas had come to save her.

With amazing speed, Bernardo scooped Joan up and turned with her in his arms. "Ah, Sir Thomas. You catch me in the act of rescue. It is most fortunate that after a long night in the war room I came out to clear my head. I discovered Lady Joan asleep beneath the tree. The fog moved in so quickly—she is cold to the touch."

"Yet warm enough to cry out, my lord. My squire will see her safely to her quarters," Thomas said firmly. He handed Joan's shoes to Hugh and then lifted her from Bernardo's arms, steadying her as he set her down.

She was crying by now, her relief overshadowed by her humiliation. She frantically scrubbed at her forehead. "Come, my lady," Hugh whispered, holding out a hand to help her balance as she stepped into her shoes, let down her skirt. He began to lead her out through the trees, guiding her with his voice and a hand gently holding hers, but Joan stumbled as they reached the paving stones, blinded by her tears. "It's best that I carry you through to the great hall, my lady. Do I have your leave?"

Joan nodded. "Take me to the queen's chamber."

Hugh lifted her as if she were a small child and carried her through the warm kitchen and into the great hall. There Lady Lucienne rushed across the tiled expanse toward them, crying out their names. The sight of her brought on a fresh torrent of tears.

❖ ❖ ❖

PHILIPPA TOOK IN THE SHIVERING GIRL, HER HAIR WILD AND TAN-gled with willow leaves, her gown and shoes wet and stained with grass and mud, her eyes swollen from weeping. Clapping her hands, she sent her ladies and the servants scurrying for a cushioned chair, blankets, heated stones for Joan's feet and hands, and strong brandywine.

Lucienne told her what she knew "Sir Thomas is escorting the Sire d'Albret from the abbey grounds, Your Grace."

"Bring Holland here when he returns," Philippa ordered. "No mention of this is to leave this chamber. Do you hear me?" All present bowed their heads in submission. "Now go, wait without."

She smoothed Joan's forehead and squeezed her shoulders, then, easing into the chair across from the girl, she took the icy hands in hers. "Tell me everything, as best you can."

Joan haltingly described what happened.

Philippa was relieved to hear that Holland had arrived in time. The girl was frightened, but intact. God be thanked. What was Albret thinking, rubbing the child's feet, such an intimate touch? "Do not for a moment believe that you are in any way to blame, Joan." Philippa kissed the girl's icy hands. "Lady Angmar will escort you to your bed in the nursery, where you are to remain for a good, long rest—I shall send along a soothing draught for you. Angmar, tell Princess Isabella and all in the nursery that Lady Joan frightened herself with a silly spell and Holland found her curled up and weeping beneath the willow." Bella would eventually find out the truth, but a few days' delay would give Joan time to recover her composure.

Felice and Mary would be reprimanded for their negligence, and all the household would be ordered to ensure that from now on neither Bella nor Joan left the nursery without a companion.

As Joan departed in the company of Lady Angmar, Thomas Holland arrived. Philippa noted the cold look he gave Lucienne as their eyes met. A romance gone sour? Or did he blame her for the negligence of her lady's maid?

"I commend you on your timely arrival and swift, decisive action, Sir Thomas."

Hands crossed over his heart, he bowed. "It was the cook, Brother Piers, who alerted me, Your Grace. He knew Lady Joan was alone in the orchard, and, seeing Lord Albret out there, he sent a boy for a guard."

There was the potential source of the gossip—the kitchen staff. Philippa summoned the cook, commending him and then ordering him to silence his staff.

Such a disturbing morning. Philippa thanked God over and over that Brother Piers and Holland had saved the day. But what were they to do about Bernardo Ezi?

She wondered what Edward thought when Albret did not return to the council room. She sent word requesting that her husband come to her at the first opportunity.

"Fetch Lady Clare. Tell her to bring her lute. I would be soothed by her music and sweet voice."

Grim-faced, Edward ordered her ladies out of the room, then turned on Philippa. "What happened? On whose order did Holland escort Bernardo Ezi out of the abbey?"

"Albret disgraced himself in the orchard this morning," Philippa said, keeping her voice low. "He frightened your cousin, Lady Joan, rubbing her feet and kissing her. He insulted her and us with his familiarity. She is a child under our protection."

Edward shook his head. "I've had a messenger from Brabant, outraged by the insult to his friend Albret. He says Albret treated my cousin as he would his daughter. She was cold, frightened. He was warming her before she took a chill. And for this he was treated so dishonorably? I asked you on whose order, wife."

"On no one's order, my lord, but spurred by the affront to Lady Joan, your cousin, our ward. You would defend him? She is not his daughter, Edward. How can you possibly condone such behavior? He offended her honor and ours."

"Well, now he's taken ship for home precisely when I need him most, thinking it best that he remove himself."

"So says Brabant, the very man Albret chose to bring to us his complaint that Joan was awkward, her gowns unbecoming and marking her as a poor relation. It was cleverly done. Then his daughter urges Joan to accept Albret's gifts, assuring her that he is just a kindly uncle who makes young girls laugh by pretending to be a lovesick suitor. And so she softens and is blamed when Albret, a man old enough to have fathered a son Joan's age, does not have the moral fortitude to keep his hands to himself. They have played us, Edward. They have betrayed us and frightened and shamed your cousin. Where will it end? Has your mother's ambition brought you so low? How far will you crawl for Brabant's amusement?"

"I do not crawl!"

"No?"

"And leave Isabella out of this."

How, when it was she who had driven him to such ends? But Philippa knew by his red face and angry eyes that she'd said enough. "Leave me now. Return when you've ears to hear the truth." She turned her back on her husband, a gesture so alien to her nature and her love for him that she prayed it would shake him awake. It was not for Joan she did this but for her husband's honor.

Behind her he growled as he poured himself some wine,

then began pacing the length of the room, pausing only to drink deeply and refill his cup. Standing sentinel, she reminded herself to breathe.

At last he came to rest so close to her that she smelled the sweet wine on his breath as he asked her forgiveness. "God blessed me with a wise helpmeet, and the wit to know I will regret it if I do not give ear to your words."

She turned, holding out her hands to him. His eyes were sad now, his temper cooled. He grasped her hands and kissed her tenderly on the mouth.

"You are right. Our honor has been challenged by Albret's too familiar behavior. So what should be done, Philippa?"

"We coolly correct Brabant's account, instructing him in the nature of Albret's transgression. And, when the time comes, if he pursues the marriage bond we reject him."

Edward was shaking his head.

"This match has been poisoned, my love," Philippa said.

"We shall see. For now, you will move the household to Ghent as soon as I march south. Albret will not bother you there. He distrusts the Flemish merchants as much as does Brabant."

"So it shall be done, husband."

"I have not said I've given up on this match."

"As you wish, my love."

PHILIPPA WAVED LUCIENNE ASIDE AND LOOKED WITH STUDIED DIS-passion at the girl standing before her, pale, with dark circles round her defiant eyes, her hands curled into fists, demanding that Albret be punished. "Be easy, my child. He has taken ship for Gascony."

"If he still pretends to negotiate a marriage between me and his son?"

She had hoped the girl would not ask quite so specifically about that. "I am confident that the Sire d'Albret will keep his distance henceforth, especially if you are betrothed to his son. His wife would see to that, I assure you."

The girl inhaled sharply. "I will *never* consent to wedding his son. Never!" Turning on her heel, she stormed from the chamber.

Philippa cursed her mother-in-law for so poisoning Edward with her ambition that he would yet consider a liaison with a man who had so insulted his family. "Go after her, Lucienne. Assure her that you know me well, and you are certain I will prevent any such betrothal." She herself promised nothing, but the assurance from Lucienne might calm the girl, prevent her from doing anything rash.

"I understand, Your Grace." Lucienne bobbed her head and swept from the room.

9

Sunrise lit the lion of England, rampant on the standards and banners fluttering above the king's company gathered in the yard of Antwerp Castle. Joan stood on the battlements between Lady Lucienne and Lady Angmar. Since the attack, one or the other was ever beside her, except when she slept, and then it was Felice who sat up whenever Joan moved. Fearing that Albret might have only pretended to depart Antwerp in order to catch them all off guard, Joan appreciated their watchfulness, but it had prevented her from seeking out Sir Thomas to thank him properly.

Now she searched the crowd below for familiar faces, but the sun was not quite high enough. And then she heard his laugh. Following the sound she picked him out of the crowd and rushed down the steps to go to him. But, once on the level of the troops, she lost him.

"Lady Joan?" Earl William came up behind her. "You're in danger of being trampled. We're too many for this space. The horses are restive."

"Have you see Sir Thomas Holland?"

"Holland, is it? Where's your Gascon shadow?"

"My Gascon shadow departed with the tide days ago, Earl William, God be thanked."

"Good. I did not like how he looked at you. I wrote to Countess Margaret of my concern."

Heartening news! "I am grateful to you, my lord earl. God bless you. *Have* you seen Sir Thomas?"

He gave her a questioning look, but gestured to her to follow him. "I'll guide you through the horse dung."

Sir Roland punched Thomas in the arm as Joan approached, saying, "Sly knave." Thomas looked from her to the earl, puzzled.

"Lady Joan wishes to bid you farewell, Holland." The earl patted Joan's hand. "Let his squire escort you back to the wall when you're ready, child."

"You've come to see me off, Lady Joan?" Thomas drew her away from his friends. "Are you recovered?" He searched her eyes.

"He is gone, and I pray I never see him again." She pulled the silk square from her sleeve. "Would you do me the honor of carrying my colors, Sir Thomas?"

The dimples appeared. "I am honored, my lady." He reached for the silk, but seeing the white hart he shook his head. "Not this, my lady. Your father's emblem?"

"Yes, this, Sir Thomas. You have proved yourself a most worthy champion. All they'll see is a bit of silk. It will be our secret."

He bowed, then kissed her hand. It was nothing like Lord Bernardo's kisses. Chaste, sweeter by far.

"Is he truly gone?"

"The king and queen promise me that he is. And tomorrow we move to Ghent, a city controlled by a man Albret despises. I trust I shall be safe from him there." She stood on tiptoe to kiss one dimple, then the other. "May God bless you and keep you, my champion."

He gently touched her cheek with the back of his hand, looking down on her in a way that made her heart race. "May God bless you and keep you, my lady."

❖ ❖ ❖

WILLIAM MONTAGU LOOKED UP AT LUCIENNE ON THE BATTLE-
ments after delivering Lady Joan to Thomas. Good. Lucienne
had feared that he might not see her in the crowd. He glanced
back at the two, then nodded, indicating that he understood this
was precisely the sort of thing Lucienne had warned him of. She
had spoken of Joan's vulnerability, the danger that she might
form an attachment to Thomas, her rescuer, and how that
would inconvenience Montagu, who counted on him as one of
his best captains. *I come to you, the king's most trusted adviser and
friend, asking you to convince His Grace that a marriage connection
with Albret is beneath him. For the girl's sake, my lord earl. She is so
very frightened. You'd meant her for your brother, but that did not
happen. Have you not another Montagu to suggest?*

Lucienne had worked on him over an intimate supper the
previous night. She'd confided to him how, when she'd been
but a year older than Joan, a fox like Albret had robbed her of
her innocence. Even so many years later, she could still taste the
suffocating fear, the despair of knowing the worst of men, the
dark side of their desire. Smiles and teasing words that had once
made her feel pretty and loved, then made her ill. To dance or
to sing had been to invite dangerous attention. In one heinous
act, her cursed uncle had sucked the joy from her life. She had
suffered in silence, telling no one of the deed, believing her uncle's threat to kill her if she accused him. Only in marrying the
elderly Lord Townley had she finally felt safe, protected by his
love, his wealth, his power. *You can do this for Lady Joan.*

Lucienne did not blame Joan. She understood her pain and
her need for the reassurance of a champion. Just not Thomas.
He was Lucienne's. Her husband was failing, he would soon
die, and she would be free to marry Thomas.

But at the moment Joan appeared to own him, heart and
soul, damn her. What man could resist the adoring gratitude of

such a beautiful young girl? The image of her golden hair curling so alluringly as she lifted her wide blue eyes to him, offering her favor, her light step as she was led away by the squire—all this would be fresh in Thomas's mind as he rode out to war. He would turn it over and over on the long ride south, contrasting it with his memory of the girl weeping and frightened on the morning of the attack.

She saw now how Thomas caressed Joan's cheek. *Sweet Mother in Heaven, watch out for my Thomas.* He was on a collision course with the king's intentions for his pretty cousin, and that could only end in Thomas's disgrace, and that of his family, who had put their hope in him as the one to restore their honorable standing. His eldest brother, Robert, was now Lord Holland, but he was focused on keeping his lands rather than on serving the king. The second of the four living Holland sons, Thomas had distinguished himself in the king's service. He meant to build on that, even going so far as vowing to join the Teutonic Knights' crusade against the Lithuanians as soon as King Edward could spare him. Lady Joan was a dangerous distraction. Lucienne could save him.

Now Montagu pressed his heart and bowed to her. Lucienne threw him a kiss. God grant him success. He was her best hope.

10

Ghent

Princess Isabella spun round and round, admiring how the flower border on her hem added a richness to her favorite gown. "Is such elegance wasted on our hosts?"

"No, not wasted," said Sandrine. "Jacob Van Artevelde is a very wealthy broker with a home fit for a king's dwelling, or so I'm told. And his wife, Katarina, is quite elegant."

Joan was at last to meet the man so detested by Albret and Brabant. Van Artevelde's notoriety among the nobles of the Low Countries was due to his having shrewdly taken advantage of an armed rebellion against Louis of Nevers, Count of Flanders, to rise to power. Though he was officially but one of five captains governing the city, everyone knew that he held the power in Ghent and had influence in the great merchant cities of Bruges and Ypres as well. With his small, well-trained army, he'd put down rebellions in those cities, making it clear that he was not to be crossed. He was said to be a persuasive speaker, inspiring loyalty, and for those who did not fall under his spell he engaged personal guards who were skilled assassins. Joan had lain abed the past few nights imagining those assassins surrounding Bernardo Ezi and first hacking off the offending hands, then . . .

Felice was suddenly behind Joan, fussing with her hair.

She had an impatient way with a comb, nothing like Sandrine's gentle ministrations. Joan looped her arm though Bella's and swept her away to the hall, joining the cluster of ladies awaiting the queen.

She enjoyed this moment before an event, everyone aflutter with anticipation, the whisper of silk, the excited voices. The queen's ladies wore bright-colored gowns glittering with gems, their hair finished with feathers and crispinettes of gold and silver wire.

"I've never been to the house of a commoner," Joan said. "Will we dance?"

Lady Lucienne laughed. "This is not so grand an occasion, nor are the Van Arteveldes, for all their airs. At best, we might have an opportunity to stroll about their house and gardens."

Now the household knights arrived, the few King Edward had not taken with him on campaign, and the women's voices rose to greet them. But the chatter ceased abruptly as the queen entered the hall, regal in red brocade, with a gold surcoat powdered with precious stones. It was one of the formal robes that she kept fresh and elegant, despite their financial straits, to signal her superior rank. Joan was surprised that she'd chosen to wear it for this occasion.

But when they arrived at the Van Artevelde home and she saw the handsomely liveried guards and well-trained servants, she understood. The large, imposing hall was crowded with elegant strangers shouting to be heard above the others talking loudly in many languages. The effect was dizzying, and Joan was glad of Philippa's strong grip on her arm. Her second surprise of the day was the queen's downward pressure on her forearm, indicating that she was to bow to Jacob and Katarina Van Artevelde—she, of royal blood, bowing to commoners.

A trumpet called the guests to attention, and all eyes were upon the five. Jacob Van Artevelde led the procession to the high table, escorting Queen Philippa. He had a plain but open face and a slender frame, a man perhaps in his fifth decade, with a quiet refinement. His wife escorted Joan and Bella. She was taller and much younger than her husband, and darkly beautiful. Her green velvet gown was bordered with gold silk, her crispinette aglow with emeralds that caught the light of the candles and torches. Joan focused on not showing her surprise at the unexpected elegance.

She was seated between her hostess and her eldest daughter, Thea, a plump, impishly smiling young woman who immediately barraged Joan with questions about England and Antwerp, and life at a royal court. As she answered, Joan watched the spectacle, the high table allowing her a clear view of most of those seated at the other tables in the hall. The cacophony of voices had risen as soon as those at the high table had been seated, forcing her to lean close to Thea at times. It was a relief not to worry that Albret might suddenly appear by her side. Even so, he was the subject of one of her companion's questions. *Is it true that he is the handsomest man alive?* Joan had assured her that, in her opinion, that crown went to her cousin King Edward.

Hoping that any moment Thea and her siblings would spirit her away from the high table for some fun, Joan asked what they did for entertainment—hawking, riding, chess, musical instruments, singing, dancing? Thea's responses were disheartening. It seemed they had little time for "idle pleasures," so busy were they assisting their mother in running the household when they were not at their lessons, or accompanying her on visits and errands.

Joan must have looked a little disgruntled, for Dame Katarina kindly asked whether there was any food she particularly favored.

"I am not of a delicate appetite," said Joan.

"But there must be dishes you particularly enjoy, my lady. Perhaps venison?"

Joan smiled.

"Ah! I thought so. What of fish? What would most delight you?"

Curious as to the limits of her host's hospitality, Joan said, "Sturgeon."

"And honeyed sweets, I would dare to guess. Yes, I see by your ever-brightening smile that it is so."

Within moments, a servant arrived with a platter of sturgeon. Joan slipped some onto her side of the plate she shared with Thea. Wine was offered, and she asked that it be watered a bit.

"You are a sensible young woman," said Dame Katarina. "My daughters complain when I water their wine."

"I am more curious than sensible, Dame Katarina. I'll see nothing if I fall asleep."

They were interrupted by a servant. Katarina excused herself. "I am called away to see to a matter of some urgency in the kitchen."

"The kitchen? But you are the lady of the household."

"I am the *mistress* of my household, Lady Joan. My servants receive their orders from *me*." She bowed. "If it please you, it might be kind to rescue Princess Isabella from Thea. I believe she's just gone to interrogate her."

Joan gladly rose to see how Bella was faring. Crossing behind the high table, she overheard a snippet of conversation as she passed the queen and Jacob Van Artevelde.

"You challenge his honor?" the queen snapped.

Joan slowed so that she might hear their host's response.

"It is said that the Sire d'Albret cares little whether he kisses the ring of England, France, Brabant, or the Holy Roman Empire as long as his own palm is crossed with enough silver to maintain his extravagant court and fund his border wars," Jacob said. "I believe it in my best interest to demand that, in exchange for my promise to support your cause, you provide me some assurance that Albret's and Brabant's power over you will not jeopardize our alliance. They do not approve of commoners bonding together to rule."

"Power over us?"

"I pray you forgive my bluntness, Your Grace, but you *are* in debt to Brabant, at least." Van Artevelde's hooded eyes were inscrutable from Joan's vantage point, but by his posture and the hint of a smile on his wide mouth she had an impression of self-satisfaction. He could not be more different from his wife, or from Joan's first impression of him.

Where would His Grace draw the line in wooing supporters, this king to whom his barons' and subjects' respect and love meant everything? Honored and beloved monarchs did not lose their thrones, as his father had. How much, then, would King Edward tolerate from a commoner like Van Artevelde? Or a lord like Albret? Too much, it seemed to Joan.

She shivered and continued on. Bella's tone was querulous as she tried to interrupt Thea's flow of questions.

"I see that this is the lively end of the table," Joan said as she joined them.

"Cousin!" Bella looked relieved. "Allow me to introduce you to Thea's brother and sister." She commanded Thea to step back and make room for Joan.

"But I—" Thea began to protest, then thought better of it and moved aside.

Cecilia, a few years younger than Thea, was a slender, rather solemn girl; Phillip, her brother, was a sturdy, pleasant-looking boy, though at the moment he seemed on the verge of falling asleep from boredom. But when Joan suggested that they all escape out into the garden, she was met with horrified looks. All three felt it an honor to be at the high table with a queen, a princess, and a lady.

The venison had just been served when Joan and Thea resumed their seats. Dame Katarina leaned over to tease her daughter that she must not make Joan feel as if she were being interrogated.

"You must forgive Thea," Katarina said with a smile. "She is excited to meet a young woman of royal blood. I do believe she and Cecilia expected you, Princess Isabella, and Her Grace to wear heavy crowns to the feast."

"I assure you, Dame Katarina, I asked almost as many questions in return."

"Good! Thea and Cecilia need practice in social discourse. You have been gracious in your responses. I noticed your reticence in describing the Duke of Brabant's children. And I apologize for her mention of the duke's friend, the Sire d'Albret. I noticed your discomfort at mention of him."

Joan felt herself blush and wondered at her hostess's admitting to such close observation. "He is an unpleasant subject."

"My daughters have heard him described as the most handsome, most amorous noble in France, and they heard a rumor that you and he ... Well, you see how silly they are. You are far too young to be mentioned in the same breath with such a man." It seemed she only then noticed Joan's distress. "I am as thoughtless as my daughters, it seems. I pray you, forgive me."

It was no wonder such things were said. Joan had walked right into his snare, and to the world it would look as though she had done so willingly. But to hear her shame so widely known ... "I would prefer to know what people are saying about me, unpleasant though it may be. As I would have appreciated knowing more about why he's called the Gascon stallion before suffering his company."

Katarina gave a surprised laugh. "That seems too amusing a description for such a man as he."

Joan agreed. "What do you know of him?"

"That he is feared by his people, trusted even by his allies only so far as their interests align with his. That he does nothing without consulting astrologers, alchemists, and geomancers, which suggests to me a man desperate for power yet mistrusting his own wisdom. But perhaps nobles are less wary of such guidance. Merchants put no faith in such purveyors of mystery. We are practical people, trusting in God and the fruit of our own labor."

"I am glad to know these things."

"Let us pray you are free to forget all you've learned of him."

She won Joan's affection with those words.

On the way back to St. Bavo Abbey, Joan and Bella shared what they'd observed, declaring their favorites. Neither cared for Jacob Van Artevelde. Bella thought Thea a bore—all those questions!—and Dame Katarina dressed above her station.

"I liked Dame Katarina's honesty and thought her more worthy of respect than many a noblewoman," said Joan. "As for Thea, I agree. But she's a collector of information, like you."

"You mean a gossip."

"I don't know how much of it she shares."

"Then what's the point?"

Joan shrugged. "How did you like Cecilia and Phillip?"

"She is a sly one, with funny names for everyone in the room. He was asleep with his eyes open throughout the feast. And he farted a lot." They laughed.

On their return to the abbey, they knelt with the queen and her ladies before the travel altar in her chamber, praying for the king and his men. "Even now they may be preparing for battle against my uncle," said Philippa.

Joan prayed for Thomas's safe return, and that her experience of Bernardo Ezi was well behind her.

11

In the morning, Queen Philippa greeted Joan with unusual warmth.

"I've just had a message from Katarina Van Artevelde. My dear Joan, you have triumphed. You share your father's affability. When Queen Isabella and my Edward first appeared at my parents' court, Margaret and Edmund had just married. They were such a handsome couple, and so lively. They were the talk of Valenciennes. All their best attributes have come together in you. Countess Margaret will be proud of you. You won Katarina with your beauty and grace, your maturity and courtesy."

"I am honored, Your Grace," Joan said, though her heart was hammering. Such praise usually came at a cost.

"What? So serious?" Philippa reached for Joan's hands and pulled her close to kiss her on the forehead. "She invites you and Bella to accompany her with her daughters to a local fair two days hence. Indeed, she expresses a desire for you to befriend her daughters, hoping that by your example they might grow in courtesy and grace. How say you? Is that not praise indeed? And something you might enjoy?"

"It is, Your Grace." Despite her impression that Thea and Cecilia were all duty and no play, Joan looked forward to exploring the markets and fairs. But, considering the queen's purpose in Ghent, she knew that something more than befriending Thea and Cecilia was expected of her. Particularly as Bella had not been included in this conversation.

And now she saw the look that presaged a more serious discussion.

"Let us sit by the brazier, my dear."

She was charged with learning all she could of the Van Arteveldes' tastes, their circle of friends, their loyalties.

"It is not so difficult as it sounds," the queen assured her. "Listen, observe, and when the opportunity arises ask questions—such as the identity of someone Dame Katarina has addressed, whose livery the messenger is wearing. Your mother has entrusted me with your training in diplomacy. Here is your first test."

Her mother had asked for no such thing, but Joan merely nodded. It was dangerous to cross or disappoint Queen Philippa, and Joan felt the weight of this new responsibility.

To spy on those who were likely using her to spy on the queen? A delicate mission, particularly as Joan saw in Katarina Van Artevelde a potential ally against Bernardo Ezi, should she need one, considering the enmity between her husband and Brabant, and, by extension, his good friend. She must find a way to please the queen while endearing herself to Dame Katarina and her family.

"One more thing, my dear." The queen, smiling, told her that the Sire d'Albret's knight, Sir Olivier, awaited her in the courtyard with a gift.

Joan recoiled. "I will accept nothing from him!"

"It is meant as a peace offering, an apology, and you *will* accept it. I order you to do this, Joan. It binds us to nothing. Lady Angmar will accompany you."

The sorrel palfrey was bright-eyed and eager for the apple Lady Angmar had given Joan to offer, delicate in taking it. Joan thanked the knight in the name of Queen Philippa, and as he

spoke she realized that she'd seen him before, most recently in
the abbey church, though never before had he worn the livery of
Albret. At the market and elsewhere in Antwerp, he'd dressed
plainly—so that she would not know he was Lord Bernardo's
spy? She tried to tell the queen about him after he left, but she
waved it off.

"It is necessary to keep the peace, dear Joan. You see? You
are learning a great deal about diplomacy."

Or betrayal, Joan thought, biting her lip as she took her leave.

ESCORTED BY TWO KNIGHTS FROM THE QUEEN'S HOUSEHOLD AND
the armed guards who accompanied the family at all times,
Thea and Cecilia Van Artevelde led Joan and Bella through the
city to the waterfront, where they would board a barge to take
them to the fair. All the while, the girls regaled them with colorful gossip about the townsfolk. Their witty exaggerations had
Joan laughing much of the way.

On board the barge, Joan chose to sit in the covered area
with Dame Katarina and Sandrine, who escorted Bella everywhere, while the other girls stayed out in the sunlight flirting
with the two knights. For a little while, Joan was content to
drift in and out of the polite conversation, noticing the flatness
of the landscape, the scents of the river. Equally of interest to her
was Dame Katarina, expensively clothed in a gown and cloak
of brunette, and a hat that seemed woven of peacock feathers.
Such wealth. Even the barge would have been quite acceptable
to the queen.

Catching Joan's eye, Dame Katarina asked, "How do you
find my two magpies? I hope they do not weary you—they have
so looked forward to showing you their city."

"Not at all, Dame Katarina. They are very funny, and they
seem to know everyone in Ghent."

Dame Katarina looked out. "They are amusing. Ah, look,

they've fallen asleep in the sunlight. Do you think Princess Isabella is warm enough?"

Sandrine took that as a suggestion to see to them, and went out to tuck a lap rug round the girls.

"I understand that you are pursued by the Sire d'Albret even here," said Katarina. "That his man, Sir Olivier, presented you with a fine sorrel palfrey."

"Her Grace assures me it is no pursuit but meant as a formal apology. How did you hear of it?"

"My brother witnessed the purchase. The palfrey is of noble lineage, like you, and impeccably trained. A costly gift for an apology. I should think it would trouble you."

Joan nodded. "*And* the man who presented it—I believe he has followed me from Antwerp to Ghent. But to what purpose? I do not agree with Her Grace that accepting the gift binds me in no way to the Sire d'Albret."

Katarina's eyes widened. "I do not like the sound of this. Point this man out to me if you see him. At least when you are in my company you will be safe from him."

Katarina's response troubled Joan, seeming to confirm her suspicion. It stayed with her throughout the day, dampening her enjoyment of the fair, though she did her best to keep up with the others, tasting unfamiliar foods, dancing with Thea to songs in languages she did not understand, choosing colorful feathers and ribbons to present to her new friends on the journey home.

In the following week, she and Bella accompanied Dame Katarina and her daughters on a tour of the gardens of Ghent, dined with a peat baron and his four daughters, and spent a night at the country manor of a minor noble whose daughter Jacob Van Artevelde hoped to win for his son Phillip. It was on their approach to one of the gardens that Joan pointed out Sir Olivier standing beneath the eaves of a house across the narrow street. Dame Katarina had called to her guards and quietly identified the man as someone who should be encouraged to move on whenever he was spotted in their vicinity. Not seeing him again on any of their excursions that week, Joan began to relax and enter into the enjoyment of exploring Flanders.

Queen Philippa seemed satisfied by what little Joan gleaned for her. "You have befriended the most important family in Ghent, my dear. I could not ask for more. As a token of our gratitude, I have a gift for you. It is high time you had a skilled lady's maid of your own. Mary is ill suited to the task. Go on. Helena awaits you in the nursery." She looked quite gratified by Joan's surprised thank-you. "She comes highly recommended by your new friend, Katarina Van Artevelde. The young woman was trained by her sister-in-law, who married very well—a minor lord in the service of Jan of Brabant. Alas, she died in childbirth a few months past, and Helena needed a new position. Their tragedy is our good fortune. Now go! You've much to discuss!"

Gowns and a lady's maid. Joan distrusted the queen's uncharacteristic largesse. But she liked Helena at once. A pleasant-looking young woman, small, plump, and efficient, she had impressed Felice and already befriended Sandrine and Prince Lionel's nurses. Indeed, all in the nursery seemed cheered by her arrival—except Mary, who scowled and sulked and waited for Joan to prompt her before following any of Helena's directions.

As the days grew shorter, Joan, Bella, and the Van Artevelde girls spent more of their hours together indoors, often talking over needlework, Dame Katarina and her friends rounding out the group in a pleasant corner of the Van Arteveldes' hall that had the benefit of southern light. How easily they all took their turns in the conversation. No one was queen here—not even Bella, with her royal title. The servants often interrupted Dame Katarina, who wore the household keys on her girdle when at home. Master Jacob sometimes paused in his coming and going to tease his daughters—he was a different man with them than he was in public, jovial and warm. Phillip and his younger brother Jan studied with their tutor at the opposite end of the hall, often calling out to ask what had set the women laughing. Joan envied them this life of ease and daydreamed about what it might be like to wed a wealthy merchant, or a lesser knight, such as Sir Thomas.

12

On a stormy day in late October, a herald, his hauberk muddy, his banner limp, rode through the gates of St. Bavo Abbey to announce King Edward's approach to the city, returning from campaign. He and his troops would enter Ghent on the morrow.

Queen Philippa was closeted far into the evening with the herald and another knight, who arrived later in the day, while her household rushed about readying the king's rooms in the abbey and the barracks at Gravensteen Castle for his knights. When at last Philippa came into the hall, pinched-faced and agitated, Bella reached for Joan's hand and whispered a prayer that her father was safe.

"My uncle Philip of Valois refused to engage his troops with ours despite the devastation wrought in Cambrai by our army," Philippa announced.

"But that is good news, is it not, Your Grace?" asked Lady Angmar. "Are His Grace and his men unharmed?"

"There were few casualties. No barons or knights suffered harm but for the unpleasant aftertaste of a chevauchée. But all hope of a quick settlement to this conflict was dashed by my uncle's refusal to fight."

No knights suffered harm. Then Thomas must be safe. Joan crossed herself and said a prayer of thanks.

At dawn the rains ceased, and the city burst into life preparing a fitting welcome for King Edward and his army, hastily erecting stands from which the citizens of the city and the royal household might watch the procession, stretching red-and-gold banners with the lions of England across the streets and squares. While the queen was yet at Mass, Jacob Van Artevelde and his fellow captains appeared in the hall to consult with her, resulting in a flurry of frantic whispers and early departures from the abbey church, though Philippa herself remained kneeling in her pew, head bowed, until the end of the service.

In the nursery, Bella could not contain her excitement at her father's return, fidgeting so while being dressed that Sandrine thrice pricked herself while repairing her hem, and waking her baby brother with her loud chatter and laughter. Joan's own heart fluttered in anticipation, and, halfway through dressing, she changed her mind. "The rose-and-blue. I meant to wear the rose-and-blue. This green will seem dull beneath the gray sky," she said, blinking back tears of frustration. She wanted to outshine Lucienne. Without any fuss, Helena asked Mary to shake out the rose-and-blue gown. "Do as she says," Joan snapped when the maid hesitated.

"Is he not like Arthur of old?" Bella sighed as her father rode through the gate, his armor polished, his pale hair streaming out from beneath a simple gold crown, his cloth of gold cloak and the gold-trimmed caparisons on his mount brightening the gray day. Behind him his barons rode beneath their own coats of arms, the earls of Salisbury and Derby first in line, with the bishop of Lincoln between them. As the crowd cheered, Master Jacob and his fellow captains rode forward to welcome King Edward and join the procession into the city.

At last, behind Salisbury's banners, Joan saw Thomas, sitting tall in the saddle, his head high, his dimples showing as he caught a flower tossed from a balcony, laughing with his squire, Hugh. Then he turned, his eyes searching the stands. Joan lifted her arm, and he lifted his to reveal the gold silk tucked into his sleeve. She bowed to him, pressing her heart.

Bella giggled. "You are wicked! Lucienne is searching the stands for her rival. Lower your hand. Did you not see the silk in his sleeve? She will think it is yours."

Joan did not correct her.

Gravensteen, the castle of Louis de Nevers, Count of Flanders, would be home to the king's men while in Ghent. The count had fled to France when the merchants took over the principality, and his castle, built a century earlier in the fashion of crusader castles, was little used. It was perfect for housing the king's men, with barracks, stables, and practice yards to occupy them. They would need distraction, for they'd marched for weeks with little to show for it, no glorious battles, only burning and pillaging, leaving a bitter taste in their mouths that required copious amounts of ale and wine to dispel. They found the heroes' welcome they'd received embarrassing, the banners, the flowers strewn in their path all undeserved. It was up to Thomas and his fellow captains to ensure that they took out their frustration in the practice yard, and eased their comfort with camp followers, not the daughters of the citizens who had so warmly welcomed them.

It was several days before Thomas and his fellow captains felt easy enough to leave and partake of a feast at the abbey. As they entered the hall, Roland and Guy made straight for the table already crowded with their fellows, but Thomas hesitated, searching the crowd for golden hair. He found Lady Joan seated between a man he guessed to be the abbot of St. Bavo and an elegant, dark-haired woman to whom she was talking with much gesturing and laughter. His breath caught in his throat.

Joan was as beautiful as he'd remembered, and so close. In three strides he could be beside her, kissing the top of her head, drinking in her scent. She would glance up, her eyes widening. Her smile lighting her sweet face, she would lift a hand to touch his cheek—

"Six days, Thomas. I feared you'd forgotten me." Lucienne slipped her hand in his and leaned close, roses and spice, breasts almost tumbling out to welcome him, those violet eyes searching for a sign of his desire.

His body betrayed his heart, lusting for Lucienne, though he'd thought little of her since they parted.

"Food or pleasure first?" she asked.

He glanced past her, saw Lady Joan turn to smile at him only to notice with whom he stood and quickly look away.

"Food first, pleasure later." He kissed Lucienne's hand.

"Behind the stables after vespers. I know a place." She kissed his cheek and moved on.

He made a point of crossing in front of the high table, hoping to catch Joan's eye. When she glanced up he bowed, hand to heart. For a moment, she looked uncertain and he cursed Lucienne, but then came the smile he so loved. He stepped close, and she introduced him to the abbot and to Dame Katarina Van Artevelde, who studied him closely. Little was said, nothing of consequence but that Lady Joan gave thanks to God that he and all the king's men had returned safely. He kissed her hand and withdrew, joining his fellows at one of the lower tables.

She'd noticed, the Van Artevelde woman—she'd seen how he lingered over Joan's hand. She must think him mad, obsessing over this royal child. But Joan had him, heart and soul, and he could no more stop thinking of her than he could stop breathing.

There had been a moment when, had he acted on his first impulse to keep his distance from his royal charge, he might have preserved his heart. On the third day on the road to Ipswich, Joan had ridden up beside him offering a wineskin—*You look pinched and thirsty.* In truth, he'd been hung over from the previous night's strong ale and wanted nothing more than to ride silently on until they stopped for the night and he might sleep. But he'd thanked her and taken a good, long drink, then forced himself to smile at her as he returned it. She'd put her hand over his—*No, keep it with you.* And he'd found himself grinning like a fool.

"Thomas! Here!" Roland shouted, opening a space for him at the table, slapping him on the back as he took his seat. "She's been waiting for you, eh? Lucky dog. I know. Lucienne favored me once. Before *you* came along."

It proved a long, tedious feast, without the distraction of dancing, which might have allowed him a few precious moments with Joan, and as soon as he spied her departing with the other young guests he slipped away.

By evening an icy drizzle chilled Thomas, despite his fur-lined cloak, as he waited for Lucienne behind the abbey stables. He could not remember a tryst with her that had not been fraught with risk and discomfort. She preferred it that way.

A whisper of silk, and suddenly she was there, stroking his cheek, radiating warmth. "Come, Thomas. We have a room with a bed for a few hours."

She led him across the courtyard, between buildings, dodging the light of the torches.

"A monk's cell?" he hissed as she drew him in. "Are you mad?"

"Even a monk may like the jingle of coins in his secret purse, Thomas. The bed is hard and narrow, but he assures me the walls are thick enough to mask the sound of our passion."

But there was little to hear.

"It's Lady Joan you desire, isn't it?" She put a finger to his lips. "I saw how she drew your eyes. She is not for you, Thomas. Stay away from her, I beg you. You have too much to lose. She is meant to secure Gascony for the king."

"She is still intended for Albret's son?"

"Why else would he present her with a costly palfrey?

"He is here?"

"No, one of his knights, Olivier, delivered it. But what else could it mean? She did not refuse him, Thomas."

"Even after what Albret did?"

Lucienne shrugged. "That is unimportant. You must see that he is crucial in protecting the Aquitaine, now more than ever. Such damage in Cambrai—where will Philip of Valois wreak vengeance?"

Thomas did not want to believe that Joan would accept anything from a man who had so frightened her. "Surely she was ordered by the queen to accept it."

A shrug. "Of course. An apology. Certainly a pretty one. When she rides the sorrel, the sweet silver bells on the harness Albret bought for her in Antwerp jingle merrily." Lucienne stroked Thomas, kneading him, moving above him, waking him to her charms.

13

Gravensteen Castle, Ghent
10 NOVEMBER 1339

King Edward and Queen Philippa had chosen Gravensteen
Castle's great hall for Martinmas Eve, a celebration of the harvest before the long fast leading to Christmas. All the household,
the local merchants, and an army of borrowed servants decked
the grand hall in tapestries and banners and filled it with white-
clothed tables that would soon be groaning with the bounty of
the season past, for many the last fresh meat from the culling
before winter. The queen's ladies wondered among themselves
where the royal couple had secured the funds for such extrav-
agance, given the healthy amounts still owed the allies they
wooed in the Low Countries and the Holy Roman Empire. Yet
such regal display was as necessary as military might, and this
night the royal couple honored the captains of the city of Ghent
and their wives as their special guests, warming them up for a
meeting the following day at which King Edward would negotiate for their military support against Philip of Valois. It was
said that he meant to promise he'd return to them the towns of
Lille, Douai, and several others Valois held.

Her arms outstretched so that Helena could make a few
final adjustments to the open, hanging sleeves of her overgown,
Joan thought about the changes a year had wrought. Just before
Martinmas a year earlier, she and Ned had stood in the porch of

St. Mary Magdalene pledging their troth. Now he was intended
for Marguerite and Joan for the son of a man she feared and
despised. As Mary held up a mirror so that she might see herself
in the gown Helena had transformed for the celebration, Joan
saw reflected not that girl who had dared hang the white hart
banner in the hall at Woodstock but a young woman. It made
her sad. A lady's maid, the gowns, the lessons learned from
being too friendly to Albret, the pain Joan suffered whenever
she saw Sir Thomas and Lady Lucienne together—the past six
months had brought a mixture of grace and torment, so alien
to her cares back home. Better? Worse? It did not matter. This
was now her life.

"My lady, do you not like it?" Helena asked. She had decorated the wide-sleeved deep azure overgown with pearls and
silver buttons in celestial designs, and the long, tight sleeves and
skirt of the pale blue underdress shimmered with mother-of-
pearl.

"I cannot believe what I see in the mirror, Helena. Is this
me? So beautiful?"

"It is, my lady."

In the hall, she and Bella paused to gaze with wonder at
the extravagantly costumed guests balancing fantastical head-
dresses fitted with ships at full sail, knights with lances poised
for the joust, birds taking flight. The queen had ruled that her
daughter and Joan were too young to cope with such fanciful
headwear. Joan was glad, but Bella complained that she felt
small and underdressed, and rushed over to complain to Thea
and Cecilia. Catching sight of William Montagu, Joan joined
him, admiring the hawk on his hat. It was quite lifelike, and
posed so that it seemed to be studying Montagu's own beak of
a nose.

"A hawk for a hawk, my lord—a perfect choice for the far-
seeing Salisbury."

He bowed to her with a laugh. "You grow more beautiful

every day, Lady Joan. What do you hear of your mother and brother?"

"Very little. I had hoped you might have heard something of Mother's feelings about my proposed betrothal to Albret's son."

"Not yet. His Grace persists in this?" Montagu cursed beneath his breath. "Is Lord Bernardo in the city?"

Joan shook her head. "But his knight, Sir Olivier, spies on me."

"Unacceptable! And I am troubled that Countess Margaret has not written to you. I shall ask Her Grace about it."

"And what of you? *You* promised to write."

"Rest easy, young Joan. I have proposed a plan that I think both you and Countess Margaret will find to your liking."

"My lord Salisbury, forgive me, but I must interrupt." The queen had swooped down on them. "Come, Joan. We must take our places at the high table." Philippa nodded to her page to bring Joan along in the royal procession, then spoke softly but sharply to Montagu.

Joan wanted to rush back to him and demand to know his plan. But the page brought her to the king himself, and all other thoughts flew from her head. He often borrowed themes from the tales of King Arthur for his feasts and tournaments, and had never seemed more like her image of King Arthur of old than at present, his long purple robe shimmering with gemstones threaded on gold and silver wire, his pale hair, so like hers, glimmering beneath a gold filigree headpiece that represented a helmet of war with eagle feathers in silver. It gave him the appearance of a wise elder, though in fact he was but a few years older than Sir Thomas.

"My fair cousin." Edward reached for her hand and placed it in the crook of his arm. "You will dance with me later, Joan. I have not had the pleasure for many a day." He looked down at her with shining eyes. "What a beauty you're becoming. I do hope Albret's son proves worthy of you."

She caught her breath. "I pray that I am never so cursed as to know, Your Grace."

Though he still smiled, one side of his mouth twitched, and he moved his gaze to the top of her head. "My son tells me you are clever and see the truth of people. But I trust you also weigh their importance to the good of the realm. We must never lose sight of our duties as the royal family, must we, cousin?" He awaited her answer.

"Have I ever disappointed you in any way, Your Grace?"

"No, dear cousin, you have not. But in our great endeavor to win back our birthright—yes, I fight Valois for all our family— we might be called upon for greater sacrifices than in times of peace. I meant only to spur you to our cause." He paused to look her in the eye, serious now. "You've made no promises, you and my son, have you? You are not holding yourself for him?"

Joan forced herself not to look away. "What a question, Your Grace. Has Ned said so?"

"Perhaps I misunderstood."

"We are the best of friends, as you know." She smiled. "But we were yet children when we parted."

"Children. Indeed. Though my son thinks he knows his mind." He bowed to her. "I will not permit any harm to come to you, sweet cousin."

An impossible promise to keep, Joan thought as she bowed to him, her pearl-encrusted sleeves brushing the tiled floor. "Your Grace, I will be honored to dance with you." She did not gift him with a smile.

At the high table, she was relieved to be seated between one of the queen's Hainaulter cousins, an affable man, and Dame Katarina, who was proving a good friend. Indeed, she'd been true to her word, keeping Albret's man Olivier away from their house. Joan had perforce tolerated him at a few of the queen's dinners, but in the company of the Van Arteveldes she breathed freely, confident that he would not appear. And, so far, he seemed absent at this feast, an appropriate concession she'd counted on.

Katarina commented on Joan's entrance. "The Earl of Salisbury, Her Grace, King Edward—you are considered an important guest, Lady Joan."

"I chose to speak to Earl William and was interrupted by Her Grace, whose page took me to His Grace. Not important but potentially troublesome, Dame Katarina."

"Troublesome? Would they be right?"

"I cannot predict what I might do should they continue to favor my marriage to Albret's son. What think you of Helena's handiwork?" She raised her arms so that the pearl-encrusted sleeves caught the candlelight.

"Beautiful! I thought you would be just the young woman to appreciate her gifts."

Katarina was describing some of the work Helena had done for her when King Edward interrupted them with a hand on Joan's shoulder, claiming his dance. Looking up, up—he was so tall he loomed above her, she felt a shiver of dread at what she might suffer from him should she choose to disobey. But she took his proffered hand with a smile.

He led her into a slow dance in which the partners approached, withdrew, joined and turned, hands touching, palms touching, then apart, eyes meeting, then turning away. The king's body seemed to hum with power, and Joan felt herself warming to him, relaxing into his lead, enjoying the dance. It was over too soon.

As the king led Joan back to her seat, she asked him about his fascination with King Arthur.

He smiled down on her and pressed her hand, which she'd lightly rested on his forearm as they walked. She felt his warmth through the purple sleeve encrusted with gems.

"Do you not enjoy the tales of King Arthur's court?" he asked. "Do you not hope to live on in song and legend as he has?"

"I do enjoy the tales, Your Grace. But, as for living on in songs, I give that little thought. I should be content to be remembered by those who loved me, judged on how I lived my life, not on my status."

"That will never be so for you, cousin. You are not simply a beautiful young woman, you are of royal blood, close cousin to a king, with all the duties and honors that entails. As to your question, I set such themes in costume to remind us of who we are. All the court. Indeed, I've considered establishing a Round Table to inspire my barons and knights, a reminder of our higher purpose."

"Alas, Your Grace, you shall be too busy with your war to see to such fine endeavors."

"Ah, but it will be the perfect vehicle through which to unite the nobles of both kingdoms." He bowed to her with a victor's self-satisfied smile, and handed her over to her next partner, Count William of Hainault. A few more partners brought her back to William Montagu.

"We were speaking of my mother's thoughts regarding the Sire d'Albret, my lord."

"Forgive me, but Her Grace has asked that I not poison your mind against the man. Still, I will inform Countess Margaret of my continued concern. It is not right that she should not be told of this proposed match."

"And the plan you spoke of?"

"I leave it to Countess Margaret to tell you, if she approves."

Joan saw by the set of his jaw that she must be satisfied with that for the present.

She danced with other lords and merchants, growing pleasantly tired.

"Who was your favorite partner?" Dame Katarina asked when Joan returned to her seat.

"All of them," she said, laughing. But her mood soured as

she caught sight of Lady Lucienne, smiling up at Sir Thomas as they danced.

Dame Katarina noticed. "Watch how Sir Thomas glances your way, and then turns on her his most dazzling smile. You have nothing to fear from Lucienne."

Joan felt herself blushing. "Don't be silly. He's nothing to me." Since his return a fortnight ago he had said little to her, seeming to go out of his way to avoid conversation.

Katarina smiled, clearly seeing through Joan's protest. "Prudence is wise, particularly when your heart is set on someone other than the man whom your guardians have chosen."

"I have no intention of following my heart. I must uphold my family's honor."

"Now you have made me sad. You'd sounded so fiery earlier, threatening trouble if they persisted in pushing you toward Albret's son." Katarina put her arm round Joan and gave her a squeeze of affection. "God has given you beauty, grace, and courage. For what? Have you asked yourself that question?"

Joan had not noticed until now, as she studied Dame Katarina, that the seed pearls powdering her sea-green silk gown suggested fish scales, and that the flowing feathers in her headpiece imitated the motion of seaweed, or a woman's long hair underwater.

"Are you a Siren?" Joan asked.

"A simple mermaid."

"I do not believe there is anything simple about you, Dame Katarina."

"No?" She smiled dreamily as she watched the dancers. "Would it not be a welcome change if the woman might ask the man to dance? Why should we always be the ones to sit here, yearning? Why should they always be the ones to choose?"

Joan sighed. "Why indeed?"

"There is one who does not wait. I was watching when

Lucienne strolled by Thomas Holland and brushed his arm, tilting her head toward the dancers when he looked round, a sly smile, a slow blink, as if reminding him of the pleasure of moving together to the music. She may be a strumpet, but she lures him with such art I find I quite admire her."

"She has earned the right to please herself," said Joan. "She married an elderly lord, immensely wealthy, and bore him sufficient sons to ensure his legacy. But I—one misstep and I'm for the convent."

"Truly? Are women of the royal blood deemed so untrustworthy that they may not choose with whom to dance? One dance? My father was quite stern about his daughters' reputations, but even he would not deny us a dance with a handsome knight."

Perhaps Joan might tease Thomas into a dance, but she wanted more. Before the campaign he had watched over her, lovingly, she'd thought, and he had accepted her favor, worn it on his return, smiled at her once in the hall, and then—nothing. She wanted to know what had happened. She wanted him back.

Joan turned to the queen's cousin, engaging him in a few moments of chatter. But when she saw Thomas part with Lucienne and move toward the door to the yard she excused herself and followed. Outside, the air enlivened her—fresh, crisp, and though the sun was low in the sky it was not so chilly as to make her regret having no cloak. Men stood about in clusters, knights and barons mixing with the wealthy citizens of the city. The king would be pleased. The only women Joan saw were the wife of one of the captains, coming from the privy with her personal maid, and a few maidservants pouring ale and wine. Joan searched for Thomas, at last sighting him walking near the chapel. She hurried after, skipping ahead of him so that she might block his escape.

"Sir Thomas!"

"My lady, you should not be out here alone, and without a cloak. I pray you, fetch your maidservant." He made as if to move past her.

Joan reached for his hand, turning it palm up. It was calloused and chapped, but the lines were clear. "I wonder which of these might have warned me of your discourtesy?" With a finger she traced the longest line, pausing in the middle. "Might it be here, where it suddenly divides?"

"Discourtesy?" His voice had softened considerably, and his expression was one of surprise as he met her gaze.

"I offered you my favor, my father's emblem, and you accepted with such a beautiful smile, I thought you understood. Yet since then you have kept me at a distance. Did my gift mean nothing to you?"

"Of course it did. I hold you—" He withdrew his hand, balling it into a fist, and looked away.

They stood just outside the chapel. "Come within." She took his arm and led him through the door, slipping onto a bench just inside. A few candles fluttered on the altar, the sacristy lamp softly illuminated the painted walls, but here, near the door, only a small lantern lit the entrance. And they were quite alone. "Something has caused a rift between us, Thomas, and I would know the cause."

He sank down with elbows on thighs, forehead in hands.

"Thomas?" She touched his shoulder. "What have I done to push you away? I counted you as my friend, my champion."

"I am confused about Albret's costly gift. What the queen intends by having you accept it."

"You know of that." She felt herself blush. "I don't wonder. I did not want the palfrey, but Her Grace insisted that I accept it as a formal apology. To do so does not bind us, she assured me. But His Grace has set his sights on Albret, warning me to remember my duty."

He straightened. "I feared as much."

"I will not obey them in this, Thomas, I will not." Her voice broke. Mother in heaven, not now. She must not cry now.

"Sweet Joan, forgive me. I'm a witless gudgeon." He brushed a tear from her cheek.

She leaned close, looking into his eyes, then kissed him on the lips. Her heart pounded at her boldness. "I think I love you, Thomas."

His large, warm hands were on her shoulders. "You're just a child, Joan. A child. What can you know of love?"

"I am not a child, Thomas. I am nearly a woman. Albret certainly noticed. So have you, and the king." She slipped her arms around him, pulling him close, and kissed him again. He tasted of sweet wine and spices. His breath caressed her cheek as his arms came round her waist. She kissed his cheek, then his mouth again—

They jumped apart at a sound, then laughed to realize it was a candle settling in its sconce.

"Heaven help me," Thomas groaned, and rubbed his face as if to wake himself. "I need air."

Joan caught his arm as he rose and moved toward the door. "Can you not say it? Do you not love me?"

He pressed his forehead against the wood. "God's blood, Joan, do you need to ask? I have loved you since that night on the ship."

She stood on tiptoe and pulled his head toward her, kissing him once more. "I will tarry here a little while. When I return to the hall, ask me to dance. I *will* have a dance with you this Martinmas Eve." She stepped away. "Now go!"

Before following him she knelt at the altar, praying to the Blessed Virgin to watch over and protect her, protect Thomas. She jumped as the door creaked open behind her, letting in a chill draft.

Helena stepped in, holding out Joan's fur-lined cloak. "My lady, I thought you might need this."

"It is most welcome. But how did you find me?"

"Dame Katarina told me you'd gone out, and when I saw Sir Thomas leaving the chapel I thought I might find you here. Princess Isabella and Her Grace have both asked after you, my lady. We might slip round the chapel to the privy, then enter through the far door."

They stepped out into a biting wind that presaged a cold rain.

BLINKING IN THE SUDDEN BRIGHTNESS OF THE GAILY LIT HALL, Thomas stood in the doorway of the screens passage and considered his next step. He must not seem to be waiting for Joan to appear. Nearby, Jacob Van Artevelde spoke with William and Edward Montagu. They would be a poor choice of companions from whom to break away to claim a dance with Joan.

"Before you engage in conversation, you might check your clothes for pearls, like this one on your shoulder," Lucienne whispered, so close behind him that he felt her breath on his neck. She plucked a sliver of mother-of-pearl from his jacket. "So she wrapped her arms round you?"

"Who? I see a number of gowns with pearl decorations."

Lucienne laughed and joined the Montagus and Van Artevelde, and soon Sir Edward was leading her out to join the dancers.

Of all the dangers Thomas and Joan faced, Lucienne was the most immediate, her jealousy a warning. He went in search of a mazer of wine, but changed direction when he spied Joan at the far end of the hall, handing over her cloak to her lady's maid. As she moved, the mother-of-pearl on her arms shimmered, drawing eyes to her, and before he reached her she'd accepted the hand of one of the captains of the city. Thomas must wait his turn, sipping some wine, letting it warm him. When the music slowed, he moved to claim his dance.

"Why, Sir Thomas. It is so long since we last danced."

Was it possible that this vision of beauty and grace loved him? She was flushed from the previous dance, her eyes bright, and he wanted to scoop her up and kiss her before all the crowd. But he settled for dancing two sets with her. Then she asked him to escort her back to the high table.

Katarina Van Artevelde smiled up at him. "You must escort Lady Joan and Princess Isabella on one of their frequent days away with my family, Sir Thomas. I should like you to see our countryside from the gentler aspect of a palfrey or a barge rather than a warhorse. Do say you will." Her tone was casual, but her remarkable cat eyes warned him to accept.

He remembered how she had watched him lingering over Joan's hand a few weeks past. "I can think of nothing I would enjoy more, Dame Katarina." *And I shall watch you like a hawk,* he added silently.

14

Bella shook Joan awake. "You spoke Ned's name in your sleep. What was the dream?" she whispered.

Joan sat back against the pillows, hugging her knees, trying to blink away the afterimage of the raised axe, the severed head. Thomas's head. "It was a darksome dream," she whispered, remembering Ned's words a year past: *We now are betrothed and you cannot accept another gift like Bruno.* If he'd killed Bruno out of jealousy, what might he do to Thomas? Not the axe, a more subtle revenge, but deadly nonetheless? She drank deeply of the posset Helena brought her, letting its potency slow her racing heart, draw her back down into drowsiness. "I dreamed of Ned in battle with the bloodlust upon him. It frightened me." She shivered.

Bella pressed her head against Joan's. "He would love that you dream of him fighting bravely."

For days Joan prayed that it had not been a premonition, that she had not condemned Thomas by loving him. The fear shadowed her, robbing her of appetite, sobering her mood, inspiring expressions of concern from Bella, Thea, Cecilia, Helena, Sandrine, Dame Katarina, even the queen. At last she confided in Katarina, telling her of the dream, of the vow Ned had coaxed from her a year earlier, his resentment of the puppy given her by a potential suitor, Bruno's death.

"If you were my daughter, I would warn you to keep your distance. I am troubled that such character is manifest in the future king and can only pray that his tutors and trainers inspire in him a radical change. He is quite a contrast to your Thomas, a man of honor if I ever met one." She kissed Joan's hand. "Be at peace, my lady. The prince is not free to choose you for his future queen. He knew that when he coerced you into pledging your troth."

"Nor am I free to choose Thomas."

"No?" Katarina looked toward where he stood at the front of the barge with one of his men, watching the shore. "That is still to be seen. Sir Thomas picked out the surrogate Sir Olivier had set to follow us and removed him from our tail, and I've complained of Albret's ignoble tactics to Her Grace, as well as sharing with her quite damning information about him. Of course, the queen received it without comment. She could not admit to favoring him after he disgraced himself. But I pray she is as sensible as she seems."

"It is not for her to decide. My cousin the king will do what he must to save the Aquitaine. That goal is the seed to the wider war he now wages. If Albret is the key . . ." Joan shrugged. It always came back to that.

"I understand the terrible burden of ambition. My life changed when Jacob and his fellows came into power. Suddenly nothing was safe. Our home was guarded day and night, we could go nowhere without armed protection. Ever vigilant, ever juggling rivals. But I made one vow—that I would never allow Jacob to force our children into unions with families who represented everything we abhorred but would further his ambition. Never. I understand the queen's loving support of her husband, but I cannot believe she will be so ruthless toward you. And if she is—no, your mother would curse her to the end of time, and she could not bear it. Already the queen is grieved by the pain she's adding to her own mother's mourning by supporting her husband's attack on her brother's crown. When she finally *sees*, she will not allow this."·

"The dowager queen Isabella once loved my mother, held her closest among her women, and she loved my father as a brother. But when he threatened her ambition she stood back and watched her lover destroy him."

Still, despite her protest, Joan found comfort in Dame Katarina's words. The queen attended Mass every day, spent hours in prayer—surely God and the Blessed Mother would guide her. And perhaps even Earl William might have a hand in changing her mind.

Always, the nearness of Thomas calmed her. She felt his presence as a shield against all danger.

But this comfort was to be short-lived, for by late November he had been sent away on a mission for the king.

15

Westminster
NOVEMBER 1339

Hot with fury, Margaret pressed her forehead against the shutter, letting the snowstorm's icy breath soothe her brow, William Montagu's letter crumpled in her hand.

Her anger at the betrothal Edward and Philippa proposed for Joan was laced with guilt. She might have accompanied her daughter—indeed, she knew that many considered her a negligent mother to have stayed behind. But she had fought too hard, too long, to recover her late husband's properties and honors for their surviving son and heir to go abroad for a protracted period and leave it all unguarded. Her daughter had been but eleven, yes, but her son, John, was only eight. He needed her protection more. Or so it had seemed.

Such a choice! Of all the men in Christendom, Philippa and Edward had chosen Arnaud Amanieu, Bernardo Ezi's son and heir, as a husband for Joan. Idiots! Margaret remembered Bernardo's wife, Mathe of Armagnac, a shrew who would have sold her soul—and probably had tried—to win a place at the French court. Margaret's only daughter was to be traded for such a feeble alliance? No. She would not accept this insult. She would not give her permission for this.

But she must speak up quickly. A messenger must be sent, with William's weight in the king's regard added to her objection. William had warned that they were at war and Albret was part of Edward's strategy; to oppose the match could be construed as treason. Yet, in the same letter, he'd complained about the marrowless, cold-blooded alliances on which Edward was building his northern army, how little it would take for Philip of Valois or the pope to break the resolve of the barons and captains of the Low Countries and the Holy Roman Emperor.

Did William waver from their long-held plan? Would he not fight to keep Joan free to wed one of his kin? He wrote that King Edward had already lost one planned marriage alliance, that of his daughter Joan with the heir to the Frankish kingdom, so was all the more determined to secure Albret's support, placing his hope in Gascony.

Margaret would not capitulate; she would not give up Joan's chance for safety among the Montagus. There were others she might have taken as lovers, some of them marriageable, but she had chosen William for who he was, what he might mean for her daughter. That she had come to love him complicated matters, but her family came first.

She called for her clerk, already composing the letter to the king in her head, weighing whether or not to mention William's suggestion of a better mate for Joan. In so doing, she would force William's hand. She deemed it time. The king would know, in any case, that William had written to her about the proposed betrothal.

Forgive me, William, but you would do as much for your children.

16

St. Bavo Abbey
EARLY FEBRUARY 1340

Suddenly, just after Candlemas, Joan found herself crying at the slightest discomfort or sharp word. She had no appetite, nor did she find any joy in her usual occupations. Even Queen Philippa's suffering as her lying-in grew near brought on tears. Joan's dreams were weighted in sadness and her body was frighteningly sensitive.

And then, early one morning, she woke with a deep, dull stomachache. Her limbs felt leaden as she fought to untangle them from the bedclothes, and as she sat up she felt a slithery wetness between her thighs. Reaching past Helena to open the bed curtain, she saw in the faint light from the brazier a dark stain spreading beneath her. Blood.

Awake now, Helena whispered for Joan to follow her.

Within moments, Joan sat by the brazier wrapped in a warm bearskin, a rag between her thighs, a mazer of brandy-wine in her hands. "Too strong," she protested after a taste.

"Sip it slowly, my lady. It will warm your stomach and soothe you."

She did not think anything could soothe her. This was the event she had most dreaded, the sign that she was ready not only to marry but to consummate the union. It would be impossible to keep it secret. Already the nursemaids were whispering, and Mary, not one to miss the opportunity to trade gossip for a favor, had slipped from the room. Joan could only pray that Sir Olivier had no spies in the household. And that God would not forsake her.

FROM BEYOND PHILIPPA'S CHAMBER DOOR EDWARD'S VOICE RANG out in sharp commands. He and Jacob Van Artevelde had just returned from Bruges and Ypres, where they were to discuss with the other city captains the spring campaign to regain control of Lille and Douai. Clearly, something had gone wrong.

"Plump up my pillows, then leave us," Philippa told her ladies and the servants. "And leave the wine." As the women swept out the door Edward strode in, taking charge of the chamber, his dark blond brows drawn together in temper. Ignoring his scowl, Philippa flashed her most radiant smile and opened her arms. "Come kiss me. Then sit beside me and tell me all your news."

He pecked her on the cheek, and she caught the scents of fresh air, sweat, and the ale he drank with his men to express his bond with them—a combination of smells prefacing marital discord. He paced away, tossing his gloves on Lady Clare's lute as he passed it. The strings sounded, as if inviting him to play. But Edward was deaf to pleasure at the moment. As he turned on his heel, Philippa sighed at the churning emotion distorting his handsome face.

So it had been more often than not of late. Many a night he paced her chamber, railing against Parliament for its failure to send the money needed to move forward with his war. He had already awakened the dragon in accepting the double crown of France and England; to back down now would be a humiliation no king could survive. But in truth all the alliances were proving dangerously fragile, some dissolving before his eyes. Their youngest daughter was on her way back to Ghent, negotiations having broken down with the Franks. Pope Benedict continued to stall regarding the dispensation for Prince Edward's marriage to his cousin Lady Marguerite.

Philippa's own temper had been razor-sharp, particularly on the days when she received a letter from her mother criticizing Edward's actions, and the previous day she'd had a passionate argument with her brother William, Count of Hainault, after which he'd stormed out of the guesthouse and ridden off before the feast planned in his honor.

"My men caught several spies for Louis of Nevers engaged in discussions with captains of Bruges and Ypres, carrying letters from Pope Benedict threatening excommunication for taking up arms against Philip of Valois."

"Would you expect otherwise of the Count of Flanders? Of course he is trying to wrest control from you. But you have foiled his attempts."

"Thanks to Thomas Holland. He has the instincts of a hunter and has trained his men well. Yet too many waver. They turn toward the highest bidder. Bernardo Ezi is a case in point. Where is he? I invited him to my crowning. Why did he not attend?"

"Perhaps he has what he wanted all along. You publicly named him one of your two lieutenants in the Aquitaine. Let it rest for now. There is little time and much to do before you leave and I withdraw for the birth." Edward was to take ship for England in a few days to confront Parliament.

He turned back to the window, flinging open the shutters, inviting in the fading, misty light, a scent of rain. "Curséd place."

"In truth, I am relieved that Bernardo Ezi did not come," Philippa said. "After his behavior toward Joan, I do not trust his intentions. And now that she has flowered I could not risk a meeting. . . ." She pressed her swollen eyelids. "If he could not control himself then—"

That brought Edward back to the bed to pour a cup of wine. "Her flowering? You've told no one?"

"The household knows, perforce, but of course we keep such matters to ourselves. What we need to discuss is Bernardo Ezi and his insult to your authority. Everyone seeks to inform me that his reputation preceded his time in Antwerp, that he has an insatiable sexual appetite, that he has intercourse with virgins so that their blood restores him, that half his men-at-arms are his bastards, and there is the nickname, the Gascon stallion—"

"God in heaven, wife, these are old slanders. Who is resurrecting them?"

"That is not the point, Edward. Despite my efforts to silence the household regarding the insult, it appears that it is common knowledge. I understand why you made him lieutenant in the Aquitaine, but the proposed marriage is now out of the question. It would look as if you were turning the other cheek."

Edward muttered a curse. "You sound like Montagu."

"Good." She knew he was thinking of Montagu's proposal, which had Countess Margaret's full support.

"What else have you heard?" he demanded.

"Your captains believe that Albret's man Sir Olivier is here to observe their preparations for war. To what purpose, Edward?"

This, at least, concerned him. "I *am* disturbed about the captains' distrust of Olivier. I must know Albret will be loyal, that Brabant did not mislead me. I will have Holland look into it. If all the rumors point back to Van Artevelde, I can discount them. There is some old enmity between him and Albret, older than that between Van Artevelde and Brabant. I would not trust anything he or his wife says regarding Albret or his man."

"I pray you are wrong about the Van Arteveldes. I've arranged for Joan to stay with them during my lying-in."

"Why? Would it not be better for Bella to have her friend here?"

"It's for Bella's sake that I'm sending Joan away. Since her bleeding, your cousin has suffered such nightmares that she's upset all the nursery. I thought to give them all a respite. Bella's already worried about me. Dame Katarina has ample room to provide your cousin with a private chamber where she will not disturb the rest of the household. Helena can tend her."

Edward patted Philippa's swollen hands. "Good, good. Artevelde will see her presence as an honor. Well done, my love."

"And when I am churched we should send your cousin home. Once our Joan arrives with her entourage, we will be too crowded here. To make room, I plan to send Lady Lucienne and a few others back to England. Your cousin can join them. It is best, Edward. If we wish a chance at another, more suitable marriage for her among our allies, her absence should silence the gossip. In time."

Heaving a great sigh, he agreed. "Her presence served its purpose. Albret saw in what high regard I hold her, what honor she would bring to his family."

"Edward!"

"Peace, wife. I've come to no decision." Edward drained his cup and looked round, at last noticing that her chamber was already crowded with her women's cots, the birthing chair, and all the rest of the necessities of her lying-in. "I see I returned just in time."

"Yes, I sense the birth is nigh, and we've much to do." She held out her arms to him. "Come, rest beside me for a few moments."

In the early hours, they planned several meetings for the next day. When all else was settled, Philippa handed him a sealed letter, to be opened with the children if she died in childbirth. He shook his head, pushing it away. She knew he did not want to think of the possibility of losing her. She was his anchor, his ablest adviser in matters of diplomacy, his protection against evil.

"I pray you, Edward."

"Give this to the chamberlain, not to me. I cannot bear to see this. And you are healthy, yes? You have borne four babies without trouble."

She stroked his forehead. "You dislike how powerless you are against nature, I know. But you must be prepared, husband. If God should choose to take me now, I will be at peace knowing that you have this safely in hand." She tucked it into his girdle. "Put it in your scrip, then come lie down with me again—hold me before we must rise and meet the day."

He left their bed at first light, returning shortly after Mass. "I prayed for you, my love." He sat down in the chair she'd had brought near the bed, beside a table with the necessary documents. "Let us complete our business so that you might be easy in your mind as you withdraw for the birth of our child."

EARLY MARCH 1340

HAUNTED BY THE MEMORY OF A DREAM OF A SAVAGE BIRTHING, Joan found comfort in Queen Philippa's serene air as she lay back against the silken pillows listening to Lady Lucienne read from tales of King Arthur's court. The chamber had been freshened with sweet-smelling herbs and filled with bright-colored hangings and cushions. Lady Clare softly played her lute in the background. All bespoke tranquillity, comfort, sanctuary.

Every now and then, Philippa interrupted Lucienne to deliver one more instruction, particularly to Bella. The princess had suffered several nightmares of late after overhearing the wet nurses trading tales of horrifically difficult births, and had earlier beseeched her mother to permit her to stay in her chamber.

"Your sister Joan and her ladies will almost certainly arrive while I am indisposed, Bella. You must welcome her into your bed and comfort her. From all accounts this has been an unpleasant experience for her, and she is much diminished in spirit. She will need you far more than I will."

Bella had dabbed her eyes and shrugged. "Cousin Joan could welcome her."

"No, your cousin cannot. Come the morrow she will bide with the Van Arteveldes to make room for your sister and her entourage. I am depending on you as the elder sister."

Bella made a face at Joan. But her testiness was nothing against Joan's fear. From the moment she had awakened with cramps and found blood on her chemise, she had been terrified, counting the days until she was safe in the well-guarded Van Artevelde home. Dame Katarina spoke of unusual activity at the lodgings of Sir Olivier, as if the household were preparing for an honored guest. Albret? Did he know of her flowering? Had he come to claim her?

"Of course, we might be wrong," Katarina had said to Joan. "And it is only hearsay. But I wished to warn you to have a care."

Now the queen was asking Joan whether Dame Katarina had been filling her head with stories about the Sire d'Albret.

"Nothing that I have not heard from others, Your Grace."

"I advise you to weigh all that you hear against the fact of a long-standing unpleasantness between Jacob Van Artevelde and Bernardo Ezi."

At vespers Joan, Bella, and Lady Clare left the queen's chamber and gathered in the chapel with all the household to pray for the queen's safe delivery. Then, for this one last night, Joan cuddled beside Bella, whispering words of comfort, doing her best not to sleep and frighten her cousin with her troubled dreams.

17

During the night the temperature dropped precipitously, freezing the water so that in the morning the household came to a halt while sufficient water was heated for Her Grace. Bella grumbled and declared that she would lie abed until she had her hot tisane. Unable to sleep, Joan dressed in her simplest gown and accompanied Lady Clare to Mass in the abbey church. She was glad of her decision when she stepped out into the courtyard. Thick snowflakes drifted down, and though clouds obscured the sun, the morning was bright with a lacy white coating. In the church nave, the scent of incense and the flicker of torches, though offering little warmth, wrapped her in a sense of cozy comfort, quieting her mind. The nave was far from crowded, so she was able to see more of the congregants than usual, noticing the mix of elegant and threadbare cloaks, and how many were sniffling from the cold. A group of men stood in the back by the doors, haggling about something in loud whispers; two women stood near them trying to shush a wailing child. And just beyond them—Joan gasped as her eyes met those of Bernardo Ezi. He grinned and bowed to her as bells signaled the end of Mass.

Grasping Helena's arm, Joan whispered that they must hurry out with the crowd, they must not be left behind.

"What is it, my lady? What's frightened you?"

"The Sire d'Albret. He is there, in the back of the church, and he saw me. He knows that I saw him."

Helena looked where Joan pointed, and crossed herself.

"What's amiss?" asked Lady Clare.

"I'm cold," Joan said. "Let's hurry back to the guesthouse."

Outside, snow blanketed the abbey grounds and came down in graceful whirls on a wind that lifted their cloaks and left them momentarily breathless. Helena, Lady Clare, and her lady's maid exclaimed as they bent into the wind for the short walk back to the guesthouse. Cloaked against the swirling snow, Joan lifted her skirts and hurried on ahead of the other women. This would be the perfect time for Albret to snatch her, when they were busy battling the capricious wind.

Suddenly Thomas was at her elbow, startling her as he offered her his arm. "God bless you, Thomas. My champion, even in the snow!"

"You rushed out of the church as if something happened."

"Did you not see him there? Albret?"

"In church? No."

"He stood in the back corner of the nave. Helena saw him as well. He has come for me, Thomas. I saw it in his eyes."

"I'll take you directly to the Van Arteveldes. Sir Roland is at the guesthouse. He'll accompany us. Helena can follow later." One arm around her, he steadied her along the slippery path.

Though he was a comfort, she was relieved when they were within sight of the guesthouse, light spilling out the open hall door, and Van Artevelde's guards, a half dozen, mingled at the entrance with the king's men.

Inside, Dame Katarina apologized for arriving early.

"I hoped to take you away before the storm worsened," she said. "But you went to Mass! Helena, make haste to prepare. We must leave at once."

❖ ❖ ❖

WHILE JOAN AND BELLA SHARED TEARFUL EMBRACES, DAME KATArina took Thomas aside.

"Did she see Albret at Mass?" she asked.

"How did you know?"

"One of my husband's men saw him enter the church and came to warn us. My heart goes out to her. I pray you, dine with us today. She could use some cheering, don't you agree?"

"Of course I will come."

Within no time Joan and Helena departed, leaving Thomas to stew about how soon he must be away. He had so little time to ensure Joan's safety.

When he made his way to the Van Artevelde manse several hours later, the snow had ceased and the day had warmed, turning what had been a muted wonderland into a cacophony, roofs and trees dripping, the melting snow crunching underfoot. By the time he arrived at the manse, his left boot had sprung a leak and he cursed himself for a fruitless detour past Sir Olivier's lodgings, where he'd seen no sign of life. A servant helped him off with his boots, offering him a pair of soft leather shoes for his comfort. Dame Katarina swept by to welcome him, assuring him that Joan was settling in.

"We've given her the visitor's quarters, set apart with her own little parlor and bedchamber, to allow her some privacy. My daughters might else drive her back to the abbey with their constant attention." With a flustered smile, she was off to see to something in the kitchens.

Now Jacob appeared to invite Thomas to his private office for a talk "while my wife sees that all is ready." His welcome was carefully staged, Thomas thought, even down to his glimpse of Joan in the hall, smiling up at him from her seat between the Van Artevelde daughters. God in heaven how he loved her, how it hurt to think of her smiling so at another, how impossible it was to accept that she might marry another and be gone from his life forever.

"Lady Joan is safe here, I assure you," said Jacob. His smile—was it truly what it seemed, knowing, slightly amused by Thomas's infatuation? He hoped he was not so transparent.

Inviting Thomas to take a seat on a cushioned bench, Jacob settled across from him, a small table with a flagon of brandywine and costly Italian glass goblets between them. A servant poured, then withdrew. After the usual courtesies, and a surprisingly frank explanation of the business deal gone wrong that had caused the initial enmity between him and Albret as well as an admission that he made it his business to know Olivier's movements, Jacob Van Artevelde apologized for his wife's earlier behavior.

"Clearly she upset the entire household, rushing Lady Joan away as she did. When she learned of Albret's arrival in the city last night, and that he'd gone to Mass in the abbey church, she believed her worst fears—" He paused, sipped his brandywine as if to steady himself against his wife's emotions. "To be blunt, Katarina insists that Albret purposes only to seduce Lady Joan, that she's not meant for his son. My wife means to propose to you a plan to rescue Lady Joan from Albret's clutches once and for all. It is, of course, not my place to advise you. I mean only to give you fair warning."

"She would have us wed?"

Jacob closed his eyes, bowed his head. "Ah. I am too late. I had not anticipated that."

"No, Dame Katarina has said nothing to me. We are merely in accord, if that is her plan."

"You are both mad!" Jacob gave a pained laugh, squeezing his brows together, shaking his head. "Forgive me. It is not my place. But to abduct the cousin of His Grace the King of England and France . . . He would not forgive you. You, one of his most trusted captains."

All true. His mother, his elder brother—they trusted Thomas to restore honor to the family. Knighted young, he was meant to rise in the ranks of King Edward's army. He had prayed over this, begged God to clear his mind of her, his heart. But from the moment she offered him her friendship Joan had possessed him, body and soul, and God had left it so.

As for Albret, Lucienne had left Thomas with no doubt as to the Gascon's intentions. He had noticed how she avoided Albret, never smiling at him, this woman who could not rest until she had aroused every man in the room, touching them, looking deep into their startled eyes, convincing each that it was he she desired. Except Bernardo Ezi.

"You've shared his bed and he frightened you."

"No. He prefers younger flesh."

Thomas had begged her to warn Queen Philippa.

"Not *so* young as your Lady Joan, I assure you. Besides, Her Grace has heard all the stories about the man."

It seemed it was up to Thomas to save Joan. He prayed that his family would understand. "Would you and your wife stand as the witnesses to our vows?" Thomas now asked Jacob.

"You would do this?" Jacob waited for his nod. "If it is truly what you wish, and if the lady agrees, we will stand as witnesses. But, as I told my wife, I have one condition—that you keep this secret until after the campaign to free Lille and Douai. If His Grace should learn of our part in this, he might choose not to honor our agreement, claiming I had betrayed his trust. And he would be right in that."

"But Albret—"

"Nothing will be agreed before then. Lady Joan is to return to England after Her Grace's churching. By midsummer, you will be free to write to your mother and brother. There is time."

His knowledge of the queen's intentions and the makeup of Thomas's family set up alarms. "Might I speak with Lady Joan in privacy before dinner?"

"Do you not need more time to consider what this might mean for your future?"

"No."

"Ah. Perhaps I do not give my wife enough credit. She swore that it was so, on both sides." Jacob rose. "After dinner, I pray you. My wife wishes that we first break bread together."

SHAKEN BY THE EVENTS OF THE MORNING, JOAN HAD RETREATED TO her bedchamber for an hour before emerging to engage with Thea and Cecilia. The room had its own entrance through the courtyard, protected yet discreet, with an anteroom set up as a private parlor. As she rested on the great bed, a plan had insinuated itself into her mind. She and Thomas would pledge their troth, with the Van Arteveldes as their witnesses, and consummate their union in this very bed. This was their chance. The queen was closed away, the king at sea—this was their chance to choose their future. Who was to say that this moment wasn't God's gift, that he hadn't meant them to be together? *If* they had the courage to choose love over all else. This might be their only chance of happiness.

She pricked her courage to broach the subject with Katarina.

"A betrothal!" Katarina's eyes lit with pleasure. "You have found your courage, my lady. I thought you might. Of course we would stand witness to your vows. But consummation, no, you are too young."

"Once only. So that I am not a virgin."

"Oh, my dear—"

"In my dreams that is what he wants, my first blood."

"I think you will find yourself much comforted by the betrothal, Lady Joan. Leave the other for a later time."

"If he agrees?"

Katarina would not commit. But how could she prevent it? It was Thomas who must agree. Joan was asking him to risk everything for her.

All through the dinner she watched him, smiling whenever she caught his eye, softly bringing the conversation round to him again and again—his prowess in tournaments, his status among the king's guards, asking after the health of his mother, Lady Maud, his siblings. In a fine forest-green wool tunic with the king's new heraldic device of the French fleur-de-lis quartered with the lions of England, a Lincoln-green hat making some order of his dark curls, as wild as hers from the weather, he sat tall and proud at the table, his dimples charming Thea and Cecilia, his exploits impressing their brothers, Phillip and Jan. It was only afterward that she remembered how quiet their hosts had been, neither Jacob nor Katarina saying much, busy casting enigmatic looks toward each other.

It seemed an interminable meal, but at last Dame Katarina rose, inviting her daughters to come with her to take some alms to an elderly neighbor. After they departed, Jacob said that he would send a servant with some hot spiced wine to Joan's private parlor.

"You would like some quiet conversation, I should think."

ONCE THE SERVANT DEPARTED, THOMAS SEEMED AWKWARD WITH Joan, perched on the edge of the chair across from her as he spoke of the weather, the Van Arteveldes' hospitality, some of the conversation at dinner. She had never seen him so uncomfortable.

When he rose suddenly, she did as well, snaking her arms round his waist, fearing that he meant to leave. "What is wrong, Thomas?" She pressed her head to his chest and felt his heart beating wildly. He took a deep breath. She looked up, expectantly.

He was gazing down at her with an uncertain smile. "I fear I am about to be the biggest fool in the realm, Joan. At Martinmas you spoke of your love for me. And ever since—I have convinced myself that you might against all reason agree to marry me. Would you, Joan? Would you have me as your husband?"

Relief brought warmth and giddy laughter. "Yes, oh, yes, I will take you as my husband, Thomas, for I love you above all other men." She stood on her tiptoes to kiss him.

"Even if Albret did not exist? Would you still take me?"

"Even so."

He gathered her close, whispering into her hair, "I cannot express how happy I am, my love."

After a long kiss, he spun her around with a great shout, then carried her over to a bench where they could sit side by side. She lifted his hands and pressed them to her cheeks, then kissed each calloused palm.

"You make it difficult for me to think," he said, laughing. Those beautiful dimples appeared. "I've asked Jacob Van Arte- velde if he and his wife would stand as our witnesses, and they have agreed. On one condition. That we keep our betrothal secret even from our families until after the campaign to Lille and Douai. He fears that King Edward would withdraw his support."

She was a little disappointed by how quickly he moved on to the practical. She'd expected more kissing. But she took a deep breath and considered what he'd said. "The king would not withdraw his support, he has worked too hard to gain theirs."

"Jacob is firm on this. He says there will be time, that Queen Philippa is sending you back to England after her churching."

"It is the first I have heard of it."

"He is certain that nothing could be decided with Albret until the king returns, and by that time you will be in England."

"This begins to feel like a trap, Thomas."

"I know, though I cannot fathom what they have to gain. Still, their knowledge of the queen's plan troubles me, and I will warn Salisbury. But I mean to use their scheming to our advantage. I've thought of nothing but this for so long, and now they have provided this chance."

"Thomas, you come to this freely, do you not? They have not coerced you?"

She was relieved to see a flash of anger.

"On my honor, Joan, no one decrees where my heart shall go."

"God be thanked." She took his hands again, kissing both of them. "Hugh and Helena must also witness. Their word would not carry as much weight, but if Queen Philippa surprises us and we need to reveal our betrothal—"

"Yes, of course."

"There is one thing to which Katarina would not agree, but she has no power over us. I want not only to pledge, Thomas, but to consummate our vow. Tonight or tomorrow night. Before you depart on your mission. Then no one can come between us. We will be husband and wife."

"No, Joan, you are too young."

"I have flowered, Thomas." She saw that he understood. "Albret may know of this. We must lie together, just once. So no one can deny it. It is important to me, Thomas. It will stop the dreams."

He studied her face for a long time. "I will lie beside you. Just that, nothing more, unless you invite me."

It was enough. "On this very eve, my love, we will pledge our troth with Dame Katarina and Master Jacob as our witnesses." She slipped onto his lap, and with each kiss she felt less sure of her bearings, a sensation that was perversely pleasurable.

AFTER THOSE FIRST TENDER MOMENTS, SHE AND THOMAS WERE separated when Dame Katarina arrived to see that Joan rested awhile. Helena poured the two women some wine, and they sat in high-backed chairs by the brazier in the bedchamber. As the unwatered wine relaxed her, Joan sat back, appreciating the beautiful room—the painted walls, the tapestries, the carved chairs, tables, bedstead, the fine linen on the bed—the whole surpassing all but the queen's own chamber both here and at Windsor.

Katarina interrupted her reverie. "I trust you understand the import of what you and Thomas are about to do, and that my family accepts a grave responsibility in assisting you."

"I am aware of the solemnity of what we do tonight."

Katarina took Joan's hand and looked her in the eye. "Thea and Cecilia must not know of this. You shall pledge here, in this private parlor."

"I swear."

Katarina glanced over at Helena. "I am glad you have a lady's maid you can trust. Is Thomas's squire as trustworthy?"

"Thomas would not otherwise keep him."

"I pray that you long have joy in Thomas, and he in you."

They were quiet a moment. Joan risked a little more wine, feeling it warm her.

A knock on the door, and a servant called out, "The master and Sir Thomas are here."

Katarina patted Joan's knee and rose. "Stay a moment. I've something to fetch for you."

With steady hands and a comforting silence, Helena freshened Joan's hair.

"How beautiful," Dame Katarina said from the doorway. Draped in her arms was a linen chemise embroidered with butterflies. "If you mean to lie with Thomas tonight, I have a gift for you." She extended her arms, and Helena lifted the soft garment. "If you choose simply to talk awhile, save this for your wedding night."

"Thank you for trusting that I know my heart," said Joan.

"Ah. You have decided." Katarina kissed Joan's forehead and held her a moment. "Come now, it is time."

In the antechamber, Master Jacob bowed and kissed Joan's hand.

"My lady Joan. It is an honor to witness such a joyous event."

"*Benedicite*, Master Jacob." She bowed in turn. "May God bless you and your family for the hospitality and friendship you have shown me."

At the door stood Thomas, with his squire, Hugh. Seeing the latter's uncertainty, Joan thanked him for standing witness as well. Helena went to stand beside him.

Thomas stepped forward, upright, proud, his face alight with affection. Smiling at him, Joan suddenly felt light.

"You are sure of this, my love?" he whispered.

"I am, Thomas." Giving him her hand, she turned with him to face the Van Arteveldes.

Thomas took the ring Hugh held out to him and slipped it on Joan's finger, a gold ring with a small green stone. "I, Thomas Holland, vow that I will wed you, Joan Plantagenet, before a priest, as soon as I may, and thereby I pledge you my troth."

Joan repeated the vows in her name.

"It is only a bauble, but I had no time!" Thomas whispered as he drew her into his arms.

She did not care. She felt safe, loved, happy, imagining her father smiling down on them. She did not care to imagine her mother's reaction.

A quiet toast was shared in the antechamber, and then Katarina led Joan into the bedchamber to change into the delicate garment. Joan was suddenly cold, when just moments before she had felt overheated. Helena combed out her hair as Katarina poured her a cup of brandywine. It made Joan's eyes tear, but she welcomed the heat it created in her belly. She was terribly aware of her nakedness, barely concealed by the gauzy fabric. She drank more.

"Not too fast!" Dame Katarina cautioned with a laugh. "You do not wish to be drowsy when Thomas comes to you."

They led her to the bed, and plumped the cushions so that she might sit up. Dame Katarina kissed her on the forehead.

"Good night, sweet Joan. May you and Thomas be happy."

She and Helena left the chamber. Alone there for the first time, Joan felt as if she had fallen off the edge of the world into a void so vast there was nothing to stop her, no hope of a safe landing. Her stomach ached, her vision blurred, she gasped for breath.

And then Thomas was in the room, silently stripping down to a fine linen shirt, his legs bare. As he slipped into the bed beside her, he must have seen her distress. "Joan, my love, what is wrong?" He drew her close, warming her, breaking the spell.

"Oh, Thomas." She wept with relief.

He held her, stroking her hair, reassuring her that he would never do anything to hurt her. "We need do nothing but this tonight," he said. "You are safe with me, Joan."

"No! No, Thomas, we must do what a husband and wife do. I cannot lose you!"

"You will never lose me. You have my heart forever."

A kiss, another, and soon Joan lifted off her chemise.

Thomas touched her breasts, her waist. "God help me. Do you know how beautiful you are, my love?"

She blew out the bedside candle and slipped back under the covers, drawing him to her.

AT DAWN, BIRDSONG WOKE THOMAS, AND WHAT HE'D THOUGHT WAS a long dream of yearning proved to be impossibly true. Curled up beside him, her pale hair covering his chest, was his beautiful Joan. His wife. God in heaven, his wife! As he lay there, the heat from her young body tantalizing him, he prayed for her happiness, that she would never find cause to regret their union.

"Thomas?" she whispered, opening her eyes, smiling up at him. "Oh, you *are* here. I feared I'd only dreamed it."

"A good dream? That dispelled your nightmares?"

A sleepy smile. "No nightmares." She shyly covered herself as she propped herself up on one elbow, and now, in the light from the window, he saw a sadness in her blue eyes.

"I pray I did not hurt you, Joan."

She touched his cheek. "I love you, Thomas. A little pain does not change that. I am sad because this morning you must go, and I must pretend that nothing happened. I want days with you—weeks, months, years."

He held her close for a little while, but it was true that he must return to his men, to his duties. "Shall I return tonight?"

"Of course, husband!"

SHE LAY WATCHING HIM DRESS, ADMIRING HIS BODY, MUSCLED AND lean. "You are perfect. My perfect husband."

"I do not know what I did to deserve you."

As she eased herself off the bed, she discovered deep, unaccustomed aches. She pulled aside the mound of covers to show him the bloodstains.

"Proof!"

He set down the mazer and gathered her up, lifting her so that they might be eye to eye. "No regret?"

She shook her head and planted a kiss on his lips.

As they shared the wine, he wondered aloud what their next step should be. "For the moment, I must go back to the abbey, attend to my duties."

She forced a smile. "And I need to behave to Thea and Cecilia as if nothing had happened."

But Dame Katarina helped her put that off for a day, suggesting that she tell Thea and Cecilia that the previous day had so wearied her she would keep to her bed. Joan noticed shadows beneath her hostess's eyes as she advised Helena on how to fold the sheet so that the stain would be easy to display as proof that Joan and Thomas were husband and wife, but not immediately visible and so might be safely stored until needed. Katarina assured her that all was well; she was happy for Joan, and looking forward to the following day, when they would all attend Mass at the cathedral.

"What about Albret?"

"Apparently, he has left the city. Olivier as well. You are safe, Lady Joan." As Katarina took her leave, she kissed Joan on the forehead in a distracted manner, her gaze far away, and at the door she glanced back for just a moment with a slight frown.

As Joan stepped into the hot bath Helena had prepared, she wondered at Katarina's demeanor. And Albret's sudden disappearance. Yesterday he had leered at her in the abbey church and today he was gone. That was so unlike his previous behavior as to make her question whether she had actually seen him. But Helena had seen him as well, and the Van Arteveldes had been alerted to his presence.

No matter, she had what she wanted. And more. The feelings aroused in her as she and Thomas lay together—so that was how it was when a man stirred a woman. She closed her eyes, sinking into the hot water, smiling to think of how it had been, praying God's forgiveness for her wantonness.

18

William Montagu paced in the dining hall at Gravensteen Castle, awaiting Thomas.

"My lord earl." Thomas bowed, hastening to apologize for his absence.

Montagu tilted his head to study Thomas with his good eye. "You've the look of a man who spent the night in bed sport. Good. You'll have little of that in your future. You ride south tomorrow."

"Why the change, my lord? I had planned to leave three days hence."

"Two nights past, the Sire d'Albret's man packed up his household and disappeared. His landlord says they left in great haste, leaving food, wine, even some clothes behind. It smells rotten to me and I want you to follow him south, see whether he's communicating with Valois's men in Lille and Douai. If you find them, escort them over the border into France to ensure that they do no more harm, and then hasten back to report."

Two nights past? "What of Albret himself? Van Artevelde claimed his men saw him here yesterday."

"That is news to me. His man distracts us while he's lodged elsewhere?" Montagu cursed under his breath. "Duplicitous bastard. I warned the king. Lady Joan would be wasted on his son."

"What do you think is Albret's purpose?"

"Damned if I know. I'll double the guard on the abbey—Her Grace's time has come, and all is in uproar at the guesthouse. It is up to us to keep the royal family safe."

"To that end, I would warn you to watch the Van Arteveldes. I was troubled when I spoke to Jacob yesterday." Thomas told Montagu of the man's knowledge of things he should have no way of knowing, and prayed him to warn the queen when she returned to public life.

As soon as the earl departed, Thomas sent Hugh in search of the guards who had escorted the queen's ladies to church the previous day. Questioning them, he did not like what he heard—that neither of them had noticed Albret in the church. Had Joan seen what she feared to see? Could Van Artevelde's men have misinterpreted what they had seen? One or the other he could believe, but both? And Helena? Could the Van Arteveldes have hoodwinked him? How? Dame Katarina could not have learned so quickly of Joan's fright in the church.

"Stay a moment, Sir Thomas," said one of the guards. "I did notice Lady Joan take fright. But at Durand, Van Artevelde's man. He was watching her. Dressed up in fine clothes, he was. Fancy boots for a snowstorm. He might look like the Gascon at a glance. Same hair, nasty dark eyes."

"Durand, the ox," said the other guard. "He does have the look. As long as he neither speaks nor walks—foulmouthed and lumbers like an ox. But standing still at the back of the church, he could look like him."

Thomas sent men out to scour the streets, the taverns, find out whether anyone had seen the Sire d'Albret in Ghent within the past day. Or Olivier.

THE MOMENT SHE OPENED THE DOOR TO THOMAS, JOAN SENSED trouble. He kissed her hands, then strode past her into the parlor, poured himself some brandywine, and slumped down on one of the high-backed chairs, taking a long drink.

She brought a stool so that she might sit at his feet, resting her head in his lap. "What has happened?"

"My orders have changed. I am to make haste to Lille and Douai, departing at first light. I can stay only a few hours."

"No! Why?"

"Olivier has disappeared. Albret is nowhere to be found. Salisbury suspects he is in communication with the French. If I find either, I'm to escort them to the border."

"I will be safe."

He stroked her head. "From the Gascon, aye."

She looked up, searching his face. "There is something more, Thomas."

"Is that not enough? That we have so little time together? Who knows when I will return? Whether you will still be here?" He dropped his head back against the chair.

"Then let us treasure what little time we have." She rose and took his hand. "Come to bed, my love."

"I will not hurt you again."

"Then just hold me."

He followed her, but refused to undress, removing only his boots and stretching out on top of the covers.

"Why did you leave your maidservant Mary at the abbey?"

Joan climbed onto the bed, sat back on her heels beside him. "Mary? What do you care about her?"

"I wondered why. Whether Dame Katarina said anything to you."

"If you mean had she warned me that Mary is a gossip, that was nothing I did not already know, though I had not guessed the extent of what Dame Katarina told me the other day. Mary regularly went to Albret's man Olivier with news of the queen's household. Jacob's men followed her. So Katarina thought it best to leave her behind."

"Why? Mary already knew where you would be biding. What harm would her being here do?"

"What are you thinking?"

Thomas shook his head. "I can find no one apart from you, Helena, and the Van Arteveldes who claim to have seen Albret yesterday."

"Are you accusing me—"

He put a finger to her lips. "No," he said, his voice tender. "Not you, my love. Them. I fear they went even further than we had guessed to push us together. One of their men was in the church, dressed to look like Albret."

"Why would they so trick us?"

"I do not know, and that is what worries me."

"Thomas, you are frightening me. We pledged our troth and lay together as husband and wife. We are husband and wife. You will honor that? You *will* tell your family?"

At last he looked at her, startled. "Of course I will, Joan. As soon as I may." He pulled her down so that her head rested on his shoulder. He stroked her hair. "My beautiful Joan. You are my love, now and always. My regret is in rushing you. And now to leave you. I have not behaved honorably."

"You are my champion always."

He kissed her then, and she wrapped herself around him, tightly, tightly. For just a little while. He'd frightened her. A knight was all about honor. She prayed that his doubts would not strengthen while they were apart.

In Jacob's office, Katarina and her husband studied a contract regarding one of their ships. She suddenly shook her head. "I've no patience for this right now."

"Our guests?" Jacob asked. "Are they difficult?"

"Not at all."

"Then what?"

"I feel unclean. Helena's spying, how we tricked them. The lies about Albret, the virgin blood. She would not have insisted on lying with him. She is so young. She will suffer. They both will."

"In time, perhaps. We do not do this for personal gain but for the good of all the merchants. King Edward must see that his strength is here, in the north, not in Gascony. By killing his chance at such an alliance in Gascony, we force him to continue to support us."

"She's but a child, Jacob."

"You shed tears over her? We have *saved* her from the cursed Bernardo Ezi, made certain she has an honorable man. Helena assured us that Lady Joan loves him. Whence come these tears, wife?"

"They will punish her. Mark me, the queen will take out her frustration on the girl because she cannot afford to attack us." She looked back in the direction of the chamber that Joan and Thomas shared. "I fear for them."

"They are lawfully wed."

"A king and queen might do as they wish."

"Precisely why this was necessary."

"For us. But for her, for him—at what cost to them have we secured our treaties, and had our revenge on Albret?"

Jacob sniffed at her concern.

For a moment, instead of pitying the couple, Katarina envied them. To know such love. Surely it was worth any difficulties they might face, to have known one night of such joy.

19

Gently brushing back Joan's hair to kiss her forehead, her cheeks, and then her lips, sweetly tender kisses, Thomas whispered, "I must leave you now."

"No!" Joan sat up sharply. She had promised herself that when he turned for one last glance he would see her smiling, radiant with love, so that the very thought of her would bring him joy. But when the time came she wept and begged him to stay. "Who am I now without you?" She tried to pull him back down onto the bed.

"God help me, what have I done to you?"

She was furious with herself, yet could not stop the tears, could not forbear telling him how frightened she was that he would forget her, hoping that she might still gain control of herself and send him away with tender words of love.

"Forget you? Never! I swear to you I will make this right, Joan, my beloved." Thomas departed in a cloud of doubt and self-loathing.

And now she must behave as if nothing had changed, though everything had.

❖ ❖ ❖

DAME KATARINA HAD ARRANGED TO INVITE ALL THE KING'S CAP-
tains, one by one, so that her children would not attach too
much significance to Thomas's dinner with them. Joan became
a player, acting as if she were still virginal and unmarked by
all that had happened with Albret and Thomas. Thea and
Cecilia giggled and shared their thoughts about the captains,
and Joan did her best to participate, offering her own witty
observations, forcing laughter, encouraging Sir Roland, Sir
Guy, and their fellows to talk about their families and their
experiences.

All the while she felt as if she were hovering above a young
woman playing herself as she might have been had Albret never
overstepped the bounds of decency, had she not fallen in love
with Thomas and bound herself to him. She wondered how
everyone could be so blind as not to realize that they were not
interacting with the Joan they knew.

When word came that Queen Philippa had been safely delivered of a healthy son, Joan thought she might return to the
abbey—but she was ordered to remain at the Van Artevelde
house until the queen's churching, after which she would depart for England in Lady Lucienne's company, freeing up room
in the queen's crowded household.

Just as Jacob Van Artevelde had predicted to Thomas.
The queen should be warned of Jacob's detailed knowledge of
her plans. But if Joan stirred up trouble between the queen and
the Van Arteveldes, she risked losing the witnesses to her betrothal.

Secrets upon secrets. Living among the Van Arteveldes,
whom she no longer trusted, was torture. She hesitated before
uttering a word, searched all theirs for hidden traps. Darksome
creatures stalked her in her dreams, snapping at her arms and
legs, driving her off cliffs, into crowds waiting to butcher her.
Her eyes, and Helena's, were ringed in shadows. Her moon

blood arrived a few days late. She did not know whether to mourn or rejoice. She wept.

ON THE DAY ON WHICH LUCIENNE'S PARTY WAS TO TAKE SHIP, Philippa received Joan in her chamber for a brief farewell. She wished to be the one to deliver the news to the girl, feeling responsible for the change in her, the paleness accentuated by the shadows ringing her eyes, the thinness, indeed the loss of the curves that had been the cause of her troubles. Philippa hoped that the news might do much to restore Joan's vitality before she alighted on English soil, before Countess Margaret beheld her daughter.

"My dear Joan, be easy in your heart. The Sire d'Albret is no longer a threat to you. We have withdrawn our proposal to betroth you to his son." The girl's smile was not what Philippa had hoped—a movement of the mouth, but nothing in the eyes. "Do you understand? You are free, you can forget the frightening incident at St. Michael's."

"I cannot forget it, Your Grace, but I am grateful I am safe." Joan bent to kiss Philippa's hand a second time.

"I am entrusting you to my beloved Lucienne for your journey home. All the household will be praying for your safe passage." Though Philippa suspected that all would be relieved to have Joan gone. Her daughters complained about this subdued Joan, how she was no fun. Even now Bella and Joan merely pecked at their cousin's cheek in farewell, then drifted away in search of entertainment. Philippa prayed that her son would find his cousin tiresome as well.

As Joan withdrew in the fragrant embrace of Lady Lucienne, Lady Angmar sniffed. "Your Grace, she will hear a different tale from others, and then you have lost her trust."

"My dear Angmar, I *did* plead her case to His Grace, implored him to reject Albret. In the end, the result is the same.

If she hears now that Albret withdrew on the insistence of his wife, she will be doubly relieved."

Albret had assured them in the message that he held it as the highest honor to serve as one of Edward's lieutenants in the Aquitaine. As Philippa had told Edward when Albret did not appear for the crowning, the man had what he wanted. Clearly, he meant to save his son for future negotiation.

20

LATE APRIL 1340

Breathing in the fresh, slightly salty air as the queen's barge floated down the Lieve Canal to Sluys, Joan tried to think of nothing but the passing landscape, grateful that, for now, Lucienne was quiet. She was confused by her behavior. Days before the queen informed Joan that Albret had quit the marriage negotiations, Lucienne had called at the Van Arteveldes', wishing to be the one to break the news. But she'd undermined Joan's relief by making vague allusions to a much more suitable union in her future. "But I can say no more!" Joan had found it maddening.

Now it was her servant Mary's turn to irritate, morosely pointing out the number of guards standing watch, how closely they studied the banks, the other barges. Lucienne suddenly snapped at her, warning her to cease whining or she would find herself left ashore.

But when they arrived in Sluys the next morning they were all unsettled by the unnatural quiet of the docks.

"Who threatens us?" Joan asked Sir Drogo, the captain of their escort.

"Be assured, my lady, no harm will come to you. Until all is ready, you will bide in a worthy merchant's home, well guarded, where you will find comfort and ease."

"I am grateful for your protection, but it does not answer my question."

"The French are watching this harbor and the waterways leading here. They will know by now that someone is traveling under King Edward's protection."

The merchant's wife opened the door herself, her posture stiff, yet she welcomed them with courteous words and showed them to an enclosed bed near the fire circle in the narrow hall, where they would sleep. Joan understood her reticence. The king's officers commandeered lodgings; they did not ask. Readying for her departure the next day, Joan offered a gift of what little money she had to the couple who had hosted her, but they proudly refused, assuring her that all had been arranged with the king's men. Knowing how seldom such promises were fulfilled, Joan tucked a jeweled comb beneath the bedcovers, to be found after she'd departed.

At the dock, they were escorted onto a small galley and stuffed into a roughly built cabin fitted beneath the forecastle. It contained a bed so small it would be a tight fit for two of them, and some benches, the only light a lantern hanging just inside the door.

"We sail with the tide after sunset, my ladies," said Drogo. "I apologize for the crowded cabin, but you must remain in here, out of sight, for your protection."

Once their chests of clothes had been stored, there was little room to move about. They sat quietly listening to the crew prepare to sail, and when at last they felt motion they all crossed themselves.

Lucienne suggested that they eat while they all had stomachs. Mary, Felice, and Helena bumped into one another as they brought out the basket of food and wine the merchant's wife had provided for their journey. After they'd silently picked at the food and emptied the jug of wine, there was nothing to do but try to sleep through the crossing. Joan chose not to join

Lucienne in the bed, curling up on a deep bench by the door, wrapped in her cloak, her dagger at hand.

She woke in the night to the sounds of men shouting, their boots thundering on the deck. Her heart pounding, she rose and pressed her ear to the door.

"A grapple starboard!" "We're boarded!" "Cut the cable!"

"What is happening?" Felice cried.

"I fear pirates have boarded the ship," Joan said, her throat tight. "Or French raiders."

"God help us!" Mary whimpered.

Joan opened the door just enough to peer out. The deck was a writhing mass of men slashing, wrestling, shouting in French and Italian, all masked in smoke.

"God help us," she whispered, then shouted to the women, "The ship is burning!"

The door was yanked out of her hand, opened wide by a thick-necked man bristling with weapons. "I've found the women!" he shouted to those behind him. In Italian. Joan prayed for strength as she lunged up, driving her dagger under his ribs. With a howl of pain, he threw her aside. She screamed as she fell toward the corner of a chest.

She woke coughing, facing back toward the burning forecastle. *God help me!* She was being dragged out onto the deck.

"Portside! English!" a voice shouted in French as a violent shudder rocked the ship.

The hands on Joan's shoulders began to slip, and a woman softly cursed.

"Helena?"

Gently, her lady's maid let Joan down onto the deck and bent over her, tears running down her sooty face. "God be thanked! I feared you were dead, my lady."

Joan tried to stand up, but the deck was spinning and she fell back, gasping at the pain in her forehead.

"Here!" Helena called to someone.

Footsteps approached. "My lady?" Sir Drogo lifted Joan in his strong arms. "I have Lady Joan! She's alive!" he called out to the others.

Out from the burning cabin Felice staggered, shrieking, her clothes on fire.

"Help her!" Joan cried.

Felice began to run. God knew how she had the strength.

No one was near enough, though two of Drogo's men struggled toward her, one with a cloak to roll her in, but the fire was spreading quickly and the smoke made it difficult to negotiate around the fallen. Eyes wide in horror, her mouth open in a heartrending shriek, Felice pulled herself up over the rail and plummeted down into the waves.

"No!" Lucienne shrieked, reaching out toward where Felice had gone over as if she might pull her back. One of the men caught her up and carried her away.

"God grant her peace," Joan prayed as Drogo carried her to the plank so she might be helped across to the waiting ship as the English rescuers milled about, beating at the fire.

"They came up so silently." "Genoese." "A three-masted ship." "Ours now. The king will be pleased."

Wrapped in a warm blanket, Joan curled into a ball on the deck and covered her ears against the soldiers' chatter. She lay like that, with her eyes tightly closed, through the rest of the journey, praying, but God would not release her from the horror. Felice's screams echoed inside her head.

When at last they anchored in the harbor at Ipswich, Sir Drogo helped her down the ladder and into a small bark. Helena and Mary were already seated. Lucienne was helped down next, moving awkwardly with one arm wrapped and bound to her side. Her eyes were swollen from weeping. She sat beside Joan, murmuring prayers.

"Why did they attack?" Joan asked Drogo.

"They suspected the queen and the young princes were on

board, following the king to England after Her Grace's churching. The guards at the cabin were their first victims, believed to
be protecting the royal cubs and the queen."

Joan hugged herself, wishing Thomas were there to hold her.

"Did I kill him, the man I stabbed?"

Drogo shrugged. "I could not say what killed him in the end,
my lady. But you did well. You saved yourself and the others."

"Not Felice," Lucienne whispered.

Drogo dropped his head and crossed himself.

Joan leaned over the side of the boat, emptying her stomach.

21

Ipswich

Countess Margaret had been a day away from Ipswich when a messenger recognized the livery of Kent and stopped to tell them of the pirate attack. "The women are being nursed at Trinity Abbey in Ipswich. Lady Joan suffered injuries, but we are assured that she will quickly heal."

All Margaret heard was that her daughter was injured. She was not reassured until she saw with her own eyes that her daughter was alert and whole. "Praise God you are safe," she cried when at last she held Joan in her arms. "I was so afraid for you!" Her head and a hand bandaged, her eyes haunted, Joan clung to her mother as she had not done since very small. "You are safe now, my child."

A deep cut on Joan's forehead had been stitched and bound, her minor burns soothed with a poultice of chamomile. The abbey's physician declared her well enough in body to travel in a few days. Lucienne would require a longer stay, the burns on her right arm and both hands needing more time to heal so that the blisters would not break and fester during her journey north. None of them slept well, Helena coughing most of the night, Mary weeping. When Joan woke in the night, gasping for breath, Margaret held her, assuring her that she was in Ipswich, safe at Trinity Abbey. "Sleep, child. Rest in healing sleep."

❖ ❖ ❖

But it was not healing for Joan. The moment she closed her eyes, the horror returned—the knife in the man's belly, her head hitting the chest, blood running down into her eyes, the burning forecastle, and, worst of all, Felice engulfed in flames, screaming as she leaped from the ship— over and over, unceasing.

On the second day, the physician advised that Joan walk out into the town with her mother so that the air and the solid ground might rid her of the dreams. But even in the noise and smells of the market the world was dimmed and muted, as if a veil separated her from life. Her mother tried to engage her in choosing among costly silks for a new gown, but she could not choose, not caring, the smell of pitch from the harbor reminding her of the terrible night at sea.

Barking Abbey
MAY 1340

The buildings of Barking Abbey glowed golden in the distance as they approached; it was only as they drew close that the high walls dominated, hiding the beauty within. Countess Margaret prayed that here her daughter might feel safe enough to emerge from the armor in which she was hiding, under the protection of Earl William's sister, Abbess Matilda. Heaven only knew what Joan was feeling. She expressed no emotion except for the terror that woke her in the night.

Inside the abbey gate, a small crowd had gathered in front of the guesthouse. Servants quickly came forward to assist the arriving company. Abbess Matilda, a tall figure in black, her close-fitting white wimple emphasizing the Montagu nose, stood before the door to greet them.

"It is an honor to receive you both. Welcome, welcome to Barking." The abbess embraced each of them, then led the way to a spacious apartment with separate bedchambers connected by an antechamber. "I thought it best that Lady Joan have all the quiet she required," said the abbess when Margaret exclaimed over the generous lodgings. "But I had not known the extent of her injuries. Perhaps she should spend a brief time in the infirmary?"

"No. I wish to nurse my daughter myself."

"Of course. You have only to ask for whatever you require."

Hours later, Margaret slipped into her sleeping daughter's bed and held her close, at last permitting her own tears to flow. She should never have put the girl through such an ordeal all alone. She should have agreed to let Blanche Wake accompany her. Unnatural mother.

DURING HER FIRST FEW WEEKS AT BARKING JOAN KEPT TO HER BED, eating little, saying less, and Margaret left her side only for daily Mass and a midday meal with the abbess. When sitting in Joan's chamber, Margaret kept her hands busy taking in and shortening one of her own gowns for her daughter's much slighter frame. All Joan's belongings had been lost on the crossing except for her tattered and stained gown, a ruined pair of fine boots, and a simple gold ring with a green stone that Joan wore round her neck on a leather thong, refusing to remove it even while bathing. All questions about the ring's provenance were met with silence, and sometimes tears. Helena claimed ignorance. Even Mary, whom Margaret had come to see was useful as a source of gossip—apparently her only skill—did not know whence came the ring. She suggested that she might venture a guess, but Margaret cut that off, lecturing her on spreading unfounded stories.

As Joan's external wounds healed, Margaret began with

simple questions about the queen, the infant princes, the cities she had visited. But when all was met with silence Margaret grew certain that the crossing was only part of whatever troubled her daughter, and that the ring held the answer.

"You have not heard a word this whole meal. What troubles you?" The abbess reached for Margaret's hand across the little table, comforting in her warmth and kindliness.

"Forgive me. I selfishly forget that you have your own worries about your brother." Earl William had been badly injured when taken by the French at Lille in April, a head wound that left him confused. Like Joan, Margaret thought, sick that her daughter should share such an experience with a seasoned warrior.

Matilda did not know that her guest was her brother's mistress. Few did, hence Margaret's pretense of forgetting. "My daughter's failure to thrive frightens me. I believe that it is not only the attack that troubles her, but what it is—I do not know how to help her."

"Have you told her of your plan?"

"She knows it has long been my intention that she should join your family. But no, I have not yet spoken of it to her. I await the king's pleasure."

"Countess Catherine wishes her daughters to become better acquainted with Joan. She desires to know when she might expect you at Bisham."

"Never if King Edward refuses us once more, late summer if he agrees to Joan's marriage to young Will Montagu." The earl had first approached the king and queen with a proposal for a match between his son and Joan at the beginning of the year, as Albret's behavior grew worrisome—and Margaret's own missive to the king had forced William to step forward.

"Surely His Grace will agree, after such an embarrassment, and my brother's courage, his sacrifice."

Margaret had shared with the abbess Lady Lucienne's account of Albret's reprehensible behavior, and Earl William's last message, sent just before Lille: *I do not know the whole of it, but Her Grace is now inclined to support our petition to the king, motivated by her deep regret.*

"I pray you are right," said Margaret. "Sometimes I wish I were a merchant's wife, free to speak my mind without losing all."

"No one is so free as to lay blame at the feet of the king and queen, my lady." The abbess rose. "Shall we kneel before the Virgin and pray for our loved ones?"

22

Sluys and Ghent
JUNE 1340

The metallic tang of blood and the sour odors of tar and sweat filled Thomas's head, a ringing in his ears muffled the battle sounds round him as he slashed his way across the deck of the ship, lurching over bodies, sliding in the blood. Lunge, turn, slash, shout a warning to one of his men, duck, roll, slash, kick the corpse out of the way—he danced the deadly dance, afire with bloodlust. Rising up on the lee side of the listing cog, he came upon a man whimpering that he was just ship's crew, not a soldier, imploring Thomas to let him live. He let go of his hold on the side and dropped to his knees with hands pressed together over his head. Unmoved, Thomas raised his battle-axe and brought it down, severing the man's spine below his neck. As he kicked the body aside, he saw another crewman trying to crawl away. Down came Thomas's axe, the ringing now a roar in his head.

Afterward, he celebrated with a two-day drunk during which he was hailed as a hero of Sluys, which had been a resounding victory for the English. The French fleet was destroyed. The tides ran red for days.

He came to on his cot, his head pounding, his tongue thick in the desert of his mouth. Shielding his eyes from the light shining in through the open door, his stomach burned as he remembered the crewman's pleas. God help him, he'd become a

monster, a mindless slayer. In his rage, all the men aboard the
French ships, soldiers or crewmen, had become Joan's attackers
and he'd felt free to slaughter them with impunity. Vengeance,
not courage and honor, had fueled his bloodlust. Vengeance and
frustration.

He had not learned of the pirate attack on Joan's ship until
more than a month after the event. It had happened while he
engaged the French outside Lille, then followed Montagu's cap-
tors across into Cambrai in a failed attempt to rescue the earl.
The pirates had meant to kill her, his beloved, and he had not
even known that she was in danger.

But this slaughter was not the way to protect her. As soon
as he could walk in a straight line, he sought out the chaplain to
make his confession.

The priest quickly absolved him of the blood on his conscience with a standard reminder that as a soldier he'd merely
been honoring his duty to King Edward. But in response to
Thomas's confession about Joan, how he should have investi-
gated the man in the church but instead used Joan's fear to the
end he'd so desired, the priest had more to say. Thomas's sin
was not his love for Joan but his betrayal of his king, the king
for whom he'd bloodied his hands. He must ask King Edward's
forgiveness. *You pledged your troth to your lady and lay with her.
It is fitting that you should strengthen your vows together before a
priest, but you are already bound in law. That you took her to wife
without your lord's permission, and he her cousin and guardian,* that
is your transgression.

Thomas sought out a clerk to pen a letter to his brother
Robert, Lord Holland, and his mother, Maud. Van Artevelde's
insistence that he wait be damned—he'd stalled long enough.
His family must welcome Joan and take her in, ensure that no
harm came to her. Only then would he make his peace with
King Edward, when he knew that she was safely in the protection of his family.

23

Barking

LATE SUMMER 1340

In late summer, Margaret sent for her brother's wife, Blanche, Lady Wake, hoping that Joan might confide to her beloved aunt what she hid from her mother, as she had in the past, and in doing so begin to recover. On the day Blanche was expected, Joan declared herself well enough to ride out along the road to Barking to meet her. But by the time she was dressed she was breathing shallowly and admitted with some surprise that she had not the strength to ride out. Instead, she would sit by the fire in the guesthouse hall and let her aunt come to her. Even this was a change from the past months, though, and Margaret welcomed it.

They had not long to wait. Within the hour Blanche arrived in the company of two pages, three serving women, two lady's maids, as well as a tailor, a seamstress, and their servants. As always, Margaret felt as if she were bracing for a storm as she welcomed her brother's wife, a formidably large, handsome woman with a voice that demanded attention and an energy that left most breathless.

"Where is Joan?" Blanche cried as she dismounted from her palfrey. "I expected to see her miles before we reached the abbey." While the abbess quietly ordered lay sisters to prepare more rooms in the guesthouse as well as the cottage in the outer yard for the men, Lady Blanche hurried into the guesthouse hall, halting with a soft cry of dismay to find Joan nodding by the fire. "Is it the head wound, Margaret? Has she healed properly? Did a physician see her?"

Margaret assured her that a physician had declared the wound healed, and that this lethargy was of the spirit, not of the body.

"Lethargy? She is asleep in the middle of the day. Our Joan!" Blanche bent down to her niece, whispering her name.

Blinking awake, Joan threw her arms around her aunt's broad shoulders. "I meant to ride out to meet you, Aunt. I have missed you so."

"Oh, my dear, I so wish I had been with you."

Margaret smiled at a sudden image of the redoubtable Blanche fighting off the pirates. "Would that you had."

"We'll walk twice a day. Good long, brisk walks. You'll be back to your accustomed health in a week," Blanche declared. She held her hands out to Joan. "Shall we begin?"

"But you have been riding for hours."

"I need a good walk before I sit down to my needlework. Come, my love." She urged Joan to rise. "Janet, Agnes, come walk out with us." The two lady's maids seemed dismayed by the prospect, but they smiled graciously and joined their mistress. "You, too, Margaret. It will put roses in those sallow, sunken cheeks of yours."

"Someone needs to see to the rest of your company, Blanche. Do go. It will be good for Joan." With a smile, Margaret turned to the task at hand, her way of dealing with her sister-in-law for the first few hours, until Blanche exhausted her momentum.

Margaret had just sent off the last of the servants when the four women returned, Joan in tears, Blanche unusually quiet, Janet and Agnes talking softly between themselves.

Blanche took Margaret aside. "I fear I blundered, asking about Lady Lucienne's burns."

"I should have warned you—she does not like to be reminded of the attack, the horrible death of Lucienne's maid.
Perhaps you are right, I should consult another physician regarding her head wound." Margaret watched her daughter
settle back into the chair she'd vacated for the walk. Within
moments, her chin dropped to her chest. "Did she walk far?"

"Far for an aged invalid, not for our Joan."

HER SLEEP WAS CURSED. AS SOON AS JOAN CLOSED HER EYES, THE
terror returned—the ship ablaze, Felice shrieking, the knife
sinking into the pirate's stomach, his warm blood gushing
down her hand. The priest said she was shriven, that God had
accepted her penances. Why, then, was her sleep cursed? The
women fluttered about her, coaxing, cajoling her to tell them
what haunted her, then shook their heads at her terror, assuring
her that it was over. But it wasn't over. It would never be over.

She wanted Thomas. But she must not speak his name.

Westminster
SEPTEMBER 1340

BLANCHE'S REGIMEN STRENGTHENED JOAN SUFFICIENTLY TO MAKE
the journey home to Westminster on horseback, a feat Margaret
had not thought possible a month earlier. But Joan still tired
easily, and her heart seemed no lighter for being in familiar sur-
roundings. Long hours she would bide in the garden, sitting,
walking, always in silence, her eyes seldom resting on the beauty
before her, and never venturing down as far as the river. Silence
enshrouded her. Even the bees seemed subdued in her presence.
And when someone addressed her, no matter how carefully

they had made noise on their approach, she would startle and look round with such wary eyes that it broke Margaret's heart.

Still Margaret skirted the truth when Joan asked why she was being fitted for so many gowns. *To cheer you, of course. And your birthday grows nigh. I cannot believe it was thirteen years ago I carried you.* Blanche warned her that she must tell Joan soon, *else she will never trust you in future.* Joan did not trust her now, not enough to unburden herself; Margaret intended to choose her moment.

London

A BEAUTIFUL LATE-SUMMER DAY HAD CLOUDED OVER, AND RAIN threatened, but Margaret hoped to finish one last piece of business before the storm broke, the glover's shop being but a few streets from Blanche's town house, where they were biding for a few days. When Joan removed her gloves, Margaret noticed that she was now wearing the little gold ring on her left hand.

Clearly, Blanche did as well. "Come now, do not keep the good man waiting. For a proper fit you must remove the ring. Why must you be so stubborn?" Irritated, Blanche took Joan's hand and began to pull.

"No!" Joan cried, and slapped her aunt's hand. "I will not remove it."

Taken aback by the outburst, Margaret made her excuses to the glover, took her daughter firmly by the arm, and departed, not pausing until they were in Blanche's hall. She sent her daughter, breathless from the pace Margaret had kept, to her chamber with Helena, then rounded on Blanche.

"How dare you attack my daughter! I involved you because she has always trusted you."

"We need to know what that ring means to her, Margaret. I hoped to startle her into a confession."

"In a shop? Are you mad?" Margaret called to a servant to bring brandywine to the guest chamber, where she would be with her daughter. "Knock before you enter." She held up a hand to Blanche, who prepared to follow. "You have done enough."

"You must tell her what lies in her future, Margaret. You have waited months. It is a shadow between you."

She was right about its being months. The messenger had arrived in mid-June, as King Edward was preparing to return to the Low Countries. *His Grace prays that you and your daughter are in good health and regrets that he is not at leisure to come himself. But he wished you to know that he approves your petition, indeed blesses the proposed union. May the young couple be happy and prosper in their lives together.* The parchment bearing King Edward's seal had lain in Margaret's chest since then, awaiting the right time to tell Joan, when she had the strength to understand the security it promised. Perhaps it was time.

"My lady is resting," Helena said softly when Margaret and the servant who followed slipped into the guest chamber she shared with her daughter. Though she resented the Flemish maid for her evasive answers to many questions about Joan's time with the Van Arteveldes, Margaret appreciated the woman's skill in creating a soothing environment for her daughter.

"I have brought wine, and Cook is heating a stew that my daughter and I can share while we talk, just we two." Margaret nodded to the servant attending her to put the tray by the bed. "You may leave. And you, Helena, go enjoy a warm meal. I shall send for you when we are ready for the food."

When all had withdrawn, Margaret perched on the edge of the bed and kissed Joan on each cheek. Her daughter seemed an angel with bruised eyes, her skin so pale yet glowing, as if she were lit from within.

"My heart is full, Joan. I pray that you can forgive me for sending you alone to Philippa. I know what it is like to be in your situation. When they betrothed me to John Comyn, I was so young. Though it never came to pass, I dreaded going to Scotland, living among strangers. I was so frightened. I've dreamed of that many a night while you were away, and I feared for you."

"I am sorry I have frightened you, Mother."

Margaret shushed her, stroking her shoulder, kissing her hand. "You have nothing to apologize for. My fear strengthened my resolve to secure you a safe haven, and I have. I have good news! With the king's blessing, you are to marry into the Montagu family after all. As soon as Earl William returns, you and his son Will are to pledge your troth." She smiled her encouragement, but in vain. Joan did not look at her but down at the ring. Margaret gently lifted her daughter's chin. "Montagu, the king's champion, who has loved me for so long. Where could you be safer?"

Joan grasped Margaret's forearm so tightly that she winced. "I cannot marry him."

Margaret patted her daughter's cold hand, imagining that this strong emotion was fear of the wedding night. "You will wed, but not live together—not for several years, I promise you. We simply wished to settle this while we enjoy the king's pleasure. He commands only that we wait for Earl William's homecoming for the official betrothal, which he promises will be no later than the autumn. That is soon, my love. Soon you will be free of any fear of Albret."

"You don't understand. I am pledged to Sir Thomas Holland." Joan extended her left hand. "He gave me this ring on our betrothal."

God in heaven. Margaret closed her eyes and worked to steady herself. "Thomas Holland, of the king's household?"

"Yes. You see why I could not tell Aunt Blanche." Blanche was a Lancaster; it was her uncle whom Thomas's father betrayed.

"Why have you done this?" Margaret had not meant to shout, startling her daughter.

"I had to help myself escape Albret, Mother. No one else would. I knew Thomas would save me. And I love him."

Love him? What did a child know of such love? Margaret poured herself a modest amount of wine, but it was Joan who lifted the cup to her lips and drained it.

"Since when do you drink like that?"

"It's for courage. I have a tale to tell. Will you hear me out?"

Margaret poured some wine for each of them, placing the jug out of Joan's reach. "Tell me all."

She held her breath as Joan began, telling her of Sir Thomas's kindness on the crossing, her first impression of Albret, the news of the prince's proposed betrothal, her growing understanding of the king's desperation, the effect Albret had on her, Sir Thomas's friendship . . . Margaret wanted to cover her ears as Joan tearfully spoke of her changing body, with its unfamiliar and frightening sensations, and Albret's seduction. She thanked God that Holland had found Albret and Joan beneath the willow—what had the queen been thinking to allow her to walk about by herself when so many men were gathered under their roof? And then the Van Artevelde scheme ripened. They had used Joan and Thomas's infatuation, spinning stories to enhance her daughter's fears, exaggerations. Gascon nobles were proud, far too proud to ever tolerate a man such as the Van Arteveldes had painted Albret to be, fathering so many bastards that they made up his personal army. But children believe such tales. And he *had* attacked Joan. Her fear was too strong for it to have been imagined, surely. When her daughter, breathless, stopped at last, Margaret let the silence expand until she felt that she might trust her temper.

"I've heard them saying that Thomas is considered one of the heroes in the Battle of Sluys. The king holds him in high regard, Mother."

Not for long, if he hears of this. A man more than twice Joan's age. How dare he entrap her! Margaret's head was spinning.

"I have not heard whether he was injured," Joan said. "Do you know?"

Would that he had been gelded. "I know no more than you." She watched her daughter twisting the ring. "You care for him deeply." *But you hardly know him.*

"I do, Mother, and I believe he loves me. Have you heard anything from his family?"

There it was, the telling detail, the lack of any communication from his family—proof that he had toyed with Joan, then abandoned her. Margaret's heart hurt. "Nothing, my dear. Nothing."

"I don't understand. But, of course, to find a messenger—it could be months before his letter makes its way to his family." Twisting the ring. Twisting, twisting.

It had already been months. Margaret understood well enough. Even had Thomas been in earnest, his mother would not be such a fool as to condone his abduction of the king's cousin. Maud Holland had fought as hard for her family's survival as Margaret had for hers. She would have forbidden the match.

"Do you swear that you have heard nothing from Lady Maud or Lord Robert Holland?"

"I would not keep such a thing from you, my child."

"Perhaps they await some word from me?" Joan wondered.

"The king has given his blessing to your marriage to Will Montagu. He would never agree to your marrying Thomas Holland now, nor do we or the Hollands dare ask it."

"I would have been free of the king's control. Free of the court."

Was she so naïve? "Oh, my dear girl, you cannot escape who you are—the king's cousin." Margaret shook her head. "You are to forget him, Joan."

"But our vows! I love him, Mother. I gave myself to him. We lay together after pledging our troth. We are husband and wife."

The words pierced Margaret's heart, and for a moment she could not remember how to breathe. Her child, her angel. She could forgive much, but not that. "What? Where?"

"At the Van Arteveldes' home. I insisted."

"*You* insisted," Margaret snapped, "and a man twice your age knew no better than to heed you? God's blood, you are not such a fool as that, daughter, I know you are not." She winced at her daughter's pain, wishing she could retract her angry words. But the girl must face the truth. "I know it is difficult for you to see, but Holland is as much to blame as Albret. He took advantage of a frightened child, an innocent."

"You intended me to marry Earl William's brother Edward two years ago. He is of an age with Thomas."

"That is not the point, child. Nor would we have permitted you and Edward to lie together for several years." Margaret hated how her voice shook.

"I love Thomas," Joan sobbed. "I am bound to him. Helena was witness, and the Van Arteveldes. They will vouch for us. We vowed before God and consummated our marriage. We are husband and wife."

Helena witnessed it. Margaret closed her eyes and waited for the flush of anger to subside. But it would not. "You vowed before scheming shopkeepers and a maidservant they provided you, no doubt to spy on you, to find your weaknesses. You have told me enough for me to see that the Van Arteveldes led you to this." She saw a recognition in Joan's face. "I see that you know it. You understand how they manipulated you." But why had they pursued this? So that they might use it with the king? To what purpose?

Joan sniffled. She was still such a child. "I know they did, Mother, but we chose to seize the chance. Thomas discovered the next day that they had exaggerated my danger. He was so angry. He would not lie with me the night before he left on a mission."

"Would that he had come to his senses sooner. What he did—had you bled yet?"

"I had. I never would have forced him—"

"Forced him?" Margaret closed her eyes and waited until her heart slowed.

"I frightened him away," Joan said, sobbing

Margaret set aside the wine and climbed into bed beside her daughter, holding her, gently rocking her. "Hush, my sweet Joan. Rest. Rest now. All will be well." She lay there until her child's breathing slowed and deepened and her slight body re- laxed, all the while praying for God's guidance in coping with this crisis. At least Joan was not with child.

When Margaret left to have some food, she found Blanche pacing the hall. "Well? What did you learn?"

For a moment Margaret considered saying, *Nothing*. But Blanche would find out. Nothing could be kept from her for long. "Joan believes herself betrothed to Thomas Holland."

"Never!"

"You must swear you will say nothing to shut her up, Blanche, else I will take her away as soon as she wakes and you shall not see her again until after she is betrothed to Will Montagu."

"So you will not waver in that?"

"Of course not. I have fought too hard for such security for my daughter."

"Then I have no need to say anything. Come, let us share some food and talk of this." Blanche was helpful with questions of a practical nature Margaret might pose to Joan that would help her see how impossible such a marriage was. How would they live? Where?

"I daresay he never spoke of such things. He'd no intention of honoring his vow," Blanche sniffed.

By the time Margaret returned to the chamber, her heart was too heavy for sleep. Rather than wake Joan with her tossing and turning, she settled in a chair by the fire.

Damn you, Edmund, for challenging Isabella and leaving me to raise our children among your predatory family.

Slats of sunlight striped the bed when Joan woke. Helena smiled from the window seat.

"You slept late, my lady. Are you hungry?"

With a jolt, Joan remembered telling her mother everything. And then she'd held her until she slept. "Where is Mother?"

"Down in the hall. She told me to let you sleep as long as you wished. Shall I dress you?"

In the hall her mother and aunt greeted her warmly, inviting her to take a seat in the sunshine. They talked quietly about nothing in particular as she broke her fast, then her mother suggested a walk in the garden.

"Might we talk some more about Thomas Holland?"

Margaret asked in such a gentle voice that Joan felt no threat. "Of course."

"It would help to hear what plans he made for your life together. As a second son, he has no property. Did he say where you two would live?"

"Not really."

"As a knight bachelor he would seldom be home, wherever that might be. You know that, don't you? The king sends him where he needs him. France, the Low Countries."

"I would go with him."

"Indeed? Where would you bide, child? The king makes no arrangements for wives."

Joan's stomach hurt. She shrugged.

"And if Edward renounces him for marrying you without asking his leave—which he very well might, you know your cousin—then what? Crusading? Thomas would surely not take you with him to live among the infidel."

"I would go where he went, Mother." Joan was sorry she had eaten.

"Perhaps he would become a mercenary in the Italian city-states. He would be ever on the move. Even if you went with him, you would rarely see him. And mercenaries often go a long while without pay. That's why they become raiders. That's no life for a young woman, a life of danger and poverty."

Joan covered her ears. "You're being hateful."

Margaret gently pulled her hands away, looking on Joan with eyes full of love and concern, no rancor. "I am only pointing out the truth, my dear Joan. Surely you do not choose such a future. Surely, if he loves you as you say, he would not ask you to share such an uncertain future with him. Perhaps that is why he has not written to me. He has thought it through and sees that it is impossible."

Joan turned away from her mother. "He loves me. He'll find a way."

Margaret rubbed her back. "Look into your heart, my child. Consider what I have said. That is all I ask."

"You are wrong. You'll see."

Her mother did not bring it up again. She even yielded to Joan's plea that Helena should remain her lady's maid, in gratitude for risking her life to save Joan from the burning cabin. For a time Joan enjoyed a fragile peace, giving thanks for the respite each morning that she awoke in her own bed in her mother's house. Margaret honored Joan's wish not to talk of the planned betrothal even as work continued on her new wardrobe. She spoke of household concerns, the work at hand, local gossip, sweet memories. She was there when Joan woke from frightening dreams, comforting her, promising her that she was safe. Joan made an effort to engage in the design of her gowns, applied herself to much of the needlework, and did her best to be a pleasant companion to her mother. And all the while she waited for some word from Thomas, chewing on all that her mother had said.

She had no answers. Thomas had never spoken of how they would live. Perhaps it had never been as real to him as it had been to her. Had it seemed real to her then? She could not be certain now. It almost felt a dream, the entire sojourn in the Low Countries someone else's memory.

24

Westminster
29 SEPTEMBER, MICHAELMAS

Her hooded falcon, Jolie, danced on Joan's arm as they neared the river, and when at last the bird was released she soared up, up toward the scudding white clouds, and then dived with terrifying grace, hitting a heron with such force that for a moment all that could be seen of them was a cloud of feathers. Joan's companions congratulated her.

"Praise Jolie, not me," she told Ned, uneasy beside him. So much had happened since they'd parted, yet he behaved as if he'd seen her yesterday. She lifted her arm and the falcon returned, already watching for her next catch.

Bella cried out in triumph as her own falcon brought down a bird.

Joan tried to lose herself in this, her favorite sport, to thrill with Jolie as the falcon soared and dived, but she could not relax with her cousins, and the knowledge that Will Montagu was near, hunting rabbits with her brother, John.

The morning's hawking party had been planned by the Wakes as a surprise celebration of Joan's thirteenth birthday. The prince, the princess, and Will Montagu had joined Joan and her family at the end of morning Mass in St. Stephen's, the abbey church. As if by chance. But Joan knew better.

"Why did you do this, Aunt? I'm not ready."

"They're your friends, Joan, my dear. I thought on your birthday . . ."

"You thought what would please you."

"Joan!" Her mother frowned and shook her head.

She'd not seen any of her cousins since her return, even though Bella and her sister, as well as the infant princes, had been sent home from Ghent a month earlier. She'd known they would expect her to talk of her coming betrothal, what happened in the Low Countries, all the things sitting precariously on quicksand while she regained her purchase on solid ground.

She'd particularly dreaded seeing Will. In the flesh, he was hardly threatening. In truth, all three of them seemed terribly young to her. Will had shot up several inches since she'd last seen him but was more awkward than ever, ducking his head as he greeted her, then slipping to the far side of her uncle as they left the church.

Ned had been the first to greet her, taking her by the hand to tell her how much he had missed her. She'd averted her eyes, not wanting him to sense her ambivalence. He seemed such a child.

Bella immediately brought up all that Joan wished to forget. "We all said a prayer for Felice. Is it true that Lady Lucienne lost her fingers when your ship burned? You should have waited. Mother sent us home after our victory at Sluys, when the channel was quiet."

Margaret kindly responded. "I was with Lucienne for several days. Her fingers were badly burned, but they will heal. As for the decision to sail when they did, it was your mother, Her Grace the queen, who made it."

Joan thought to deflect more questions by asking her own. "Have you any news of your father, Will?"

"I'm told he will be back by Martinmas." There was a smear of dirt on his freckled cheek, and he should have taken a comb to his hair, which looked a bit like a bird's nest. Poor Will—the

Montagu hawk nose and full lips looked odd on his round face, with his small, dark, close-set eyes. "We all pray that is so."

"As do we," said Joan, despairing as Will looked away, allowing Bella to pipe up with more uncomfortable questions.

"Is it true that you gelded the pirate who found you in the ship's cabin?"

"Who says they witnessed what I did to the pirate?" Joan demanded. Whoever it was must have been close enough to save Felice. Why had he let her die?

Blind to Joan's discomfort, Bella shrugged. "It's common gossip now."

Meaning Joan was common gossip now. How much did Bella know? Or guess? What had she told her brother?

"We've tired you," said her uncle as he came up behind her, startling Joan.

Her falcon was back on her wrist, and Ned and Bella were now far down the trail. She'd wasted most of the hawking wallowing in her resentment.

"We've more than enough fowl for the larder," said her uncle. "It's time to head back."

The Wakes did a better job of crowding Bella out of the conversation at dinner. And Ned entertained them with a lively narrative of a hunting mishap, told with much gesturing and a hilarious assortment of voices. He was a gifted mimic.

"Thea and Cecilia Van Artevelde miss you," Bella managed to intersperse afterward, "though I think, in truth, it is all the king's guard who dined with them while you bided there whom they truly miss. Thea dreams of Sir Roland, and Cecilia believes Sir Guy is in love with her, though she thinks Sir Thomas is more handsome."

"Sir Roland is a *much* better dancer." Joan distrusted any mention of Thomas in this company.

"Are you going to marry Will?" John whispered.

"So says Mother." She watched Will, wondering what he

thought of all this, and how Ned had coerced him into coming. She had known him all her life, but they had never been friends. Her brother knew him better. "What does he like?"

"Whatever pleases his father."

"John!"

"It's true. He excels in nothing that the earl values. So he tries at least not to excel in what his father despises."

She tried again to draw Will into conversation, but, as he behaved as if it were a punishment, she gave up, bored with the effort. John was not entirely right—it would have pleased the earl had Will tried to engage her in conversation.

"Why don't the four of you go out into the garden?" Margaret suggested when the last course was being cleared.

Why don't you all go home? Joan silently countered. With a sigh, she rose from the table and with John led their guests out through the kitchen to the garden beyond, and the river. She halted at the low garden wall, as close to the riverbank as she wished to venture at present, still uneasy around water. Bella, Will, and John continued down to the bank to toss pebbles at the passing barges. Ned straddled the wall beside her, taking her hand.

"I saw you watching Will. Do you really think to wed that coward?"

"Might we talk of something else?"

"What about our vows, cousin?"

"Your father warned me away from you."

"Bella told me about that bastard Albret, how he touched you. He will pay for that."

"I very much doubt it. Your father needs him."

"He had no right to touch you like that." He kissed her hand. "No one does. Not him, not Will. You cannot lie with Will!"

"It would not happen for years. Mother swears. Just as with

you and Marguerite of Brabant. I like Marguerite, Ned. She will make a gracious queen."

"The pope will never agree to that marriage. But he would to ours. It would not threaten Philip of Valois."

"The pope might agree, but not your parents."

He turned her hand palm down and touched the stone on her ring. "Who gave you this? Albret?"

"I kept nothing of his. You should know I would not."

He kissed her cheek. "I will avenge your honor, Joan. I swear."

"Ned, please—let's talk of something else."

"I would do so to any man who dared touch you." He nodded at Will. "He knows that."

"Ned, stop it."

"Who *did* give you the ring? Bella says you returned from the Van Arteveldes with it."

"I bought it at a fair."

"You? Or Thomas Holland?"

That Ned would mention him—she felt breathless but forced herself to say with a laugh, "Why him? Why not Sir Guy, Sir Roland, Sir Piet—all were guests at the Van Artevelde dinners while I abided there. All were pleasant to me. Unlike you—" She tried to withdraw her hand.

"Such a paltry thing." He grabbed her finger and tugged.

"Ned, don't! You're hurting me!" It stung as he forced it past her knuckle.

He tossed it out onto the muddy riverbank. "I'll give you something more suitable to your station."

"I don't want your ring, I want mine. Why are you so hateful?" She started toward the spot where it was sinking, but the tarry smell from the river gagged her, too like the smell of the ship, intensified as it burned. She covered her mouth and stumbled back toward the hall.

"Joan!" Ned reached for her hand as she passed him. "I'm sorry if I hurt you."

"No, you aren't. You're sorry I'm walking away from you." She picked up her skirts and ran, not stopping until she arrived, breathless, in her bedchamber. She threw herself down on the bed, shaking with anger and grief. Her ring, the beautiful ring Thomas had given her, lost in the mud. "May God smite you, Edward of Woodstock. Smite you for your pride and your cruelty!" She pressed her face into the feather bed, imagining Ned's shock at being disciplined by the Almighty himself, the lightning bolt shooting toward him. . . .

"May I enter?" Bella asked from the doorway.

And how would God punish Bella for her intemperate mouth? Joan rolled over and sat up, wiping her eyes. Strike her speechless—that would be appropriate. The entire court would breathe a sigh of relief. "What did you tell Ned about my ring?"

Bella shrugged as she crossed the room and perched on the edge of the bed with a dramatic sigh. "You are so tetchy today. I told him only what Thea Van Artevelde told me—that you wore it the first morning you joined them in the hall for sewing, and when she asked about it her mother told her not to be rude. And, since I'd never seen it, we guessed Sir Thomas might have given it to you."

What else might they have guessed, those two master gossips? "Why did you even mention it?"

"I just did."

"Why would Sir Thomas give me such a thing?"

"It's no secret that you like him, and he likes you. Mary said you often shared a bench in the abbey garden, breaking your fast together."

Of course Bella would quiz Mary. "What else did she say?"

"She grumbled about being left behind when you went to bide with the Van Arteveldes."

Joan pointed to a pretty ring on Bella's finger. "You owe me a ring. I like that one."

Bella covered her hand. "I didn't take it from you, Ned did. Let *him* give you a ring."

"You taunted him with it, didn't you? Do you have nothing better to do than gossip about me?"

"I'm sorry." Bella slipped off the ring and held it out to Joan.

"I don't want it. Go away. And stop telling tales about me. You don't know anything."

GOD IN HEAVEN, WHAT NOW? MARGARET HAD WONDERED AS JOAN rushed by, her hair flying, shaking her head at her mother's exclamations of concern and stumbling up the steps to the solar, seemingly half blinded by tears. Soon her companions returned, quiet, avoiding adult eyes, the prince and the princess signaling to their servants that they were ready to depart.

Ned asked Margaret to convey his apologies to Joan, his tone more resentful than apologetic. She might have known it was he who upset her daughter. Bella kissed Margaret on the cheek and asked permission to go after Joan. She reluctantly agreed. As the prince went over to bid goodbye to the Wakes, Will slipped something into Margaret's hand.

"I tried to clean it with my sleeve, my lady," he said in a voice meant for her ears only.

Joan's ring. "What happened, Will?"

"He would not believe she bought it for herself and he threw it away. I pray you, do not let him see it."

She tucked it into her girdle. "Thank you. I will tell her it was you who retrieved it." She kissed his forehead and restrained herself from wiping the smudge off his cheek.

Will bobbed his head, giving her an endearingly crooked smile, then hurried to catch up with the prince and the princess as Bella returned from the solar, red-faced and muttering about Joan's foul temper.

Margaret turned back to her brother and sister-in-law with relief after the three young visitors had ridden from the yard. Sitting down beside Blanche, she took up her needlework, enjoying a moment of peace.

But her brother Thomas was curious about the exchange with Will. "Might I see the ring?" Holding it up to the light, he exclaimed, "Holland gave her this?"

"That man!" Blanche hissed.

Thomas ignored her. "It is no cheap trinket but a fine stone, Margaret. Had you noticed?"

She confessed she had not.

"What is your point, husband?" Blanche demanded.

"A gift of such quality from a knight bachelor suggests that he was in earnest. He is an honorable man, much admired for his martial skills and his leadership in the field." When his wife protested, he reminded her that her uncle had been a scoundrel and a traitor to his king. She herself had called her father's campaign to have his brother declared a saint rubbish. "The man was a devil, and the elder Holland did a great service to the realm when he betrayed his lord."

"So you would have your sister encourage him?" Blanche asked.

"After his brother has already congratulated me on my niece's betrothal to Salisbury's heir? Of course not."

"What is this? When did you speak with his brother?" Margaret asked.

"Did you not tell her, wife?" Thomas asked. "It was days ago I encountered Lord Holland."

"Of course I did. Margaret, you remember. The vintner's shop?" Blanche tried to look bemused, but in truth she looked uneasy.

"No," said Margaret. "Tell me, brother."

Thomas was now regarding his wife as if she'd just begun to caw like a raven. "Robert, Lord Holland, strolled into the vintner shop I frequent, it must be a week past, now. I cannot believe you missed the chance to tell this, Blanche."

"Thomas, tell me what happened," Margaret implored.

"He congratulated me on my niece's betrothal to young Will Montagu, that is all. A trivial thing, except that his brother had hoped to wed her. The family must have decided it was not in their interest. Which, of course, it is not. To go against the king's intentions for his cousin would ruin Holland. I, for one, am grateful they made him see reason. Sir Thomas is a captain we cannot afford to lose as we face war with France. He has many friends among his peers in the Low Countries, and his men trust him." He handed Margaret the ring. "You might advise Joan not to wear that in the presence of the prince. Too valuable to lose." He shook his head. "I pity young Montagu. Anyone marrying Joan will need to stand up to Prince Edward, and I do not yet see much backbone in Will."

So the Hollands had decided the matter for them. Margaret should be relieved, but it hurt to think how betrayed her daughter would feel, and she had a nasty taste in her mouth about Blanche's part in this. When she finally went to Joan, who was curled up in a window seat, staring at herself in a small mirror that she held before her, Margaret felt a stab of pain for her lovely child. Helena moved a chair near the window for her, then withdrew.

"Will retrieved your ring." Margaret held it out to Joan.

The mirror was quickly set aside, Joan's eyes shining with tears as she slipped the ring back on her finger. "Bless him. Ned will make him pay for this kindness."

Margaret told Joan what her brother had said about its worth. "He suggested that you not wear it in the prince's company." She kissed her daughter's forehead. "You had forgotten how unpleasant he could be."

"Hateful. He cannot let me be. He threatens anyone I care for."

"He may be the crown prince, but he's still just a boy of ten."

"Remember when he broke John's nose for laughing at him in the practice yard?"

How could Margaret forget? She had removed her son from the prince's household after that, sending him to be fostered with Blanche's brother Henry of Grosmont, Earl of Derby.

"And what of my dog Bruno?"

"We do not know that that was the prince's work. But, for the sake of the realm he will one day rule, I do pray that Ned grows beyond his bullying ways." She kissed Joan's forehead again, smoothed back her curls. "As for the Hollands . . ." Margaret told Joan of her brother's chance meeting with Lord Holland, her heart aching as Joan's tears gathered and her shoulders slumped.

"So that is why you have heard nothing." Joan turned to look out the window. "It was kind of Will to rescue my ring."

Margaret took her daughter's hand, delicate, with long fingers, sadly cold at the moment, and kissed it. "Have you decided?"

Still staring out into the soft late-summer rain, Joan said, "It seems Thomas's family has decided for us."

"Shall we share a cup of wine?"

Joan shook her head. "I just want to be alone for a while."

IN THE EVENING, AS MARGARET SAT WITH HER BROTHER AND SISTER-in-law by the hall fire, she started as Joan silently appeared, a ghostly apparition, her fair hair and pale gown reflecting the flickering light from the hearth fire.

"Come. Rest against me," Margaret said.

"Better now?" Blanche asked.

Margaret felt her daughter shrug. "Tell me about Robert Holland," Joan said to her uncle. "What is he like?"

He described a "remarkably ordinary" man who carried himself with an aggrieved air. Blanche muttered something about the Hollands playing the victims. Thomas shushed her and repeated what he had told Margaret about their encounter.

"He said nothing about his brother and I being wed?" Joan asked.

Margaret noticed her brother look to his wife, who arched a brow in warning.

"Not a word, Joan."

Margaret smoothed Joan's hair from her forehead and kissed her, but said nothing. It was the best answer for Joan, though she guessed it was not the whole truth.

Shortly afterward, the Wakes withdrew to their bedchamber. Joan moved to the chair Blanche had vacated, drawing up her legs, wrapping her arms round them, curling into herself. She'd become a young woman of grace and light, Margaret thought, and cursed Thomas Holland for breaking her daughter's heart. Yearning to raise Joan's spirits, Margaret spoiled what she had meant for a surprise on the morrow.

"Would it please you to hear that Efa is going to join the modest household accompanying you into your marriage?" With all that Joan had recently suffered, Margaret thought the healing skills of her children's childhood nurse made Efa an ideal choice to round out the servants her daughter would take into her marriage.

Joan unfolded, her brightness returned. "Efa! Have you sent for her? Truly?"

Margaret opened her arms to her suddenly joyful daughter, who slipped onto her lap and hugged her tightly. She laughed as Joan rained kisses on her cheeks.

"I will heal now. Efa will know what to do."

"But have a care. No spells. No tales of fair folk leading you astray. I sent her away once for that, I can do it again."

Joan hugged her again. "Bless you!"

EFA'S BROAD, FRECKLED FACE RELAXED INTO A WARM SMILE AS SHE pushed back her hood and opened her arms for a welcoming embrace. Joan breathed in the familiar flowery scent of Efa's red hair, which she wore loose, having never wed. She was a small, buxom woman who walked with a swing that suggested that she moved to a music only she could hear. A few years older than Joan's mother, she looked at least a decade younger, though as Joan stood back she noticed a few silver strands in the dark-red hair and perhaps a few more laugh lines radiating from the wide hazel eyes that closely studied her. Efa's smile faltered.

"You have much healing to do, little one. But your heartbeat is strong. A good sign."

They talked into the evening. Joan told Efa everything—all that had come to pass, all that was in her heart. Two things made the woman lean close, an ear cocked, as if listening for more than just Joan's voice in the telling. One was the circling of the old willow—*and he suddenly appeared*, she'd whispered to herself. The other was Joan's feeling since returning home that she had been away for a long, long time, during which she had aged but no one else had; nor did they notice that she was not the thirteen-year-old they expected her to be.

"You fear that Albret might be of the fairy folk, that he took your soul," she guessed.

"Mother says I'm not to talk to you about fairies or spells." But Joan leaned close, wondering.

Efa rose and began to hum to herself as she rummaged among the jars in the chest she'd brought.

"Well? Might he be?" Joan finally asked.

"You *are* changed, little one. You became a woman and lay

with a man you love. I *feel* your bond when you speak of him. It's no childish love, not with that warmth." She shrugged as she picked up one of the jars.

"There's no cure?"

Efa paused with the jar half unwrapped, regarding Joan with a sympathetic frown. "Oh, little one, I fear the only *cure* is to be reunited with your Thomas."

"That's impossible."

"Is it?" She arched her curly brows as if disagreeing. "As for the Gascon, there is an undercurrent. But that is all behind you." She finished unwrapping the jar and sniffed, wrinkling her nose. "Have you continued with archery?"

"No. The queen thought it unseemly. And since I returned I haven't had the strength. But what has that to do with all this?"

"It was archery that gave you the strength to stab the pirate. Now you must hide your feelings while you wait and watch. Practicing at the butts will steady and strengthen you, and sharpen your patience. We shall play chess each evening as well."

"Wait and watch for what?"

"Opportunity, little one. Joy."

"And what of Ned? How can I protect Thomas from him?"

"Thomas is a man, the prince a child. I would not worry overmuch about that."

"And Will?"

"Ah. He will prove the most difficult, to be sure. But do not give up hope."

Joan slept well that night, and many nights afterward. Until she was summoned to Bisham.

25

EARLY NOVEMBER 1340
Westminster to Bisham

Joan watched her mother's reaction to the news from the Earl of Salisbury's man, saw the stricken look on her face, hands to her mouth, heard a little cry. She guessed that Earl William had died. But then the messenger grinned, ear to ear, and Margaret clapped her hands and said something in a voice high with glee. So he lived.

She steeled herself as her mother turned and swept toward her, arms outstretched.

"Earl William is in London with the king! We leave in a fortnight for Bisham, for your betrothal, my love." Margaret's eyes sparkled.

Joan did not mirror her mother's emotion. The betrothal ceremony was the moment when, with the exchange of property, a proposed marriage between noble houses became an official entity. It was precisely what her betrothal to Thomas lacked. Her mother's careful scheming was coming to fruition.

But, as they organized the packing of her new wardrobe, Joan noticed a brittle quality to her mother's laughter. After all her effort, could she be uneasy about the coming betrothal? Or was it the prospect of biding under the roof of her lover's family that troubled her? It was one thing to come face to face with

Catherine Montagu at court, quite another to be received by her in her own home.

Margaret looked aghast when Joan offered to go alone. "Miss your betrothal? I will not! It is all arranged. We will share a barge upriver with Abbess Matilda."

JOAN HAD ALWAYS LOVED TRAVELING BY RIVER. BUT SINCE THE PI-rate attack the very thought of being on the water turned her legs to jelly. She approached the dock at the bottom of the garden with jaws set, her eyes locked on the awaiting barge, not on the water. Abbess Matilda lifted a hand in greeting—she had boarded downriver near Barking. It was a small, flat, open barge, nothing like the ship on which Joan had sailed from Sluys, and the river did not even smell like the sea. But as Joan stepped onto the planking her breath caught in her chest and she could not release her grip on Efa's arm to take the page's proffered hand. There was no need. Sure-footed, Efa led her on, seating her just within the small pavilion that would shade them from the sun.

"Keep your eyes on the land to either side of us," Efa said. "Safe, solid ground."

But Joan closed her eyes and prayed. They were well away from Westminster by the time her heart stopped racing and she managed to look out at the riverbank. It did help to see land so close at hand. But she did not let go of her nurse.

Her tension eased once she stepped off the barge and felt the earth beneath her feet. Their party was to finish the journey to the Montagu manor of Bisham on horseback through green, rolling countryside. Her mother and the abbess flanked her now, chatting amiably about passing landmarks and the indifferent harvest. Margaret's cheer sounded flat to Joan.

As the imposing stone-and-timber manor house came into

view, the sound of hammers and the shouts of men pierced the stillness.

"Bisham Priory," said Abbess Matilda, pointing to one side of the house. "My brother founded it several years ago, for Austin Canons."

The larger buildings within the priory walls were bristling with scaffolding.

"So close to the house," Margaret noted.

"William no doubt hopes the proximity strengthens the effect of the canons' prayers for their founder and his family." Abbess Matilda laughed, despite her evident pride in her brother's good work. "So what do you think of your new home, Lady Joan?"

Her new home? Joan took a deep breath. "It seems a fine house, well suited to such an impressive man as your brother, Mother Abbess." But she could not imagine considering it her home.

Margaret reached out to pat her daughter's hand. "I pray you will be happy here."

Well she might pray, but it would be for naught.

The Montagu family awaited their guests in the manor-house yard, richly garbed in jeweled colors, bright against the hard-packed earth. Will stood at one end of a semicircle, with his father, the earl, and his brother and sisters filling in the middle, and his mother, Countess Catherine, anchoring the far end. As a groom assisted Joan in dismounting, Will stepped up to greet her, his shoulders thrust forward as if bowed beneath the weight of his responsibility. Apparently, he was no happier about this than she was. He stumbled over a prepared speech, blushing crimson to the roots of his red hair by the end. Earl William quickly seconded his son's welcome, and smiled fiercely as he delivered Joan into the enthusiastic embraces of Will's three sisters. A courteous greeting from Will's brother, John, brought her all the way down to Countess Catherine.

Though in coloring and the rich dark hair she was a match for her cousin, Lucienne, she had a more passive beauty, a delicacy more appropriately worshipped from afar, and a nature as changeable as the weather. On this day she stood quietly, her air somewhat sorrowful. Countess Catherine was the daughter of the first Baron Grandison, at whose death she'd become William Montagu's ward, and eventually his wife, a gift from King Edward II for the earl's services. Much the way Joan was a gift from the present king for young Will, the earl's heir.

Catherine bowed slightly, greeting Joan and her mother with chilly formality, and, without further comment, turned to lead them into the hall.

"I pray you don't take offense at Mother's coolness. She slept little once we learned of Father's capture," said Bess, the eldest daughter, slipping a hand through Joan's free arm. "And, even now that he's home, she is worried. But you are very welcome." She turned and tsked at her brother for hanging back.

Shy, awkward, chubby, with strawlike light-red hair, pale brows, pale eyes . . . Joan tried not to compare Will with her beloved. He was just a boy. But she could not imagine him maturing into such a man as Thomas. His hand had been clammy and limp in hers. As Joan followed Bess through the great hall, an airy space with a fine tiled floor and glazing in the main windows, Joan told her about her brother's kind retrieval of her little ring.

"He dared antagonize the prince? I would never have imagined it. He must hold you in high regard."

"High regard?" Joan looked back at her intended, his full lips slightly open as he listened to her mother. He looked such a dullard, she did wonder what had possessed him to make that gesture. "I suspect he merely thought it the proper thing to do. I understand that you are to be wed soon as well."

"Yes. To Hugh Despenser." Bess's flat tone suggested that she was no happier with her lot than was Joan with hers.

"Has your father brought any news of Prince Edward's betrothal?" Joan asked. "Has the pope approved?"

Bess had heard nothing, but begged Joan to tell her all about the court of Brabant, and the most fortunate Lady Marguerite. The other Montagu sisters, Sybil and Pippa, crowded round to hear as well, and in a tight little pack they swarmed up the steps to the bedchamber they would all share. They showered Joan with kindness, and she pretended to be happy to be there with them.

MARGARET FOLLOWED THE GIRLS, FOR SHE WOULD ALSO BED WITH them for the several nights of her stay. She avoided looking around, feeling like a spy in her lover's home, grateful for his wife's habit of looking over the heads of those she addressed rather than meeting their gaze. If Catherine had looked into Margaret's eyes as she greeted William she would know, and all hope for Joan's safety in the bosom of this powerful family would be dashed.

While the servants moved about the bedchamber, Margaret opened the shutters and looked out on the rolling countryside, studying a tangled wood round a pond as she worked to collect her emotions and tuck them safely behind her court façade.

The Truce of Esplechin in September had allowed William's release from captivity near Paris so that he might return to England and raise funds for his ransom, as was the custom with noble captives. But, according to Abbess Matilda, he had little time for that, as he had taken it upon himself to investigate who was responsible for bringing to such a dangerous halt the flow of war funds the king required in the Low Countries. From the look of him, William needed more time to recover. His appearance shocked Margaret, his hair whiter, thinner, his body gaunt, his face even more unbalanced than his wounded eye rendered it—there was a slight droop to the left side of his face, so that on one side he now looked startled, on the other drowsy. Pain shad-owed his smile. His head wound might have healed outwardly, but according to his daughters' chatter he was not himself, his moods wildly fluctuating. He and Catherine must be a volatile pair at present.

Margaret hoped to find a moment to speak with him in private, ostensibly to offer Efa's services as a healer. She also wanted to warn him of the situation with Holland. Though she took a risk in telling him the truth, she could not in good con-science allow him to proceed with the betrothal of his son and heir in ignorance.

EARLY THE FOLLOWING MORNING, AS SHE APPROACHED THE STABLES, Margaret heard an angry shout followed by someone howling in pain. Peering around the opened door, she witnessed William boxing the ears of a young groom with such viciousness that one of his own knights called out, "My lord!" and stepped in front of the lad, protecting him from further blows. William roared something unintelligible, then turned sharply away. Margaret had never known him to be violent to his servants. She ached to see how his elegant clothes hung on his diminished frame, though from the state of the groom it was clear that William was still strong, even though not himself.

"Well met, brother!" Abbess Matilda called out as she stepped past Margaret into the light. "I'm glad to have found you. Would you walk out with me? I should like your opin-ion on something." She lightly touched his elbow. He nodded and made to follow her out. "The sisters of Barking have daily prayed for you, dear brother. God be praised that you are home safely."

"Cur of a groom," William growled, kicking a chicken out of the path. "Came at me from behind." He gestured to his left rear.

"You are not wearing your eye patch," Matilda said. "Perhaps the lad didn't know not to approach you from that side."

William growled again, but brightened as he caught sight of Margaret. She held her breath, praying he would not say something that gave them away.

"Out for an early-morning walk, my lady?" He gestured to her to come forward, bowed and made a show of kissing her hand while whispering, *After dinner, the far cottage*.

She smiled. "I thought I should seize the chance for a morning walk, my lord earl. I am so seldom at leisure in the countryside."

He bowed to her again and moved on, a page and a knight following close behind.

The abbess put an arm around Margaret. "I am sorry you witnessed that. I've never seen my brother in such a rage. You know of the injury he suffered at Lille, and then to be forced to ride all the way to Paris. Suffolk, who was with him, says a physician attended him, but something is not right." She was silent as a servant opened the hall door to them, then paused again just within, her hands on Margaret's shoulders. "Pray for William, my lady." She hurried after her brother.

But Catherine and William were already loudly arguing in the hall. Margaret slipped back out to continue her walk. God be thanked. William's head was not so addled as she had feared. But his attack on the groom troubled her.

A soft rain fell. Joan and the Montagu girls shrank at the discovery and disappeared back into the hall.

Raising her hood, Efa said, "I wondered how we would lose them. God smiles down on you, my lady."

"Or weeps," said Margaret. By the time they reached the far cottage, her hem was soaked and she shivered with cold. "Perhaps you should come within right away, Efa." Their plan had been that she should wait outside until summoned. Margaret could not predict whether or not William would agree to a Welsh healer. And, perhaps, he would be in an amorous mood. "You will be cold."

Efa pointed to a bench sheltered by the eaves. "I'll be dry enough, and I can warn you if anyone approaches."

"Earl William's certain to have one of his men with him."

"Then I shall have a companion." Efa waved Margaret inside.

Indeed, William's squire opened the door, bowing to Margaret, then stepped outside, closing the door behind him.

Margaret pushed back her hood and walked into her lover's arms, relieved to feel them enfolding her. "I did not dare to hope for such time with you," she said, kissing his forehead, his cheeks, then lingering on his mouth.

He lifted her chin, studying her in his one-eyed, birdlike way. "The time apart has been far kinder to you than to me. You are as beautiful as ever, Maggie." With a finger he traced the outline of her lips. "We have much to talk about. But first this." He drew her down onto hides piled close to the fire circle.

That he would risk this with his family so near assured her that he'd missed her as much as she missed him. When they were naked, she kissed the new scars on his chest. Several looked angry. "Efa has unguents—"

He growled. "Not now."

Later, when they lay quite still, his head on her chest, she said, "Something happened in Ghent that you must know, William—"

"Joan and Holland. Edward told me." He smiled up at her. "I wondered whether you would tell me. I am glad you did."

Edward told him, the king. "Does Philippa know as well?"

"Van Artevelde bragged of his part in it to her. Threatened to make it public if she or the king tried to leave without paying their debts. Edward had already departed, and Philippa's household were ready to slip away as soon as she rid herself of Van Artevelde." William laughed.

It was no laughing matter to Margaret. "My poor Joan, caught in the claws of such creatures as those Flemings."

"Or was it Holland who was snared? Joan is not gowned as she was there. Holland was not the only one who could not keep his eyes off the sweet young flesh on display."

Margaret rolled away and sat up, covering herself with a hide. "Her gowns were provocative?"

"Very."

She felt sick. "I had not heard this. Was this the cause of it all, Philippa so eager to please Albret that she made a strumpet of my daughter?"

"Who chose the cut of her gowns I do not know, but she was not unwilling, Maggie."

"She was a child, William, twelve years old!"

William tugged at the hide. "Let it be, Maggie. She's under my protection now, and Catherine's strict rule."

Margaret held tight to the hide while she struggled with her anger at the implication that Joan had been at fault, that she needed discipline. If Catherine knew about Thomas, she might make Joan's life a hell on earth, scolding moralizer that she was. "Does Catherine know about Holland?"

"No. And it's best that she does not hear of it."

"Does the king know she is not to be told?"

"He knows. Now let us not talk of Catherine." He plucked at the costly hides. "This is their love nest."

She'd had eyes only for him when she entered the cottage. Now Margaret noticed the quality of the furnishings, smelled the apple wood burning in the brazier. Catherine and the king. She'd heard whispers but had not known whether to believe them. William had always pretended indifference. He'd come to Margaret's bed long before Catherine declared her duty finished, five healthy children being sufficient. Theirs had never been an affectionate marriage, William having no patience for his wife's erratic humors. He'd sworn to Margaret all along that Catherine did not know about them, but her choice of lover, William's lord and good friend, seemed to her a carefully chosen arrow with a poisoned tip.

"If she ever discovers us, do you think she would turn on Joan?"

"Has she said something?"

She'd said as little as possible to Margaret since she arrived. "No."

"Do you now doubt our course? Too late, Maggie. I've worked too long for this." He reached past her for a cup of wine but suddenly sank back, pressing his temples. "Christ on the cross."

Margaret rose and fetched Efa. The squire took the opportunity to warn his lord that it grew late.

"Escort me to the hall," said Margaret. "Then return for your lord and Efa."

"My lord?"

"Do as she says," William growled.

It had gone better than she'd hoped, but as she followed the young man out into the gentle rain, her eyes fixed on the bobbing light from the lantern he carried, she felt sick with doubt. How could William blame Joan? Why had she thought her lover's family a safe place for her daughter? For so long she'd been intent on Joan's marrying into the Montagu family, it had not occurred to her to consider Thomas Holland's interest. She'd never thought to approach his family.

He is a knight in the king's service, not a future earl but a respectable suitor, Efa had said, wondering at Margaret's refusal to at least hear him out.

You forget your place, she'd snapped.

Forgive me, my lady.

Efa's outspokenness was both a blessing and a curse. At the

moment, Margaret silently cursed her for watering the doubts already seeded.

Robert Holland said nothing about the prior vow. Surely he would have said something had the family been told of it.

How did he know of the planned betrothal, my lady? Who told the Hollands? Does Sir Thomas know his family has not approached you?

It is done, Efa. Do not dare give my daughter false hope.

I am your servant, my lady.

God was her witness, Margaret wanted only what was best for her daughter. Why, after all this time, was this such a bitter victory?

As the day of the betrothal ceremony dawned, Margaret was beside herself with worry over the absence of her brother and his wife, who had promised Joan a generous dowry. But the Wakes arrived at last, just hours before the ceremony was to begin. Their party included her son, John, who had at the last moment demanded to be present. Margaret now interrupted his fond reunion with his sister so that Joan might dress. As she sat with the Montagu girls, tearfully watching the transformation, Margaret tried not to imagine the low-cut gowns the beautiful young woman before her had worn in Antwerp and Ghent. Joan had blushed when Margaret asked about them. *I did not like how they made me feel*, she'd admitted.

As Joan entered the hall in her modest gown of azure-and-crimson silk, pearls and amethysts entwined in her pale hair, she drew all eyes to her. She moved toward young Will with a natural grace, straight-backed and serene, an unfortunate contrast with the boy, who fidgeted beside her. His short padded jacket rode too high, emphasizing his fleshiness, his round head. A beauty on the verge of womanhood and an awkward boy. Margaret was sick with doubt. Joan's account of her night with Holland haunted her. The king had assured her that they needed no papal dispensation for this betrothal, that Holland had been in the wrong. But what if *they* were wrong?

A hush fell over the hall as the canon signaled for the couple to come forward. Taking Joan's hand, Will haltingly pledged her his troth, his voice reedy and tense. Head bowed, Joan moved her lips, but it was clear from the puzzled looks from the canon and Will that they could not hear her. The hall grew so quiet that Margaret heard Joan apparently whispering prayers. Asking God's forgiveness? Or Holland's? A dog barked far away, an owl answered. As the silence lengthened, Margaret held her breath. Then, at long last, Joan lifted her eyes to Will and softly repeated the pledge. Margaret shivered. It was done. God grant them joy and abundance.

As the guests began to move about, William strode up to Joan and loudly welcomed her into the family, briefly embracing her. Margaret was gratified to see that, after only two days in Efa's care, he showed signs of improvement in the balance of his facial features and his posture. She smiled as she watched Joan bow to him and quietly respond. Will had already disappeared, as if he could not escape his betrothed fast enough.

"May no harm come to them," murmured Blanche, suddenly beside Margaret and nudging her forward. "Find the lad and congratulate him, Margaret. The children have done what you wished. Now they need your support."

Children. Of course. That was what Efa had forgotten; Joan was far too young to choose for herself. Thomas was an opportunist, and Margaret had foiled him at his course. She straightened up and went in search of young Will.

JOAN HAD PRAYED FOR GOD'S FORBEARANCE BEFORE WHISPERING the pledge, then waited to be struck down for her sacrilege. She was already wed to Thomas. He had her heart, her body, her soul. How could she bear this? Afterward, Earl William strode forward, roaring his welcome to the family as he enfolded her in an embrace. *To this pledge you will be true. I will see to it*, he said in her ear, with a coolness that made it clear that his welcome held no affection, that his pretense of fatherly concern had been a sham. To him she was merely a vessel of royal blood with which to ennoble his family line. She was no less his pawn than she had been Van Artevelde's, who used her to prove his power over King Edward, or the king, who saw her as bait.

She wished she had the freedom to spit in his face. Where had he been when she needed protection in Ghent? While he turned around, arms held wide, inviting everyone to the feast in celebration of the happy event, she sought an escape. But people crowded round, wishing her joy. She moved through the following feast mouthing the words people wished to hear, fighting with her impulse to rush out of the hall and find somewhere to hide. The earl's threat frightened her. Was Thomas in danger? Her mother watched her with relief mixed with something else—was she still unsatisfied? After all this? Bess, Sybil, and Pippa declared her their new sister and lavished her with gifts of ribbons, buttons, and bouquets of the last beautiful leaves of autumn. Will gave her a pretty gold hand fasting pin, two hands clasped over a heart, and a falcon. She dutifully presented him with a linen shirt that her mother had embroidered with their initials, and her uncle Thomas announced that he was adding three thousand pounds to her dowry, Aunt Blanche beaming at the expressions of surprise. Joan wondered whether it was meant as compensation for spoiled goods. Will kissed her chastely on the hand as she withdrew to her bedchamber with her mother and the Montagu girls. It was done.

26

London, the Tower
DECEMBER 1340

Kneeling in the Tower chapel, Philippa gave thanks for hers and Edward's safe crossings, the joy of their reunion with their children Ned, Bella, Joan, Lionel, and John, and for the continued health of the babe in her womb. She felt bathed in the joyous warmth of God's grace.

She was home, despite Van Artevelde and all the others who had thought to keep them hostage until such time as Edward paid them all he'd promised. They'd slipped away like thieves in the night, she and Edward. Some would see it as a humiliation.

In truth, she'd enjoyed it. The journey proved an ordeal, as it would have been even had she departed in splendid ceremony; but she had the pleasure of reliving her last meeting with Van Artevelde over and over as she lay in the cabin aboard ship. The little weasel.

He'd strode into the hall, chest puffed out. "I pray that the king is much improved and might grant me a brief audience, Your Grace."

"I thought I made it clear in my message that that is impossible. The thigh wound His Grace suffered at Sluys has festered and his leech is bleeding him for the next several days. He must rest."

"I pray you, Your Grace, I ask for but a glimpse of the king. I do not like to say it, but a rumor has caused great concern among my fellow captains, a river man reporting that His Grace took ship two nights hence, slipping away by night from us, his creditors."

It was true. Edward was by now halfway across the North Sea, heading home. As she would be within hours. Tonight she would follow by a different route. She rose up, indignant. "You accuse my husband of abandoning me, his wife and queen, when I am with child? I say again, you shall see him in due course." Even as she spoke to the arrogant little man, her household was readying her departure. Some already waited in the ship at anchor downriver.

Van Artevelde shrugged. "I have no control over the rumors spread among the captains of the city, Your Grace."

"No?" She'd feigned surprise.

He'd seen through it and bristled. "I pray you do not think to steal away to attend the betrothal of Lady Joan and young Will Montagu, Your Grace."

She wondered who had told him of the plans for Joan and the earl's son, but had no doubt why he'd brought it up—he would now think to shock her with the news of Joan's earlier vow. Foolish weasel. She'd known about his betrayal for months. For every Helena planted in her household, there were three servants in his who kept Philippa informed.

"Their betrothal? It is none of my affair. But you seem to find it significant. I suppose your daughters thought to see Joan again. They had become such friends."

"In faith, Your Grace, I am unhappy for Lady Joan, being forced to break her pledge to another."

There it was. At last.

"How thoughtful. But you should know that she fooled you. She was betrothed by proxy to Will Montagu several months before she repeated those vows with Holland. He had quite swept her away, with your considerable assistance, but we had seen the trouble brewing—Albret's change of heart, Holland's interest—and bowed to the Earl of Salisbury's petition." It was partly true. Montagu *had* presented the petition just after the turning of the year, but Edward had not yet decided against Albret, so they had put it aside.

She'd smiled sweetly as she sent her regards to Katarina and the girls and called a servant to show the gawping little weasel to the door, where two guards awaited to escort him to a monk's cell for the night. It would not do to have him raise a hue and cry. Her only regret was that Katarina had not accompanied him. How Philippa would have enjoyed seeing the harpy declawed, her wings clipped.

Yes, she had enjoyed that last meeting with Van Artevelde, the upstart commoner. But enough reverie. She rose from her prie-dieu in the Tower chapel, anxious to settle in the great hall before Edward arrived so that she might witness the dowager queen's reaction to the announcement of Joan's official betrothal. It should be entertaining, as Isabella blamed William Montagu for her lover Mortimer's capture and execution.

"Your mother has no love for Montagu. What has she to say of this match?" she'd asked Edward the previous night, drawing a curse. "You've not yet told her, have you?"

"I thought you might. You did encourage this match, my love." He'd leaned down to kiss her forehead. "Catherine Montagu is one of your favorite ladies of the chamber, is she not? Are you not happy that she will be further linked to our family?"

Philippa had closed her eyes and snaked a hand round his neck to bring him closer for another kiss, smiling as if savoring the moment. He must never know how she watched him with Catherine, noticing every smile, every touch. Were they lovers? She did not believe it, but Catherine was beautiful in a way Philippa could never be, and Edward's clear admiration hurt. Still, she was fond of the woman, which is why it hurt so that Catherine returned Edward's looks.

But a queen must rise above such things. Philippa would receive Catherine back into her household after Christmas. Unfortunately, with this betrothal Lady Joan would become a more permanent member of Philippa's household as well, whether she bided with her mother or her mother-in-law, for both were frequently with the queen. That troublesome young woman underfoot again. At least she would soon be wed, and Ned would understand that his cousin Joan was out of reach once and for all.

"You are right, my love. I have encouraged it, I benefit from it."

"My dear Philippa, my heart's ease." Edward drew her from her seat and kissed her warmly.

"But it is you who must break the news to your mother. She will simply argue with me, believing it possible to dissuade you. She must hear it from you."

From the chapel Philippa made her way into the hall, having her servants set up a comfortable resting place in a corner shielded by a carved wooden screen that would allow her to witness the dowager queen's reception of the news without discovery.

In the event, Isabella's performance lived up to Philippa's expectations. She was livid, spitting out "the Earl of Salisbury" as if it were a curse, pacing away, then turning sharply, her silk skirts swirling. "Montagu's blood mingling with ours? Do you not see the abomination of such a marriage, the insult to me?" Rage distorted her features, her beauty unseated by her temper.

"Be relieved that the trouble is laid at Montagu's feet," Edward reasoned. "For Joan will be trouble, you can be sure of that. Remember the white hart banner at Woodstock."

"There is nothing wrong with my memory, Edward," Isabella snarled. Philippa saw her husband flinch in the heat of his mother's eyes. "She's just a girl. You might have tamed her. Instead you've bent to Margaret of Kent, the countess of schemes. Next she'll demand one of my granddaughters for her son."

"Never."

"You say that now." Isabella strode from the room, majestic in her fury.

Philippa rose from the window seat to embrace her beloved. "You expected nothing less, my love. As for Margaret's son, we shall find a foreign wife for him, eh?"

"I count on you to arrange that when the time comes." He rested his head on hers for a moment, holding her tight. "You are my anchor, Philippa, you and William." He kissed her, then called to his dogs and strode out into the falling snow.

And William. And Catherine. Philippa folded her hands over her heart. She would not think of that.

27

Ditton Park
LATE DECEMBER 1340

Bundled against the cold, Joan, Bella, and Bess sat on a bench at the edge of the practice yard watching the prince take on a series of opponents in sword practice. Since his first lessons, Ned had excelled in the arts of war, and he'd only improved while Joan had been away. But, much to her surprise and secret delight, her own brother, John, was proving a challenge, quick and impetuous, catching the prince off guard at every turn. Ned rallied in the end and brought John to his knees sans sword, but he was sweating as he loudly thanked her brother for giving it his all. Joan tried not to cheer so enthusiastically that she insulted Ned.

And then there was Will, poor Will, limping away after a fierce attack that left him with his shield arm hanging oddly.

"Ned's a bully," Joan muttered.

"Will has no backbone," said Bella.

Joan feared it was true. She kept searching for something to admire, or at least like, in Will, but so far there was just the incident with the ring.

It did not help that Ned looked more and more like his father every day—tall, fair, with sharp blue eyes and a smile that rivaled the sun. Even now, his face flushed, his hair wild, he pleased the eye. Despite knowing Ned's dark side all too well, Joan often caught herself envying Marguerite of Brabant. Watching the first few exchanges with the next combatant, Joan guessed that he would best Ned. Choosing not to witness the unpleasantness that would surely follow, she declared herself too cold to sit there any longer and took her leave, catching up to Will as he limped back toward the hall.

"You should fight back, Will. You're several years older and surely stronger."

"He's my prince. Someday he'll be my king."

"In the practice yard he's your equal. Stand up to him."

Will started to shrug, then groaned, pressing his injured arm to his side. His face was white and pinched with the pain.

"Come. Let Efa see to that." Joan led him into the kitchen and sent a servant for her nurse while she poured Will a cup of watered wine.

"He'll need something stronger than that," Efa said when she'd examined the shoulder. "It's been pulled out of joint, and popping it back in will be painful." She saw to it that he took a generous mouthful of brandywine, and then some more. "Now, up onto the table with you and lie down." She recruited two muscular servants to hold still Will's torso and legs while closing her eyes to feel round the joint. "Hold now," she barked, and with a quick, forceful yank resettled the arm in its joint, accompanied by a howl from Will. He skipped the feast in the hall later that day.

Joan wished she had as well, or that her companions at table were better able to distract her from watching Ned. How beautiful he was in a deep blue jacket embroidered with celestial bodies in silver and gold thread. But the short jacket, tight leggings, and ballock knife strategically arranged reminded her of her first encounter with Bernardo Ezi. It embarrassed her to remember how she had allowed him to touch her neck, ply her with strong mead. And when Ned drew her out to dance she found herself blushing at the intensity of his gaze, how his

hands held hers a beat too long, how he mirrored her movements as if he could anticipate her. How had he come to remind
her so of Albret?

"Someone has given you dancing lessons," she noted as he
led her back to her seat.

He took her hand and kissed it. "You love to dance, so I
learned."

"It will serve you well with Marguerite. She, too, loves to
dance."

"Marguerite. Pah. The pope will never agree to my marrying her." He knocked John's hat down onto his face as he strode
away.

John laughed as he shook out his hat and put it back on. "Did
you criticize his dancing, sis? We all let him win, you know. It's
the only way to have peace. Be nice to him, I pray you!"

"I praised his dancing, you ninny. He just objects to any
mention of his intended."

"Because she's not you, ninny."

Much later, after many partners, she looked up to see that
Ned had returned, taking her hand from her aunt Blanche's
brother, Henry, Earl of Derby.

"Have a care that you do not pull my lady's arm out of joint
as you did that of her betrothed," Derby said with a wink at Ned.

"His injury was due to his limp grasp of his shield, and he
knows it," Ned muttered as he led Joan into position. "If Will
blamed me, he would be here in the hall seeking sympathy instead of hiding his shame."

How little he understood Will.

"What? You are not jumping to his defense?"

"I was so thoroughly dazzled by your skill I noticed little
else, my prince," she said with a laugh as the dance began.

He muttered a curse. But by the end of the dance he was
smiling again. "Come out to the stables at dawn tomorrow.
We'll have an early ride."

"The guards will never let us pass."

"They will. You'll see."

"If I'm awake." She had no intention of meeting him.

BUT IT SNOWED IN THE NIGHT. SHE'D AWAKENED IN THE CROWDED bedchamber to a telltale light shining through the chinks in the shutters and tiptoed across the cold floor to peer out at fat flakes swirling in the light of the guards' torches down below. How could she resist? Dressing in simple riding garb, she'd made it all the way to the door of the bedchamber before Helena called out to her, waking the Montagu girls.

"It's snowed in the night," Joan whispered. "I want to walk out in it before it's all trampled."

"But it will be cold and wet," Bess whispered.

"I don't care! Catch up with me at the stables, Helena."

In the great hall, Joan picked her way past the noblemen and their servants snoring on their pallets, shaking the guard at the door awake so that he would let her pass. "My lady's maid will follow shortly," she told him.

"Brace yourself, my lady," he warned as he opened the door against a wind that sent the banners thrumming overhead.

Joan rushed out into the swirling snow, her boots crunching on the inch or two that had already fallen, her cloak flapping round her legs. The wind sucked the breath out of her, but it was worth it, the courtyard quiet and so beautiful beneath the blanket of white. She bent her head against the wind and followed the torch-lit path. By the time she reached the stables, she was glad of the shelter, standing still for a moment to catch her breath.

Someone came up behind her, catching her hand and spinning her around.

"Ned!" She laughed to see all the snow in his hair. "Isn't it glorious?"

"I knew you'd come." He called softly to the groom, who led out two saddled palfreys and helped them mount.

"My lord prince?" Earl William stepped in from the yard, shaking the snow from his fur-lined hood before pushing it back. "Joan? What is the meaning of this?" He grasped the bridle of Joan's palfrey with a leather-gloved hand. "You mean to ride out before dawn in such weather? And with no guard?" He turned his head sharply to consider both of them with his good eye.

"We saw a chance to ride out at dawn in a fresh snowfall," said Joan. "I pray you, do not spoil our fun."

"You don't know the land round Ditton Park." It was not a royal manor but one recently confiscated from the king's treasurer, one of those he held responsible for his fiscal humiliation in Ghent.

"My cousin does," Joan lied.

The earl turned his eye on Ned. "In truth? How so, my lord prince?"

"By riding out it in, my lord earl," Ned said with a laugh as he brought his horse round so that the two formed a wedge pressing in on either side of Montagu, forcing the earl to let go the bridle and back away. "Why are *you* abroad on such a morning, my lord earl?"

"I am off on a mission for your father the king."

"Then we should not detain you. We're off!"

Ned slapped Joan's horse, startling it into a canter, and took off after her. Through the yard they rode, servants and chickens flying from their path, dogs barking as they took off after them. Joan loved the wildness of it, though she fully expected to be stopped at the gatehouse. But the drawbridge was down, the guards distracted by the earl's party, who were already mounted and waiting. She laughed at the surprise on their faces as her palfrey carried her under the archway and out onto the wooden bridge, clattering across as voices now cried out for her to halt. Too late!

She and Ned galloped down the road, snow-blanketed fields on either side, then slowed to a walk as they turned off onto a woodland track. Her hood fell back, her hair escaping to stream behind her. She could not remember the last time she'd felt so free. As they cleared the wood and rode out into a meadow, Ned's palfrey's tail sent up a snowy spray, dampening her face. So cold! She nudged her horse into the lead, heading due east toward the brightening dawn glimmering through a high hedge. Riding through, she came to a small clearing bordered by ancient hollies.

She halted, struck by a memory of just such a place, just such a snowy morning. She was eight. Efa had taken the children out into the wood to enjoy the snow, she and John as well as Ned and little Bella, only three at the time, struggling through the snow on her short legs as if it were several feet deep. Joan had rushed on ahead and, finding a treasure trove of snapped holly branches and hazel wands, she'd tucked holly beneath her hood, the deep green leaves and red berries poking out around her face like a garland, albeit a prickly one that left scratches that would take days to heal. Brandishing a hazel wand, she'd stepped out before the others on the path, declaring herself the queen of fairies and demanding that the mortals bow down before her. Bella whined for her own wand. John started to cry that he wanted his sister back.

But Ned had caught the spirit of her play and knelt, imploring the queen of fairies to knight him. Solemnly she had touched both his shoulders with the wand and named him Sir Edward of Fairy. Like this morning's ride, it was one of the moments that endeared him to her.

Ned dismounted. "Why did you stop?" he asked as he reached up to help her down.

"To enjoy it before it begins to melt in the morning sun." As soon as she was steady on her booted feet she spun round, arms wide, but there were no more flakes to catch. "The snow's already stopped!"

Ned grabbed her by the waist and held her facing him.

"I ask for a token from you, a promise that you will be mine when the time comes."

"Oh, Ned, don't spoil the morning."

"I promise that for now I will honor your marriage and be kind to Will, all right? After all, he does me a favor, keeping you safe until we've won France. Then there will be no need for me to forge an alliance with my marriage and we can be together."

"Don't be an ass. I'll still be Will's wife."

"He will never bed you. I'll make sure of that. We'll petition for annulment on the grounds of impotence."

"And what of Marguerite of Brabant, Ned?"

"I told you, the pope—"

"What if he does, Ned? Or your father's had you wed someone else?"

"We'll accuse her of something. Witchcraft. Treason."

"Ned, don't say that. As the future king, you must have a care about accusing the innocent." Her joy in the snowy dawn was beginning to fade.

"Now who's spoiling this moment? We *will* be together, Joan. It *will* be so. Give me a token."

The magic had gone from the morning. "You are being silly. I'm cold. I'm going back." She reached for her palfrey's bridle, but Ned grabbed her hand.

"Give me the white hart emblem, the one I rescued for you."

"I lost it with all my clothes in the fire on board ship." Not true, Thomas still had it. Or she hoped he did.

"The little ring, then."

Her heart pounded. Did he know that Thomas had the silk,

and the significance of the ring? But how could he? "You called it a paltry thing. Why would you want it?"

"Because you cherish it." He pulled her close and kissed her. "Are Will's kisses as sweet?"

"Stop this!" She pushed him away, and in that moment, as his face darkened with anger, she heard several horsemen crashing through the wood just behind them. God bless their timing. "Someone's coming. Help me mount."

"Remember the holly circle? Where you declared yourself queen of fairies and knighted me? You put a spell on me that day."

So this place reminded him of that morning long ago as well. Too late. "This is silly. I was eight years old, Ned, and we were playing. Help me mount."

For a few breaths he stared into her eyes, and for a moment she feared him. Then, suddenly, he let go of her shoulders. "You're right. We wouldn't get far." He helped her mount, then hooked his booted foot into a stirrup and mounted as well.

Her palfrey danced beneath her, sensing her agitation. She leaned forward to calm the horse as Earl William's guards rode into the clearing.

Once inside the gatehouse Joan was whisked away by her mother, who informed her that the queen was furious, blaming her, and Countess Catherine was moving Joan's things into her bedchamber.

"I hope it was worth it to you."

"For a moment, it was so glorious. Then Ned ruined it."

They had stopped near the hall door. Margaret gathered Joan's hair and tucked it into her hood. "It is ever so, daughter. You take flight with his fancies and then wonder how it all went so wrong."

"I won't again."

"As you said when he threw your ring into the mud."

This time was different. He'd frightened her. For the rest of the Christmas and New Year's festivities, Ned treated Will with good cheer and Joan kept her distance as much as possible. She distrusted the peace. As did Efa.

"He is accustomed to having his way and, for whatever reason—it cannot be passion at his age—he wants you to be his queen. Let us pray that the pope blesses the prince's marriage to Brabant's daughter. Though, God help her, she will be miserable with him."

"You've no spell to dampen his ardor?" Joan asked.

"I don't dare, little one. He will rule this land one day, and we want him to be whole."

28

Westminster Abbey
JANUARY 1341

In the soaring grace of St. Stephen's in Westminster Abbey the guests milled about, the jewels and buttons on their silks and velvets twinkling in the light of the candles and torches, rivaling the beauty of the sun shining through the stained-glass windows. In a short while, Margaret's dream for her daughter would be realized. *Bless their union, my Lord*, Margaret silently prayed. She stood to one side with Blanche, who gave off such waves of animosity that no one dared join them. Before Christmas, Margaret's brother Thomas had briefly been imprisoned in the Tower with several others in the home administration for failing to raise sufficient funds for the king's war, and though he been released quickly, without further punishment, Blanche still bristled at the insult to her husband in the presence of the royal couple. Thomas Wake, for his part, chose to wait out on the porch with Edward Montagu to avoid conversation with the king. Queen Philippa and her ladies flocked round Countess Catherine, whispering behind gloved hands as they cast glances at the young couple, while the ladies' husbands quietly talked to King Edward and Earl William. The young Montagus and royals surrounded Joan and Will, trying in vain to make them laugh. Even Joan's brother was making an effort. John's father would be proud of him, Margaret thought. But she did not like the prince's behavior, how often he touched Joan—her arm, her hand, her hair—as if he had a claim to her. Will did not seem to notice. Indeed, he seemed to have eyes only for the prince, smiling when Ned smiled, laughing loudly at his japes, straightening with pride when the prince looked his way.

William's brother Simon, Bishop of Ely, who would perform the ceremony, had been deep in conversation with Blanche's brother Henry, Earl of Derby, but now turned to face the gathering, motioning for the young couple to join him.

Will and Joan stepped forward, he moving woodenly in his elegant new jacket and high boots, she graceful and assured in crimson satin and cloth of gold, her fair hair tumbling down her back in riotous curls as if enjoying one last performance before being swept up into the coif of a married woman. The church grew so quiet that the whisper of their silk attire and their fine leather shoes on the tiles echoed in the stones overhead. No one would guess, seeing Joan now, that she had emptied out her stomach before dressing, sick with fear that God would strike her down for betraying her pledge to Thomas. As Will fumbled for Joan's hand, she gave him an encouraging smile. Margaret relaxed a little. The boy's voice cracked as he vowed to keep and protect Joan, but he managed to slip the ring on her finger without mishap. Joan's voice, in response, was low, almost a whisper. Will pecked her on the hand when the bishop finished his little sermon on the sanctity of marriage, and then the guests bore down on them. Margaret watched as Joan searched the crowd and, finding the prince, smiled shyly. Ned repaid her with an angry thrust of his chin, then turned on his heel and hurried down the nave, pushing past Margaret's brother and another man standing just inside the door.

"What's a Holland doing here?" Blanche hissed.

"A Holland?" Margaret squinted, trying to see the man more clearly, but he stood with the light behind him, his face in shadow. "You know them so well that you recognize one from this distance, in this light?"

"Know thine enemies," her sister-in-law muttered.

"How did he come to be here, Blanche?"

"Anyone might have told him." Blanche gave her head a little shake, the emeralds in her crispinette darkly glimmering. "Let us go and congratulate the sweet couple." She moved away, stopping to share a word and a laugh with the queen, at whom she'd glared only moments before.

Margaret had known there was more to the story of her brother's encounter with Lord Robert, but she'd brushed aside the thought, wanting peace. *God help me, have I been hoodwinked by my brother's wife? Have I been so blind? Did Blanche frighten the Hollands away?*

As Will spoke his vows, Joan remembered Thomas as he looked that night in the Van Arteveldes' guestroom, pledging his troth. She heard his dear voice, then her own rise in answer. She felt the lightness, the joy. And then Bishop Simon was prompting her. *This* was real—the awkward boy slipping the ring on her finger, her dry throat, the heaviness of her limbs. She'd whispered the vows in anguish, fighting back tears.

And now, watching Ned storm out, pushing past a man at the door. *Thomas?* Had she conjured him? She caught the eye of the man in the doorway and her heart soared. Thomas had come for her! But no. No, though he was very like, he was not her Thomas. The mouth, the jaw, his heft, they were all wrong, yet, overall, the resemblance was there. A brother, perhaps, and, considering the narrowed eyes, the set mouth, she guessed he despised her. For betraying Thomas, or for attempting to entrap him? Either way, he condemned her. She wondered how he had come to be there.

"Where's Ned going?" Will loosened his hold of Joan's hand. "He can't be angry. He knew what this was."

"You know his temper. We were the center of attention. He was forgotten. Come, let's bring him back." She grasped Will's hand and tugged him toward the door.

"Such a sweet couple!" her aunt Blanche cried as she stepped in front of them, enfolding them both in a velvet embrace. "May God bless your union with joy and abundance."

Joan managed to wriggle out, rushing to the door, but the man was gone, replaced by her uncle, uncharacteristically grim-faced.

"Was that one of Thomas Holland's brothers?" she asked.

"Return to your guests, Joan. You are a married woman now, the future Countess of Salisbury. It is a great honor for our family. Do not disgrace us."

"I've done all you asked of me, Uncle. Did you see him?" When he remained stone-faced she pushed past him, running out into the bright January morning.

Clusters of squires and pages stood on the steps, cheering as she appeared. She'd almost forgotten that she and Will were the occasion for this gathering. Smiling, she waved to them while scanning the crowd.

"There's Ned, across the square," Will said, catching up to her. He pointed over her shoulder to where Ned stood with several of the young nobles from his household.

"Let's go!" The Holland was rounding a corner just beyond.

Will gripped her elbow. "No. Come back inside. Safety in the crowd. Ned's planning something unpleasant, I'm sure."

Having lost sight of Thomas's brother, Joan let herself be led back into the nave, where she and Will were teased for attempting to escape betimes.

That night in bed, she curled up in a little ball while the Montagu girls whispered excitedly about their conquests at the feast, examining in her mind's eye the features of the man at the church door. He had Thomas's hair, his eyes, and there was something about his cheekbones, but she'd spied no dimples, no cleft in the chin. He might be anyone but for his expression of disgust, disappointment.

Efa said that only Thomas could heal her. But how could he believe in her love now? One night. She had been happy for one night. Mother in heaven, she had made a colossal mess of it. Secrets layered upon secrets—she would be wise to take a vow of silence.

29

Prussia
LATE SUMMER 1341

When King Edward slipped through the hands of his greedy allies in the Low Countries, he left a considerable cohort of English soldiers to find their own way home, Thomas among them, despite being one of the men in charge of the royals' nighttime escapes. He had hoped to spend Christmas with Joan and his family, celebrating his marriage, but it was not to be, for he could not afford the price of the journey. A letter to his family must suffice, and even that was difficult to arrange and quite costly. Once it was known that both the king and the queen were gone, the remaining English troops were charged exorbitantly for everything, particularly sea passage but even letters home. Praying that Joan was safe, Thomas found a courier to carry a letter to his brother, in which he'd enclosed a letter to Joan. Then he joined a company of his fellows heading east to seek their fortunes fighting alongside the Teutonic Knights against the Lithuanian infidel.

He soon regretted his choice. He found the Teutonic Knights to be so poisoned by hatred for the Lithuanians that it seemed to him they were the true enemies of Christ, not those they called pagans. They reveled in butchering the women, children, elderly, and infirm villagers they came upon—after raping the women. Their commanders made halfhearted speeches

about chivalry and Christian charity, but most left the perpe-
trators unpunished even when those not of the order bore horrified witness. In the ashes of their villages, Thomas and his
comrades often found crucifixes and paternosters. Rather than
purging the infidel from Christian lands, the Northern Crusade
was a brutal campaign to clear land the order coveted. Thomas
doubted that God would count this as a holy pilgrimage that
erased his sins and those of his father. And, as for making his
fortune, the Knights were so greedy that they cheated their fellow crusaders out of booty and ransoms. For the sake of honor,
he must quit the crusade.

On what he'd intended to be his final foray for the order,
Thomas found a way to beat the Knights at their own greedy
game and perhaps salvage some of his soul. On a long midsummer evening, he and three of his men came upon an enemy
camp tucked under a rocky outcrop, the soldiers heavily armed.
He guessed they were guarding a cave in which they'd hidden
treasure or someone of importance. Retreating to where Hugh
and other squires waited with the horses, he discovered Raoul
de Brienne, son of the Count of Eu, Constable of France, taking
his ease with several of his men.

Thomas cursed himself for being so easily tracked.

"We followed you from the Knights' camp," said Raoul.
"Not the same as tracking, which you do so well. I have a prop-
osition, for our mutual benefit." He offered Thomas a wineskin. "Will you hear me out?"

Thomas nodded as he took a swig, then handed back the
skin.

"If we combine forces, we don't need the Knights to attack.
We take whatever it is they so closely guard, keep the booty for
ourselves, and no one the wiser."

"Why should I trust you?"

"Trust?" Raoul shrugged. "That will take time. For now, I
hold out the promise of a fair split of the booty, and less carnage.

Those who surrender can walk away—disarmed, disgraced, but alive."

"The Knights will eventually discover our deception."

"We shall ensure that they profit just enough to look the other way. Eh? Is this to your liking?"

It was. And, by late summer, as the order prepared to withdraw for the winter, having pushed the Lithuanians back far enough to satisfy them for the moment, Thomas looked forward to going home. Raoul urged Thomas to return with him to France as a captain in his retinue. "I will be constable of France when my father dies, and count of Eu. A powerful patron. We shall send for your betrothed. I will provide you a fine country house with a vineyard."

Thomas knew it was not an empty offer. They'd developed a mutual trust watching each other's back and working together toward a common goal. Over many a dinner they had discovered a shared humanity and a dedication to honor. In another time, he would have considered it a privilege to serve under Raoul, but not now.

"When my liege lord Edward, King of England and France, comes to claim his crown, I would go to battle against my brothers?"

Raoul shrugged. "A small matter. The war will be quick, decisive, Edward will retreat, and you will reconcile with your brothers."

"Your offer is more tempting than you could know. I cannot depend upon my king's patronage once he knows I've robbed him of his beautiful cousin." He nodded at Raoul's surprise. "Joan is the daughter of the late Edmund, Earl of Kent, the king's uncle. But I must find my own way, my honor intact."

"I offer you my patronage, and my help in securing her."

"I cannot accept."

"I am sorry. For both of us. But I toast your boldness in

love." They drank. "Let us at least pledge that when we meet in battle we shall treat each other with honor."

Thomas could agree to that, and did.

So it was that his brothers Otho and Alan found him riding in the company of Raoul de Brienne as the crusaders withdrew toward the order's castle of Marienburg. The two Hollands had broken from their company when they heard that their brother was not far behind. From a vantage point beside the crowded road, they hailed him as his company appeared.

At first Thomas doubted his eyes, they had changed so, Otho having gained a formidable bulk and a scar across his cheek, Alan missing a piece of his left ear and some of his hair. They were no longer the boys who had followed him everywhere, eager to grow up and experience the world. They'd had their fill of experience, by the looks of them.

Alan grabbed Thomas's arm and held it, grinning as he studied his brother's face. "It's been four years, Thomas, and you've not changed. You've had it soft, I see."

"Hardly. I'm just better at ducking, you ass. Did you lose the ear here?"

"Scotland."

"And you, Otho—God's blood, you're an ox." They embraced. It was good to see them both.

He asked if they had any news of Joan.

Alan glanced at Otho, eyebrows raised. "You've not heard? She's wed young Montagu, heir to the Earl of Salisbury."

"You're still a poor liar."

"It's no lie. Tell him, Otho."

"It's true. This past winter I went to Westminster for our writs of safe passage and stumbled upon her wedding in the abbey church. There is no mistake." Otho punched Alan's shoulder. "I told you we should seek him out when we first arrived."

Thomas was shaking his head. "I wrote to Robert and

mother. They were to speak to her mother the countess on my behalf."

"You wrote, yes, but so did Blanche of Lancaster, married to Thomas Wake, Joan's uncle. She warned us to stay away from Joan, else we would find ourselves in court defending our land against the powerful Lancasters. She is a litigious bitch, Lady Wake. We cannot afford her as an enemy. It's done, Thomas. No mistaking."

Thomas stared at him, unbelieving. "We pledged our troth before God!"

"But not before a priest, or so you said in your letter," said Alan. "Our parish priest assured Mother that you might in good conscience wed another."

"Then I have no right to this." Thomas pulled the white hart silk from his sleeve. It was filthy, stained with sweat and blood.

"A white hart?" Otho noticed. "From Lady Joan?"

Thomas tossed it to Hugh. "Burn this." *And may Robert burn in hell for his betrayal.* This was his doing. It stank of his spinelessness.

Hugh caught the silk, and was turning to tuck it into his pack when he cried out, "Sir!" He pointed at a skirmish on the road below them.

It was Raoul. He must have turned back for Thomas and been set upon.

Hugh held out the silk. "You will want this."

Thomas ignored his squire's outstretched hand. "Bring my horse, damn you." Without another word he mounted and flung himself into the fray, swinging his sword. He pushed toward Raoul, who was matching his sword against that of the leader of one of the companies of Lithuanians they had plundered and set free. Thomas swung, slicing down through the man's neck to sever it from his fighting arm. Now he, too, was surrounded, and as he thrust and slashed he was joined by Otho, swinging a

mace, Alan a battle-axe. The trio cut, slashed, splintered, shouting warnings to one another.

But it was Raoul who called out, "To your left, Thomas!"
Too late. Thomas's head exploded with pain and his left eye
went dark, unbalancing him. Shouting at the top of his lungs,
he swung to the left and slashed the arm raised to strike again,
then the neck above, but as he yanked loose his sword he began
to fall. Otho was suddenly beside him, pushing him upright,
holding his shield over him. "Be still, Thomas, let me lead." He
struggled to stay upright, but he slipped farther and farther to
the left, collapsing into the pain and the roaring in his ears.

GOLD SILK, THRUMMING IN A STRONG WIND. THE COUNT'S TENT.
Otho, the ox, frowning down at him, lips moving. Thomas
opened his mouth and the pain sliced across his face, spiraling
round and round his head until he sank back down into the
blessed dark.

Another moment, a litter, curtains swaying, someone asking
him if he could sit up to take some water. He turned away.

Again he swam up through the blood-streaked darkness,
this time toward the creak of oars, the scent of tar and vomit, a
gentle rocking. Raoul smiled down on him. "Awake at last, my
friend? Do you think you might drink some brandywine from
a bowl?" Thomas clenched his teeth against the pain as a young
man helped him sit up, then stuffed cushions behind him. His
head pounded, and his vision—he reached up to the bandage
covering the left side of his head.

"You saved my life, Thomas. I am taking you home, where
you will have the best physicians."

"My eye?"

"If it can be saved, it will be done." Raoul guided Thomas's
hand to a bowl of brandywine.

"My brothers?"

"They've hardly left your side."

"And Joan. Did I dream that?"

Raoul shook his head. "I regret to say it is true."

"She is better off. She would not want me so, with one eye."

"The loss of an eye is bad for an archer, but not a knight. I've fought beside many a knight with such wounds and never found them lacking."

The brandywine burned down Thomas's throat. He held out the bowl for more.

Guînes
LATE AUTUMN 1341

LATE IN THE YEAR, KING EDWARD SUMMONED HOME ALL ENGLISH knights fighting on foreign soil. John, Duke of Brittany, had died the previous spring and the ensuing conflict over the succession was Edward's chance to gain a foothold in Brittany from which he might invade France. He meant to make a show of strength with his own men—he was through with trying to rally the Low Countries.

When Raoul announced the news at dinner, Otho and Alan began at once to plan their route home. It was their duty as knights to obey their king's summons.

"You will be disappointed in the spoils," Raoul warned them. "What about you, Thomas? Will you go with them, or take up my offer?"

Through the autumn Thomas had suffered two excruciatingly painful surgeries, drunk countless potions, endured endless poultices, unguents, and even a few charms, all to no effect. His left eye remained dark, the angry scar visible beyond the silk patch over the blind eye. Where else would he now find a patron who wished him to be a captain?

"The Countess of Kent might take pity on you and hear you out," Alan said.

"There is nothing to say. Thanks to Robert, Joan is married to young Montagu. Yet honor forbids me to take up arms against my countrymen."

"Brittany is far west of us," said Raoul.

"Edward will not stop there."

"And you need to confront your brother Robert."

"Confront? To what end? He has neither conscience nor courage. I've nothing to say to him." Thomas could see by Raoul's raised brow that he wasn't convinced. "I doubt that I'll see him. He'll be in Westminster defending himself against a dozen lawsuits."

"But if you do?"

"Then God help him."

"Do not spill your brother's blood, my friend." Raoul grinned. "Or perhaps just a little."

They parted friends, swearing once again that if they met in battle they would treat each other with honor.

Thorpe Waterville Castle, Northamptonshire
SPRING 1342

As Thomas dismounted in the yard his mother hurried forth, then stopped a few feet away, hands to her mouth. "Mother in heaven, Thomas, your eye!" She reached out to touch the scar that crossed from eye to ear. "We must send for a physician."

He caught her up in a warm embrace. Throughout her husband's troubles, Lady Maud Holland had kept a steady, good-natured mien, comforting to the children, and had fought hard since his death to keep an inheritance for Robert, the eldest. All her children held her in high esteem. Thomas did not blame her for her blind spot regarding Robert. He was her firstborn, the heir, now the lord. His word was law to her. "I've had the care of the best physicians in Christendom. Be at ease, Mother. There's nothing more to do."

As he stepped back from her, she focused on tidying her hair, avoiding his gaze. "Regarding Lady Joan—"

By then his brother Robert had joined them, slapping Thomas on the back. "You're almost as broad as I am, though I'm sure you padded yourself with muscle in battle, rather than eating well." He laughed, patting his ample middle, oblivious of the gloved hand racing to his jaw until he was lying on his back in the dirt.

"What right had you? What right? You bastard!" Thomas spat, pulling off his gloves so that he might feel Robert's throat as he crushed it.

"Thomas! Let go of your brother." Maud took hold of his arm, trying to pull him away. "I agreed with Robert. We have not the means to fight Lady Wake or the Montagus."

"We would if Robert were not always dragged to court by those he's cheated of property or honor." Thomas broke away, diving down onto Robert. "Whose wife are you bedding now?"

"Alan! Otho! Help him!"

They managed to pull Thomas away.

"Did you even send on the letter I wrote to her?"

"What was the point?" Robert muttered.

"She must have thought I'd deserted her," Thomas shouted. "You bastard!"

Robert spewed curses as he massaged his jaw.

Maud pressed Thomas's arm. "My son, in time you will see it is better this way. The king will forgive your transgression—"

"Forgive?" Thomas shook her off. "I fought beside His Grace at Sluys and Tournai, ate at his table in camp. He showed no animosity toward me. Faith, he praised my leadership. You'd no right, Robert, you, who know nothing of what it means to fight for your king, nothing of honor."

"Enough!" Maud commanded.

Thomas cursed and turned his back on them, shrugging off Alan and Otho as he strode away. He'd not told Joan of Robert's violent clashes with neighboring landowners. Any English court would side with the Wakes and the Montagus; how easily they would twist his love for Joan into ambition. His only possible hope was to petition the pope, arguing the legality of the vows he and Joan made in Ghent, which would require a fortune he did not have.

No matter how hard he and his mother worked to regain the Holland honor, it was never enough. There must be some taint on their blood. He should not sully Joan with it. He must let her go.

30

Eltham Palace
EARLY SPRING 1342

The tournament honoring the visit of William, Count of Hainault, the queen's brother, attracted all the knights summoned for the coming invasion of Brittany. A city of pavilions had grown up in the meadows surrounding Eltham Palace, and the jousting would take place over several days, interspersed with elaborate feasts.

Thomas, Otho, and Alan had welcomed the chance to make some money in wagers and attract sponsors before sailing for Brittany in late summer, all three hoping to come out of it with funds for some new gear, or, at least, to repair what they had. Alan and Thomas were to show off their swordsmanship in the vespers events on the eve of the tournament, the crowd naturally betting against the half-blind brother, unaware of the hours he'd spent in the practice yard in Guînes and later at home. Otho found out through eavesdropping that Will Montagu would be acting as squire to one of his kinsmen, which surely meant that Joan would be present. Alan looked forward to finally seeing her. Thomas dreaded it. Seeing her would be a torment.

The three strolled about the tents renewing acquaintances, urging friends to come support them. It was then that Thomas beheld Joan for the first time in two years. Her fair hair caught up in a jeweled crispinette as was appropriate for a married woman, her long, slender neck exposed. God's blood, how beautiful she was. How he loved her. She was talking to a squarely built squire he guessed to be Will Montagu—he had the Earl of Salisbury's hawk-like nose.

Just like that, his resolve snapped. What right had Montagu to her? She had pledged herself to Thomas. Seeing her stirred memories of the love in her eyes, the passion with which she had come to him. By Joan's frown and gestures, he saw that she was arguing with Montagu, at the last turning away in apparent disgust as he hung his head. She had never looked so at Thomas.

Another young man strode up and slapped young Montagu on the back, then chucked Joan under the chin. Thomas caught his breath. The newcomer lit his Joan up like the sun, and in the warmth of his light she straightened and smiled. Though it was not her full smile, not as she had smiled at Thomas. Will shrugged and walked away.

"Trust Prince Edward to find the loveliest lady attending," Alan muttered.

"That is Joan, my lady," said Thomas.

"By the rood she is fair," Alan breathed. "You'd said she was, I know, but my imagination never envisioned such perfection. I see why you wanted to kill Robert."

"Rumor is the marriage is unconsummated," said Otho. "Can you imagine, being forbidden to bed her when she is within your reach?"

Thomas could not. "So that is Will Montagu. He's just a boy."

"He is," said Otho. "Go challenge him."

"Tempting, but it would gain me nothing. Still, seeing her again, I am resolved. I cannot give her up. I will win her back. But honorably."

"You and your bloody honor." Otho scoffed. "But I'm glad you've not given up. She's worth a battle or two."

More like a king's ransom.

"Come on, it's time," Alan said, taking Thomas's arm.

The two brothers had performed their swordplay routine at many tournaments, becoming so accustomed to each other's style that they could take risks that thrilled an audience. Now, with practice, they'd learned to compensate for Thomas's blindness. Alan and Thomas had attracted an enthusiastic crowd with their first round, forgetting everything in their focus on their thrusts and parries. Then Joan appeared on the arm of the prince. Thomas lost the rhythm.

Alan thrust at him. Thomas began to modify the routine to compensate for his lack of focus, but his brother forced him back to riskier thrusts. He tried to forget that Joan was standing there, tried to get back in step with his brother. But he failed, and suddenly Alan stumbled backward, blood blooming on his arm. Thomas backed away, indicating that they should end it there. But Alan pushed himself up and thrust, Thomas parried, and they were off, the rhythm taking them. Thomas won the round to loud applause and shouts for more. He looked to see how Joan received his triumph. But he could not find her in the crowd. Blinded, scarred, performing for bets—he should not be surprised that she ran from him.

Men crowded round, slapping him on the back, praising his technique, curious how he'd lost the eye. One noble invited him to sup with him so they might discuss the training of his son and heir, born blind in one eye. Thomas answered all as courteously as he could manage through the noise in his head, and withdrew with the noble. This, at least, he might do to please God, win back some grace.

BLINDED BY TEARS JOAN PUSHED HER WAY THROUGH THE CROWD, stumbling, whispering her apologies, shaking her head at expressions of concern, running as much from the sound of Ned's voice as from Thomas and his brothers, running from herself, from the hopeless tangle of her life.

She had begun the day arguing with Will about his inability to stand up to his parents. She'd prodded him to tell them that it was not she who made certain Ned was always about but Will himself.

"They accuse me of insulting you by flirting with him, and you say nothing in my defense. Why can't you tell them it's you who can't bear to be far from him? It's you who hangs on his every word?"

He stared at her.

"Say something!"

He'd shaken his head. "Half the time the two of you walk off without me. You don't want anything to do with me. *That's* what angers them."

He was right. She didn't, and they knew, and that was never going to change, ever.

And then Ned had interrupted, both of them smiling at him, grateful to be rescued from each other. He'd rushed her off to watch two battle-scarred men performing for the money they would make on the crowd's bets.

"I'd rather not, Ned." She tried to break his hold on her hand. But he insisted, though he knew it angered her that the king's best men should be reduced to this. She'd heard how Edward had abandoned them in Flanders without a thought to how they would afford the passage home. Including Thomas. Yet now, seeing an advantage in the confusion over the Breton succession, the king had ordered them home, threatening to confiscate their lands if they did not break off from the mercenary bands that had been their salvation and honor their pledge to him. And here they were, awaiting the king's pleasure, following the tournaments in hope of attracting patrons.

The two before her had no armor, no helmets, just worn

boiled leather jackets. She expected Ned to make fun of them, their penury a sign of their lack of skill, in his opinion. But he was watching them intently.

Suddenly the one with the eye patch ducked and spun round, grinning mischievously at his opponent, revealing a dimple. "Thomas!" *God in heaven*. She'd not heard he would be present. What had happened to his beautiful face?

Ned glanced at her, and she realized she'd spoken Thomas's name aloud. "Yes, the brothers Holland," said Ned. "Alan and your Thomas."

"His wound!" She'd not known. How could she not have known? "How he must have suffered." Her ears rang, her vision blurred with tears. If only he'd come home, come to her . . .

"He's half blind now, but watch him, how quickly he moves his head. He has trained until it is second nature. In so short a time! They say it was late summer that he was blinded protecting Raoul de Brienne, the son of the Constable of France. In Prussia. In gratitude, the Count of Eu sent for the finest physicians in France, hoping to save his sight. But the eye had been too damaged."

How could she help? Late summer? The scar should no longer be so angry. She would send Efa to him. She felt Ned watching her. "You admire him," she said.

"How could I not? Such a crippling wound has bested better men than he."

There *was* no better man. Joan forced herself to look away from Thomas, fearing she would run to him. She scanned the crowd to see if she recognized the man from her wedding. She found him standing next to Hugh, Thomas's squire. He was shorter than Thomas, stockier. Hugh noticed her now, his expression unfriendly, accusing. She looked away, feeling sick.

"How does he do that?" Ned marveled. "My uncle William greatly admires Thomas Holland. He tried to lure him away from Father. Did you know that?"

He meant the queen's brother, the Count of Hainault. Joan had not known that, but she did not bother to answer, afraid to say anything to him about Thomas, worried about Ned's motivation in telling her this, what he knew about them, that he meant by his chatter to draw her out.

"My uncle insisted that Thomas be included in the tourney participants tomorrow," said Ned.

She could not help herself, she looked back at Thomas. Mother in heaven, he'd noticed her. He paused, looked as if about to say something. He neither frowned nor smiled. Joan could not breathe. Alan, noticing the pause, glanced her way, but quickly moved to defend himself as Thomas burst into action, whipped by a fury. The crowd grew louder, cheering them on as, with a fierce slice, Thomas drew his brother's blood. That is when Joan turned and ran.

Now Ned grasped her elbow, shaking it. "You've never run from blood before. What is this? Tears? What is Thomas Holland to you, cousin?"

"He was a good friend to me when I was far from home." Joan tried to shake off his hand. He knew. He was goading her. "Let me go. Earl William is approaching us."

"Another half-blind warrior," Ned muttered under his breath, stepping way from Joan.

Earl William bowed to him. "My lord prince, I would have a word with my daughter. Alone."

His daughter. Never. Ned looked ready to challenge him, but Joan feared what he would hear.

"Go, Ned, please." She feigned a smile and shooed him off.

"You were told to stay away from Holland," the earl growled when Ned was just a few steps away. He paused. She held her breath until he moved on.

"I did not seek to see him, my lord. I did not know he was here, but only came upon him."

The earl grunted, disbelieving. "He's a fine captain, Joan,

even now. Do not ruin him with your attention. What's done is done. You are Will's wife."

"So you all tell me," she muttered, sick of him, sick of all of them. With a little bow, she turned and walked away, her legs wobbly but holding her up and functioning. The earl called after her, commanding her to stay, but she continued on.

As night fell, the bright-colored silk-and-canvas pavilions, lit from within, seemed to float on the dark field. When Joan finished a game of chess with Bella she was drawn outside, caught by the beauty of the floating pavilions, the starry sky, the sound of laughter, a singer mourning the death of his lady love, the lute playing counterpoint to his clear voice. The blood and sweat, the conflicts, the desperation of the impoverished knights—all were hidden by the gentle night, tucked into the shadows the lanterns did not reach.

Someone called her name, softly, almost secretly. She followed the sound. He stood beneath a tree very near the royal pavilion.

"Hugh!" Her heart raced. "Your lord has sent for me?"

"My lady." He bowed, holding out the white hart silk. "Sir Thomas says he has no right to keep this."

The silk felt rough, stiffened by Thomas's blood? His sweat? She kissed it and handed it back. "No. He has every right to this. He is my husband, my beloved. There is no one else."

"But my lady, you are—"

She put a finger to his lips. "I could not fight them all. But I pray that His Holiness the pope will uphold Sir Thomas's claim. If we can find a way. I saw him, Hugh, his terrible wound. Tell me how—this silk, was he wearing it?"

"No, my lady." He told her how Otho and Alan had told Thomas of her marriage right before he rushed into the fray to save Raoul de Brienne.

He'd thrown away his protection, thinking he'd lost her. They'd both been betrayed by their families. "My nurse, Efa, is a gifted healer. I will send her to him tonight. Expect her." Bella appeared at the entrance to the royal pavilion, squinting into the dark. "Go!" Joan whispered, and waited until Hugh was away before stepping out into the light from the entrance torches.

"Joan! Who was that with you?"

"Your brother, of course, wanting my help in a prank. But I'm for bed."

Joan caught her breath as Ned's voice rose from the royal tent, singing a round, then joined by others.

"He arrived on one end as you departed from the other," said Bella. "Why did you lie to me? Who is he? Was it Thomas Holland?"

Joan grabbed the princess by the arm. "Do not say his name, do you hear me, or I'll have Efa cast a spell that will see you wed to an ancient, toothless cripple!"

"You're hurting me! I'll say nothing, I swear. But how could you want him? He's a cripple now."

Joan squeezed hard before she let go of Bella's arm. "It wasn't him, anyway."

"No? Then who?"

Joan laughed. "I would be a fool to tell you." She kissed Bella on the cheek and stepped across the way into the Montagus' pavilion.

The lanterns had been dimmed and all but Helena and Efa were abed. Joan drew Efa to one side, whispering to her of the encounter, what she had learned of Thomas's wounding, including the part she believed the white hart silk had played, and asked her to go to him, help him.

"This was the silk you embroidered to hang at Woodstock, to honor your father?"

Joan nodded. "Is that important?"

"With charms, everything is. Go to sleep now, rest your

heart while I see to your beloved." Efa stroked Joan's forehead, kissed her cheek, and withdrew to collect her things.

"Sir, she is true." Hugh held the cloth out to Thomas. "She kissed it and handed it back, saying you have every right to this, you are her husband, and she loves you still. She is sending her nurse to you, the healer Efa."

"She saw me and she still speaks of love?" Thomas crushed the cloth in his hand, trying to constrict his surge of hope. "She's wed to Salisbury's heir. I dare not go near her."

"My lord?" A woman stood in the doorway, wimpled and carrying a basket. "I am Efa. My lady sent me to you."

Thomas motioned her to enter, offering her a camp chair. "How is my lady?"

"Incomplete without you, my lord." She refused the chair. "Better that you sit and I look at your wound." She was a small woman, the top of her head just barely reaching his shoulders, but her grasp was strong as she guided him into the chair.

"The best physicians in France worked on it," he said as she untied the silk patch to expose the eye. "It is too damaged. What do you mean, 'incomplete'?"

"Hush now." She ran her fingers over the wound, with the back of her hand felt his forehead, bent to peer into both his eyes, whispering to herself all the while in Welsh. He felt a warmth spreading through him, though she had given him nothing to ingest, and he began to fear that she was casting a spell. "Efa, as in the first woman, Eve?" he asked.

Her laugh was light. "There are many Efas in my village in Wales. Sisters, daughters, granddaughters, nieces of Eve." She went over to the basket she'd set down on a bench. "They were right, the eye itself is too damaged. But it is the condition of the wound that is my lady's concern, and mine now that I see it. Half a year? The fine physicians gave him no unguents to soothe it and keep the scar soft and supple?" She asked it of Hugh, who stood over her, closely watching what she did.

"They did, Dame Efa, but Sir Thomas is not keen to use them."

"Ah. Mine you will. And, while we are all here, I shall work them in each morning and each evening, as my lady wishes." She rejoined Thomas, holding a small bowl to his nose.

Thomas was surprised by the pleasant scent. "All their unguents stank."

"So that you believe in their healing power." She laughed softly as she spread some of the ointment along his scar.

"Joan sent you to me?"

"How else would I be here, my lord? Now hush, feel this."

Her touch was light, yet all along the puckered skin he felt a prickly warmth and an easing, as though skin, muscle, and bone opened the fist they'd formed against pain. He gave a great sigh as he felt his entire body relax. "What spell is this?" he whispered.

"No spell, just fine medicine," said Efa.

Before he knew it, he was lost in a dream of reunion with Joan, holding her in his arms, kissing her. . . . "I need to talk to my lady."

"Not now, not yet. Earl William and Prince Edward watch her every move. What you need to do is go to Brittany as planned and capture someone who will bring a fine ransom that you can spend in Avignon."

"Petition the pope? There is no time. By then she might have borne him an heir—"

"Do not be so certain. She is more your wife in deed than she is young Montagu's. Countess Margaret and Earl William are uneasy in their minds about this match, whether it will be challenged, and they've kept them apart, though even had they not there is nothing between the two. Young Montagu's affections lie elsewhere as well." She sighed. "You have generous friends who love you. What you most wish for will come to pass."

"I do not believe we can foresee the future."

"Whether you believe is unimportant, my lord. It will be so. Now hush."

His resistance to her words began to ease. "How am I to bear being so close and not speaking to her?"

"As you bore this wound, Sir Thomas, with courage and prayer." She stepped back, her wide hazel eyes considering him. "Already I see a change. It was beginning to pull up your left cheek, hiding the dimple my lady loves so dearly. Might I touch the silk she spoke of?"

He handed it to her. "She said she used your charms."

Efa handled the white hart emblem gingerly, sniffing, running her fingertips across it. "More than my charms, there is much of my lady in it, and you have strengthened it with your blood and sweat." She handed it back. "Do not lose it again, my lord. Do not break my lady's heart." She gave him a little bow. "Until the morrow."

Thomas reached for her arm. "Tell her I love her."

The healer's smile warmed his soul. She was on his side. "I will. May God smile on the two of you."

When she was gone Thomas lay back on his cot, thinking to rest a moment, then join his brothers in Count William's pavilion. But for the first time since his blinding he fell into a deep, dreamless, healing sleep, not waking until morning.

Joan curled up to Efa when she slipped into bed, and though she dare not speak and wake the Montagu women, she felt comforted.

In the morning, Efa took Joan aside to tell her about her meeting with Thomas, her certainty that they would complete their vows, the strength of what Joan had woven into the silk— her enduring love for her father, and his for her.

"Your Thomas is protected by your love."

"You taught me well."

Efa smiled. "Not me. These charms are yours."

Joan hugged Efa tightly. "Mother was wrong to send you away."

"She was frightened, that is all, my lady. Our priests cannot explain this power, and so they fear it and preach against it. But it is so simple." She shrugged and pushed Joan toward Helena. "You must dress so you might watch him from the stands."

THOMAS LOOKED UP AND SHE WAS THERE, LUMINOUS, A LIGHT among the women, the light of his life. He touched his heart, she touched hers and smiled, and, just as the healer's hands had done, Joan spread a warmth like a benediction through his being. All doubt ceased. He would win her back.

31

AUTUMN 1343
Woodstock

It was a perfect autumn day, sunlight falling through the bright, thinning canopy of beech and hazel, the air just sharp enough to make her grateful for the wool of her gown and surcoat but not so chilly that her hands were clumsy with the bow. Joan was laughingly showing Bella what was wrong with her form, bending her wrist as the princess had done, then straightening the wrist to show her how much steadier it would be. Bella whined that she hadn't the strength.

"That is the purpose of practice, to build strength," said Efa, nodding her approval of Joan's correction.

Joan let go the arrow, cheering as it landed close to center. Bella sighed loudly—she was lately of the opinion that a noblewoman should not express enthusiasm. Efa was oddly quiet, and as Joan turned to her she saw the cause.

"Almost perfect, cousin!" Ned called out as he joined them, kissing her neck, then snaking his arms round to adjust her hands in a slightly different grip. "See? Even steadier." Another kiss.

He'd made a habit of this of late, catching her by surprise and drawing her close, kissing, touching, breathing in her ear. Countess Catherine had quickly gone from being pleased with his omnipresence, seeing Will's delight, to shrilly criticizing Joan for encouraging the prince. She was not wrong. Ned made up for the chilliness of the Montagus. He reminded Joan that, even in the midst of so much unhappiness, she could experience magical moments. He made her laugh.

Efa disapproved. *There is a darkness in him. Keep him at arm's length.*

Joan would remember Bruno, the ring, countless smaller incidents, and vow to heed Efa's warning. But, the moment he was near, she found a reason to keep him there *just this time*.

"I hear your maid Mary has been sent away for being with child. Your husband's child. Can you forgive him?" Ned meant it as a taunt, not as a question.

"I don't want to talk about it. Go away if you're going to be hateful."

It was true about Mary. She'd gone to live with her parents on a farm on one of the Kent estates. Countess Catherine blamed the situation on her son's understandable frustration in being forbidden to sleep with Joan, his wife. They were both sixteen, old enough. The wait had given Will no choice but to ease his frustration with a maidservant. Catherine had declared that, after the Christmas court, the two would commence living as husband and wife.

Will did not yearn for her; he was content with their situation as long as Ned was near. He'd taken up with Mary to quell rumors that he'd lost his heart to one of the royal grooms.

Ned grinned. "Mother has summoned Lady Lucienne back to court now that her year of mourning is finished. Did you know?" Lord Townley had succumbed to a fever the previous autumn, and Lucienne had surprised everyone at court by retiring to the country to grieve. "Thomas Holland will be happy to see her. Now that she's a wealthy widow, he has a fortune within his grasp."

Handing a servant her bow and quiver of arrows, Joan turned around to slap Ned, but he was already past the hedge. Sometimes she truly hated him.

"He knows you so well," said Bella. "He knows just how to annoy you."

London
LATE OCTOBER

It was Thomas's favorite London inn, near the Thames but not too near, a short walk to St. Paul's, past the elegant homes of the cloth and wine merchants. The food was good, the ale thick, and the regulars strangers to him. When he returned from months of fighting in the field, he stayed there for a week or more for quiet, peace, before facing his family. So he was irritated to find that he'd been cheated out of the extra coin he'd paid to sleep alone, albeit in a room in which he could not stand up straight for the slope of the roof above. It was already occupied.

"You must have taken a wrong turn," he growled, turning up his lantern to see who was seated on the bed. But even before she turned he knew her by her perfume, roses and spice. How easily they came together. She gasped to see his wound, hushing him when he called himself hideous, covering his face with kisses.

Only after a long while did they talk. She wanted to hear how he'd been injured, was curious about Raoul de Brienne and his father's household, but not too curious. And then *she* talked. She knew much of what had happened with Joan in Ghent. How? She laughed at the question, but quickly grew serious.

"You must have a care with the prince. He has asked me many questions about your rescuing Lady Joan from Albret, about your relationship with the Van Arteveldes. He is obsessed with Joan. Protect yourself. Petition the pope."

"I haven't the money."

"I do." She leaned over him, kissing him lightly, smiling through a perfumed fall of midnight hair.

"I cannot accept—why would you do this for us?"

"Because I love you." She smoothed back his hair, kissed the brow above his wrecked eye. "And I know she has your heart."

"I do not deserve you, Lucienne." He kissed her hand. "I am grateful for this, for all you have been for me. But I cannot accept your offer. I must do this on my own."

They argued, made love again. "For the last time," she told him. "You are no longer free." As he led her down to the room where her servant awaited her, she repeated the warning to be careful with the prince.

Thomas looked to see if she was smiling. But no, she was serious. "He's just a boy."

"Do not underestimate him, Tom. Joan's marriage to young Montagu serves him for now. Rumors are young Will prefers boys and pines for the prince. Poor Joan. But you—*you* the prince would consider a threat. Get the pope on your side as soon as you can. And Countess Margaret. I am certain she looks on her daughter's situation with dismay and must wonder if this is God's sign that the marriage was in error, a punishment for breaking a solemn vow." As her servant draped a cloak around her, Lucienne said, "My offer stands."

He could not imagine accepting such a gift from her. But he was moved by her selfless generosity and grateful for her advice. If anyone knew the temper of the court, it was Lucienne.

Westminster
NOVEMBER 1343

LEAVES SKITTERED ACROSS THE GRAVEL PATH LEADING TO THE carved oak door. Thomas took off his hat, smoothed down his hair, checked that his patch was securely seated, replaced the hat, then nodded to Hugh to knock.

A page opened the door. "My lord?"

"Sir Thomas Holland to see Countess Margaret."

A bow. "A moment."

They stood at the door, Thomas staring up at an abandoned nest tucked into the overhang as Hugh rocked on his feet.

The door opened once more, but it was the countess's brother, Lord Wake, who stood on the threshold. "Sir Thomas, come in, come in." He reached out to grasp Thomas's arm in a soldierly gesture of welcome. One of the northern lords responsible for protecting the realm from marauding Scots, he had seen his share of battle.

"My lord, I hoped to talk to your sister." Thomas had been told that the Wakes were in Lincolnshire. He prayed he'd not been misled about Joan, that she was truly away at Bisham, not here with her mother. He did not want his purpose misconstrued.

"I've sent a servant to her." Wake showed them into the hall, a large, airy room, ordering a servant to escort Hugh to the kitchen for some food and ale.

Thomas stared up at a white hart banner hanging proudly from the rafters above the table at the head of the hall.

"My niece sewed that, but of course you know." Wake gestured for Thomas to sit. "Be at ease, Sir Thomas. I do not share my wife's grudges. I will hear you out, even if my sister will not." He held up a hand to silence Thomas. "I trust she will join us in good time."

Servants arrived, bringing wine, bread, cold meat, cheese, winter apples.

Wake settled on a high-backed chair, sitting tall, as if at attention. "You were caught between my niece's desperate attempt to avoid a marriage meant to buy the king an ally and Montagu's ambition—a wife of royal blood for his heir. Most unfortunate."

Thomas was relieved to get right to the point. "Joan and I are lawfully wed."

"Witnessed by a couple who wished only to embarrass the Sire D'Albret. It was not only His Grace who questioned the validity, considering who coaxed Lady Joan into it, and why. My sister was not at all easy in her mind about it."

"Nor was she easy about my father's history, I imagine."

Lord Wake looked sympathetic. "In that his actions so weakened your family's influence, yes, that is part of my sister's prejudice against you."

"Lady Joan's maidservant, Helena, and my squire, Hugh, were also witnesses."

"Three years have passed since the wedding, in Westminster, attended by the royal family, Joan's kin. What do you hope to gain after all this time?"

Thomas stared into his wine. "I understand the marriage is unconsummated."

"As to that—" Wake stopped.

Countess Margaret stood by the dais, beneath the white hart banner. "Sir Thomas. If you will come with me." She did not wait, but turned toward a door, which a servant rushed to open, stepping aside to let his mistress, then Thomas, into the small room fitted out as a parlor.

As the countess took her seat in a high-backed, cushioned chair, and whispered instructions to the servant, Thomas settled on a camp chair across from her. Except for her eyes, there was little resemblance between Margaret and her daughter, the mother having a darker complexion and less even features. Handsome rather than beautiful.

As soon as the servant departed, the countess attended him with a polite half-smile. "Tell me why you have come, Sir Thomas."

"To try to convince you that in the eyes of God your daughter and I are husband and wife. I cannot believe Joan did not tell you that. I believe you chose instead to silence us."

He told her of the threat Lady Wake had made to his family. Quietly, without emotion. He had not expected her look of surprise. She had not known, or, at least, not the whole of it. She covered her confusion with anger.

"You should be ashamed of yourself, taking advantage of a young girl."

"My lady, it was not like that. Joan must have told you. It was her idea, to consummate it so that she might be safe from the Sire d'Albret. And she assured me that she was a woman."

"She was only twelve years old. Shame on you!"

"Was she not a woman?" His breath caught in his throat. "My lady, I never doubted Joan's assurance." Had she done this? Had she lured him to commit such a grievous act? She had been frightened, desperate. . . .

"I am not insensitive to your pain, Sir Thomas. The Van Arteveldes caught you in their trap as well. But three years have passed since His Grace declared her free to wed Will Montagu, and blessed the union. Three years, Sir Thomas. What would you do now?"

It was no time to succumb to doubt. "I do not hold that she was free to wed another, my lady. I believe that her present unhappiness is proof of that. She is my wife in the eyes of God."

She rose up, those remarkable eyes flashing with anger. "Of what do you dare accuse me?"

He rose in respect to her. "It is you who accuse, my lady. You accuse me of being dishonorable. And I say you are wrong in that. You accuse me of having taken advantage of a girl who had not yet matured. I still believe you are also wrong in that. But of what do I accuse you? Nothing. What I have done is point out our disagreement and assure you that all I did was out of love for your daughter." He bowed his head, then met her angry gaze. "God forgive me if it is true I made love to a child. I vow to make this right."

"She was a woman," Margaret whispered. "I do not mean to mislead you. But it is too late. The deed is done. You must forget my daughter."

"I can no more do that than forget to breathe, my lady."

"You do love her. I see that."

Was that a softening he heard in her voice? "Will you tell Joan of our meeting?"

"No. And I forbid you to try to see her."

"I cannot help but see her, my lady. I've been summoned to resume my duties in King Edward's household guard."

"After what you did?"

"Since Joan and I pledged our troth, I've fought beside His Grace on several occasions, my lady."

"Then do not waste this chance to redeem yourself, Sir Thomas." She moved toward the door, paused to let him exit first. "I am sorry for your terrible injury."

Which one, he wondered as he strode across the hall, calling to a servant to fetch Hugh.

32

Bisham
DECEMBER 1343

Layers of soft gray and watery blue silk swirling about her in the brisk wind, Catherine commanded the doorway. William dropped his diplomatic pack to embrace her. "My dearest Catherine."

She stopped him at arm's length, offering a cheek for a kiss. "You are not glad to see me?"

"Your cloak is wet, William. Come within, warm yourself by the fire." She stepped aside so that he might enter the hall, then followed. "We have much to do. His Grace has sent beautiful velvets and silks to adorn you for the Christmas court. And a new fur-lined cloak, just in time—yours reeks of horse and dampness. Your page is not so well trained as I'd thought him. He hasn't been fully drying your clothes." She nodded to a servant to remove William's cloak.

"Nights in the field do not afford me such luxuries," William snapped. "I must dress up for a Christmas court?" He muttered a curse. "I am too old for all this, Catherine, I grow weary. I shall make my excuses to Edward when I deliver my report. What say you to Christmas here at Bisham?"

"William," she chided, "His Grace honors you." The truth of it was that Catherine could never bring herself to disappoint

Edward. "And the queen expects me at Windsor within the week. Before moving on to Woodstock for Christmas, we must settle arrangements for the tournament for St. Wulfstan's Day in January."

With a grunt, William sat down on a stool so that his page could pull off his boots.

"Those look old and worn," Catherine said, frowning at the young man.

"Leave him be, wife, the boots are worn. They've served me all the way to Spain and back. I don't suppose Edward sent leather for new boots?"

"No, William, but—"

"Ah, there's my excuse. I must bide at home while I'm fitted for new boots. That will delay me halfway to Twelfth Night, I reckon." His bouts of dizziness and nausea had increased in frequency and duration of late, and he'd spent too much of his strength toward the end of his last campaign hiding these disabling spells. He yearned for some quiet in which he might rest, settle his affairs, and make his peace with God. But the king commanded his presence, and Catherine had no intention of disappointing Edward, that was clear. He sighed. "Faith, wife, I know I must not dawdle here. Edward expects me five days hence." And Margaret expected him along the way. "But a tournament so soon after Christmas?" He sighed again.

"Prince Edward has told Joan that his father will announce a grand brotherhood of the Round Table at the tournament, and we're all to wear red velvet trimmed with miniver." For a moment, Catherine glowed with anticipation, reminding William how lovely she could be. "That girl—she's transferred her affections for Holland to the prince. Poor Will. No wonder he's sleeping with maidservants. It's time Will and Joan bedded, William."

So she knew of the Holland affair, yet had said not a word

about it to him. That did not bode well. "In faith, wife, one worry at a time. Brotherhood of the Round Table, eh? Hmm . . . Where is Joan? I would speak to her."

"You ask after her before seeing your own children? Is it because you agree, or do you prefer—"

"Everything is a battle for you, Catherine. I am doing your bidding. Talking to her about being a wife to my son. I wish to save my reunion with my children until I might relax and attend them with an unfettered heart."

By the time Joan appeared in the doorway to William's chamber he'd fallen asleep in his chair, spilling wine on his jacket. His servant woke him.

"Lady Joan, my lord."

"Forgive me for the delay, my lord," said Joan. "I was out in the fields—"

Confused, he stared for a moment at the elegant young woman in the doorway. Which daughter?

"My lord, did you not send for me?"

He remembered now. "I did." Sitting up straighter, he felt the dampness through his jacket. Pathetic old man. "There is no need to hover in the doorway." He gestured for her to take the seat his servant had placed across from him. "I'm in no state to attack you."

Joan perched on the edge of the stool, her clothes giving off the pleasing scent of roses, as if in her deep rose silk and green velvet gown she *were* a rose. This blossom had thorns; he had no doubt of that.

He picked up the letter he'd left on the little table beside him, opening it so that she might see the general shape of the contents, that it was a missive to Holland. By the lift of her chin in defiance, he saw that she recognized her own childish script.

"Your hand is not as legible as your mother's. 'My must be-

trothed brigand'? Ah, 'most beloved husband.' 'I live for the—'
I cannot make it out." He held the letter out for Joan to decipher.

"'I live for the day we prove the falseness of my marriage
to Will and are free to live together as husband and wife.' It is
simple enough. But of course you are familiar with my mother's
script, and she has had years of writing to you in which to perfect her form." Her blue eyes seemed violet. Was it the dress?
Or her pique?

"Is that what comes between you and my son, your resentment at my love for your mother?"

Her full lips curled in the ghost of a smile. "Perhaps a little,
but as you read, you know that I consider myself already married to Thomas in the eyes of God. And I love him. Even had
Will behaved honorably, I could not consider him my husband
and would not willingly go to him."

William had hoped that by delaying the consummation of
their marriage the young couple would have found a compromise by the time they set up a household. But clearly that would
not happen. "Honorably. Yes, I know about his bedding your
maid. Yet you encourage the prince in *his* affections. What is
Will to make of that?"

"Have you ever tried to control the prince?"

"Perhaps a clear no would suffice."

"My lord, was that all?" Joan asked.

Her boldness angered him. "You will be a wife to my son,
Joan. After the Round Table tourney, the two of you will retire
to Mold." She sat quite still, unsmiling. "Your nurse Efa will
come in handy in Wales. You may go." His head was pounding. "Leave me," he growled as she sat there staring at him with
those cold blue eyes. Ice, they were.

Woodstock
DECEMBER 1343

MARGARET ARRANGED TO MEET WITH WILLIAM IN A COTTAGE ON his way to Woodstock, the inhabitants grateful to be paid for a few hours' absence. They'd not been together since Joan's betrothal, in the workman's cottage at Bisham. Margaret had not been certain he would come. He entered the cottage warily, peering into the shadows. Heaven knew what he thought to find. She waited. His greeting would tell her how it would go. With a nod of satisfaction, he shrugged off his fur-lined cloak, letting it slip to the rushes, and approached, reaching out for her hands. She saw the lines that the pain had etched around his eyes, above his brows, around his mouth. Efa had guessed he must be in constant pain. She said she had warned him that if he did not take his ease he would not have long to live. He'd re-fused her ministrations after that. Willful ignorance. Margaret would not have thought that of him. He took her hands now, kissed them, then kissed each cheek. "Maggie, it is good to see you." This was not the greeting of a lover.

So it was over. "And you, William." As he let go of her hands she stroked his brow, kissed his cheek. "Come, sit and have some brandywine."

"You are angry about my son and your daughter's maid-servant." He settled on the camp stool she'd brought for him, rubbing his temples, opening and closing his jaw as if clearing his ears.

As she poured, she chose her words, telling him of Thomas's visit, what he'd told her of Blanche's interference. She spoke of Joan's unhappiness, and Will's. William did not interrupt her, sipping the brandywine, occasionally grunting. When she paused, he held out his cup for more brandywine.

"Trust me, Maggie, the solution is simple. After the January tourney, they will establish a household together at Mold.

Once they consummate their marriage, neither of them will have cause to stray."

"I know you are not so blind as to believe that. William, let us go to the king—"

"No!" He grabbed the filled cup from her, the brandywine spilling down his arm and splashing on her gown. He paid it no heed. "Edward will destroy your daughter, perhaps even withhold your son's inheritance if we petition for an annulment, and I dare not guess what he would do to my son. He's never liked him. Holland would suffer as well. Edward has summoned him and his brother Otho to the great tournament next month. They are to be knights of the Round Table, Margaret, a great honor. But not if you remind the king of Holland's transgression."

She had lost, as she'd known she would when he did not take her in his arms. He had what he wanted from her—Joan's marriage to his son, the addition of royal blood to his line. "We've made a mess of it, William."

"Joan and Thomas are the ones to blame, not us."

"They acted in good conscience. Followed the forms. It is we who have erred, we who have transgressed."

William drank down his brandywine and rose. "It grows late."

She stood, reaching up to kiss him on his sunken cheek. "God go with you and keep you safe, William."

He patted her back.

She turned away so that she would not witness him striding through the door without a backward glance. Blessed Mother, she had always thought he was the one desperate for her love, she the one who used him. Not so. Her heart was breaking as she heard him ride away. She'd been used and discarded, and she'd taken her daughter down with her. Yet she could not find it in her to wish him harm.

33

Windsor
JANUARY 1344, THE ROUND TABLE TOURNAMENT

Joan stood atop a tower, gazing down on the stands and barriers for the jousting and the colorful tops of the pavilions so crowding the upper and lower wards of Windsor Castle that they now spilled out into the fields just outside the walls. Tournaments had punctuated her life, welcoming the knights and barons home from the field. But this was on such a scale as to be overwhelming. She was grateful to be above the din and jostling of the crowd, the smoke of the fires. But her companion, Lady Lucienne, grew restless, complaining that the sharpening breeze cut through the thick wool and fine fur of her cloak. She laid a gloved hand on Joan's. It was a gorgeous glove of the softest leather, stitched in contrasting colors, adorned with beads of silver and gold, so that her gestures caught the eye. She leaned close, her perfume of roses and spice mingling with the freshening air, and suggested that they descend, she had someone she wished Joan to meet. Joan would as lief stay up above the throng, but she knew that Lucienne was not as robust as in the past. She'd had to pause frequently on the climb, her breathing labored. And so they descended, Lucienne hurrying Joan along, drawing her through the crowd to the lower yard and into a building that housed clerics and some of the king's household officers. Joan regretted her unquestioning trust. Lucienne was still the queen's spy, and she feared a trap. She was certain of it when Lucienne pushed wide the door and Joan beheld her beloved quietly conversing with Efa. Joan backed down the corridor, shaking her head as Lucienne hurried back to her.

"Would Efa betray you?" Lucienne reached out a hand. "I pray you, accept this gift. We have plotted and schemed to bring you together."

"Why?"

"Not out here. We will be discovered!" Lucienne took Joan firmly by the arm and propelled her down the corridor and into the room.

As the door closed, Efa touched Thomas's arm. He turned. "Joan!"

And all her hesitance vanished. They rushed to each other.

"My beloved." Thomas gathered her close.

For a long while she did not move, breathing with him, calmed by his strong heartbeat. Then she leaned away, looking at him, drinking him in with her eyes.

"Am I very ugly?" he whispered.

She traced the scar that radiated out from his eye, beneath the silk patch. The skin was soft. Efa's gift. "No, my love. Never."

Joan felt her nurse's gentle pressure on her back, "You have two hours," Efa whispered. "Listen for the noon bell. I will return for you then." A rustle of silk, and the door closed behind the two women.

"We are alone," said Thomas.

"In a bedchamber." Joan giggled, as nervous as her first night with him.

He carried her to the bed, and there they lay for a while, side by side, wondering at the miracle of being together. Slowly they undressed each other, touching, kissing, making love the first time too quickly, then more slowly. Lying in Thomas's arms afterward, Joan remembered Catherine's threat—Mold, she and

Will setting up household—and she wept. Thomas kissed and held her, and though she had vowed not to tell him, she broke her promise to herself, her unhappiness spilling from her in a pitiful rush as the sext bell chimed.

When Efa knocked on the door, Thomas was telling Joan of Lucienne's offer.

"No. She is the queen's spy. We dare not be beholden to her."

"Then I must confront the earl," he said. "I cannot live like this."

Doubt assailed her when he was gone and Efa was putting the finishing touches on her dress.

"Am I wrong?" she asked her nurse, seeing that she looked troubled. "Should we accept his mistress's generous offer?"

"I cannot fully fathom Lucienne's heart, my lady. I believe she wants to do this for you—now. But how long she will sustain this selflessness I cannot guess, whether her yearning for him will gradually outweigh her wish for his happiness."

"We must wait." Joan kissed Efa. "Thank you for these hours with him."

FEASTS TOOK UP THE SUNDAY OF THE TOURNAMENT, PRESIDED OVER by the king and queen resplendent in ermine and red velvet. With them at the high table were their children, the dowager queen, Joan, Margaret and the other countesses, along with two French knights who had risked King Philip's displeasure to be present. At the other tables were the wives of barons, nobles, knights, and the citizens of London. The men feasted in pavilions out in the upper ward. After escorting his mother to the hall, Thomas paused in the doorway exchanging pleasantries with the guards as he watched how Prince Edward leaned close to Joan, his lips almost kissing her ear as he spoke, how he touched her hand, then cupped both his around it. Thomas forced himself to look away, out over the sea of gorgeously dressed women. As it had been in Ghent, it was difficult to distinguish the wives of the wealthy merchants from the noblewomen, their hair as skillfully arranged, their silks as bright, their jewels as brilliant as those of their betters. More brilliant, certainly, than his mother's. He turned away from the crowded hall.

It was not until the next day, the opening day of the tournament, that Thomas found Earl William without a coterie of barons surrounding him. He was in his pavilion, being prepared for the lists, his squire kneeling to buckle his greaves. Taking heart at the timing, when Montagu could easily send his men away for a few moments while the two had a quiet word, Thomas told him that he wished to discuss Joan. Montagu cleared the tent, inviting Thomas to have some wine, which he declined. Montagu shrugged and poured himself a goodly bowl, drinking it down, then refilling it before turning back. He leaned against a table, his armor preventing him from sitting. His face was flushed by the wine.

"I've intercepted and read enough of the letters that have passed between you and my son's wife to know how it lies with you." He nodded at Thomas's surprise. "That ends now, or I will tell the king of your treachery, your allegiance to the Count of Eu and his heir, what a danger you are to his claim to France, how inappropriate it is to have either you or any of your family in his service." He was shouting by now, the veins on his forehead and neck standing out. "Pursue this at your peril, Holland." He coughed, and suddenly dropped his bowl as he lurched forward, his eyes glazed.

"You are ill, my lord."

Thomas reached out to assist Montagu, but the earl weakly repulsed his hand and with a curse ordered him out.

"Father?" Will hesitated in the doorway, looking from his father to Thomas. "What have you done to him?"

"God's blood, boy, nothing. Your father is ill."

Color blotched the young man's round face. He lunged at
Thomas, a fist coming for his jaw. Thomas blocked the punch.

"Reason with your father. Keep him from the field. He's too
weak for the lists."

"Get out! Have you not shamed us enough?"

"Shamed you? You might have asked your wife if she was
free to wed before exchanging vows. Pah." Thomas strode from
the tent as Will softly tried to reason with his father. The elder
Montagu roared for him to go snuggle with his page.

Hiding from her mother-in-law's sharp tongue, Joan was
sitting in the Earl of Derby's pavilion with her brother, John,
the earl's squire, quietly discussing Lucienne's purportedly selfless act. John professed himself no more a believer in Lucienne's
selflessness than was Joan. He was expounding on a crazy theory that Lucienne meant to distract the queen from her own
pursuit of Ned—the prince had bedded one of Bella's maids,
why not a more experienced woman?—when the prince came
strolling into the pavilion.

"Lucienne after me? Is that what you imagine?" He punched
John in the shoulder and grasped Joan's arm. "I'm more interested in the favor Lucienne did for your friend Holland." He
pulled her out of her seat. "Coupling in a cleric's bed. God's
blood, he must have wet himself that night."

John threw his hat on the floor and rose, poking a finger
in Ned's face. "Leave my sister alone. You're always making
trouble for her."

Ned made as if to bite John's finger, then laughed when he
backed away. "Go watch the tourney, John. See how it's done."

John lunged, "You—"

Shaken by Ned's knowledge—who had spied on them?—
and disgusted by his behavior, Joan stepped between them.

"Stop this, both of you!" She was about to say more when a crowd buzzing round four men carrying a knight laid out on his long shield strode past, most in the livery of the Earl of Salisbury. Rushing outside, she caught the arm of a page hurrying after them. "What has happened? Is it Earl William?"

"My lord earl fell and did not rise. And when he finally opened his eyes he did not know his own lady wife."

"What is his injury?"

"They've found naught. But the queen's physicians will now examine him. He breathes, he is awake, but he could not stand on his own. I must go, my lady."

She shook her head at Ned as she watched the boy dodge through the crowd, catching up with the group as it disappeared behind a large pavilion. "Not now. I must see what's happened." In the distance, the crowd cheered. A knight greeted her and the prince as he passed, his squire rushing after him with his gauntlets. The tourney went on, of course. A fallen jouster was nothing unusual.

Her fate was tied to the earl, whether or not she wished such a connection, and she made her way through the crowd to see for herself his condition. Grim faces acknowledged her. Will, stiff with shock and expressionless, stepped aside to let her see his father, covered in furs, only his head and neck exposed. Countess Catherine was stretched out on the cot beside her husband, as a mother would to warm and comfort her child.

"He did not know me when I first ran to him," Will whispered. "It is Holland's doing. They argued about you. But your knight will be disappointed. Just now Father recognized Mother. He will recover."

Joan noticed Efa off to one side and joined her. "Will he?"

"Briefly, perhaps. But the damage is done. What is this about Thomas?"

Joan shook her head. "I know nothing."

Outside, a trumpet sounded, and as all heads turned toward

the doorway King Edward appeared, a magnificent presence in full armor. The occupants of the pavilion parted to either side, bowing as the king strode through, doffing his helmet.

Catherine sat up, her eyes red from weeping, her veil hanging to one side, her hair in disarray. "Your Grace." She fought against the layers of silk twisted round her, trying to rise from her husband's pallet.

"My lady Salisbury, there is no need to leave your husband's side," Edward said.

But her feet had found the floor and she stood, one side of her skirt hitched up in a tangle, a stocking drooping as a garter came undone and fell to the floor. "Your Grace." She bowed.

The naked tenderness on the king's face as he reached out to help Catherine rise sent a shock through Joan. He felt for her as she did for Thomas. Such a love. She had never guessed. The king bent as if to pick up the garter, but his armor prevented it. A servant knelt to retrieve it, handing it to the king.

"My lady." Edward held the garter out to Catherine, but she had already turned to crawl back onto the pallet, cradling her husband's head in her lap.

A flash of gold in the doorway caught Joan's eye. It was the queen, who had arrived just in time to see her husband kiss the garter and tuck it into his breastplate.

"So much pain," Efa whispered.

BY THE NEXT DAY THE EARL SEEMED HIMSELF AGAIN, THOUGH HE had withdrawn from the jousting. Countess Catherine sat beside him in the stands, her eyes softer, less judging, holding his hand, stroking his cheek. Joan sat behind and to one side of them with her mother, who struggled to ignore the couple.

Joan had found her mother kneeling beside the bed, praying in the middle of the night.

"Efa says he does not have long. He has been my strength."

Joan had knelt down beside Margaret, kissing her cheek, rubbing her hands to warm them. "You are the strong one, Mother. You are the one with the great heart."

"They say he argued with your Thomas."

"So they say. I know nothing of it."

Thomas jousted well that day, besting three opponents out of four, his blind side tripping him up at the last. Joan yearned to wave to him from the stands, but there were too many eyes on her, too many eyes.

ON THE LAST MORNING OF THE TOURNAMENT, THE GUESTS CROWDED into the chapel in the lower ward for a solemn Mass, at the end of which Montagu and Grosmont, the earls of Salisbury and Derby, led the knights and barons behind the king in a procession of chivalry, all in regal red velvet and miniver, at the end of which King Edward swore an oath to establish the Round Table. Work was to begin at once on a great circular building in the upper ward of Windsor Castle that would hold all the members when they gathered at Whitsun. The earls of Derby, Salisbury, Warwick, Arundel, Pembroke, and Suffolk, the barons and knights present—all vowed to observe, sustain and promote the endeavor. Joan was relieved to see Thomas and his brother in the procession. So far no harm had been done by the rumor that Thomas had argued with Montagu right before his fall.

Afterward, the squires were to joust, Ned challenging all comers. He'd asked for Joan's colors and she'd given him a piece of rose-hued silk that matched the bodice of the dress she wore beneath her fur-lined cloak. She'd thought to give it to Will, as a peace offering, knowing how his father's fragile health worried him, but he had not approached her.

Ned had slipped his hand beneath her chin and turned her for a kiss on the mouth, lingering, practiced. "Am I improving?"

She stepped back. "Don't make a spectacle, Ned. Your parents will blame me."

"And Thomas Holland? Will he blame you as well? Poor, deluded man, crowded out by young Will and the prince of the realm." He kissed her hand. "Sit close to the front so I can see you from the field."

Shivering, she did so. Bella tsked and shared her warm lap rug with Joan. Ned was triumphant, and, with every win, he kissed the air and bowed to her. She felt the queen's eyes on her and cursed Ned. But she feared angering him in such a mood. She had never felt so trapped.

34

Within a few days of the festivities, the earl fell once again into confusion. Countess Catherine expressed her wish to take him home to Bisham, where he might feel safe. Queen Philippa was puzzled by that. Here, at Windsor, he had the benefit of the royal physicians. But Catherine spoke of signs and portents, a menacing shadow that had stalked William throughout the tournament, a darksome dream the night before his fall, whispers all round her as he'd ridden out onto the field, a shaft of light in the shape of a sword. Philippa had seen this panic in Catherine before, after the birth of each child. Taking her hand, she assured Catherine that William would be guarded day and night.

"Calm yourself, Catherine. He should not travel in such a perilous state. We will do all in our power to save William."

How kind Philippa was to her rival for Edward's love. Joan glanced at Lucienne, her own rival, and found the violet eyes trained on her. Seeing that Joan had caught her, Lucienne glanced at Catherine and made a face, as if to say, *She's quite mad, isn't she?* Confused, Joan looked away. Why was Lucienne pretending to be her friend?

❖ ❖ ❖

LESS THAN A FORTNIGHT AFTER HIS COLLAPSE IN THE LISTS, EARL William was dead. A solemn Mass was offered for him at St. Paul's Cathedral in London, with all the royal family attending. Joan had asked permission to stand with her mother at the service, but Catherine had insisted that she accompany Will. She felt out of place, aching more for her mother than for the earl. She imagined her mother back in the crowd, mute with grief, stoically determined to maintain her dignity. Surely God had not meant this. Surely he had intended that a man and a woman should come together in love, not duty, and from their love beget new life.

At the end of the ceremony, King Edward stepped forward, draped in black velvet, and nodded to his herald, who let it be known that the first meeting of the Round Table would be postponed, Pentecost being too soon for such celebration after the death of the king's dear friend.

As the assembly departed, Countess Catherine knelt before William's brother Simon, Bishop of Ely, and took a vow of celibacy.

"Are you certain, Catherine?" he asked.

"God has guided me in this," she whispered.

"Why is she doing this?" Will muttered.

Repentance for loving the king more than her husband, Joan guessed, but kept her own counsel.

JOAN WAS SUMMONED TO THE KING'S HALL. HER HANDS WENT COLD when she saw Countess Catherine seated near him like an angel of death in her black mourning, her eyes huge in her bloodless face. Edward greeted Joan coolly, gesturing for her to sit. She did, though her instincts told her to run, especially when he re-

mained standing at the back of his chair. Surely he'd not blame
her for Catherine's vow.

"I've heard disturbing rumors about you and Thomas Holland, cousin—that you still claim him as your husband."

"Your Grace, I am lawfully wed to Thomas."

She watched not the king but Catherine, seeing her hands
clench, her lips move. Cursing her? Thomas?

"You are the wife of Will Montagu, who will in time be
granted the earldom of Salisbury, as his father wished. And you
shall be his countess, *as his father wished*," Edward proclaimed.

*While Will gets bastards on my maidservants and pines for all
the pretty grooms in the stables*, Joan thought. *And longs for Ned's
approval, Ned's love.* But, looking at the king, she said only, "I
am not his wife."

"He is unmanned by your love for another. It is your duty
to comfort him, to reassure him." There was no mistaking the
rising anger in the king's tone, and his eyes warned of danger.
"I value Holland's service. Do not make me strip him of his
knighthood and send him into exile. Stop this nonsense and
be a wife to your husband." Edward slammed his fist down on
the back of the chair, making it rock. "I've appointed Sir John
Wingfield as Will's guardian and granted the lad some of his
father's estates in Somerset and Wales."

Mold, Joan thought, looking at Catherine, who kept her
gaze on her gloved hands.

"You and your husband will from this day forward live as
husband and wife. Am I clear?"

Joan bowed her head. "Yes, Your Grace. I pray that I—in
faith, *we* do not pay too dearly for breaking a solemn vow. A
curse on our families . . ." She whispered the last, watching
Catherine twitch. Curses. That reached her in her madness.

Edward rested one of his large, long-fingered hands on
Catherine's shoulder as he gently assured her that the arch-

bishop of Canterbury and several bishops, including Will's
uncle, had blessed the marriage. "Not one of them warned of
God's ire," he said.

Catherine shrugged off his hand. "Yet William is dead,
Your Grace."

"Go now," Edward commanded Joan. "Comfort your husband in his grief, and speak no more of divine retribution."

Joan bowed and withdrew. Out in upper ward, she stood in
the shadow of the great stone walls moist and dark with the icy,
relentless drizzle, watching two dogs sniffing at the debris left
behind by the departed guests.

"What did Edward say?"

Joan started as her mother slipped a cloak around her shoulders. She described the meeting.

"Ah. So Catherine and William were united in this. No
wonder he was so cool when I tried to convince him that the
marriage had been a horrible mistake that we might remedy
with an annulment, that it was not too late to make things right."

Joan peered at her mother, disbelieving. "What changed
your mind?" For the first time she heard from her mother
of Thomas's visit to her, and her remorse. "Did you know of
Blanche's part?"

"I suspected it. I will never forgive her. Still, I had hope. But
the king—" Margaret shook her head. "If my heart can change,
so, too, might the king's. At least I can pray it is possible." She
hugged Joan. "I must not keep you. Thomas and his brothers
are at the stables, preparing to depart. Go to him." Margaret
kissed Joan's cheek. "Hurry."

If her mother's heart could change . . . Joan grasped at the
slender hope and hurried across the inner ward. As she neared
the stables, she felt her neck prickle and glanced back, thinking
her mother still watched. But she had disappeared. Looking up,
Joan saw a lone figure in the middle of the battlements, a man.
Something about the intensity of his gaze spurred her to run,

causing the scavenging dogs to take up the chase, barking excitedly.

She found Thomas with his brothers and stood for a while,
unnoticed, as they sorted out their packs. She watched him
laughing with them, giving instructions to Hugh and a groom,
moving round his horse, examining any blemish. Though they
were bound together, she knew little of his daily life. There was
so much she yearned to know—if his eye pained him, what he
enjoyed most in a tourney, what weapon he favored in battle,
what he'd seen in Prussia. But there was no time now.

Alan noticed her standing there and bowed. "My lady!"

Thomas drew her in, kissing her forehead.

"We'll leave you two," said one of the brothers. "You've
not much time. We want to be well away from Windsor before
sunset."

The grooms and squires withdrew as well.

Joan caught Thomas's hand, kissing it and pressing it to her
cheek. "Mother told me where I might find you." She nodded
at his surprise. "You changed her heart, Thomas. Not that it
does us much good. It's too late." She told him of her meeting
with the king. "So I shall leave on the morrow for Bisham, and
I don't know when I'll see you again."

"Bisham." Thomas pulled her to him as he cursed under his
breath. "What if you conceive?"

"I will not."

"But—"

"Efa will see to that. I will not conceive, not his heir or anyone's, unless it be ours, yours and mine."

"I pray you never regret it."

"I must believe that we will be together. I will be waiting.
No matter what you might hear to the contrary, I love no one
but you." She touched his scarred temple. "Did Efa replenish
your ointment?"

"She did." He cursed again as he heard his brothers return.

"So. I am off to find a hefty ransom to free you, my love. May God see his way to helping us, and may he watch over you."

A long kiss, and then she rushed away, calling to his brothers to watch over him.

Through the mist she ran, laughing as the dogs pursued her, picking up a stick to throw for them. Her heart was momentarily light. She had hope. In through the great hall she ran, a guard shooing the dogs away as they tried to follow. Bella caught her as she was twirling in her cloak.

"You are soaked! Were you up on the battlements with Ned?"

The solitary figure she'd seen earlier? Had Ned watched her go into the stables, and Alan and Otho step outside? Her happy run with the dogs? "Is he still up there?"

"Didn't you just leave him?"

She yearned to strip off her wet clothes and curl up beneath a mound of blankets, but that must wait. Out she went again, out away from the building so that she could look up at the battlements. Whoever it was still stood there. She waved. No response. The dogs jumped up, thinking she had something in her hand. If it was Ned, his lack of response did not bode well. She ran to the tower stairs, the dogs happily following, but they fell back when she started to climb. Round, round, round she climbed, higher and higher, composing her lie as she went, until, as she reached the top, breathing hard, she walked out onto the battlements with her speech on her lips. But she found herself alone.

Looking out, she saw someone exiting the next tower, crossing the yard toward the stables. "Ned!" she shouted, waving. He walked on, never turning.

35

Bisham
FEBRUARY 1344

Seated on the dais in the great hall at a solemn feast following the earl's burial a fortnight after his death, Countess Catherine announced that she was withdrawing into silence and fasting for several months to pray for her husband's soul. Joan was to run the household during this time, and Will was to acquaint himself with the stewards of their various estates. "And, as my husband wished, they will now live as husband and wife."

At first, no one moved, the noble guests, the family and their retainers uncertain of the proper response. How uncomfortable Catherine made them, draped in black brocade, her dark hair caught up in a dark silver crispinette, onyx beads her only jewels, the pallor of her face and hands funereal. Seeing none of the earl's family making a move to save the moment, Joan rose and thanked the guests for gathering around the family in their grief and honoring Earl William. She mentioned a few of his triumphs, including the capture of Mortimer, which won a quiet cheer here and there in the hall, and then welcomed others to pay tribute to the earl.

As Joan resumed her seat, Sir Edward Montagu rose to say a few fond words about his brother, then several of his retainers, the Earl of Derby, and last, Ned, who was here with Bella representing their parents.

The room hushed as Ned rose, regal in dark velvet patterned with gold fleur-de-lis. Joan had caught Bella grasping her brother's arm as he shifted on his chair next to Countess Catherine, shaking her head with a look of concern. Joan held her breath, waiting for the nastiness she was sure Ned was about to unleash. He acknowledged his father's long friendship with the earl, briefly sketching Montagu's rise to the earldom and beyond, and his courageous behavior when captured by the French. Then, smiling down at Countess Catherine, he assured her that his family would pray for her in her grief, mentioning with a smirk her long friendship with his mother and "your love for my father, and his for you."

God in heaven. Joan saw how the guests shifted in their seats, exchanging uneasy glances. When Catherine rose with an agonized moan, Joan quietly suggested that Bess and Sybil escort their mother out of the hall, and told Will to stand up to thank the prince and the princess and end it all with a toast.

As Catherine was led from the hall, Ned pretended not to notice, launching into a description of his father's plan for a Round Table. Will lurched to his feet and interrupted Ned, thanking him and Bella for their presence. He then raised high his jeweled mazer, tossed back the contents, and called to a servant to refill it, then belched for all to hear. The guests lifted their vessels and drank, the volume quickly rising as they clattered for more.

"The belch was a *noble* addition," Joan said to Will with a roll of her eyes. Though it had relieved the tension, and he had done as she asked, she was too worried about their living arrangements to be encouraging. Upon their arrival the previous afternoon, the servants had put Joan's belongings in Catherine's bedchamber, a spacious room with a large bed curtained in a red brocade and hung with tapestries portraying stories from the Bible. Will's things were put in his late father's chamber, right next to it. The adjoining door had remained shut through the night. But tonight? Will's laugh was too loud, his face too red, the whites of his eyes too visible, like a terrified horse. Unpredictable.

Ned laughed when she reproached him for goading the countess, saying he could not resist exposing the lie of her simpering piety, and expressing disappointment that Joan had been too busy organizing the Montagu children to hear his account of the earl's bargaining for a grandchild with royal blood, Plantagenet blood. God help her, she hated him then. She called for a servant to light him to his room and disappeared into the kitchen to give instructions for the guests to be seen to in the morning as they made their departure.

Back in the hall, Joan found the Montagu sisters huddled together by the fire, talking softly so as not to disturb the guests spread out on pallets all around them. Bess thanked her for taking charge during the feast. "Mother has retired to the cottage in which she means to keep her retreat. Your Efa gave her a strong sleeping potion to ease her through the night. Thank you." How strange it felt to have Will's sisters deferring to her as the lady of the house. But they seemed relieved.

Joan stayed up late playing chess with Efa, though she was bleary-eyed from the long day and had trouble thinking through the moves.

"My lady, you need sleep."

"What if Will comes through that door tonight? Could you put something in the wine?"

"There is no need, my lady. He is already cursed. He reeks of it."

"Someone has put a curse on him?"

"That, or he imagines it. Either way, it has hold of him." Efa rose. "I shall take my leave now, but I shall be right outside." Joan's women were sleeping in a small anteroom, as if she and Will were sharing the bed, hoping to fool the household.

As soon as Efa closed the door behind her, Joan slipped beneath the bedclothes, exhausted. She was drowsing when she heard the inner door unlatch. Sitting up sharply, lifting the covers to her neck, she called out, "Who is there?"

Will stepped through, the brazier softly illuminating his bare legs sticking out below a loose linen shirt. He climbed onto the bed and peeled back the covers, pulling her down beside him. "You will do your duty to me, wife. I need an heir." His breath was mead-sweet, his hands sweaty, his lips cracked and dry, scratching her skin as he kissed her. "I have a right," he said when she did not respond.

"So take me," she challenged, hoping it was his pride speaking and not a newfound lust for her.

He tried. But his own body defeated him and he finally turned away from her, cursing the prince.

"Ned? What did he do?"

"He got me drunk after the funeral Mass."

"Is that all?"

"He is the devil, I swear it. But he won't have you. You are *my* wife." He buried his face in the pillows.

Poor, stupid boy. With her foot she poked him in the side. "You've all the time in the world."

"Mother will know," he mumbled into the pillow.

"How? I'll prick my finger and smear some blood on the bed. We'll behave as shy newlyweds in public and go our own ways behind our chamber doors."

Will rolled over. "He'll not have you. I won't give you up."

Which one? She did not ask. "Go now." She pushed him again with her foot. "I am rising with the servants to bid farewell to the guests. You should as well." She turned away from him as he sat up, sniffling, and finally padded off to his room.

She had hoped sleep would take her after he left, but her mind spun with riotous abandon through the earl's fall at the tournament, Catherine's madness, the funeral, the burial, Will's misery. At some point she fell asleep, only to wake hot, the bedclothes twisted round her. Rising to open a shutter, she turned around and gasped to see Ned sitting in a chair by the bed, the brazier softly illuminating his golden hair.

She scrambled back into bed, covering herself. "What are you doing in here?"

"Ensuring that he doesn't return once sobered." He leaned over to kiss her cheek. "How beautiful you are, cousin. When you are my queen, you'll bathe in goat's milk and sleep between silk sheets."

She ignored that last part, wondering if it was Ned who had cursed Will. "You'll be gone tomorrow. Who will guard me then?"

"He won't bother you. Tonight he meant only to show me he's won. Sleep well, my love." He touched her hair, then went back to sit.

She lay there pretending to sleep until he departed shortly before dawn, his visitation far more disturbing than Will's.

In the morning, Helena discovered the blood on the bed-clothes. "Shall we save these for the dowager countess, my lady?"

"Yes, of course."

Efa shook her head. "How could that be? I was so sure."

"I pricked myself," Joan said for her ears only.

Despite knowing she should be present as the guests departed, Joan took her time dressing, waiting until Helena noticed the prince and princess riding out of the yard.

Will, too, had missed them, arriving in the hall so close upon Joan's heels that she suspected he'd listened for her. He made conversation with the guests still breaking their fast while Joan bustled about seeing that all had what they needed for their journey home.

Word spread through the servants within days, gossipers

all of them, that the young earl and his countess were at last happily bedded, supported by rumors that Will had banished his favorite groom from his bed. But Ned had been right. Will did not return to her chamber. Relieved, she threw herself into the task of managing the household. Though now and then she wondered how long the curse would hold.

"As long as he believes in it," Efa ventured.

36

Westminster
AUGUST 1345

Margaret was proud of the grace with which Joan had taken up her responsibilities as Countess of Salisbury, knowing that her daughter believed her place was with Thomas. All at court spoke of her with fond admiration. She was so like her father, so fair of face and form, with a captivating charm, all eyes turning to her as she entered a room.

It pained Margaret to deliver the terrible news she came to bear, but better that Joan hear it from her. In July, the king had sailed to Sluys to determine the truth of reports that the Flemish cities were in turmoil and therefore in no position to support his war. He hoped also to win back the support of Philippa's brother William, Count of Hainault, who'd shifted his allegiance to the French king. He learned that the crisis in the cities was largely due to Jacob Van Artevelde's increasing unpopularity. His power had gone to his head, and the Flemish merchants accused him of setting his henchmen against them. Yet, because of his relationship with King Edward, Van Artevelde was chosen to represent the Flemish towns at the meeting on board the king's ship anchored off Sluys.

Joan expressed no surprise. Margaret shook her head and motioned for Helena to refill her mazer. "There is more."

After the meeting, Jacob departed for Ghent with obvious reluctance. For good cause. Shortly after he returned to his house, it was surrounded by a hostile mob led by the councilmen who opposed him, all shouting, "Come out and tell us what the English king said!" When he called out that he would report to them on the morrow, the mob said they would break down his doors and kill him.

Joan had listened quietly, hands to mouth as the end became clear to her. "He sacrificed himself for his wife and children?"

"No. It seems Jacob was not quite so ready to suffer martyrdom," said Margaret. "He fled out the stable block, hoping to reach sanctuary in a nearby Franciscan priory. But he was caught and beaten to death by the mob."

Helena gasped.

"May God grant him peace." Joan crossed herself. "No matter their motivation for befriending me, the Van Arteveldes welcomed me into their home and gave me sanctuary."

"I know," Margaret whispered.

"And now Thomas and I have lost the key witness to our betrothal. God has abandoned us."

"Perhaps not. The king has rescued the Van Artevelde family. They should arrive in London within days." Margaret turned to Helena, who had gone quite pale. "What do you think? Will your kinswoman still support your lady?"

"I believe she would, my lady."

"I pray you are right."

London
SEPTEMBER 1345

THOMAS HAD LEARNED TO EXPECT A VISIT FROM LUCIENNE SHORTLY after arriving in London, though how she knew so precisely when he would appear mystified him. He seldom knew until he boarded what vessel would carry him across the Channel from Brittany, and where he would land. She came to talk, to tell him all the court gossip, to relax with an old, trusted friend. But this day she was agitated.

"Is it Joan? Has something happened?"

"Not to her. But something that might affect your cause. Sit and I will tell you."

He listened to her description of Jacob's end. "The Flemish tyrant butchered. God have mercy, I have half a mind to cheer the bloody rabble."

"He was your main witness."

"But Dame Katarina is here, you said. In London? Do you know where?"

Lucienne said yes to all. "And Countess Margaret wishes us to speak with her. She would prefer to do it herself, mother to mother, but as it might jeopardize her son's proposed betrothal to Elizabeth of Juliers—"

Quite a match, thought Thomas. *The queen's niece for Joan's brother, John.* "You will do this?"

"Yes."

He kissed her cheek. "I should have loved you more."

"I should soon be bored with you."

He smiled, though he knew her too well to miss the false note in her voice, the lack of laughter in her eyes. "I trust you already have a plan."

"Of course!" Secrecy was important—Katarina must not offend the king, her benefactor. Henry Vanner, a vintner who lived a street away from where Katarina Van Artevelde and her children had taken lodgings among their fellow Flemish merchants, agreed to host the meeting as partial payment of a debt he owed Lucienne. Thomas and Lucienne were to appear at his home late the following Sunday afternoon when Katarina was dining with the Vanners, who would put on a show of being uneasy about their appearance.

❖ ❖ ❖

A SERVANT WELCOMED THEM, RECOGNIZING LUCIENNE, TAKING their cloaks and showing them to the group seated round the fire, only to be met with a stern rebuke by his master. Katarina Van Artevelde, elegant in her mourning, assured him that Lady Lucienne was a welcome acquaintance. "But I do not know this gentleman." She had not seen him since his wounding.

"Sir Thomas Holland," he said, bowing to her.

"Sir Thomas!"

Vanner's wife turned with feigned concern toward Dame Katarina, who had half risen, then sunk back down, her hands to her heart, her face ashen. "Are you unwell, my dear? Should I send them away?"

"I must not see you, Sir Thomas. His Grace, he has been so kind, but if he knew . . . My children—"

Lucienne sat down beside the flustered woman, taking her hands. "No one will know of this visit, I promise you."

Katarina looked at Thomas. "Do you come to gloat, Sir Thomas?"

"I hoped you thought better of me than that. I pray for you and your children, and for your husband's soul. No matter your purpose, you provided sanctuary for my lady, and comfort. Faith, I came here today to ask one more favor of you."

Henry Vanner cleared his throat. "My wife and I will leave you for a little while so that you might talk." Their hosts withdrew.

Lucienne still held one of Katarina's hands, stroking it. Thomas settled across from them, awaiting a sign that Katarina would hear him out. Her arresting eyes bore the signs of much weeping—a puffiness, a redness poorly masked. Listening to the wind without, the whispering behind the closed door, he waited for her to break the silence.

In a little while she slipped her hands from Lucienne's and

reached out to touch Thomas's scar. "Did this happen in combat?"

"Yes."

"He saved the life of Raoul de Brienne, the son of the Constable of France," Lucienne said with pride.

"A noble deed. It must have caused you much pain."

"That pain was nothing compared with learning that my wife was wed to another in my absence. But that did not surprise you, did it?" He tried to keep his tone flat, unemotional.

Katarina bowed her head. He'd not expected an apology.

"Your husband's death has left us with only you as witness to our betrothal. Will you still stand behind us when we bring our case to the pope?"

"I must think of my children." She lifted a scented cloth to her eyes.

Thomas nodded. "I encourage you to do so. You must not deprive them of the king's protection. If he were to hear the complete story of your interference in his plans for Lady Joan—" he stopped. This is not how he'd meant to proceed.

The feather on Katarina's black velvet hat quivered as she met his gaze. Now she looked like the Katarina he remembered, challenging him with the ghost of a smile in her eyes. "How cruel you are, Sir Thomas. And ungrateful. Did we not bring the two of you together?"

"For your own ends. Shall I go to the king?"

"There is no need. My late husband and I signed a letter attesting to your betrothal, the night spent with Lady Joan, the bloodied sheet, and I have it with me. I'll keep it safe until you have need of it."

"You will give it to a messenger I will send to your home, Dame Katarina. Tomorrow."

"You do not trust me?"

"I trust no one, with good cause. You will also be available to my lawyer and to any representatives of the pope when the time comes. If His Grace should move you to a different location, you will get word to Lady Lucienne at once."

Katarina began to play with a button near her waist.

"My lawyer will take every care to be discreet."

"Thomas is an honorable man," Lucienne assured her.

Thomas rose and thanked Katarina for her time. "I am sorry to come to you in this way while you are in mourning, Dame Katarina. My lady and I will not forget your help."

"And if the pope decides in young Montagu's favor, will you blame me for that?"

"As long as you do all that we ask of you, we will let you live in peace."

"Peace." She looked at him as if he'd lost his mind. "You did not see what they did to Jacob, his body so pounded and slashed our servants needed shovels to retrieve his remains. Someone had tried to saw off his head, but gave up and smashed it in, again and again. My children thought their father beloved by the people. Now they know how easily such love turns to hate. I've lost my husband, my status, my country, and you speak of peace."

Thomas's father had also met a violent end at the hands of those who had once been his comrades. He was no stranger to such suffering. "Forgive my intrusion on your mourning. Admit my lawyer tomorrow, that is all I ask for now."

"Will she help us?" he asked Lucienne when they were out in the street.

"I will see that she does." She slipped her arm through his, kissing his cheek.

He asked if she might arrange for him to see Joan.

"I do not think it wise. But I shall tell her all that was said." She kissed him again and crossed the road to her town house.

Thomas continued on to his lawyer's home, a sour taste in his mouth for intruding on a widow in mourning. But he could not afford to leave Katarina in peace.

/   ❖ ❖ ❖

SITTING BENEATH THE OLD LIME AT THE EDGE OF THE GARDEN, JOAN was sorting rose hips with her mother and Efa, their voices only slightly louder than the drone of the bees collecting the late-summer pollen and frequently drowned out by the calls of the bargemen on the Thames. Half the city seemed to be out on the water that afternoon, basking in the warmth. They spoke of Lucienne's visit the previous day, her account of the meeting with Katarina Van Artevelde, picking apart the particulars, turning them over and over to see what they might hide. Joan found it hard to take much comfort. A letter such as Thomas now held was useless without the means to petition the pope.

"Oh, my dear," Margaret said as she glanced up toward the house. "Your cousins approach."

Bella and Ned were advancing down the path, followed by servants carrying baskets.

"We brought refreshments!" Bella announced, flouncing down on the bench beside Joan. "Why have you been avoiding us, cousin?" she whispered. "We hardly see you anymore."

"My responsibilities as lady of the manor keep me away, dear cousin," Joan said, adopting Countess Catherine's haughty voice.

Bella had begun to ask about the countess when Ned interrupted, sitting cross-legged at Joan's feet and reaching for her hand.

"You don't want to touch me, I'm sticky with rose hip juice." She held her palms out to prove it.

It was the first time Joan had seen Ned since he accompanied his father to Sluys. For the next hour, he entertained them with stories of his adventure. His descriptions of the dissembling and self-important Low Country officials were amusing, his boasts of his part in the proceedings unbelievable. But none of them challenged him, not even his sister. Joan waited, knowing that he was likely saving for last his real reason for this visit.

"Since then I've had the pleasure of meeting Jacob Van Artevelde's family. What a strange pair they were—he a river rat, she a swan. And their daughters—such magpies!"

"Dame Katarina would agree," Joan said as her mind raced—what might the girls have told him? Would he betray Katarina to the king?

"Do you not wonder how culpable they were in their father's unpopularity, with their careless gossip?"

"Not at all. They loved him. They spoke openly only with those they trusted. How they must have thrilled to meet you. You have guaranteed their success in London society."

Joan spent the afternoon deflecting the bait and beating Ned at his own game. He did mention a sighting of Thomas and Lucienne together in London, and appeared disappointed in Joan's lack of reaction. It reassured her. He must be unaware of Lucienne's continued support. And Thomas's lawyer had Katarina's letter. Thank God for that.

37

Guildford Palace
MAY 1346

From atop the crumbling keep of Guildford Castle, Joan and Bella watched servants and squires struggling to fold the huge banners, standards, and pennons the women had sewn for the ships in the king's fleet. All must be packed by morning, when king and company departed for Portsmouth, where the invasion force was gathering. By midsummer they expected to be in France. A dozen servants held on to the huge streamer with the quartered arms of the king, blue garters, and the figure of St. Lawrence. The heavy worsted cloth had to be carefully folded to take up as little space as possible, for already the carts were laden with several hundred standards and pennons, smaller but still bulky and heavy.

Joan and Bella had not worked on these. Their fingers were pricked and sore from the needlework on the king's and Ned's gorgeous jupons, and the hangings for a grand bed for the king—for, no matter that they were on campaign, a king must be suitably magnificent when entertaining noble guests. The ladies of Philippa's chamber had sewn hundreds of small azure-and-silver garters on the blue taffeta bed hangings and spread, the king's latest favorite emblem, with the motto "Hony soit qui mal y pense," or "Shame to those who think evil of it." Two jupons, one of taffeta and one of silk, had been powdered with the silver-buckled garters. There were also satin doublets and velvet jupons with the king's arms. The work had begun in midwinter, when Edward chose the chivalric design.

Bella had teased her father that the garter emblem might be misconstrued as a woman's undergarment rather than as straps for armor. The queen's smile had frozen, and Joan guessed that in her mind she was back in the pavilion, seeing Edward kiss Catherine's garter and tuck it away. This was the very image of that garter.

"Nonsense," the king had said, laughing at his daughter. "Such buckles must never chafe the soft flesh of a woman's thigh." The guests at the high table had laughed with him and toasted to the great cause, as the queen excused herself, saying she felt unwell.

Bella had slipped over to Joan's seat to continue her plaint. "Garters. Why didn't he choose something more chivalric? Arthurian. And the motto—shaming those who think evil of Father's campaign—it's bullying, not chivalry. Of all his mottoes, I like this one the least."

Joan noticed the king frowning at the queen's departure. She agreed with Bella. "He might have consulted your mother on the symbol. She might have warned him."

"Mother? No. She cares about quality, not meaning."

Not always, thought Joan.

Shouts rose up from the castle yard, pulling Joan from her reverie just as Ned appeared down below, laughing as he ducked past the sagging banner. He enjoyed the adulation, waving to the crowd, stopping here and there to make someone laugh.

"He will be knighted upon landing in France," said Bella. "He'll be insufferable then. How awful it is to be a girl, always left behind."

Joan's brother was also to be knighted upon landing, and Will, too. Poor Will. He'd asked her to share his bed the previous evening, to hold him through the night, and she'd done so,

seeing his fear. He'd stayed away since that one night at Bisham.
She could afford to be kind. She waved to him now as he entered the yard with several of his fellows, scanning the battlements to see who watched. He proudly waved back.

"You waste your kindness," said Ned, leaning over the battlements beside her. "He'll have his pick of pretty boys in the
field."

"Oh, hush," she snapped, leaving him.

He hurried after her, stopping her on the tower steps, his
hands cupping her face. "You must pray for me every day, Joan.
Will you promise?"

His hands were damp with fear. Poor Ned. He strutted
about like a peacock pretending that nothing touched him,
nothing moved him, but it was all an act. "Of course I will,
cousin. All of you."

"I know why you say that. But, just this once, could you let
me know you'll pray for me especially?"

"Ned, you know I will."

"And stand on the battlements when I ride out so that I can
see you. I must know that your heart is with me, Joan. I fear that
if you are not up here seeing me off, if I look up and don't see
you lifting your arm in farewell, I won't return."

Just this once, she slipped her arms round him as he kissed
her, and held him close. "You will return triumphant. I feel it
in my bones."

IN THE MORNING, JOAN STOOD ATOP THE BATTLEMENTS WITH SEV-
eral of the queen's ladies and the royal children, watching King
Edward, Prince Edward, and their great company ride out to
war. As they reached the gate, Ned looked up to see if Joan
was there. She lifted her hand to signal that all would be well.
He bowed to her, hand on heart, and rode out. "God watch
over him," she whispered, and was about to turn away when a

knight a few horses behind the prince caught her eye. Straight and proud he rode, his curling hair almost hiding the eye patch. Thomas. She waved, but he did not look up.

"Who is it? Who are you waving to?" Bella asked.

"All of them."

"Oh!" Bella and her sister Joan both began to wave wildly.

When the yard was empty, Bella sighed. "Nothing will ever be the same."

"I should hope not," said Lady Angmar. "His Grace means to return triumphant, the pretender Philip of Valois deposed."

"You don't understand," Bella snapped.

Joan did. Thomas's eye was only the most visible of his scars. Earl William's head wound had changed his character while slowly killing him. Long ago, she and Bella wondered at the horribly puckered scars on the men's bodies in the practice field, the missing fingers, hands, but she knew now that, for many, the deepest wounds were invisible.

"What if Ned can never dance again—if he comes back at all?" Bella whispered, slipping her hand into Joan's.

"Ned is strong," Joan assured her. "And, as the future king, he will be protected by all around him. You'll dance with him soon." She was far more certain of his safe return than of Thomas's, already half blind, though a seasoned soldier. Leaving the battlements, she slipped into the chapel to pray for her beloved. She barely squeezed in the door, stumbling over women kneeling at the back, bent over their paternosters. She knelt beside them. After several rounds of Aves for Thomas, she said one for Ned, one for Will, and several for her brother.

38

Normandy
SUMMER 1346

King Edward's army set the countryside of Normandy ablaze as it marched toward Caen. Thomas could see in the prince's eyes the confusion of the sudden violent shift from the celebratory landing, the knightings, including Ned's own, only to spend the next day ordering his men to scorch the earth behind them. Ash fell like the devil's snow when the wind shifted. The men rode with chins down, trying to breathe only the air filtered by the scarves pulled up from their necks. Thomas pitied the foot soldiers.

In camp, in the shadow of the priory of Fontenay-le-Pesnel, the food tasted of ash and everyone coughed and rubbed their eyes. But it must be worse for those within the walls of Caen, ten miles away. Thomas imagined them looking out on the burning land stretching from the walls to—the sea? They would have heard of the extent of the burning from the refugees who were pouring into the town, carts piled high with what was left of their worldly goods. Thomas had been on both sides of such a siege, though his homeland had never been under attack. He thanked God for that.

In the morning, the king's messenger would be sent to offer the citizens of the town their lives, their goods, their homes in exchange for their surrender. It was unlikely the garrison would permit them to agree.

Thomas watched Prince Edward walk through the camp, being introduced by his experienced commanders to the men they wanted him to know. In his bearing, how closely he listened, his slightly distant but courteous responses, he was his father's son, a prince indeed—but young and inexperienced, with a dark streak, according to Joan. Thomas hoped he had the sense to heed the advice of his seasoned captains. The prince approached. Thomas rose to greet his commander.

"Holland!" Ned clasped his hand, nodded to him. "I count on you to take the town quickly. No long siege, eh?" He slapped Thomas on the back, strode on.

In the morning the bishop of Bayeux, who presided over the council of the garrison at Caen, tore up King Edward's offer of clemency and threw the king's messenger into prison, sending back the messenger's squire to report the bishop's disdain. Thomas was not surprised. What did the bishop have to lose? He was a cleric. He would not even be imprisoned. Nor did he likely own anything in the town. Thomas wondered how the townsfolk felt about his arrogance, whether they had such faith in his concern for them that they willingly put their lives in his hands. He doubted it.

Prince Edward led the company north round the city, encamping to the east, intending to wait for the signal from his father to attack. But some too eager foot soldiers made a rush on a small, unguarded gate in the old town walls. Finding it deserted—the citizens had moved across the river to the newer part of town, which was surrounded by water—the soldiers rushed to open the main gate to the bridge leading to the new town. And there they found the garrison amassed, the French officers quickly retreating to the tower on the bridge.

Thomas watched the prince, who'd been pacing and muttering to his officers ever since the foot soldiers disappeared inside the walls. Now he paused, listening to the report. Would he hesitate, awaiting instructions from his seasoned elders, or would he make a decision on the spot?

"For King Edward! For England!" the prince shouted, and Thomas and all the company rushed into action, other companies following, the cries echoing against the walls.

God bless Prince Edward. It was the right choice for Thomas. The first company to attack would have their pick of the officers worthy of ransom. And there they were. As Thomas fought his way onto the bridge, he saw how the French hovered around the base of the tower.

Within moments, a wounded captain of similar rank to his own surrendered to Thomas, recognizing him from Prussia. "Holland! As you are an honorable knight, I surrender my sword to you." Better to be held for ransom than be slaughtered. Though his ransom would be small, Thomas made a show of entrusting him to two of his men. Who knew who might be watching from the tower?

"The Count of Eu, Constable of France, has retreated to the tower," one of Thomas's men reported.

Raoul de Brienne had inherited the title on the death of his father. *Let us at least pledge that when we meet in battle we shall treat each other with honor.* He would bring a fine ransom, and Thomas would see that he was treated with respect.

Thomas waded through the carnage, wary of slipping on the blood coating the ground. His head buzzed with the shouts and screams, the sound of metal on metal, on stone, his arms pushing and hacking, seemingly no longer part of him. Once beneath the tower, he called to his men, making a racket so that he might be noticed.

Down from the tower came several knights, holding aloft a great ceremonial sword.

"My lord, the Count of Eu, Constable of France, delivers up his sword to Sir Thomas Holland."

Thomas strode forward and took the sword, then ordered his men to keep the way clear for his return while he climbed the tower. In a small room at the top, his friend waited, handing over his weapons.

"God is watching over me at least in this," said Raoul. "I place myself in your hands, Thomas."

"You will be safe with me," Thomas vowed.

By nightfall, the French chamberlain, who had surrendered to another captain, had been claimed by the prince. But Thomas still held Eu.

"You've now saved me twice, Thomas. How will I ever repay you?"

"With your ransom, I'll win Joan back. That is how, my friend." He handed Raoul a small cup of his celebratory brandy-wine.

"Still loyal to your king despite the theft of your lawful wife?"

"Is your king any less arbitrary with his favor?"

The count chuckled and raised his cup. "I honor your integrity, Thomas."

"Ah, old friends, well met." Prince Edward stepped into the light of the campfire.

The count rose to greet him.

"My lord prince," Thomas bowed. "It is an honor." He nodded for Hugh to offer the prince some brandywine.

The prince declined. "I've come for your prisoner. My pavilion is more appropriate to one of his rank."

It was not uncommon for the royals to claim the most valuable prisoners as their own. Thomas and Raoul had prepared for this, knowing that, once claimed, the count would be lost to Thomas.

"How thoughtful, my lord prince," said Raoul, "but I am most comfortable here, in the custody of the man who has now twice saved my life."

The prince nodded to one of his men to take the count, but Thomas stepped between. "My lord prince, let us bring this before your father the king."

"In the morning," said Raoul. "For now, I pray you grant me this night's ease."

Thomas watched the gloved hands open and close, caught a twitch beneath the prince's right eye just before he nodded to the count.

"Until the morning."

Raoul considered Thomas with interest afterward, as the prince departed. "There is something more between you than my ransom, though that is considerable. Is it your love for his cousin the fair Joan?"

"How did you guess?"

Extending his cup for more brandywine, the count settled back against a rock, holding the cup to his nose. "This we do better than you, eh?" He laughed. "As for the prince, he clenches his jaw and puffs out his chest when he looks at you, a proud little cock. And, as it is rumored your lady leaves a trail of broken hearts—"

"That is not true!"

"The brandywine has gone to my head." Raoul leaned close. "But it is said that the garter beneath which you fight is that of the Countess of Salisbury."

"Not true. And, if it were, that would be her false husband's mother, the beautiful widow Catherine Montagu, who has taken a vow of celibacy."

"Ah." Raoul shrugged. "Still. Beware the young cock."

Thomas slept poorly that night, despite having five of his men watch over the count. In the morning he escorted Raoul to the king, who invited them to sit down to a simple meal while they talked.

"The prince sends his regrets. He is seeing to the discipline of the men who breached the walls before my signal yesterday."

"The prince did not signal, Your Grace?" asked Raoul in a way that implied otherwise.

The two men considered each other as the servants offered Thomas and Raoul meat, cheese, bread, wine. Thomas waited for the king and the count to signal that they were ready to talk. At last the king nodded.

"You wish to repay Holland for the price he paid in saving your life years ago. I understand, as does my son. Holland, hand your prisoners over to Huntington. The earl is overseeing the transport of prisoners of rank to castles in England, where they will be kept under heavy guard until their ransoms are secured. I give you my word that Eu will be held safe and secure, to your benefit." He laughed. "He'll be far more convincing in urging his kinsmen to pay you than he would my son! Hah!"

Thomas thanked the king and set to the food and wine with good appetite.

"Did your men say the prince signaled?" Thomas asked afterward as they made their way to Huntington's camp.

Raoul shrugged. "No. But *my* father would have believed it of me."

39

Windsor
AUTUMN 1346

Edward's summons was couched in effusive praise in an effort to preempt marital discord, knowing how Philippa had suffered during their long sojourn in the Low Countries. Her skill in diplomacy might more quickly bring relief to the women and children in the besieged city. He needed her. And for her company she must bring the noblest ladies of the realm. He had built a town for her. They would observe Christmas with much merriment, celebrating the great victory at Crécy.

Join you in a siege camp outside Calais? In winter? Do you think me mad? How she would love to refuse. But they were at war. To refuse was treason. He was careful not to mention that.

Catherine Montagu, recently returned to Philippa's household, expressed delight at the prospect, yearning to see her son, Will, freshly knighted, on his first long campaign. She seemed much improved, well supported by Joan, who had taken up her responsibilities with efficient grace. Philippa was well pleased with Joan's transformation, though she did grow impatient for Joan to produce an heir for Will. Such an event would surely convince Ned that he must look elsewhere for a wife.

As for the recovered Catherine, she had arrived with a lavishly updated wardrobe, dark colors in honor of her widowhood artfully decorated with beads, gems, and buttons to catch the light in a room and set her aglow, calling attention to her slender, still remarkably youthful figure. Celibacy had lost its appeal, had it? Perhaps she dreamed of lying with Edward in the great bed curtained in those insulting garters. Gently Philippa broke the news that Joan would represent the Montagus while Catherine oversaw the domestic side of the royal household here at home. *I count on you, my dear Cat.*

Joan pleaded with Philippa to reconsider, to let Catherine go in her stead. She dreaded the Channel crossing. *It is the very thing to cure your fear, sweet Joan.*

Philippa and Catherine had been at odds ever since, the countess criticizing the quantity of embroidered cushions being packed, the number of cloaks and gowns and boots, the crown, the caskets of jewels, goblets and glass—nothing pleased her. Philippa enjoyed every arch look, every sharp word, knowing it was all born of the pain of being left behind. It was a sweet revenge.

Villeneuve-le-Hardi, Normandy
WINTER–SPRING 1346–47

CALMED BY EFA'S PHYSIC, JOAN SLEPT FOR MOST OF THE CROSSING. Helena guarded her out on the deck, for Joan refused to ever again be trapped in a cabin. The queen had rejected her request to bring Efa. Joan comforted herself with the knowledge that her mother planned to offer Efa's services to Dame Katarina and her children, to help them forget the horror they had witnessed, forging a healing bond. But she felt vulnerable without her nurse.

The king's elaborate encampment southeast of Calais, *Villeneuve-le-Hardi*, or Brave New Town, straddled the causeway a mile from the coast leading to Flanders. Although Joan had heard that it was substantial, with wattle-and-daub houses and shops, and larger wooden homes for the king, commanders, and nobles, she was still surprised by its vast size, how it dominated the plain beyond Calais. The king had indeed established a town in enemy territory, complete with elegant comforts. It was said to grow by the day, with the troops and all the camp followers seeing to the needs of the inhabitants. And, as for replenishing supplies, not only was a causeway into Flanders kept open but a small fleet of ships under heavy guard regularly crossed the Channel from England with goods gathered from all parts of the realm.

The king's hall was large and airy, hung with fine tapestries. Queen Philippa and Bella had arrived the previous day and now warmly greeted the newcomers, Bella eager to show Joan round the building and escape her mother.

The hall was surprisingly beautiful for something so new and made entirely of wood rather than stone. Almost all of the furnishings were spoils of war—tapestries, carved chairs and screens, Italian glass, silver and pewter plates, fabrics of every color. They would not need half of what they had brought with them. It was not at all how Joan had imagined field camps.

"You'll have days, weeks, months to explore," said Will, appearing at her side.

He was so changed that Joan almost did not know him. Worse than gaunt, he looked as if he'd been ill for some time, his eyes shadowed, cheeks sunken beneath a scraggly beard.

"You've been ill?" Joan asked. "Were you injured? Let us find hot spiced wine for you."

"Don't treat me like an invalid."

With a whispered excuse, Bella slipped away.

"Come," Joan said, slipping her arm through his. "Walk with me and tell me about your knighting, Sir William."

He seemed to relax a little with something to talk about, and they moved along the edge of the gradually filling room.

Once, she thought she saw Thomas, only to realize that it was someone else. Later, she spotted his brother Otho. Following her gaze, Will said, "Thomas Holland is away on a mission for the prince—across the Channel. And your brother has sailed for home as well."

To come so far and still not see them was a great disappointment. Though Thomas had written to her through Lucienne, Joan yearned to see for herself that he was well, and to hear more about how Raoul Brienne, now constable of France, had surrendered to him, how much he thought the ransom might be—enough? And she'd hoped to see her brother. "It seems we women will have little to distract us from one another. I can't imagine how we'll fill our days."

She was saved from saying more by the horns announcing a royal entrance.

In strode Ned, a stark contrast to Will. He glowed with health and good cheer, his chest puffed out. He looked older than his sixteen years, so tall and broad-shouldered, but it was his bearing that had utterly changed, from a boyish flaunting of his rank to a man comfortable and confident in himself, nodding his head at the wave of bows as he strode into the crowd as if it were only his due, as if he believed all there had come solely to look on him.

"Ah, the hero of Crécy arrives." Will muttered. "Look at him."

Ned spoke to all who approached him, asking after injuries, laughing at japes, at ease with the deference even the highest of nobles showed him.

"You see? He believes he's a hero."

"It is not true?"

"Many were heroes that day. Many fell."

She sensed a personal loss. "Someone close to you?"

"Damien." One of his pages. "Others who had come to be friends."

She tried to distract him with news of his family, but it was awkward, unnatural, and did little to cheer him.

A page came forward to lead them to their seats. It seemed that Joan was to sit at the high table between Will and Ned.

"I should not complain. I would not be at the high table but for your presence," Will muttered.

Joan patted his arm.

"Joan! Let me look at you." Ned took her aside. She felt herself blushing beneath his intent, appreciative gaze, a pleasant contrast to Will's indifference. "By God, you are more beautiful than ever, cousin. If my mother's eyes were not on us . . ." He made a growling noise deep in his throat. That was a crude new skill.

"And you, cousin, the handsome prince, and a hero!"

"Don't tease me." For a moment he looked uncertain, and was again the boy who had ridden off to war.

"I am not teasing, Ned."

Someone bowed to him in passing, and he straightened, his eyes sharpened. Joan felt an odd melancholy. They'd both now left childhood far behind. As they took their seats, she asked him to tell her all about Crécy. At first, he voiced much the same sentiments as Will. He'd shared the day with many brave men, and many had fallen.

"No, Ned, *tell* me. All call you the hero of the day. I want to hear *your* tale."

He hesitated but a moment. Soon she learned the lay of the land, the battle formation—Ned took up several spoons to show her his centered position, the archers to the sides. "We expected that, as ever, King Philip would refuse to engage. But no! At last!" His face flushed, eyes brightened, as he described the mortality of the Genoese crossbowmen—they were no match for the English longbows, and when the Genoese retreated in terror the French nobles rode them down in their arrogance. Had they bothered to ask why they were retreating, the nobles might have saved themselves. And then the attack, how Ned rode through the knights and nobles on horseback, slicing at them, crushing their helmets, cutting down their horses, all the while shouting encouragement to his men. *His men.* Someone shouted that his standard-bearer had gone down. Sir Thomas Daniel pushed through the chaos to raise the standard. "And Father did not rescue me. I won the day. *I* did," he ended breathlessly.

Caught up in the excitement of his delivery, Joan cried, "You have faced your destiny and triumphed!"

"I have, Joan. No more doubt that I might not live up to Father's expectations. I *am* a warrior."

"I never doubted you. I've seen you on the tournament field, in the practice yard." She raised her mazer to him. But he placed his hands over hers, guiding the cup to his mouth. Then he leaned close and breathed deeply. "You smell like England."

"Rose and lavender. You are thinking of the gardens at Eltham and Woodstock."

"You are the queen of my heart." He took another drink, then tilted the mazer toward Joan.

It felt too much like a ritual bonding, a vow shared. She shook her head. "Your parents are no doubt watching us."

Henry of Grosmont, now Duke of Lancaster, interrupted to have a word with Ned. He rose immediately, once more the proven warrior with men under his command.

Joan looked out over the hall, curious who was present. She noticed couples happily reunited, clusters of people leaning together talking excitedly, the lonely or broken few not engaged, staring off. Beside her, Will was talking with some liveliness to Bella.

"They are so proud and happy," she said later that evening to Bella after they'd been treated to a long description of Henry of Lancaster's sweep of northern Gascony by several eager young knights. "I feel as if I've been permitted a peek into their warrior hearts, man's ideal realm."

"Mother says that bloodlust makes the most ordinary man look a dashing hero," said Bella. "Father has never looked more glorious, more powerful, more handsome."

"Your father's never suffered an ordinary moment, Bella." But the king did look fitter, stronger, more confident, certainly happier than he had when he set out from Guildford Castle. And why not? He was triumphant.

THE KING INTENDED THE WOMEN'S PRESENCE AS A SHOW OF CONFI-dence on the part of the barons and knights that their women would be safe in Villeneuve-le-Hardi, but in practice the women were confined to the encampment—they could not ride, hunt, hawk, tour the conquered towns and villages. How, then, were the French to feel the prick of their presence?

The happy mood of reunion quickly faded. The wooden structures were drafty, with no glazed windows and poorly fitted shutters, the bedchambers crowded. Few of the wives shared their husbands' bed, for the men were either in the field or defending the camp. Joan was relieved, for there was little danger that she would be expected to share a bed with Will, but as the men returned to their duties the women's quarters grew loud with bickering and complaint. The novelty had worn off, and the women wearied of their confinement.

Joan hoped to escape outside with Helena to explore this makeshift metropolis that was to be her world for as long as the king desired. But they discovered that even this they could not do without an escort.

"The men have become accustomed to camp followers, my lady. They can behave like dogs," said the guard who insisted on accompanying them.

So much for Joan's intended time to herself. But she made the best of it, asking the guard about the men they encountered, particularly the wounded—those missing hands, feet, arms, legs, those with their heads or necks swathed in bandages. They sat in doorways, leaned out windows, hobbled about, often with eyes glazed with pain, fear, despair. Some had no visible injuries, but, like Will, looked cadaverous, haunted by death. Making the circuit of streets and practice grounds, Joan witnessed the real price of the king's war. Beyond the encampment the land was flat, trampled, the trees cut down for timber and fuel. Within the encampment, desolate men; without the encampment, desolate land.

How will I bear this? When will Thomas return? Joan drank too much wine that night and argued with Ned, avoiding Will even more than usual, because now she saw in his eyes, when he thought no one was looking, the same desolation she'd seen in the eyes of the wounded that day. Her wine-induced nightmares left her shaken in the morning.

Comfort came several weeks later, in the form of a white-and-brown bundle of fur. After Mass one gloomy December morning, Ned presented her with a puppy, skinny and shivering.

"I found him scavenging in the waste outside the camp. He would have starved. I remember how much you loved Bruno. Is he not like him?"

It was the first time Ned had mentioned Bruno since she sent him away from the grave, and for a moment she wondered whether this was some sort of reparation. "When he fills out, perhaps," though she was doubtful. It did not matter. She could not resist the puppy as he licked her face and squirmed to bury his head in her neck. "Thank you, Ned. He's a dear."

She called him Jester, because laughter bubbled up where he went, his happy bark and wagging tail bringing smiles to the dourest of faces. He was her excuse to take frequent walks, hoping to overhear news of Thomas's return. After several days, she'd learned nothing new. But someone did recognize the puppy.

"Pulled him out of a burning house Red John did, poor tiny mite trapped in there. No doubt his mother lay dead within." An old soldier shook his head and spit into the alley. "Henry's what Red John called him, my lady, and he loved him so, fed him better than scraps, carried him inside his jacket when he went on watch—we all feared the pup would bark and get him killed, but somehow he knew to be quiet. It was a festering wound that wouldn't heal, that's what killed Red John. Leg swelled up thrice its size and started to smell. He fell into a fever and died. Henry stayed tucked in the crook of his arm while he suffered. At John's last breath, the pup howled and then bolted. We could find him nowhere."

Joan bent down to smooth the puppy's ears. "So you're mine now, Jester."

The old soldier laughed. "That's a good name for him. Good bless and keep you both, my lady."

Walking back to her lodgings, Joan stumbled as Jester began to pull hard on his lead, straining toward another soldier who'd crouched down to greet him. "Henry! There you are, clean and groomed. You've found yourself a good home, eh?" He rose and bowed to Joan. "My lady. You've a good dog there."

"I call him Jester," she said. "I heard all about how Red John rescued him. May God grant him peace. Do you by chance know Sir Thomas Holland?"

"Sir Thomas saved my life, my lady. Pulled me out of the way of a horse about to trample me in the field."

"Is he in camp?"

"I know not, my lady, but I pray for him every day." He told her where Thomas lodged when he was in camp, officers' quarters across from the Chapel of St. Michael.

In the ensuing days she befriended the priest in charge of St. Michael's, inviting him one afternoon to join her for Jester's walk. Don Jerome knew the Holland brothers. "Sir Thomas is the best of them in the field. You'll find many here who will enjoy recounting how he charged across a river shouting 'For St. George!' and cleaving a lone outrider almost in two." He crossed himself and nodded at her expression of dismay. "He saved many a man that day, I've no doubt, but we must pray for the soul of his victim, even so." She had no part in Thomas's honor and heroics, yet she felt so proud of him.

Christmas came and went, with still no sign of Thomas. She'd not seen him since May, when he rode out the gate at Guildford. And then, one afternoon, Joan entered the king's hall and saw her beloved conversing with His Grace, the two of them leaning over a filthy map spread out on a table. One of the ladies called out to her. Thomas looked up, and for a moment he held Joan's gaze, smiling, then returned to the map.

But for the scarring and the eye patch already so familiar, he looked unharmed, and his smile was the most beautiful sight she'd seen in a long, long while. How intently His Grace listened, how comfortable Thomas seemed. So this was Thomas in the field, confident, respected, absorbed in his mission.

She'd not thought about how impossible it would be for them to find time alone in the crowded encampment. His presence quickly proved a torment. Though Will had departed on a mission for the king, Ned was still in camp and possessive of her time. Joan and Thomas traded smiles from opposite ends of the hall at meals.

She confided her frustration to Don Jerome, the only person with whom she felt she could be frank.

"There is a chapel on the edge of the encampment used by the merchants, far from the king's residence," Don Jerome said one evening. "I have cause to go there tomorrow. Would you care to accompany me? I'm quite certain we will encounter Sir Thomas there."

Joan could not believe her good fortune. "Why are you helping us?"

"I am here to care for the souls of His Grace's men. It will be good for Sir Thomas to be with you. He will be less likely to take unnecessary risks going forward, and will allow compassion to move him when a death will not help the cause."

As promised, Jerome escorted her to the chapel the following day, leaving her at the entrance to the dimly lit space as he hurried off to the vestry. She found herself suddenly swept up in strong arms. "Thomas!" She knew his touch, his scent. When at last they broke apart, he drew her down onto a cloak he'd arranged in a corner. "Dare we, my love?" she whispered.

"In this wartime encampment, no one will bother a couple finding ease in the shadows."

And so she and Thomas came together in the tiny chapel. A brief, exquisite joy.

"I ride out again tomorrow," Thomas told her when at last they stepped out into a stormy evening. He drew her furred cloak closer round her face, kissing her lips once more. "I thank God for this time with you." He told her he'd been sent away just two days before she arrived. "The orders come through the prince, but I think it is His Grace who is determined to keep us apart." *For Catherine. Of course,* Joan thought. "But there is hope, my love, so we must do nothing to jeopardize our goal. His Grace has offered me a fine sum for Raoul, and I've accepted."

"But you deserve the whole!"

"Who knows how much Raoul will be able to raise, and when? This will be sufficient for Avignon. Until that money is fully paid, we must not antagonize him."

"I promise you, my love, I will do nothing to call attention to myself."

Thomas laughed and kissed her hand. "Now, that is impossible. All the men in this encampment worship you. I thank God for that. There will always be someone looking out for your welfare even though I'm not here." He swore that the moment the siege was lifted at Calais he would make haste to Avignon. His mother had prepared the way.

How she loved him. They stood there for a long while, drinking each other in.

VILLENEUVE-LE-HARDI CONTINUED TO GROW, ADDING LARGE houses for the great barons returning from missions in Gascony and Brittany, a hospital for the ill and injured as the casualties and the sicknesses that accompanied long sieges continued to mount. King Edward amused himself by designing a viewing gallery in his mansion, where he, his commanders, and their wives might observe the siege. Bella dragged Joan up there one night, a quiet night with a strong breeze coming off the Channel. Down below, campfires dotted the plain and lit up the base of the city walls, crossed occasionally by the dark outlines of the men on the night watch. An oddly peaceful scene but for the dark smoke rising up into the night sky from behind the walls of Calais and the sickening smell of burning flesh carried on the wind to their aerie.

"They are burning their dead, Bella, I cannot stay out here." Nauseated by the smell, Joan turned toward the door just as Ned appeared, striding over to the edge, taking a deep breath. "How can you bear to breathe that?"

"That, cousin, is the smell of victory. They cannot hold out much longer."

"They are people, Ned. Families."

"Enemies who refuse to give up their conquered city."

She rushed away, making it down to the privy just in time to empty her stomach.

NED WAS WRONG. THE PEOPLE OF CALAIS HELD OUT UNTIL EARLY August.

The town, which had long been the center of piracy on the north coast, rewarded the besiegers with unexpected wealth.

As they searched the homes, King Edward's men discovered that even the most modest were stuffed with treasures. Such wealth, yet so many had died. The previous month, the garrison had rounded up the women, children, elderly—all whom they deemed of no military use—and led them out of the gates, which were then shut behind them. The English refused to let them pass through to the countryside and the possibility of food and shelter, and the garrison of Calais refused to let them back in. They starved in the ditch between the two sides. It was a common fate in a long siege. Yet when King Edward planned to execute six burghers of Calais as a condition of the town's surrender, Queen Philippa pleaded for their lives, and was granted them.

Thomas had been one of the king's men charged with negotiating the surrender. Joan had seen the suffering in his eyes, his posture, each time he returned to confer with the king.

One evening after the surrender, Don Jerome arranged a modest meal in his lodgings for Joan, Thomas, and his mother. Lady Maud Holland had arrived in the encampment the previous day. On the morrow, mother and son would depart for the papal court in Avignon.

"The queen's intercession is what all will remember, the sparing of the burghers," Thomas predicted. "And it was mere playacting, agreed between our king and queen beforehand. It is such grand gestures that find their way into songs, and the great battles, not the deaths of those who have become burdensome to the army."

"Would you curse the source of your new wealth, son?" asked Lady Maud. "But for this war, you would not have the means to petition Rome."

Joan saw how the remark bothered Thomas, and gave him an encouraging smile. Lady Maud had not witnessed the suffering in the camp, watched the women, children, and elders starve outside the walls of Calais. She had no idea how sick they all were of this war. "It is a time of celebration, Thomas. The siege is over, you are free to ride to Avignon!" Joan reminded him.

"You are right, my love. Tonight we celebrate." He took her hand.

Maud nodded, smiling. "You are good for my son."

Joan began to relax. She'd found Thomas's mother an enigma at first. Tall and with a large frame, she was a contradiction, at once imposing and adept at blending into the background. Her visage, though outwardly pleasant, revealed nothing of her thoughts. She'd arrived in a company of barons' wives and stayed at the edges of the crowd in the hall the previous day, always one of many. Thomas's brother Otho had pointed his mother out to Joan, but she'd waited for this meeting to be introduced. Better not to draw the queen's attention to this new arrival.

"I confess I have resented you, Lady Joan," Maud had said when they were introduced at the beginning of the evening. "With your rash action you risked my son's future, his very survival. I blamed your Plantagenet blood and the privilege it affords you. I worried that you would discard him as soon as you found a redeemer in someone of higher status. But Thomas swore he would have no woman to wife but you, and Dame Katarina Van Artevelde convinced me that you and my son are bound in the eyes of God. So I came."

"It is good to know your heart, my lady," said Joan. "I pray that in time you will grow to trust me. How did you come to meet Dame Katarina?"

"Lady Townley arranged it as I passed through London in spring." Lucienne had again come to their aid. "She spoke highly of you. As did my sons Otho and Alan, but they are easily swayed by beauty. And now that I meet you"—she took Joan's hand and at last her face relaxed into a smile—"I am inclined to pray that the pope sides with you and Thomas. My sons are made of strong stuff, and His Grace knows it. I no longer fear for Thomas's life or his standing in the king's service if his petition succeeds." She kissed Joan on the cheek.

"My lady, only the pope's blessing on our marriage could sound sweeter," Joan had said.

After the meal, Lady Maud left with her page so that Joan and Thomas might have a few moments alone.

"You've said nothing of your plans for me while you are so far away," said Joan.

Thomas sat down and drew her onto his lap, kissing her forehead above the jeweled circlet. "You will go on as you have, keeping the peace with Will—"

"What if he's not so easily controlled now?"

"Who has protected you while I've been away before? Nothing has changed."

"Will has changed."

"He has been humbled by his experience of war, my love. He'll want everything as it was on his homecoming. You'll see."

Joan wanted to believe him, but a humbled man sometimes took out his shame on those who were no threat to him. "I pray you are right."

Thomas's parting gifts were an intricately carved statue of the Blessed Mother, a small beautifully illuminated book of hours, and a ring set with a rose-tinted diamond.

"Think of me, my beloved."

"Every moment, Thomas. God keep you safe!" She was suddenly frightened for him, for the danger he and his mother faced, riding through enemy territory. "You have the silk?"

"Always." He touched his heart.

"I'll pray for your safe return."

Reluctantly, they parted, Thomas slipping out first.

But for all their caution, as Joan departed with the priest, one of the queen's pages walked by, making a point of greeting her, then walked on. Had he seen Maud and Thomas precede her?

"I am as afraid for you as I am for Thomas and me, Father."

"The deed is done, my child," said Don Jerome. "We must put our trust in God."

How proud Edward was, and deservedly so. The queen stood before a tapestry of Diana, moon goddess, huntress, smiling as she watched her husband wend his way through her adoring ladies. She wished she could spare him this unpleasantness, but he would be consoled in having her support in enforcing Joan's marriage.

"My lady wife." He kissed her hand, pressed it to his cheek. "I come at your command."

"I pray I never need command your presence in my chamber, my lord." She turned toward the tapestry. "Diana, the huntress. Your son wishes to give it to your cousin Joan." She waited for his reaction.

"A good choice," he said absently.

"Really?"

Edward raised his brows and cocked his head, suddenly attentive. "To Joan?"

Good. He saw the problem. Philippa led him to a corner where she'd arranged two cushioned, high-backed chairs. They settled. A servant poured wine, then withdrew a discreet distance.

"We must resolve Joan's marriage situation, husband, and while we do so she must be kept from our Ned. She has bewitched him. He rises to her defense at the slightest hint of criticism. He showers her with gifts, including that annoying puppy. He has made her marriage to young Montagu impossible."

"You'd blame Ned? It's Joan and her stubborn refusal to see

to her duty." Edward took a long drink. "What do you mean, 'resolve her marriage situation'?"

"With the money from ransoms, Thomas Holland is on his way to Avignon. With his mother."

Edward looked pained. "Of course. That is why Ned wanted the constable for himself. I was not thinking. But do not ask me to punish Holland. He is a worthy knight. I need men like him. Montagu, on the other hand," he grunted. "If he were not the son of my old friend, I would release him. He has no stomach for war—nor for a strong woman, it seems. Still, she is his wife and she *will* honor her vows."

"If the pope rules in Holland's favor, you, I, Countess Margaret, the late earl, Countess Catherine, and our bishops will be complicit in ignoring his legitimate betrothal. The pope might use this to force his influence on the English Church."

Time and again, the popes had tried to infiltrate the English Church with their own candidates for vacant seats. Spies. "He might indeed." Edward frowned. "It would be a bitter circumstance. You have a plan?"

"Holland is going to Avignon because he doubts he would prevail in the English courts. For that very reason, Montagu should pursue a countersuit in England. We must provide young Montagu with sufficient funds to counter Holland's appeal in the ecclesiastical courts. From his inheritance, of course. Or, rather, provide his grandmother Elizabeth with the funds to bring a countersuit. Have the primate of England rule on this— he'll accommodate us."

"Pope Clement will rule against me if he has even a whiff of my part in this. He is Philip of Valois's man."

"Perhaps, but it's more likely that he'd rather not be bothered, and if the archbishop of Canterbury sends him a ruling, Clement will pocket Holland's money, stall him awhile, then rule against him."

Edward chuckled. "Lady Elizabeth loves nothing better

than a good fight in the courts." As he turned the mazer in his hands, his eyes on the tapestry to his left, he grew serious. "But will this not prolong the uncertainty? And all the while, if you are right about Ned—"

"As I said, Joan must be kept from him."

"By that look, you've already set this in motion."

Philippa smiled, knowing better than to dissemble.

Edward drained his mazer, and leaned over to kiss her cheek as he rose. "I should have married off her mother. Widows are so troublesome. They need a man's firm hand."

"You are wrong there, my love. Countess Margaret has always been on our side."

"While my old friend controlled her. But with Earl William dead . . ."

"You forget. I've promised her son's betrothal to one of my nieces, Elizabeth of Juliers."

"Ah!" Edward's eyes sparkled. "The margrave's lovely daughter. Yes. We can control her with that." He shook his head. "But we need more. Joan must also have legal counsel, through her mother. Provide Countess Margaret with a lawyer who prefers money and being in my graces to winning a case."

Philippa smiled. "I know just the man."

Edward laughed. "I thank God you're on my side."

"I shall miss you, husband. I pray that you return home before winter."

The women of the court were departing for England in a few days, which was why Philippa had needed Edward's blessing on her plan.

"You'll have little time to miss me, my love. I will be praying for you in your confinement." He laid a hand on her swelling stomach.

❖ ❖ ❖

CROWDS GATHERED ALONG THE ROUTE FROM VILLENEUVE-LE-
Hardi to the harbor to bid farewell to Queen Philippa and her
ladies. The queen's litter was in the middle of the procession,
several of her ladies on horseback fore and aft. As cheers rose
up, Philippa waved to the crowds. But many of them seemed
to be looking at something coming up behind her. And then
she heard the shouts: "Prince Edward!" "Hero of Crécy!" How
proud she was.

40

LATE SUMMER 1347

Riding right behind the royal party in the procession to the harbor, Joan witnessed Ned prancing like a peacock, waving to the crowd, averting his eyes from the injured soldiers who lined the route. He could not look on them, their gear sitting beside them, clearly hoping that someone might take pity and offer them passage. It was she who waved to them as they called out to her, wishing her a safe crossing. Jester, too, riding with Joan in an openwork basket, greeted his old friends with happy barks and wagging tail.

Ned fell back, kissing Joan's hand and asking, "Do you hear how they love me, cousin?"

"They would love you even more if you found room for them on your ship. And do not tell me how little space there is. It's the plunder that's weighing down our ships. Leave it behind, well guarded, and bring your troops home first."

"My little Franciscan. Have you taken a vow of poverty?" He urged his horse forward, raising his hand again to wave at his cheering audience.

"Might *we* accommodate some of them?" she asked Will.

"That is not how it is done." He seemed to suck in the hollows in his once round face as he straightened and looked grimly ahead.

She had thought that this war-haunted Will, no longer a boy, might find his own voice, dare to show up the prince, but he disappointed her, as fearful of an original gesture as ever. She wondered who had ordered him to rush back to Villeneuve-le-Hardi in time to escort her home. He'd appeared when Helena was already waiting in the cart with Joan's belongings, greeting her with a hug and a kiss, assuring her that he meant to see that she had a safe, comfortable crossing, all with such forced cheer that she knew he was obeying orders.

On board, she stymied him by refusing the "comfort" of the cabin. She remained on deck, Jester snuggled in her lap, while Will and his men nervously watched over her, walking along with her when she led Jester round on his leash. Several of the king's guard, none of them her friends, also kept her in sight.

"Do you fear I'll jump over the side?" she asked Will.

"That dog might trip you up, he stays so close to your skirts."

"You are a poor liar."

He protested.

She asked him to tell her of his experience in the field. She sensed a deep change in him, a maturity.

"Now you ask?"

"I've barely seen you."

"And whose fault is that? You've been playing the prince's lady. I would have been in the way."

She asked again, saying that she would certainly never see a wounded man again without thinking of the horror of stabbing the pirate on the burning ship, feeling the blade stick, then penetrate, the hot blood covering her hand, making her lose her grip on the hilt, the power with which he'd thrown her off.

"You were not trained for war. I was. Killing was nothing to me."

She did not believe him. "You are changed, Will."

"Try to rest. We have a long journey ahead." He left her.

The way he said that—"a long journey ahead"—sounded

like a threat. She grew more certain of that when she saw her
mother on the dock in Portsmouth.

"Why are you here?"

"I have not seen you in months, my child. I could not wait
until—you might come round to visit."

Joan noted the hesitation. At the inn where they were to stay
the night, Margaret evaded questions about where they were
headed by talking of the Van Artevelde family—she and Efa
had befriended them and helped them through a difficult time.

"She will bear witness to your marriage to Thomas when
the time comes," Margaret promised, briefly smiling.

Joan asked after John. If something was happening, her
brother's good fortune was most likely the cause.

"John is to receive your father's lands from the king on
Michaelmas, a prelude to his betrothal to Elizabeth of Juliers."

"What price am I paying for my brother's good fortune?"

"This is not about John."

"What is 'this,' and who is it about if not him?"

"You and the prince. You accepted many costly gifts from
him, including this dog you so cherish. The prince was ever by
your side in Calais. . . ."

A familiar charge. "And that is my fault? I never wished to
be there. And, once I was, Will was always away. How can I be
blamed?"

Margaret poured both of them more wine.

Joan pushed her cup aside. "What is my punishment?"

Her mother stared down into the cup she turned round and
round in her hands as if it might hold the answer.

Joan put her hand out to stop it. "Tell me."

"Philippa believes you are better off away from court, far
away, while the legality of your marriage is being decided."
There were tears in her mother's eyes.

"And you are cooperating for John's sake." Joan let go her
mother's hands. "She knows Thomas and Lady Maud are on

their way to Avignon, doesn't she? She misses nothing regarding me, damn her."

"Joan! It is treason to curse your queen."

"Doesn't she?"

"Yes, she knows, but in truth it is Ned's attention that worries her."

"So I am to be closed away in a convent?"

"I don't know where you are headed. No one but Will, his
mother, and his retainers are to know where you are."

"So that Ned does not discover me."

"Or Thomas. I am no longer trusted where he is concerned."
Margaret reached out to Joan. "I had no part in the plan, I swear
to you. When I received the queen's message, I asked if Efa
might be with you. She's gone on ahead. She will ensure your
comfort and health—"

Joan shook off her mother's hand, calling for Helena to prepare her for bed.

"Joan—"

"Be silent unless you mean to deliver me from this. You
have one child now. Go to him."

After all were asleep, Joan crept to the door, trying the latch.
Locked from without. She checked the one window. The drop
to the street would be risky and, even if she survived it, two of
Will's men stood watch below. She was his prisoner.

Avignon
LATE SUMMER 1347

THE ATMOSPHERE IN THE PAPAL ENCLAVE WAS A SHOCK TO THOMAS
and his mother after their journey through the French countryside. Everywhere they'd witnessed the scars of the war with
England—cities, towns, villages, farms devastated. And here in

Avignon were pilgrims seeking prayers for the souls of fathers, brothers, sons.

But within the papal enclave the bureaucracy ground on, cardinals and clergy moving about protected by retinues of clerks, approachable only after sufficient silver or other valuables had changed hands.

Thomas saw the confusion in his mother's eyes, heard the frustration in her tight voice, intuited her disillusionment from the hours she'd spent in front of her portable altar. But she spoke of none of that. In public she was all business, arranging for comfortable, affordable lodgings and quickly making friends of several goodwives certain to have the pulse of the papal city as well as an abbess in Avignon on business for her convent.

"The abbess is here seeking funds. With so many nobles dead, and the king's heavy taxation, she has lost her primary benefactors, and her abbey's crops were either seized by our armies or burned. She says that even King Philip is in financial distress. I predict that we'll learn much here that will be of interest to King Edward." It was a part of Maud's litany of hope.

"She must still have sufficient wealth if she can afford to be heard here," said Thomas. The court officials threatened to consume every last shred of Thomas's money and patience. Many made it clear that they would accept information about King Edward's plans, his financial situation, his forces, in lieu of some of the silver. Of course, Thomas refused. They found his loyalty amusing, considering his petition.

But Pope Clement took the case seriously, assigning Cardinal Adhémar Robert to handle it.

At their first meeting, Thomas and Maud knelt to the cardinal and kissed his ring.

"Rise up! You are both most welcome. Come, share some wine while we talk."

His crimson robes were of silk, his chamber filled with

carved furnishings draped in embroidered silks, the walls hung with tapestries of conquest and wonders.

"I surround myself with things of beauty to remind me of God's beneficence," said the cardinal, seeing Thomas's interest.

His smile was a contrast in white teeth and olive skin. Wolfish, Thomas thought as he settled on a well-cushioned chair. A servant offered them goblets of wine. Maud turned hers round in her hands. Thomas imagined her wondering whether the heavy pewter and precious stones had been gifts from former petitioners.

"To the satisfactory resolution of your marital problem," said the cardinal, raising his cup.

They drank. It was an excellent wine, but Thomas set it aside after the obligatory sip. "My lord cardinal, I did not expect such a notable advocate."

"It is not unusual, I assure you. I shall merely oversee the case. My assistants will do all the work." A cool smile. "I am blessed with a most industrious staff, which, unfortunately, means that they are overwhelmed with work."

By the time they departed the cardinal's chamber, Thomas and Maud had a list of a dozen clerics requiring gifts, but had been asked nothing about the case.

"I am in danger of losing my faith in this cesspit," Maud said, striding out of the cardinal's palace with such determination that Thomas did not need to shorten his stride to accommodate her. "All that they say about the corruption of the papacy in exile is true," she growled as they hurried through an elegantly cultivated garden toward the street.

Discouraged, he expressed a need to walk about the city until his temper cooled.

"We are to dine with Abbess Marianne. Our walk must needs be short, so let it be brisk!" Maud took off at a pace that had her veils fluttering despite the lack of breeze, her boots sounding a loud tattoo on the cobbles.

At the main gate of the city, they noticed a small company of travelers standing without the gates and loudly arguing with the papal guards. Servants and men in livery stood round an elegantly garbed elderly woman who had stepped out of her litter to join the fray.

"They are English," said Maud as they grew closer. "Perhaps we can be of assistance before they are relieved of all their wealth. Heavenly mother!" She stopped so abruptly that Thomas almost stepped on her skirts. "That is Elizabeth, dowager countess of Salisbury."

"Will's grandmother?" Thomas was now close enough to pick out the Salisbury arms on the knights attending her.

Maud took his arm. "Come along, it's time we returned to our lodging and conferred with Abbess Marianne. I know the dowager's reputation. There is no more litigious woman in all the realm. Worse even than Blanche Wake. Legal disputes are her entertainment."

"God help us." Thomas wondered who told Will they were here, and how the dowager countess had managed to arrive so speedily.

"Does the king see your marriage as a personal slight?" His mother had paused halfway across the sunny courtyard of their lodgings, shielding her eyes from the brightness as she looked up at Thomas. "Might he have encouraged the dowager countess to press a countersuit?"

"I did not expect him to care."

"Honor blinds you to how the world actually works, Thomas." Maud sighed and hurried within to dress for dinner.

In the ensuing weeks they dined several times with the cardinal, and it became clear that he had no intention of rushing his decision. Abbess Marianne explained that the dowager countess Elizabeth smelled of money, and keeping court in Avignon was a costly enterprise, particularly since the English armies had destroyed the French crops and supplies must be ordered from afar. But that was not the only reason Cardinal Robert disliked King Edward of England. Four years earlier, Edward had arrested Robert's lawyer and expelled him from the realm in the midst of an important negotiation. It did not help the Earl of Salisbury's case that King Edward was said to favor his claim. The abbess advised that they avoid any contact with the dowager countess and prepare to be patient. Her advice proved sound.

The cardinal informed them that he would send lawyers under the protection of the papal seal to confer with Lady Joan and Dame Katarina—in spring. He helped the Hollands find more comfortable lodgings for the winter months.

Wales
AUTUMN–WINTER 1347–48

AT LEAST HE MIGHT HAVE PERMITTED HER THE PLEASURE OF RID-ing, but Will did not want Joan to see the terrain, so she spent her days in the stifling wagon with Helena and poor Jester. At night she gave Will the silent treatment, as he pouted and swore that he was only following the queen's orders. But worse was to come. For the last two days of the journey, Will insisted that Joan and Helena be blindfolded, with their hands and legs bound. They tossed about as the wooden wheels wobbled along a rough track, freed from their bonds only to relieve themselves and eat. They slept in the cart, bound, Jester in his openwork basket beside Joan, often whimpering in his sleep at the animal sounds outside. As Joan lay awake, she cycled through her list of those she counted responsible for this insult—the king and queen, Ned, Countess Catherine, Earl William, her mother,

Will—imagining fitting torments for them, even the dead earl. She hated them all, and yearned for Thomas. Helena tried to distract her with stories, songs, tales of her childhood home, but Joan paid little attention.

On the morning of the third day, Joan heard a lookout calling, the rattle and creak of a gate opening, and the echo of the horses' hooves as they entered a walled enclosure. The cart halted.

"Where is my lady?"

Joan had never been so grateful to hear Efa's voice.

Will was suddenly in the cart, hastily removing her blindfold, then her bonds. "Forgive me, Joan."

"Never." She spit in his face.

"God in heaven." Efa's eyes were wide with disbelief, her voice crackling as Will helped Joan down from the cart. "In what world does a lord treat his lady so?" She came round to support Joan while calling to the nearest man to free Helena from her bonds.

Leaning against her nurse, Joan breathed deep, taking in the high stone walls, the ramshackle buildings within them, and the square stone keep. Mother in heaven. As Jester's barking grew sharper, she stumbled over to the cart and grabbed his basket from one of Will's retainers. Setting it down on the ground, she opened it and scooped up the agitated terrier, speaking softly to him as he sniffed her and licked her face.

"Who is this wild creature?" Efa asked, holding out her hand so that he might sniff and approve, then rubbing him behind one ear.

"A gift from Prince Edward," said Will. He stepped back when Jester barked at him, avoiding eye contact with the three women.

"This is Jester," said Joan. "He is sweet and well behaved. Come, Efa. Show me my prison." She set Jester down on the ground and grasped Efa's arm for support before her legs gave way. The past few days had taken their toll, but she'd be damned if she'd let Will have the satisfaction of witnessing her weakness.

On the first level, a wild-haired man bowed to her. "My lady."

"This is Alf, our cook," said Efa. "We are blessed with him."

Up two levels of narrow stone steps they came out into a hall, the walls hung with tapestries from various Montagu properties, and furnished with high-backed chairs and benches brightened with colorful cushions, a trestle table set with food and drink, a brazier smoking nearby. There were four window embrasures, one in each wall, wider than arrow slits but letting in little light. Two menservants bowed to Joan, one proffering a goblet.

"Hot spiced wine," said Efa. "You need it."

"I must shed these filthy clothes and bathe before I eat or drink," Joan said. "Helena as well." In truth, she feared the wine would go straight to her head.

Efa led them up another level to a chamber in which stood a curtained bed and several smaller pallets, cushioned chairs, a few small tables, and a large wooden tub near a brightly burning brazier. There were four windows like the ones below.

Two young women who had been setting out soap and cloths by the tub straightened and bowed their heads, and were about to withdraw.

"Stay. You will wash Helena after she has assisted me with Lady Joan. Watch and learn," said Efa.

They crowded onto a small bench, watching Jester circle the room, exploring. Joan told one of them to go down to the hall and bring him a plate of meat and some water.

Undressing Joan, Efa tsked and sighed over the marks left on her wrists and ankles by the bonds and the bruises from the rough ride in the cart.

"Do not stir up my anger just now. Let me bathe in peace."

Joan stepped out of the pile of clothes on the floor and into the hot water, sinking down until her chin touched the warmth, her knees rising. She closed her eyes and succumbed to the ministrations of her women, feeling the knots ease under Efa's skillful hands. When she stepped out, the two young servants added the water that had been steaming on the brazier so that Helena might bathe while Efa took a comb to Joan's tangled wet hair. Jester, fed and watered, curled up at Joan's feet. "Bring our food up here, Efa. I cannot bear the sight of my jailer." If she was lucky, Will might drink enough to tumble down the stairs and break his neck.

Much later, as Joan lay in the soft, clean bed, she told Efa of the journey, shaking her head at any attempt to forgive Margaret's complicity, instead turning her mind to the men left behind, the horrors of the siege, her farewell dinner with Thomas and his mother. Curled up between Helena and Efa, with Jester draped over one of her feet, she slept then—a sound, dreamless sleep.

In the morning, Will sent a page to summon Joan to the hall. He was clean-shaven, dressed in a jacket she'd not seen before, quite elegant, blue velvet with yellow silk showing through the slashed sleeves. Plunder, she guessed.

"How beautiful you look this morning, my lady."

His look was soft, tender. Was this what it took for him to feel for her, an abduction? She turned back a sleeve to show him the bandage round her wrist.

"And this? Is this beautiful, my lord?"

He blushed. "I've brought you a gift." He nodded to a servant, who opened one of several chests stacked by the table. "Plunder from Calais." Will shook out a fine tapestry, proudly displaying it.

"It stinks of the funeral pyres. Put that back and take these chests to one of the outbuildings," Joan ordered the servants.

"Leave them. Take the tapestry into the yard and beat the

smoke out of it." Will invited Joan to sit and break her fast with him.

"I've already eaten. Was that all, my lord?"

"You've not yet recovered from the journey."

"Yet? Do you expect me to find contentment in my prison?" She turned to leave.

He grabbed her arm and pulled her to face him. "Sit with me while I eat, then."

"What will you do to me if I disobey? What is left? A beating?" She laughed at his frustration. "You humiliate me and then expect my cooperation?"

"All the way from Calais I carried those chests, for you! For you, damn it. And that's the thanks I get? One tapestry needs airing and you refuse it all? If you made half the effort I have to save our marriage—"

"Effort to save it? Any sympathy I felt for you in France was killed by my abduction."

"Sympathy? *Sympathy?* And how can it be an abduction? You're my wife!"

"You've never been more than half a man, spineless, cowering behind your mad mother's skirts. Go lie with your pretty page and leave me be." She managed to pull out of his grasp and rushed from the room.

Will departed the following day.

41

LATE WINTER–EARLY SPRING 1348

Cardinal Adhémar Robert at last interrogated Thomas, then paid him the courtesy of showing him letters he had prepared summoning Will and Joan, or their legal representatives, to Avignon for interviews. With a rumor of a terrible pestilence killing hundreds in Italy, Thomas sent his mother home in the company of the papal messenger, planning to remain in Avignon until the messenger returned with news. She had argued to stay, but Thomas assured her that the pope and the cardinals were doing all they could to close themselves off from the sickness. Strangers were questioned about their routes to the city, and those arriving from the east were turned back at the gates.

The papal messenger sent to England returned to Avignon in late March with the news that the Montagu family had sequestered Joan and forbidden her access to her own counsel. Hearing this in the presence of the cardinal, Thomas perforce contained himself, but only barely. Another messenger, who had been sent north with an apostolic brief addressed to the archbishop of Canterbury and the bishops of Norwich and London, reported that the curial investigation of Thomas's charges had also come to a standstill because of Lady Joan's silence.

Cardinal Robert shook his head at Thomas's desperation. He had seen all this before; it was nothing out of the ordinary.

She would be denied visitors and correspondence, nothing more threatening. A wife was, after all, the property of her husband. And it was reasonable that Will Montagu should consider Joan his wife until and unless the Pope ruled otherwise. But he promised to speak with His Holiness at once and, much to Thomas's surprise, the cardinal kept his word. Pope Clement himself dictated a letter to the three prelates enjoining them to ensure that Joan was able to appoint an attorney of her own. Over a farewell dinner, the cardinal warned Thomas not to place too much hope in a quick response.

"The dowager Montagu, Elizabeth, she has much wealth and the support of your king. She means to prolong this case until you have spent all your silver." He tapped the side of his nose. "But His Holiness has no affection for your king and respects you for your part in the Lithuanian Crusade. So do not despair."

Wales
LATE MARCH 1348

WILL GATHERED THE MEN GUARDING THE KEEP AND INSISTED THAT they give up the names of those who had let in a heavily pregnant woman from the village, now recovering from childbirth on a pallet in the kitchen. Two men stepped forward, one the king's man, one Will's. Both fathers, they admitted to coming to her aid, empathizing with her husband's desperate plea for Efa's help. They stood stoically as Will berated them.

Joan had asked Will to look the other way. After all, no harm had come to her. "For pity's sake, Will, you should be proud of them for showing mercy."

He had sneered and stormed out of the keep. Now he looked a fool, vaguely threatening them with censure, for if he replaced them, that was two who might reveal to the Hollands Joan's whereabouts.

Over dinner Will was conciliatory, asking after her health, for she looked pale.

"So would you had you spent the winter here, never permitted out beyond the walls."

He hardly looked better—perhaps a little broader in the chest since they'd parted in August, his face a bit more filled out, but his eyes were shadowed and she'd heard him asking Efa for a tincture to help him sleep.

"At least you are safe from the pestilence." He told her how it raged on the continent, the rumors that a ship had brought it to Portsmouth. "You are far north and away from the coasts."

It frightened her—Thomas was in Avignon, her mother right on the Thames. He had brought a letter from Margaret, but mentioned nothing about his grandmother Elizabeth, also in Avignon.

"Ned has a mistress, did you know?" Will added, watching Joan for a reaction. "And she is with child."

Joan wrinkled her nose at the news and told Will that she wished the bastard well. But in truth she was startled by the pain of hearing it. She had helped at the breech birth in the kitchen, watched the child come forth, wailing, the mother, depleted by the long, painful ordeal, weeping for joy as she took the infant to her breast. Joan wanted to experience that joy, a joy so far denied her. She was twenty years old, betrothed to Thomas for eight years, married to Will for seven, and yet childless.

"You are not so indifferent as you pretend to be," said Will. "Is it the prince or the baby you envy?"

She slapped him. He caught her hand and kissed it. He said that he would gladly plant a baby in her as soon as the pope decided whether he would raise the child. He would not risk having his child raised by a Holland, a family without honor—

the father a traitor, a daughter the longtime mistress of John Warrenne, Earl of Surrey, the current Lord Holland a rapist.

"Robert?"

"You'd not heard? He raped Sir Gerald Lisle's wife, Margery, while Prince Lionel was in the next room. The king has disinvited him from the St. George's Day tournament. And then, of course, there's your Thomas, seducing a girl of royal blood. No one believes you were a woman when he took you, Joan. He raped a child."

"He did not!"

"No child of mine will be raised by those dogs."

"Yet you tell me that King Edward has named Thomas and his brother Otho to the new order he is forming, the one you're so proud to be a part of. An order of dogs? What is it called—the order of the kennel, the order of the hounds?"

Will shrugged. "They fought valiantly at Caen and Crécy. The king needs them for his war."

"Perhaps not the order of the kennel, then. What is it called?"

His knuckles played a tattoo on the table. "The Order of the Garter."

She had him. Now she could twist the knife. "Your mother's garter again? How honored she must feel."

He slammed his palm on the table, upsetting a flagon of wine. A servant rushed forward to stop the flow before it ruined Joan's gown.

"It is not her garter. It never was."

"You saw His Grace in the pavilion that day, Will. Why do you think she took a vow of celibacy? To atone for cuckolding your father with the king."

With a curse, he strode out of the hall. She felt no joy listening to him stomp down the steps. She felt bruised. Empty.

❖ ❖ ❖

AT LONG LAST THOMAS HEADED HOME. HE'D LINGERED TOO LONG
in Avignon, but he had made good use of the time, learning
much about the dire conditions in France. King Edward might
look more favorably on one who brought such news. Perhaps in
exchange he might be persuaded to cease interfering in Joan's
life. But it was difficult not to despair.

After the pomp and splendor of the papal court, the countryside through which Thomas rode north seemed another
world—too quiet, too empty. Most inns were shuttered, and
though Thomas and his squire, Hugh, wore no livery and
spoke a simple traveler's language that most in the countryside could understand, they were met with suspicion. For who
indeed travelled when pestilence was abroad in the land but
mercenaries, thieves, and those who might carry the death with
them?

Farther north, past the present reach of the pestilence, he
saw little improvement in the conditions. This devastation was
the aftermath of the war, the demands of the French king, the
ravages of the English armies. He wondered whether King Edward would question his goal were he to see this, whether he
would choose to be satisfied with having brought France to this
pass.

By God's grace, several weeks after departing Avignon
Thomas reached Portsmouth in good health.

He rode to Upholland, the family estate in Lancashire,
which his mother meant to cede to him on his marriage. She'd
asked him to meet her there, advise her on how to make it welcoming for Joan. They were at dinner when Otho surprised
them, walking into the hall with boots and legs muddied, calling to a servant to fetch him a tankard of ale as he slumped into
a chair turned sideways at the table so that the servant could
remove his boots.

"What is amiss?" Maud's face was tense with a mother's
concern. "You look as if you've ridden hard to reach us."

"Lady Joan is not simply being forbidden visitors at Bisham as we'd thought. The Montagu bastard's abducted her and imprisoned her God only knows where, that's what's amiss."

Thomas's chair hit the rushes as he sprang from the table, shouting for his squire. "Montagu? When?"

"Sit!" Otho shook his head at Hugh, who'd appeared from the kitchen. "Hear me out, brother. They've been gone a long while, ever since she arrived at Portsmouth in late summer."

Otho drained his tankard, called for more. Maud insisted that he eat something before he was too drunk to finish his news. He skewered some cold meat on his knife.

Thomas got up to pace behind his brother. "Talk while you eat, damn it!" He kicked over a stool.

Otho leaned over to right it. "There's nothing more to say. Montagu is not staying with her, if that is any consolation."

"Where is the king now?"

"The Tower, I think."

"I'll go to London to see the lawyer, then I'll find the king. He will answer for this!"

"Thomas! Cool your head or you'll destroy us all," Maud commanded. "I'll come with you to London. We will stop at Bisham. Perhaps we'll learn something from Catherine Montagu."

"I doubt it," Otho muttered.

Thomas was grateful for the speed with which Maud organized the traveling party. They rode hard, arriving at Bisham late the following day. The Montagu family was not in residence, Countess Catherine already assisting the queen with preparations for the St. George's Day celebration. None of the servants would talk, but they offered the Hollands lodging for the night, and treated them with courtesy.

Unable to sleep, Thomas went out to the yard before dawn and found his mother already there, walking slowly back and forth as she fingered her amber paternoster.

"He won't harm her," she said in greeting. "That cannot have been his intention."

"I pray you are right, and that he is diligent in ensuring her safety. But he is weak and easily manipulated."

They rode out at first light.

Tower of London

THOMAS'S LONDON LANDLORD LEANED CLOSE, HIS GARLICKY BREATH reminding Thomas that he'd not eaten since before dawn. "There's been a messenger from the king. You're summoned to him at the White Tower as soon as may be. Your usual room?"

Thomas handed him his pack. "I trust I'll find all as it should be when I return."

The landlord bowed. "I will take it up myself, Sir Thomas."

In the Tower yard, Thomas came upon his old friend Sir Roland talking to Will Montagu. Roland stepped forward to greet Thomas, expressing his relief that Thomas was safe returned from the south, beating the plague.

"Avignon is a fortress against all threat, even pestilence," said Thomas. "Clement and his cardinals are certain God means for them to die peacefully in their sleep in their advanced years."

"A pity you wasted a magnificent ransom on a lost cause, Holland." Will Montagu smirked.

"You will not laugh for long, bastard!" Thomas grabbed the front of Will's jacket, popping buttons as he pulled him close. "Where is Joan? If you've harmed her!" He pushed him away, and as Will fought for balance Thomas's punches hit their marks with gratifying precision—the groin, the chin, the soft spot between the ribs. Will was down before Thomas worked up a sweat. "Get up. I've only begun." He regretted he'd not worn his sword, but that might have been too quick. Batter-

ing the swine was deeply satisfying. Will struggled to his feet.
Thomas grabbed him by the shoulders and sent him sprawling,
then began to dive after him.

A gloved hand prevented him. "Enough, Thomas," said Sir
Roland. "Though he deserves this and more, it's not worth angering the king. He'd not thank you for killing the son of his
late friend."

"Just look away."

"Even if I did, *he* wouldn't." Roland gestured toward
Prince Edward, who was approaching from the Tower, looking
amused. "That's not a friendly smile," Roland whispered. "And
I cannot believe it was just chance that he called Montagu to
meet him here on the day you arrived in London, summoned
by his father."

By now Will was standing, bleeding from the nose, his
upper lip split, and one eye beginning to close.

"Go wash your face, Montagu." Thomas had lost interest
in kicking the weakling. "You cannot lose Lady Joan, for you
never had her and you never will."

"Don't be so sure of your own hold on her, Holland," Will
mumbled, glancing at the prince.

The prince met Thomas halfway to the Tower.

"Well done, Holland. Would you like the satisfaction of finishing him off in the tilting yard on St. George's Day?"

Thomas controlled himself, declining the offer with the
courtesy due his prince, though he seethed inside.

"You disappoint me, Holland. I should have enjoyed the
spectacle. Go on. My father expects you."

Thomas wondered whether the prince had goaded Will
into abducting Joan. But he pushed down that thought as the
guards at the door of the king's parlor bowed him through.

The king indicated that Thomas should join him and
Bishop Edington at a table covered with a map weighted down
with carved figures much like chessmen.

"I've need of you, Holland. We're planning a delicate mission to Calais involving the Count of Flanders. You will take ship to Flanders directly after the St. George's Day tournament. Talk to the councils in Ghent and Ypres, find out what they say of the Count of Flanders's agreements with them. Then go among the nobles you've come to know, listening. I would know before I meet with him whether Louis is bargaining in good faith."

"Your Grace, there is the matter of Montagu's abduction of Lady Joan, your cousin. I cannot leave until I've found her."

"Rest assured, Holland. I've some of my own men mixed in with the young earl's. He knows that his life is forfeit if he harms her. And, man to man, do you—"

"He already has harmed her, Your Grace!"

The king's eyes burned into him. "I am not finished."

"Forgive me, Your Grace."

"Your brother Otho will accompany you. You'll sail from Sandwich. Edington will brief you. You will be in Calais with your report when I arrive there after Michaelmas."

"But, Your Grace—"

"Sheathe your sword, Holland. Do not make me change my mind about honoring you and Otho as founding members of my new order. Will Montagu is also to be a member. Comrades-in-arms do not kill each other."

Thomas choked back a protest and bowed. "I am honored, Your Grace." Bringing shame on his family was not the way to win his place as Joan's husband.

"By the time you return from Calais, you should know Pope Clement's decision. I promise you I will stand by his ruling." Edward rose, nodding to the two as they stood and bowed. He told a servant to bring wine for the men, and some food. "They've work ahead of them."

It was dusk when Thomas left the Tower. Roland waited for him.

"Let's drink to old times, eh?"

Thomas took a deep breath, swallowing his anger. "I know just the place."

ROLAND SET DOWN HIS TANKARD, WIPING HIS MOUTH ON HIS SLEEVE while looking around the ground floor of the tavern. "So this is where you hide when in London. Good ale among strangers." He nodded approvingly.

"Not all strangers. The king knew to send a messenger here."

"I'm not surprised, nor should you be. Let me be the first to congratulate you on being chosen for the Order of the Garter."

"The garter? He's using the emblem we fought under in Normandy? Countess Catherine's—" Thomas broke off with a curse as Roland elbowed him in the ribs.

"Her name is not to be mentioned in connection with this. You could be accused of treason if overheard linking the two." He leaned closer. "Our king has never strayed from his beloved queen."

"The king baits us with this garter emblem. Once in our cups, we'll all prove traitors."

"Few know the story."

Thomas corrected him. The story was popular in France, though their version was that the countess lost it while dancing and the king quickly stepped forward, saving her embarrassment by taking up the garter and buckling it round his leg, daring anyone to question *his* honor. "It's meant as a slur on King Edward."

Roland had grown somber. "So this is his way of defying them. I see why he calls it treason."

Thomas motioned for the innkeeper to fill their tankards. This self-righteousness did not suit him. He thanked his old friend for reminding him of the honor the king had bestowed on him. "As Joan's guardian, he could by rights have exiled me, but instead he exalts me." He raised his tankard. "To King Edward and his Knights of the Garter."

Roland laughed. "I'm the one to say that, toasting you."

Ah, it felt good to laugh. "And I toast you, my savior. You stayed my hand when I would have ended the life of a fellow Garter Knight." If he said it enough, the word "garter" would cease to have such a significance. Garter Knight. His mother would be proud to watch two of her sons ride out in that celebrated company. He drained his tankard and called for more.

Westminster

COUNTESS MARGARET RECEIVED THOMAS OUT IN THE GARDEN, shading her eyes as she watched him approach. He extended his hand and smiled, determined to be a model of courtesy even to her, the woman so much to blame for this unholy mess. They exchanged greetings, she asking about his journey as she motioned him to a chair. While a servant poured wine, he described his passage through a France laid waste by war and pestilence.

"God help us." Margaret fingered the gold chain at her throat.

"Is Joan near the coasts? In the south or east?"

The simple questions roused a wariness. "Why?"

He began to laugh, but stopped himself. "Of course I want to know where Joan is, but I do not expect you to tell me, so I ask only this. If she is in the north, northwest I will leave her in peace, in safety."

"Safe from whom?"

"Not from whom, from what. The pestilence. It comes by ship."

"God have mercy." She turned to look out on the Thames at the bottom of the garden. "Surely not here?"

"Of course here, my lady."

She met his gaze. "I have reason to believe she's in the north, but I am not certain."

"Who knows?"

"Only Catherine and Will Montagu, as well as the retainers who guard her. A dozen of them. I am sorry, Sir Thomas."

"Call me Thomas. You call him Will."

"We are all on your side, Thomas—Efa, Katarina Van Artevelde, even Blanche Wake. She's incensed by Will's dishonorable behavior and has pledged to assist Joan with legal aid and more. After St. George's Day, she intends to send out a troop of men to search for Joan. Would you lead them?"

"She would do this?" There was a hint of Joan in her mother's smile. "I wish I could lead that search." He told her of the king's orders. "I suggest my brother Alan."

"Introduce me to him at the St. George's Day tournament." Margaret put her hand on his. "We will find her and ascertain her safety, Thomas. I promise you."

"I did not expect this."

"I pray that someday you and my daughter will forgive my error in ignoring your vows."

In her mind she had but erred, no more—he heard that in her voice. She had dishonored her daughter with a fraudulent marriage, kept her from her rightful husband for seven years, robbed them of happiness, cost Thomas a fortune in ransoms, and she called it merely an error. He did not trust himself to answer. He asked instead about Prince Edward's feelings toward Joan. "He takes more than a cousinly interest in your daughter."

"What has he done now?"

A most telling response. "I have been warned about his feelings toward Joan."

She looked away from him, fussing with a cup of wine, shielding her eyes against the sun as she gazed out on the water. Just when he'd given up hope of an answer and began to rise she said, "He has loved her from the moment he was aware of her as a child. He decided then that she would be his queen. As far as I know, he has never wavered in that intent. Nor have his parents wavered in their determination to prevent it. That is why Joan was summoned to Antwerp. It is why she is now hidden away—he paid her too much court in Calais. He is not her choice, Thomas. You do know that?"

"He loves her, yet does her so much harm."

"He does not see it that way. In that, he is much as you were in Ghent."

"I see you still blame me."

"You were far the elder."

Thomas rose and bowed, thanking her for the information, promising to bring Alan to her during the coming festivities. Clearly, to the countess he was but the lesser of the evils now. She had not yet forgiven him. It was good to know.

Windsor, St. George's Day

ARMOR, BANNERS, SADDLES, LONG ROLLS OF COLORFUL CLOTH FOR additional pavilions—Thomas watched the burdened servants, pages, and squires stumbling by his tent while Hugh and a page helped strap and buckle him into his armor. Alan lounged on a cot while Otho paced, already fully dressed and unable to sit. Raoul de Brienne shared their pavilion. He was still a prisoner of war but had been invited to participate in the tourney scheduled for the following day. King Edward liked to show off the highest-ranking prisoners and enjoy their company.

"Is that your handiwork on Montagu?" Raoul asked as Will

stopped at the pavilion across the way to greet a friend, who loudly teased him about his bruised and swollen face.

Thomas admitted that it was.

"Good. You've satisfied your honor. You do not need to knock him from his horse here."

"I declined the prince's offer."

"He ignored you."

Thomas thanked Hugh and his page and waved them off.

"The prince wants him publicly humiliated?" he asked Raoul when they were alone.

"He means to ensnare you, my friend. He knows His Grace will withdraw your and your brother's name from the order's roster should you attack young Montagu again."

"Then they should not pair us in the lists."

"It does not matter, Thomas."

"How do you know this?"

"It is surprising what my jailers discuss in my hearing. The prince is as feared as he is admired. He has a mistress, and she is pregnant, had you heard? But do not think for a moment that means he no longer intends your lady to be his queen. He means to rid himself of both you and Montagu. Perhaps in one brief joust."

"Both opponents die in a joust? Has that ever happened?"

"I did not mean either of you would die. The prince intends for Montagu to fall from his horse, and you're to be blamed. If it looks as if you defied the king's order in public and thus dishonored yourself, you would not likely find anyone coming to your defense should your king refuse your claim to his cousin."

Thomas cursed. "Someone else once warned me to beware the prince. I did not believe her."

"Your lady warned you?"

"No. Not Joan. She and the prince are good friends. Cousins."

A knowing look. "Surely she knows he would be more to

her, Thomas, yet it is said that in Calais she accepted lavish gifts from him and was often by his side."

"I know all this."

"Good. But I do not sense that you find this troubling, as I do. I do not like to question her sincerity, yet . . ."

"My lady is true. I would stake my life on it. The prince is another matter." Thomas called for Hugh, told him to find Will's squire and warn him to check all straps and buckles on his lord's horse and armor.

Hours later, Thomas heard that the young Earl of Salisbury would appear late in the jousting; he awaited a replacement for a damaged saddle. So it was true. The prince would do this for love of his cousin.

At the feast following the jousts, Will Montagu lifted his cup to Thomas and toasted his honor. "We have a common enemy."

It seemed they did.

42

Northeast Wales

A bank of gray clouds hid the sunshine that had drawn Joan out into the yard for a walk, Jester madly dashing about, scattering the chickens and goats. She'd grown accustomed to sudden shifts in the weather when in the yard, the high walls obscuring the broad view that warned of impending change. She saved this as another point to throw at Will in a few weeks, his first visit since March. Helena had just noted the scent of rain in the air when the clouds burst apart and pelted them with hailstones. Jasper ran yelping into the keep, and they hurried after him. In the kitchen, the cook's maid dried Jester while Joan warmed herself by the hearth, steam rising from her gown.

"I have something for you, my lady." Alf, the cook, slipped her a small sealed letter as he added a piece of wood to the fire. "I found it in the sack of beans that came this morning." He winked.

It was not Will's seal. Joan turned it round in her hands, trying to make out the curling, vinelike design while she steeled herself for disappointment. Footsteps forced her to tuck it away, just in time, as Will's man Dorn appeared, demanding a hot drink from Alf while glaring at Jester, who barked when any of the retainers invaded the keep.

"God's blood, it's cold for summer." Dorn eyed Helena, stirring something over the fire. "What's that?"

"A soothing tisane for my lady's flux. Would you care for some?" She laughed as he grabbed the bowl Alf handed him and took it out into the stairwell.

Turning her back to the doorway, Joan opened the note with trembling hands. Was it possible? Alan Holland was in the village just beyond, hidden by the families of those serving here. God be thanked for Efa's healing skill. She'd cured Alf's daughter's wasting sickness, set broken bones, eased palsy tremors, healed a number of agues and infections, and safely delivered a breech baby. Now they repaid the kindness.

Alan inquired whether she was comfortable enough to stay there until late October, when the risk of pestilence eased, and suggested that they work on a distraction during which they might slip away. Joan smiled. As children, she and Ned had devised myriad devious scenarios. It was merely a matter of remembering and choosing the right one. Efa could also be counted on to come up with a clever scheme. Joan's heart raced. It was good to feel so alive.

"Is there aught you need in tomorrow's delivery, my lady?" Alf asked. "I will pass it on to my brother tonight."

"I have all that I need for the moment. But what of your other brother? You've said nothing of him for a long while. Is he away?"

The glint of mischief in the cook's eyes warmed her as he promised to tell her about his elder brother's latest adventure. The servants disliked Will and his men and enjoyed outwitting them. And, indeed, the following day she learned of Thomas's mission to Flanders. Will's shortsightedness in counting the country folk simple had proved a blessing. Now she knew that Thomas was alive; he had escaped the pestilence in Avignon. She thought she could bear anything now that she knew that her beloved was safe.

❖ ❖ ❖

EFA HAD ADVISED JOAN TO MAKE PEACE WITH WILL SO THAT HE HAD
no reason to complicate their plans with heightened security.
But he arrived under a dark cloud.

"We will dine in a short while. You will wear your best
gown."

He settled in a chair by the brazier, shouting for his page to
remove his boots and bring him a brandywine, then prepare a
bath for him in the kitchen. When he saw Joan still standing in
the doorway, he said that he, too, intended to dress for dinner.
The hollows in his cheeks had filled out, as had his body. He'd
gained muscle, and a sharp confidence in the six months since
she'd last seen him, as well as some new battle scars. Joan hur-
riedly withdrew, uneasy about this transformation.

Over dinner Will said little, answering her questions as
briefly as possible. She'd learned in the letters he'd brought from
Margaret that the pestilence had spread across the south and the
roads were lawless, inns closed. It was not safe to travel. Joan
asked Will about the sickness— how it manifested, how he was
protecting himself.

"Ask Efa. I heard her talking to my squire."

He commented that Joan was paler and thinner than he had
ever seen her. She said that with no exercise she had little appetite.

"Take care of yourself." He made it a command. "I don't
want to be ashamed when I bring you back to court."

Joan did not know this man sitting across from her. He
sounded nothing like Will. Cautious, she turned the conversation around, asking about his broken nose.

"Holland broke it. He threw himself at me in the Tower
yard. He meant to finish me at the St. George's Day tournament, then changed his mind, warning my squire that he'd cut
my saddle strap. Your honorable Holland."

The bite of his anger began to frighten Joan. "Why would Thomas do something so cowardly after openly attacking you?"

"How sweetly you jump to his defense. He blamed the prince—that he'd ordered the strap cut so it would not hold." Will suddenly rose and grabbed her wrist, pulling her off her seat.

"Will, you're hurting me."

"Is that what you want—I die in the jousts and Thomas is accused of my murder? Are you using the two of us to stoke the prince's passion?"

"No! I love Thomas." She gasped as he tightened his hold, then suddenly twisted her hand behind her back. "My wrist!" Joan sobbed in agony.

"My lord—" Efa rushed over, reaching for Joan.

Will shoved her away. "Be gone, witch!" He ordered Dorn to take Efa down to the kitchen and hold her there, and told the other servants in the hall to follow. "The moment the prince feels free to make you his queen, Holland and I are dead."

Cradling her wrist, Joan tried to leave the table, but Will pressed down on her shoulders, pinning her to the bench.

Letting go with one hand, he reached over her for her brandywine and drained the cup, tossing it away. He'd already had far too much, and in his bellicose mood, with this new strength, Joan dared not move. He kneaded her shoulder, leaned down to whisper in her ear as he slipped his hand inside her bodice, cupping her breast, "It is time you made all my trouble worthwhile, wife. It's time you bore me a child of royal blood." His breath was hot on her neck and sickly sweet. He shouted to his page to get the women out of the bedchamber above, then lifted Joan from the bench.

She tried to fight him, but the jolt of pain from her injured wrist made her dizzy, disoriented. "Put me down, Will," she implored as he lurched against the doorframe. "Let me walk up the steps. I'll walk up the steps, I swear."

He swore and righted himself, and though he was breathing

hard and his heart wildly pumping, he made it up the winding steps without stumbling again. In the chamber he threw her on the bed, tearing at her gown, her chemise, slapping her face when she begged him to be gentle, rolling her on her back to sit on her, pinning her injured wrist beneath her. She was weeping uncontrollably by the time he took her, with a violence that tore into her very being.

Where is your prince now? Who will save you now? You belong to me. I have the right to beat you into submission. You are my wife. My chattel. My creature. How dare you turn my prince against me?

For a moment, he lay atop her, spent, breathing heavily. Then he rolled off her. "Pah. You've bled all over me, you bitch." He slapped her face, smearing her with her own blood. "I thought he'd had you."

She pressed her eyes closed, praying to die. She kept praying as he clattered down the steps, shouting for another bath to clean off the bitch's blood.

"My lady, open your eyes, look at me."

Joan shook her head, turning away.

Whispering something in Welsh, Efa gently cleaned Joan's face with a moist cloth that smelled of lavender.

"If the pope decides in that monster's favor, I will kill myself," Joan whispered.

Efa kept washing. "The Blessed Mother watches over you, my child. She brought your flow so that his seed has no purchase. She will not abandon you to such as he. Now come, let me clean you and examine your wrist, rub salve into your bruises."

"Why didn't I think to take his knife?"

"He'd left it on the table," said Efa. "Look into my eyes, my lady."

"But I didn't even think to feel for it. Did I want this?"

"Open your eyes and look at me."

Joan obeyed.

"You are God's beloved Joan. This act of violence does not

change that. Hear this, my lady. Take it in, tuck it into your heart. Your soul is untouched by Will Montagu's bestial act. It is his own soul that now holds the seed of corruption that will grow, spread, maim him. Rest now, my lady, dream of Thomas, and your love for him."

Joan woke to the sound of Will calling to his men.

"It is dawn, my lady. He is departing." Helena sat up, checking the bandage that stabilized Joan's sprained wrist. "Is the pain still dulled?"

Her wrist throbbed, but it was bearable. It was the other pain, deep within, that sucked the breath from her. "I want to sleep. Help me sleep." Joan did not want to think yet; she did not want to touch the darkness. Helena helped her sit up to drink something sweet with honey.

"You must get up and move, my lady," Efa counseled the next time Joan woke. "You must strengthen yourself for your escape."

Joan found she could do that; she could set her mind on seizing her freedom from the Montagus. Each day, as she took her exercise in the yard with Efa and Helena, she engaged Will's men, talked to them about the pestilence her mother had written about—the painful swellings, the fever, the speed with which it had spread across Italy and France, how it moved up the waterways and along the coasts. It was said to have made land in Portsmouth and to be moving up into the West Country. Did they fear it? By now, she knew from the servants that she was in Mold Castle. Might the pestilence make it so far north? Always her conversation was about the plague, so that it obsessed the men, wormed its way into every part of their minds and hearts, just as her hatred for Will Montagu threatened to poison her.

Every night Efa massaged Joan's body, whispering Welsh charms, pressing the poison from her, stirring her love for Thomas, her determination to be with him.

"But what if the pope decides in Will's favor?"

"At worst, you could take the veil. At best, you and Thomas make a life across the Channel."

Joan began to believe that she would prevail.

In October, one of the guards fell from his horse in a storm. Though he suffered multiple injuries, including a broken leg and a gash in his shoulder, he refused Efa's help, believing her to be a witch. As his wound festered and his fever rose, the other guards abandoned him in the yard for fear he carried the pestilence. They no longer came in to walk the walls.

Desperate, the injured guard finally accepted Efa's ministrations, and as he healed he told Joan all she needed to know about the other guards' habits and fears, and the lay of the land to the west.

In late October, they were ready. A villager ingested Efa's tincture of angelica, mint, feverwort, and rosemary, and when his sweat was sufficient to soak through his shirt he stumbled to the gates of the keep, crying out for Efa. As he pounded on the gate the guards stayed back, not daring to touch him. Efa and Alf opened the gate and let him in. A day later, two more villagers arrived and were taken in. By nightfall on All Hallows Eve, the guards had fallen back to the farmhouse in which they bunked, and with much shrieking and clatter the villagers went about scaring away the demons, covering the sound of Joan's escape with Efa, Helena, and the crippled guard. She brought nothing with her but Jester in his basket. Beyond the village, Alan Holland waited with horses.

Cumberland
AUTUMN–WINTER 1348–49

MARGARET AND THE WAKES HAD WITHDRAWN TO HER BROTHER'S northernmost manor to flee the pestilence, and it was there that Alan brought Joan. Through chill rains and a first snow they

rode, Alan and four of Thomas Wake's armed retainers surrounding the three women and the injured guard, intimidating
farmers to allow them shelter in barns on the nights they found
no abbey or inn. Having done no riding for more than a year,
all three women found the first days difficult, but they refused
Alan's offer to commandeer a cart that would slow their pace.
Joan would have galloped all the way but for the muddy roads
being too dangerous for horses at such speed. It was impossible
that Will could be in pursuit, but she could not shake the fear.

Curled into their hoods as they rode, there was little conversation until they stopped for the night, but it was enough to
bring Joan close to Alan, who enjoyed telling her stories about
Thomas in his youth, as well as family legends. He befriended
Jester and often rode with him enfolded in his cloak to give Joan
more ease in the saddle, knowing that her injured wrist ached
with the jostling as well as with the cold and damp.

The snow had turned to a bone-chilling sleet the day they
rode into her uncle's yard, and Margaret swept Joan into the
hall before she said a word, rushing her to a bedchamber where
she was stripped of her wet clothes and tucked into a bed soon
warmed by hot stones. Held in her mother's arms, Joan wanted
to feel safe. But this woman who now expressed such remorse
for obeying the king might do so again. It was up to Joan to
defend herself.

Alan stayed with them for a week, winning over the Wakes
and her mother as a considerate guest always ready to lend a
hand, a good listener, an entertaining storyteller. He was a man
easy in himself, with little ambition and seemingly none of the
sense of responsibility to restore his family's honor that was such
a foundation of Thomas's character. Joan's gratitude toward him
only deepened as she heard of the death toll from the pestilence
in the West Country through August and September—villages
where almost everyone died, the few survivors left half-mad
and wandering the countryside for food and shelter, towns far-

ing little better. Not even the royal family had been spared, her uncle told her. She grieved to hear that Princess Joan had died of the pestilence on her way to wed the heir to the throne of Castile, and the infant William, born in summer, had succumbed to the pestilence in a matter of months. Alan had risked far more than the king's censure to rescue her.

When Alan took his leave, Joan handed him two letters— one for Thomas, which said nothing of Will's attack, for she did not want to give King Edward any cause to deny the Hollands the honor of being Knights of the Garter, and one for Lucienne to put in Bella's hands, in which she provided all the horrible details. Joan counted on Bella to share it with Ned. She wanted him to know what Will had done. Only Ned could punish Will with impunity; only he could ensure that Will would never again feel safe. And turning him so completely and irrevocably against Will was the best revenge she could devise at present. Alan promised that he would leave it to her to tell Thomas of the incident.

She stood on the threshold of her uncle's hall, watching Alan disappear into a wintry mist, praying for his safe arrival at the royal court.

In April Joan, Margaret, and the Wakes headed south from Cumberland. King Edward had sent messengers to all the corners of his realm summoning the nobility to Windsor for St. George's Day, when they would celebrate the first gathering of the Order of the Garter. All were challenged to defy the pestilence for the honor and glory of the great realm of England, but in truth they were honor-bound to obey the summons of their liege lord. Margaret expressed outrage at his callousness in risking so many lives. *Is it so different from war?* Joan wondered. But the news cheered her. She could not wait to see Thomas.

First they would spend a week in Westminster, where Joan

would meet with Magister Vyse, the lawyer who was to record her testimony and present it to the papal legate. Her aunt had chosen him as a man who could be trusted to represent Joan's interests rather than making a name for himself or pleasing the king. Joan was eager to be heard.

They kept a brisk pace, pausing only briefly during the day to rest, eat a little, and relieve themselves, stopping at night in religious houses where they were expected, though not necessarily welcome. Lay brothers and sisters covered their mouths and noses with cloth and wore gloves to serve them, and the abbots and abbesses kept their distance when greeting them, fearful of the poisonous miasma that carried the pestilence. They rode past villages in which the only signs of life were animals abandoned and left to roam, found streams befouled by plague corpses, gagged on smoke from funeral pyres when the wind was in their direction. Joan felt as if she were back in Calais, only this time she was among the besieged. She rejoiced when they left the land on the last day of the journey to travel down the Thames by barge. The pestilence had cured Joan of her fear of traveling by water.

The house in Westminster felt forlorn, dusty and cold. Joan freed Jester to explore the echoing rooms as the servants set to work cleaning and lighting fires, but he chose to stay close to her. Walking out the following morning to the office of Magister Vyse, she found the streets largely deserted. The lawyer said the royal family had spent the months since the Christmas and New Year's revels at Kings Langley and most of the government had been shut down since the plague gained ground in late summer of the previous year. Now that it was so empty, he thought it quite the safest place to be. But he warned them not to go east to London, which was as crowded as ever.

He asked Joan to give her testimony regarding her betrothal and her night with Thomas in her own words, his clerks bending to the task of recording all that she said, the scratching of their quills an arrhythmic accompaniment to her embarrassingly explicit account. When she had finished, the magister asked thoughtful questions about the weeks leading up to the betrothal, the situation with Albret, the friendship of the Van Arteveldes, the betrothal and marriage to Will on her return to England, and, most recently, her incarceration at Mold and Will's attack. He apologized for pressing her for details, assuring her that he appreciated how uncomfortable it must be to relive it all.

Lady Margaret listened with head bowed, twisting a sachet of spices in her hands.

When at last the magister declared that he had all he needed, Joan thanked him. "As painful as it has been, I am relieved that at last I've been truly heard."

He warned her that it was only a step, that the case was far from resolved. "It's true that the marriage to Montagu would never have stood a chance in an objective court of law, but the papal court—" He shook his head. "Rome, Avignon, the corruption is the same. And, considering it was all done with the blessing of King Edward and your mother, the outcome is hardly certain. All I can do is present the truth and trust that someone respects the law."

His words dampened the hope with which she'd met the day. But she gave him a strong handshake. "One way or another, I will be free of him."

Vyse squinted at her as if wondering whether she had heard him, then shrugged and wished her good day.

43

Windsor

The lower ward was waking up, servants carrying poles and fabric for the pavilions that would house the Garter Knights and their entourages, others carting blue-and-silver pennants, trestles, wooden slabs, and benches to prepare the great hall for the celebratory feast. Joan climbed the tower stairs up to the battlements, eager to breathe the fresh air aloft. Even out in the castle yard, juniper fires burned to push back pestilential vapors. But the queen's quarters were far worse, the smoke so thick it burned her eyes and raked her throat, snaking up to coil round the roof beams, glowering down on the subdued courtiers, a constant reminder of the pestilence closing its deadly fist around the kingdom. Through the night Joan and her mother had sipped honeyed water to ease their coughs. No wonder the queen's ladies spoke in hoarse whispers their litanies of the plague dead and the debauchery inspired by the fear that the pestilence signaled the end of days—public copulation, wild dancing until dawn.

Joan had arrived bristling with righteous anger, ready for a battle with her royal cousins if they dared to challenge her escape. But the queen was a pinched and pale presence, still deeply in mourning for the two children she'd lost to the plague the previous summer. Ned had not yet arrived, but Bella had assured Joan of the success of her letter. At the New Year's joust, Ned had knocked Will off his horse. "A broken leg, a shoulder out of joint, and a broken wrist—he was carried from the field in intense pain." Bella licked her lips. "Ned outdid himself." And the king—Bella had not spared him the details of what Joan had suffered from Will, but Edward had merely admonished him to treat her with the respect that was her due as his wife and a woman of royal blood. As for Will's legal support, Philippa had handed that over to Isabella, the dowager queen.

"God help us," Margaret had whispered when Joan recounted the news. "Let me go to her. I once knew her well."

Joan refused the offer. "I will not subject you to that woman." But she'd not yet gathered the courage to confront Isabella herself.

Up on the battlements she looked down at a heartening view, the hustle and bustle of folk milling round, the beautiful multicolored pavilions, the long lines of travelers waiting to enter the gate, horses pawing the ground, people dismounting to greet friends, dogs nosing about. And already newcomers crowded the lower ward. Had she missed Thomas's arrival? Leaning farther over, Joan scoured the crowd immediately below. Her heart skipped a beat—Lady Maud looked up, raising a gloved hand in greeting. As Joan let go to wave back, someone caught her by the waist and kissed her neck.

"Thomas!" she turned in his arms and hugged him hard. "Oh, my love. I prayed and prayed the pestilence had not reached Lincolnshire."

They kissed and stepped apart, drinking each other in. Joan forgot everything in the joy of the reunion.

"God bless Alan. I would not be here were it not for him."

Pain flitted across Thomas's scarred face. He bowed his head. "The pestilence has taken my brother."

"Alan? But was he not with you?"

"With Lucienne, at her daughter's in Sussex. Lucienne,

Alan, her son-in-law, several of her grandchildren—they are all dead."

"Mother in heaven, I sent him to her with a letter for Bella. I thought Lucienne would be at court."

"You sent him the first time. He left her, then returned after delivering your letters to the princess and to me. He gave her the love I couldn't. They both had joy in the end. I pray it was enough for a lifetime. But it is not your fault." He kissed her hand.

"Lucienne and Alan." Joan crossed herself and bowed her head. "God grant them peace. They were so good to us."

Thomas lifted her chin, kissed her forehead. "We owe it to them to ensure that we are together."

"Yes."

"And you, my love? What is your news from Magister Vyse?"

She told him, wishing it were more hopeful, but he did not seem surprised. "We have formidable earthly opponents. But we have God on our side. Still, we must have a care. Come. We are too visible up here."

As she led him back down into the crowded ward, they planned how she would join him in his pavilion that night.

Otho waited for them at the bottom. Lady Maud had been taken away by Joan's mother. "And we must see to our pavilion, eh, Thomas?" Otho kissed Joan's hand. "You will forgive me, but we have much to do."

Joan urged Thomas to go. "I will find you later, and we can talk." She pushed through the crowd to St. George's Chapel, lighting candles at the Lady altar for Alan and Lucienne. A long time she knelt before the Blessed Mother, remembering two loving souls. When she rose, she was ready to seek out the she-wolf in her den, feeling Lucienne and Alan at her back, guiding her forward.

❖ ❖ ❖

OTHO HAD LOCATED WILL MONTAGU'S PAVILION. "HE'S JUST ARrived with his men. They are setting up on the far edge. I have one of our men watching."

Thomas nodded. "Come along, then."

ISABELLA SWEPT TOWARD HER, THE SILVER EMBROIDERY ON HER dark blue gown shimmering in the candlelight that enhanced the pale sunlight coming through the window at her back. Her grace belied her age, the lines around her eyes and mouth visible only as she reached for Joan's hands.

Joan tucked her hands behind her back and bowed. "Thank you for seeing me, my lady."

Isabella ignored the slight, nodding to a servant and gesturing to Joan to sit.

Refusing the servant's offer of wine, Joan chose a seat by the unshuttered window, grateful for fresh air. The dowager queen apparently saw no need for the juniper fires.

But as Isabella took a seat near Joan she held a spice ball to her nose. She was not so confident. "I know of your letter to Bella. It was clever of you, knowing that she would share it with my grandson. You meant it to be the catalyst for his humiliation of Will Montagu." She leveled her gaze at Joan. "Such a public attack. I cannot have this, Joan. Such fighting among the Garter Knights demeans my son's order."

"I have no control over Ned."

Isabella laughed softly. "You have only to curl your finger and he comes to your side. It has always been so. Perhaps it is my fault. It was my astrologer who named you his queen." She tilted her head, studying Joan. "You sit there, judging me. You. All I've done, I've done for the realm. You care for nothing but your own comfort."

"You had my father executed for loyalty to his brother, the anointed king."

"Your father changed course with the wind, Joan. He could not be trusted. Even so, I did not approve his execution."

"I don't believe you."

A shrug. "Not long ago I met Arnaud Amanieu, the husband my son intended for you. He is a handsome young man, gentle where his father is brusque, a poet of life. I think you would have loved him well. It is a pity you let such a ragtag group deceive you—the common Van Arteveldes, the trollop Lucienne Townley, and her lover, the sly Holland." Her lip curled over their names. "Bernardo Ezi was enchanted by your blossoming womanhood, no more. He never sought to deflower you. Such a pity. All this suffering you caused, for yourself, Montagu, my son, even the Hollands—to spend Eu's ransom on you rather than shoring up their lordship—such a waste."

Mother in heaven, she knew just where the blade went deep. "What is done is done," Joan said, the words sounding sharper than she'd intended. "I want you to withdraw your lawyers and order the Montagu lawyers to stand down as well."

A surprised laugh. "Why should I? How would this benefit the Crown?"

"If Will wins, I will fight against those vows as I've done for eight years. And Ned will think he need only bide his time to have me. But if Thomas wins I will happily disappear from court. Ned will forget me."

"Oh, my dear Joan, is this what you bring to the table? It is nothing. My grandson may yearn for you all he wants. But, when the time comes, he will wed whom the king chooses."

"He's avoided that so far."

"You're arrogant like your father, and as much a fool," said Isabella with a silken shrug. "I am no friend to the Montagus, it is true. But you risk much in asking for my help. If His Holiness should learn that I supported you, he would choose Montagu simply to spite me. He blames me for my son's war with France." Her smile was cutting.

"How is he to know who withdrew the lawyers, my lady? If done discreetly . . ."

"What is done is done, as you said. Withdrawing at this late date would serve little purpose, except to make us look weak—and that, my dear girl, would not do. We are at war, after all. Have you been too busy with your romantic entanglements to notice?" Isabella rose, forcing Joan to do so as well. "It was good of you to visit me. I hope you enjoy the festivities." This time she did not extend her hand, but turned to talk to her lady's maid.

Joan was shaking when she stepped out into the busy ward, her confidence in her purpose utterly undone.

THE NOISE AND CHAOS OF THE CROWD MADE IT EASY TO SEPARATE Will Montagu from his men. Otho came up behind him, Thomas grabbed Will's shoulders and pulled him round, slamming him back against the tower's uneven stones. Will's felt hat gave little protection to his skull as it made contact. Thomas took an unholy pleasure in the sound. Cursing, Will fumbled for his sword, but Thomas was there first. He pulled it from its sheath and pressed it to Will's neck.

"I'll say this once, Montagu. Touch Joan again and you die. Do you hear me?"

Will reached for the knife, but Otho had removed it. He dangled it in Will's face.

"And if the pope decides in my favor?"

Thomas pressed the sword into Will's windpipe. "You will suffer a fatal accident. Call off your lawyers. Quietly. No hue and cry, or I will finish this."

"If harm comes to me—" By now Will was shaking and soaked in sweat.

"You drink too much. Everyone knows it. You'll reek of brandywine." Thomas slammed Will against the stones one more time. "Meanwhile, do not touch her." He forced himself to let go of Will while there was yet life in him. The coward sank to the ground, pissing himself. Thomas nodded to Otho. They strode off with Will's weapons, dropping them in one of the horse troughs.

Otho laughed. "That's how to deal with swine."

Thomas spit on the ground. "Not a word to Joan. Alan swore not to tell me."

"Pray God he was shriven before he died."

"God would understand. What that bastard did—" Thomas clenched his fists.

Otho put an arm round him. "You showed remarkable restraint. Now for some ale to cool you down."

CROSSING THE GREAT HALL, DODGING LADDERS AND STEPPING OUT OF the way of overburdened servants, Joan was almost upon Ned and his ten-year-old brother, Lionel, before she saw them, their heads close as they tried to converse in the chaos. What a fine boy Lionel was—dark-haired, olive-skinned, with soft gray eyes, a wide mouth, and a laugh that rang in the rafters. She'd not seen someone so happy in many a day. Ned ruffled his brother's hair, amused, but never so carefree as Lionel, always checking to see who watched, to whom he was playing. His sweep of the room almost caught her. In no frame of mind to talk to them, Joan backed up, looking round for a quick exit.

"Come!" Bella startled Joan, taking her hand. "We're going to ride to the river. Master Adam says the wind is fresh today, we need not fear."

Joan shook her head. "I don't think—"

"You've been with Grandam. You need this more than any of us. Come!"

She pulled Joan toward her brothers, calling out to Ned. He glanced over, a smile forming, quickly turning to a frown. He bent to say something to his brother, who took a step back as if not believing what he'd heard.

"But the ride was your idea," Lionel was saying.

"Ned! Look who's joining us." Bella held tight to Joan's arm. "Fresh from Grandam's torture chamber. I don't know what she said, but look how pale our cousin is."

Ned studied Joan's face. "What did she want with you, cousin?"

"*I* begged an audience. Your mother handed the matter of my marriage over to the dowager queen, and I'd hoped—" Joan brushed it away. "I do not want to think about it now. I understand that I owe you a debt of gratitude for seeing to Will." She touched his arm.

He stepped back and glanced around as if alarmed by her touch.

"What's wrong, Ned? What did I say?"

"Nothing, cousin. You are welcome. I was just telling Lionel that I can't ride after all. I must confer with Father regarding the tourney." His bow was stiff, formal, so unlike his usual behavior toward her that she asked again what was wrong. He shook his head and backed away, striding quickly toward the king's chambers.

"Come on, John's waiting for us." Lionel led them out of the hall. "You can ride Ned's mount," he called back to her.

"Don't worry about Ned," said Bella. "He knows how you're feeling. Grandam raked him over the coals for taking Will down in such a public way. He's shied from her ever since."

"I'm not dressed for riding," Joan said, but she did not protest too long. A ride out in the fresh air was just what she needed to clear her head.

SLIPPING FROM THE BEDCHAMBER SHE SHARED WITH HER MOTHER and Lady Maud, Joan went to Thomas that night, saying nothing of her interview with Isabella, wanting to treasure their time together.

"Alan and Lucienne are smiling down on us," he whispered as he drew her to him. It was the best thing he could have said.

Before dawn, Hugh escorted Joan back to her own bed. As Lady Maud sleepily made room for her, Joan could almost believe that this was the first of many such family gatherings. Until Efa handed her the bitter drink to prevent conception.

"Patience, my lady."

Joan imagined the dowager queen grinning as she drank.

THE CROWD PARTED FOR PHILIPPA AND HER LADIES, CHEERING them as they approached the viewing stands, signaling that the tournament was about to begin. She and her ladies wore deep blue mantles powdered with silver garters—the damnable garters, Catherine's legacy.

Philippa checked her anger. Not today. Today she would remember the good in her rival. A messenger had arrived from Bisham just as Edward was leaving Philippa to join his men. Early that morning, Catherine had died of the pestilence. Edward had gone white. His lady of the garter was dead. Philippa had hated her for taking his love, but today she felt only grief.

She fought to keep her gaze high, not wanting to see the desperation in the eyes of her people, the slack faces of the ones who could not face even this day without a bellyful of wine, the disheveled garments of the heedless lovers. The first gathering of her husband's great order deserved better than this. She had urged Edward to wait until the pestilence had passed, and with it the madness—the idea that one should take joy where one may, for the end is near. Even Joan, so careful till now, had dared to cross the line, openly favoring Holland over Montagu.

Philippa took her seat at the front of the stands, calming herself as her women settled in round her, and waited until the crowd quieted. Now, to a loud fanfare of trumpets, clarions, and tambours, the Knights of the Garter rode onto the field, fanning out behind her two Edwards, king and crown prince. All twenty-six warriors sat astride caparisoned warhorses, men and their steeds draped in the deep azure livery powdered with the silver-buckled garters of the order. The brisk wind snapped their cloaks, punctuating the quiet as the fanfare abruptly ceased. A few uneasy horses jiggled their harnesses or snorted. How proud were the knights before her, how fierce, how heartbreakingly mortal. Already, in the year since Edward had named the Garter Knights, the pestilence had plucked two from the list, and he'd perforce named two new worthies to replace them. As Philippa raised her voice to announce the beginning of the tournament, she felt the crowd come alive with anticipation, and a thrill of pride pulsed through her, raising her high above the grief into which she'd fallen for so long. Perhaps Edward had been right. Perhaps this was exactly what the kingdom needed. They would prevail.

She noticed Will Montagu slumping in his saddle and gave him a stern look, gesturing with her chin that he should straighten up. His mother would have wished it. As if he'd seen her, he sat tall.

JOAN'S EYES SLID FROM THOMAS, PROUDLY WEARING THE BLUE, white, and silver of the Order of the Garter, sitting tall in the saddle, his smile so wide she could see his dimples from the stands, to the queen, lifting her chin at someone. Ned? He was not looking at her but down the line of men, then meeting his father's gaze with a nod. A sudden movement caught her eye, and she saw Will straighten. Her heart softened a little. To parade in public with his grief so fresh—it was cruel of the king to have insisted upon it. "Your Mother deserves this honor," he'd barked. Will had hung his head and gone off to dress. She glanced back at Thomas, smiled, and waved. Was that a slight nod? She slipped her hand into Lady Maud's.

"My Robert has been vindicated for all the barons to see," Maud whispered. "His Grace would not so honor the sons of a traitor. This is well done." She squeezed Joan's hand. "I'm glad to see your smile." She'd dismissed Isabella's taunt about squandering Count Raoul's ransom. "She doesn't know my son Robert. He would have used it for his own pleasure, not to strengthen the estate." She'd urged Joan to forget all the dowager queen had said. "I will not have her undermine all that Thomas, Alan, and I have fought for."

At the feast afterward, Joan bowed to the dowager queen as she passed to the second table, giving her mother her seat at the high table, walking with head held high to sit with the Hollands and their guest, Raoul de Brienne, Count of Eu and Constable of France. The gossips be damned. There was much drinking, boasting, laughing, dancing, but there were also moments of sudden silence, a memory of Alan touching them. Late in the feast, Lady Maud rose and retreated to the courtyard. Thomas held Joan back when she stood to follow. "She prefers to grieve alone." Raoul deftly turned the talk to the troubadour songs the minstrels were performing, pulling Joan and Thomas into a debate about courts of love and the chivalric code. She had not heard Thomas express himself so eloquently before. They'd had so little leisure together. She had so much to learn about him.

Occasionally Ned passed behind them, leading a woman out to dance. But not once did he approach Joan that evening. Nor did she see Will in the hall.

Again, when the activity round the pavilions quieted, Efa escorted Joan out the door, where Hugh waited to take her to Thomas's tent. Otho and Raoul withdrew on her arrival.

Just before dawn, Hugh came to escort her back to the palace. They slipped silently round couples tucked in the alleyways between pavilions and over men passed out from drink. Near the side door of the palace, a man stepped out from the shadows to bar their way.

"Let me escort you in, cousin."

"Ned. What are you doing out here?" Joan could not see his expression, could not guess his mood.

"Enjoying myself, just like you and everyone else." He waved Hugh away. "I'll not harm my dear cousin."

"My lord, my orders were to see her safely to the door," Hugh protested.

"Do you doubt the word of your prince, Hugh of Carlisle?"

"No, my lord. I—"

"Go along, Hugh," Joan said. "I will be safe with my cousin the prince."

He bowed and hastened away.

Ned took Joan's arm. "Come with me before your Thomas raises an alarm." He hurried her toward the rose garden while she protested that she was tired. He laughed. "It is no wonder. I don't imagine you've slept. Just a moment. We need to talk."

She yanked her arm from his grasp and stepped away. "You've ignored me since you arrived. Now, in the middle of the night, you accost me?"

"It's the only time I know *she* won't see us. I know what my grandam told you, and I cannot let her, of all people, poison you against the one who's always been your champion."

"What are you talking about?" The way he leaned close, imploring, unsettled her.

"I was so young, Joan, so frightened. If you'd married Edward Montagu, you would be gone from my life, and I couldn't imagine it. But it was an awful thing I did. I've done penance for that every day since, I swear. When I saw how I'd hurt you— I've never forgiven myself. But I should have told you. I am so sorry you heard it from her."

"Heard what?" she asked, though her weary mind already knew the answer, the truth that had always lain coiled in her heart awakened, filling her with dismay. She had loved him too much to believe it. She huddled into her cloak and tried to pass him.

He caught her shoulders, pleading with her. "How old was I, six? Seven? I didn't think, I just acted."

"On the advice of an astrologer?"

"She told you that? She likes to think it. But I love you, Joan. I've always loved you."

"And so you drowned my Bruno? What is wrong with you? What canker grew in you so young, a prince who had everything? Why are you telling me this now? To ruin my happiness?"

"She didn't tell you? She said if I paid court to you she would tell you."

"No. We talked of my marriage to Thomas. She said nothing of your unforgivable act."

He turned away, cursing himself. She took the opportunity to move past him.

"Joan, please, don't forsake me!" He caught her waist, pulled her backward against him, kissing her neck. "I beg you. I'll be a friend to Thomas. I'll help you anyway I can. I swear. I will be godfather to your firstborn, eh?" He kissed her again, then let her go. "Come. I'll walk you to the door. Efa will be worried."

"No." She held herself away from him. "No. I cannot be with you right now." She remembered him holding Bruno, lifeless. Her sweet Bruno. She remembered the fear in Ned's eyes, and then that gesture, the one she'd made herself forget, as he handed Bruno to her, pressing his forehead to her shoulder. Caught out. She'd refused to remember it.

"Joan!" He reached for her.

She gathered her skirts and ran to Efa, standing at the side door, lantern in hand.

❖ ❖ ❖

Thomas held his breath as Ned passed beneath a torch head-ing back to the pavilions, muttering curses, his face twisted with anger, a contrast to his pleading humility moments earlier. Then Thomas looked back to Joan, watching until he saw Efa put her arm round his beloved and escort her within.

"Come. We've seen all there is to see," Raoul whispered. "You were right. She is true. I am glad of that."

"I'd not understood how much he loved her."

"Ah. That is also good to know."

"Thank you, my friend. I'd not seen that." Lucienne had been right. He must watch his back with the prince. "It *is* good to know."

The leave-takings were as terrible as when seeing loved ones off to war. Which of them would not return? The church bell in the town of Windsor had rung several times since dawn, signaling new plague dead. The celebrants shrouded them-selves in cloaks fumigated with juniper wood, the fires dotting the upper and lower wards. In the chaos, Joan and Thomas had no need to hide. They clung to each other.

"Swear you will ride straight home, no tarrying, and light the fires all round the castle," Joan implored.

"I swear, my love. And you? Where will you go?"

"We're to Westminster to close the house, then Bourne with the Wakes."

"Listen to Efa's every instruction." Thomas kissed her once more. "I'll come for you as soon as I hear from the lawyers."

Maud embraced her, Otho pecked her cheek. When they were gone, she rushed up to the battlements to catch a last glimpse. But Ned was there. She shook her head at him and crossed to the other side of the tower, calling out to Thomas, waving. He glanced up, lifted his hand. "God keep you, my love!" she whispered.

"Joan—" Ned came up behind her and reached out for her. "She meant for this to break us apart."

"There is no us to break apart. It's Thomas I love, Ned. Thomas."

"I'll wait."

"Don't." She hurried away—from him, from herself and her willful blindness.

44

Bourne Castle, Lincolnshire
SEPTEMBER 1349

For a moment, standing in the orchard, breathing in the late-summer smells of damp grass, ripening apples, and freshly cut hay in the fields just beyond the low stone wall, Joan took joy in being alive. She slipped off her shoes and relished the sensation of moist grass and uneven earth beneath her feet, bringing as it did a rush of memories—high-pitched children's voices, hers and her brother John's, as they dashed round the trees in pursuit of each other; slipping out one night in hopes of catching sight of the owl that called, but sensing more than hearing the rush of its feathers, and then a small animal crying out in pain and terror; helping in the harvest of apples, amazing all with her agility in climbing trees.

Such happy memories were few and quickly faded as one scent overwhelmed the others. Decay. Just beyond her feet were windfall apples, pecked by birds and so brown they must have lain there for days, some so shriveled that they might have fallen months ago. The orchard stood neglected, the gardener and his family all dead of the plague. Joan bowed her head and prayed for their souls, and for all victims and their families. In June the pestilence had taken her uncle, Thomas Wake, and Maud Holland, whom she'd so quickly grown to love, and through the summer countless others. It truly seemed the end of days, the end of all hope.

Noticing the lengthening shadows, Joan dared stay in the orchard no longer. Her mother might wake and call for her. Slipping into her shoes, Joan rejoined Helena and the two armed retainers who had escorted her outside the castle walls. Fear and disorder stalked the land. Only within the castle walls did the household feel safe, yet even there the Death walked.

Like the orchard, the fields and gardens looked abandoned. Except for the cut hay, evidence that someone had made the animals a priority. Even the steward's stone-and-timber house, in which Blanche Wake had sequestered herself with a few healthy servants, looked abandoned, shuttered against the lovely day.

A man stood in the gatehouse doorway.

"John!" Joan hurried to her brother and embraced him.

"Am I in time?"

"I think so. Come."

Efa was busily shaking cushions and coverlets out the open casement. Within the great bed, the curtains pulled aside, lay Countess Margaret, so shrunken as to appear to be but a suggestion of the woman she had been. But she watched with an alertness that belied her weakened state. Joan sat on the edge of the bed, near her mother's head, and took one of her hands. It was hot, and the skin felt like dry parchment loosely wrapped round her prominent bones. So close, Joan smelled the sickness despite her fragrant necklace of herbs. She prayed, as she had done since the boils appeared, that her mother might be one of the rare survivors. She had already lived longer than most.

"You are so kind to me," Margaret whispered.

"Joan, do you dare touch her?" John's voice shook.

"Look who's here, Mother."

"Is it John?" Margaret gasped for breath. "Come so far?"

Joan motioned him closer. "So she can see you," she whispered.

He did not stay long in the chamber. "Are you mad, sister? Come, take the air." His caution was like Blanche's, though she had sat with her husband when he succumbed in London on the cusp of June. Joan, Blanche, and Margaret had then come north to Lincolnshire, hoping the pestilence might pass them by. But it had not.

When John had gone, Margaret tried to sit up, gesturing for Joan to come closer.

"I beg your forgiveness, my child," she whispered, grasping her shoulder. "You were so young, so inexperienced, and I fed you to the wolves."

"There are no wolves in England," Joan said as she eased her mother back onto the cushions. "I have it on the best authority."

"Lions, then. There are lions in the Tower."

Joan almost smiled at her mother's acuity, even on her deathbed, for the king did keep lions in the Tower of London. Caged, a symbol of the powerful whom he so yearned to conquer.

"And I foiled you all by making my own choice."

"I pray for you, Joan. That you and Thomas win, that you have children and prosper."

"Rest now. You'll need your strength to attend my wedding."

Joan had been interrogated by the tribunal of English bishops two weeks earlier, she and Margaret going to London for a night, Blanche too fearful to make the trip. They had been hopeful on their return, for the first time daring to begin planning the wedding. And then Joan had awakened in the night to find her mother burning with fever beside her. She cursed herself for asking her mother to accompany her. The manservant who attended them had died within days, and one of the two retainers two days later.

Just as dawn sharpened the shadows in the room, Margaret's hand went limp in Joan's.

"Mother!" Joan cried out as she bowed over her mother's wasted body, weeping to remember her strength, her fierce determination to protect her children from the royal family, who had stood by while her husband, their father, was butchered.

Efa knelt beside Joan, holding her close as she bent her own head in prayer.

Later, the two washed Margaret's body with loving care and dressed it in fragrant oils, then wound her in a shroud sweetened with fragrant herbs. They burned all the bedclothes and the garments they'd worn in tending her, and then, as John and Blanche accompanied the coffin to the churchyard, Joan and Efa closed themselves in together, sharing their grief and waiting to see whether the Death would take them.

45

Eltham
NOVEMBER 1349

With what trepidation Joan boarded the king's barge, sent for her to answer his summons to Eltham, where she, Thomas, and Will would learn Pope Clement's decision. As the barge approached the landing for Eltham Palace, Joan pressed her feet to the deck and stood tall, fighting lightheadedness, knowing the foolishness of quailing now, after all her efforts. Nine and a half years she had waited to be free to live with her husband. Soon she would know if it would ever be so. She thought it a cruel thing, to be denied the courtesy of receiving the news in solitude. But the king insisted that they all be present.

Frost crunched beneath her boots as she stepped onto the frozen ground. And there was Thomas, dismounting and rushing forward, enfolding her in his cloak, holding her close, his warm breath calming her.

"No matter what happens, know that I will always love you." He pushed back the hood of her cloak and kissed her.

"You are my first and only love, Thomas. We will be together. It must be so. God honors his own law. He must."

But she saw in the lines that etched his face that he held the same question in his throat: Did the pope honor God's law? She took his hand, holding it tightly—so afraid, so afraid, and yet grateful that he was here, that he had survived.

"I have a plan if the pope should fail us. Raoul offered long ago to make me his captain. He offered a château, prestige—"

"But he's here, a prisoner of the Crown."

"He's to be sent back in the new year to raise the rest of his ransom. We could accompany him."

"You're a Garter Knight. The king would never forgive you." She searched his face. Could he be serious? "It would be treason, Thomas."

"I know. And while my mother lived I could not do this. But now—what are our lives without each other, Joan?"

Her own readiness surprised her. She touched his cheek. "You are certain?"

"I've never been more certain of anything in my life."

"What of your brother Robert? What if the king punishes him?"

"Let Robert rot. He's done nothing to help us."

She rose up on her toes to kiss him. "We take our fate in our own hands, Thomas. I am with you."

Up the path, the king's household guards waited with another horse to take them to the palace. Helena would follow on foot with Joan's page. It was a cold, brisk day, frost softening the bare trees and the thorny shrubs. The company proceeded in silence until, halfway to the palace, they were greeted by Ralph Stratford, Bishop of London. Thinking he'd surely been privileged to hear the pope's judgment before the meeting, Joan tried to read his expression, but could not. That frightened her even more. Had it been good news, would the bishop not have some reaction? Was she about to become a traitor to her own cousin? In the yard, they came upon Will talking sternly to a groom. She'd not seen Will since the Garter celebration in spring. The servant turned to bow to the bishop and his companions. Will's gaze went right to Joan's and Thomas's joined hands.

"God be praised that you've both survived the Death," he said stiffly.

"And you," said Thomas.

Will nodded to Joan. "I am sorry for the loss of both your mother and your uncle." His eyes were so cold. There was so much enmity between them. How could anyone expect them to live together? She could not bring herself to speak to him.

Within, minstrels played softly in the hall. Joan withdrew to the chapel to pray until the king sent for her. She wondered what Thomas was thinking. Had he any hesitation? Could he truly love her so much? She shivered as she bowed her head and prayed that Thomas would never regret his choice. When the king's summons came, Joan was grateful that her legs did not buckle under her fear as she followed the page to a corner of the hall that had been enclosed by elaborately carved wooden screens, chairs arranged around a small table, with benches for the king's clerks forming an outer circle. A brazier warmed the area, for which Joan was grateful. Even better, the page led her to the seat closest to the fire.

King Edward welcomed her as *our cousin, Joan*, though his eyes looked elsewhere as he addressed her. Thomas stood and solemnly bowed to her. Will, a sheen of sweat on his pale face, stiffly leaned forward, as if he could not bend at the waist. Simon Islip, the archbishop of Canterbury, did not rise, but extended his ring for her to kiss. The good friend of Elizabeth, dowager countess of Salisbury, Islip was the one whose influence Joan most feared, and she prayed that he had no sway in Avignon. Bishop Stratford, perhaps to temper the archbishop's formality, took her hands and greeted her for the second time that day with a blessing. The clerks, who'd risen in respect, resumed their seats.

The archbishop now instructed them all in courtesy and restraint, and the bishop led them in a brief prayer. Then the king nodded to the clerk who held the roll.

"Speak with good voice and measured pace," he commanded when the clerk had risen.

Joan struggled to find her breath as the clerk proceeded through the preliminary greetings and blessings.

"We might have dispensed with all this," the archbishop growled.

"Amen," Will muttered.

The clerk stumbled and glanced at His Grace, who gestured to him to continue.

Praise for Dame Katarina Van Artevelde, steadfast in her friendship, and the servant Helena, the squire Hugh. Condemnation of several of the offending attorneys and a reprimand to Will that a husband's vow was to love and protect.

Joan stopped breathing. Did that mean he had won? She felt detached, as if hovering above the gathering.

Finally, the decision. The pope ruled that the contract entered into by Sir Thomas Holland and Lady Joan Plantagenet had been and still was a valid and binding marital union. Joan was to be restored to Thomas at once, and their union was to be solemnized publicly. He concluded that the *de facto* marriage between Sir William Montagu and Lady Joan Plantagenet was null and void.

Through the haze of emotion, Joan saw Thomas thump the arm of his chair with his fist. "God be praised!"

The king grunted. "Well, cousin, you have prevailed."

The king's temper brought Joan down to earth. She bowed to Edward and turned to Thomas with a full heart. "God did not forsake us, husband." Her voice broke.

Will muttered something unintelligible and sank back as if suddenly weary.

"You have heard the judgment," said the archbishop. "It shall be as His Holiness Pope Clement proclaims."

"Sir Thomas Holland and my cousin, the Lady Joan, will be formally wed at Westminster in a week's time," said the king. "Stratford will officiate."

He clutched the scrap he might yet control.

"I would be most honored, if it is the couple's wish?" Bishop Stratford looked from Joan to Thomas.

"It is *my* wish," Edward snapped. "The queen will attend with me."

"I would be honored, my lord bishop," said Joan.

"William, be assured that no blame comes to you," the king added with a nod to the still silent Will. Then Edward rose and withdrew to his inner chamber.

Islip and Stratford came forward to congratulate Joan and Thomas and wish them all happiness. When they had departed, Will rose to take his leave.

"I wish you much joy in your marriage." He said it flatly, looking down at his hands, and hurried away before either Joan or Thomas could respond.

So long separated, Joan and Thomas held hands and watched each other begin to believe. Eyes brightened, hers with tears; smiles relaxed into contentment. Slowly they came together, a quiet embrace, lacking all haste. There was no longer any need.

FOG ROSE FROM THE RIVER, GLIDING TO MEET JOAN AND THOMAS, their hoods up as they rode through a soft mist, like a benediction, toward the barge landing. They'd waited on horseback at a distance until Will's barge departed, cherishing their togetherness, loath to share it with one who had every cause to resent it.

As the barge Blanche had hired for Joan's journey swung into the dock, Helena and Hugh joined them, singing a bawdy song.

"Someone's sampled the brandywine we hardly touched," said Thomas as he swept Joan up and carried her onto the barge.

Once Thomas's packs were loaded and Helena, Hugh, and the page were settled, Thomas took Joan on his lap, holding her tight as he kissed her again and again. Her body was flushed

with joy, and she laughed to find her hands even warmer than
Thomas's.

BLANCHE CRIED OUT TO SEE THE TWO OF THEM AT THE DOOR, HUG-
ging Joan and Thomas in turn. "Seeing you together restores
my faith in a benevolent God. Now, up to the solar, the two of
you. We can talk tomorrow. Tonight you dine alone."

A fire glowed in the brazier, silver dishes and Italian glass
goblets caught the candlelight on the small table, the large bed
was piled high with cushions and coverlets.

"It is even more beautiful than the chamber Katarina
prepared for our betrothal night," Thomas said. "Do you remember?"

How could Joan forget? And the beautiful nightgown Katarina had given her, lost in the fire on her crossing. "So long ago,
but my memory is so vivid I feel I could reach out and touch the
linens in that room. And now, my love, here we are again. But
this time with no fear that we can be pulled apart."

Their lovemaking was slow, punctuated with whispers
and laughter. When Joan woke at dawn to the sounds of the
household beginning the day, she snuggled closer to Thomas
and drifted back to sleep, wondering at the blessing of this moment. By the time she once again opened her eyes, hearing Jester
whimpering and scratching at the door, pale winter sunlight lit
Thomas, sitting at the foot of the bed watching her.

"Do I sleep prettily?" she asked.

"You snore. But very prettily indeed." He crawled over to
start again where they'd left off as sleep took them.

After they'd broken their fast with the food from the night
before, which had gone untouched, they crossed the square
to church and gave thanks. On their return, Blanche awaited
them. "*Now* you must tell me all! How did His Grace take his
defeat? When will you wed? Where will you bide?"

She smiled and nodded as they recounted the meeting, amused by the king's insistence on when and where they would solemnize their vows. "Well, we cannot deny him that crumb. It would seem petty. And where will you bide? Do you need to send a messenger to prepare for you?"

"Our manor of Upholland, in Lancashire, is Mother's wedding gift to us, and I should indeed send word to Upholland that we will be there for the Christmas season," said Thomas.

"Good. Well away from the court and interfering relations. After so many years of waiting, you deserve time alone, time to become acquainted." She tilted her head at Joan's soft laugh. "You've never lived together. Mark me, you will soon discover how little you know each other." She suddenly rose to hug them each in turn and whisper an apology. "I feared I would go to my grave still bowed with remorse over my intervention. May God watch over you."

After wiping her eyes, she lifted her goblet to toast them once again. "And now—a wedding at St. Stephen's, Westminster? You'll need a very special gown for that!"

Later in the day Dame Katarina came to congratulate Joan and Thomas, presenting them with a beautiful jeweled mazer and a casket of fine wine.

Westminster Palace
LATE NOVEMBER 1349

BLANCHE, EFA, AND HELENA took turns with the three dozen silver buttons on the front of Joan's most elegant gown—a rose bodice and lavender skirt embroidered with roses and rosemary sprigs in silver and gold thread. Joan suggested that they let her aunt's maid finish, as the three, so dear to her, alternately wept and laughed.

"You and your buttons!" her aunt bemoaned. But she sighed with delight. "I wish my Thomas could see you. How your uncle prayed for this day! And Margaret. Maud, too." Tears came.

Joan leaned over to kiss her, the bell-like beads on her fillet softly ringing. Helena groaned as she lost her purchase on one of the tiny buttons.

Blanche laughed. "Bells in your hair!"

It was a gift from Bella, holding in place a jeweled gold-and-silver-filigree crispinette, one of her aunt's many wedding gifts, that cupped Joan's braided hair over her ears.

"My fair sister," John said from the doorway. "Thomas sent me to see whether you'd changed your mind and escaped over the rooftops."

"Almost there," Helena said.

"Laces are faster," John offered, ducking with a laugh as Joan tossed a shoe at him.

"There!" Helena declared as she smoothed down the fabric.

Joan swept round. Helena reached to adjust something on her head.

"It was good of the queen to let you dress here in the palace," said Blanche. "The wind would have undone all our work on the ride from London."

Down in the hall, Joan found Thomas had a partner in pacing, his brother Robert, Lord Holland, fair-weather friend.

"God in heaven, do I deserve such a bride as this?" Thomas stood in wonder.

Robert bowed low and took Joan's hand, kissing it. "Lady Joan. It is a pleasure to meet you at last."

She was saved from the retort on the tip of her tongue by John offering his arm. "It is time, sis."

The nave was well lit with torches and tapers.

"The light is Ned's doing," Bella whispered, joining Joan just within the doors of St. Stephen's Chapel. "He insisted on light as a symbol of your steadfastness."

Joan stood still for a moment, taking it in, this so long dreamed-of moment, when she and Thomas would complete their vows. "He has given us a most precious gift," she said to Bella. She was moved by it, accepting it as an affirmation of his vow to befriend Thomas, to respect their marriage.

Within moments, surrounded by Hollands, Wakes, and Plantagenets, Joan stood facing Thomas in the nave of St. Stephen's, clasping his hands, pledging her troth, smiling as Bishop Stratford pronounced them husband and wife. Nine years ago, standing with Will, she'd felt diminished here, overwhelmed beneath the soaring stone vaults. This day, she felt as if she might reach up and touch the ceiling. Only Thomas's strong grasp held her down.

Ned was the first to step forward to congratulate them. She had not seen him since she ran from him on Windsor's battlements. "My dearest cousin, the fairest lady in the realm." He kissed her, not on the cheek but the mouth, gathering her close. Before releasing her, he whispered, "I pray you forgive me. And, if ever you tire of him, I will be waiting."

As Joan pushed away, her face hot, she was caught up, in turn, by the princes Lionel and John, both of whom planted wet kisses on her cheeks. And then it was her brother John's turn, and Raoul, Count of Eu, his kiss so enthusiastic that she teased him about being too long away from his wife.

"I regret she will not meet you," he whispered. "I looked forward to that."

"It is my loss, I am sure."

Then Robert Holland gave her a solemn embrace, and Otho a rib-cracking hug. "By God, we have the most beautiful sister-in-law in all the land, eh, Robert?"

Joan was quite giddy by the time she embraced her aunt Blanche, but quickly sobered when she came face to face with Queen Philippa, uncertain what to make of the tears in her eyes.

"It is a pleasure to celebrate joy after so much sorrow. May you at long last be content and fulfilled, Joan."

"Your Grace."

Bella drew Joan away. "I'm almost envious. The way you two look at each other!" She looked Joan up and down and nodded her approval. "You'll have little need for such elegance away from court."

"Nor will I have the wealth of an earldom to support it."

"I'll miss you!"

Now King Edward stepped forward and kissed Joan's hand. "I pray that you are happy, cousin, and give birth to sons who will serve the realm as well as their father has."

"I am honored to have you and Queen Philippa as witnesses to this joyous day, Your Grace," Joan said. "Will you come back to London with us for the wedding feast?"

"A gracious invitation I must sadly decline. But surely you'll be more at ease with only your cousins." He moved on to speak to Thomas.

God be thanked. Joan had promised Blanche she would extend the invitation, but she'd prayed that the king and queen would decline. It was a day for lighthearted joy, marred only momentarily by Thomas's complaint that Ned's kiss was hardly cousinly.

"What did he say to you? Do I have a rival?"

He'd never before asked so directly about Ned. "Neither was Otho's hug very brotherly, Thomas. Or Raoul's kiss. You've no rival, my love. You know that." How could he doubt it after all she'd gone through to arrive at this day?

SNOW FELL SOFTLY AS THE BARGE LEFT THE PIER. JOAN LEANED INTO her husband's warm solidity. Thomas draped his cloak around her. "I cannot believe my good fortune," he said.

They would stay a few nights in Broughton, Thomas's

birthplace, halfway between London and Upholland, then continue on to Lancashire. Efa had gone on ahead with Jester and a load of the wedding gifts.

"To wake beside you every morning—such a simple joy, yet it is everything," said Joan. She felt at peace, wanting nothing more.

On their journey north, everything pleased her, and all who served the Hollands welcomed her with warmth. The king and queen had presented them with gifts of gold and precious stones on their marriage, but it was the generosity expressed in the hides, turned wooden bowls, stools, and animals offered by the servants and tenants that moved them most. An expression of their joy for their lord's happiness and the honor they felt in having the king's cousin as their lady.

The manor house at Upholland, where Thomas had lived much of his life, was a timber hall over a stone undercroft, the great hall simple, the solar freshly painted in bright colors and boasting a large bed, the most elegant furnishing in the house.

"You are accustomed to finer homes," said Thomas.

"Husband, this is our home, and I shall love it. But I pray you be patient, for I've so much to learn!" Though by the evidence of the meal served on their arrival and the cleanliness of the hall and the solar, she guessed that the servants would more than compensate for her unfamiliarity. And she was confident that Efa would quickly know the lay of the land. Thomas had expressed concern about how the housekeeper, Besetta, who'd been in the household when he was a child, would take to Efa, but already the two seemed easy with each other. Broad-hipped and rosy-cheeked, with jowls that strained at the strings of the undyed linen hat she wore, a peculiar thing that hid most of her hair, Besetta seemed ageless. Indeed, she squealed like a girl when Thomas caught her up in a hug. All Joan's tension fell away as she sensed the love in the hall.

As they were about to retire for the night, the steward, Andrew, pointed out a large chest in one corner. "It arrived a few days hence on a cart escorted by armed retainers in the livery of the Prince of Wales."

Efa frowned at Joan and gave a subtle shake of her head.

"It will wait till morning," said Thomas. "Right, wife?" He kissed her hand and put his arm round her, but she saw the tension in his jaw.

"Or midday," she said with a laugh as she turned to the plank steps that led up to the solar, pulling Thomas behind her. Up above, Helena and Efa had lit lamps, warmed the bed with hot stones, and a small brazier cut the chill of the December night. Joan did not look, but she was certain that beneath the mattress Efa had placed charms for their protection. She had never felt so enveloped in love.

Beginning with his boots, Joan undressed her husband, fumbling as he stole kisses and then started undressing her, too impatient to wait.

"Thank God you aren't wearing the gown with all the buttons."

"One? I have several with many tiny buttons."

With a roar, he fell back onto the bed, taking her with him. Clothes could be mended.

At dawn, Joan rose in the icy cold to open the shutter. Snow blanketed the countryside. Down below, a groom slowly made his way to the kitchen, with each step lifting his knee as high as he could.

"I've dreamed of this moment for so long, showing you the beauty of a snowfall in Lancashire." Thomas enfolded her in his arms and rested his chin on her head.

"I wish it would snow and snow and shut out all the world but this happy household." Joan turned and he lifted her, carrying her back to bed. By the time she called for Helena to dress her, the household was well into their day.

Down below, the servants excitedly asked whether they might stay to watch the opening of the great chest from the prince. Joan looked to Thomas.

"I've a mind to wait until Christmas to open it," he drawled, yawning and stretching his legs toward the fire, but Joan saw through his nonchalance. It bothered him as much as it did her. "We've plenty to do to prepare, haven't we, Besetta?"

"That we do, Sir Thomas," said the housekeeper, "but it would be cruel to make us wait any longer. We've waited for days, wondering what treasures lie within." Slowly, she ran her rough hand across the carved lid as if she might so divine its contents.

Thomas sat forward and bowed in fond acquiescence. "You've run this house for so long, I don't dare cross you."

Joan had two servants move the chest to the middle of the hall. She prayed that it was something impersonal—goblets, bowls, or perhaps matching saddles. . . . She glanced at Efa, who touched the corners of her mouth, suggesting a brave smile. Joan took her counsel, smiling as she said, "Let us see what treasures lie within, Besetta."

The housekeeper's thick arms strained against the fabric of her sleeves as she lifted the lid. Thomas went to her aid, propping it open. Besetta stepped aside for Joan. "My lady."

Holding her breath, Joan lifted out a long, flat package. Cloth, she guessed, wrapped with care in parchment. To protect a dye or an embroidery. Laying it on the table, she cut the twine, pulled back the parchment. "Help me unfold this, Besetta."

"Now that's a grand thing," the housekeeper said, wonder in her voice.

"The white hart." Thomas looked at Joan. "Your father's design, and yet not. This one seems so melancholy."

It was a green velvet coverlet, with the white hart sitting in the center, the crown round its neck, the chain pooling over a foreleg. The border was sprinkled with embroidered flowers and shrubs, the latter mostly plantagenets, or brush plants. Joan agreed that it was far more melancholy than her father's design, the hart's face and posture expressing the terrible weight of the crown round its neck.

Joan regretted her decision to open the chest. From anyone else she might have received it as a lovely tribute, the sorrowful air an accident, but not from Ned. It was a mean gesture on his part, a petty reminder of his fixation on the white hart silk she'd refused him. She quickly began to unpack the rest to dispel the strange mood the thing had cast. Jeweled mazers, green velvet drapes for the bed to match the hart spread, Italian glass goblets, lengths of the softest wool in beautiful shades of red, green, and blue.

"These are noble gifts." Joan heard a hesitance in Thomas's voice.

"The mazers and goblets are most welcome. But I would keep our chamber as it is. This is too melancholy to drape round our marriage bed." Joan handed Besetta the bed hangings. "Wrap these as they were and put them in a dry place. The chest would do, if you find room for it out of the way."

Thomas's nod to the housekeeper conveyed far more than mere agreement.

"What of the wool cloth, my lady?" asked Besetta.

"Helena should see it, so that she knows what we have to hand. Then store it where it will be easily found when we've need of it."

Later, when Thomas was showing Joan the stables, he expressed his relief in her acceptance of the housekeeper. "I know this is not the court, and our ways may seem strange."

"They will be strange for only a little while. Then they will be *our* ways."

"The prince's gifts—they are very fine."

Joan pressed Thomas's arm and waited until he looked

down into her eyes. "I chose you, and he resents it. Put him from your mind, please, my love. I have all my heart desires." She stood on tiptoe to kiss him.

"You have no regrets?"

"Only the loss of so many years."

46

As the snow deepened in the fields surrounding Upholland, Joan and Thomas spent their days and nights absorbed in each other, sharing a lifetime of stories, listening, watching, touching, while the household tiptoed around them. Joan was only vaguely aware of Helena and Efa, even less of the Holland servants. But, as Christmas approached, Thomas was drawn out of their cocoon to help with plans for a feast welcoming Joan to the wider community of the working manor and the village. And so Joan took her first tentative steps of settling into a lifestyle she'd experienced only on occasion as a child, when her mother traveled round the Kent manors and left Joan and John at one in the Midlands, in Efa's care. Joan knew little of what it meant to be lady of such a country manor—Bisham was grander, with constant guests. Upholland was small and remote.

Most of the staff had always been in the service of the Holland family. It was clear that they found her strange. Her wit was misinterpreted, taken as anger or criticism. Her clothing needed simplifying. The grooms had difficulty adjusting to her order to have a horse ready for her at all times of day. And Thomas was uncomfortable with her riding without escort.

"Poachers and weather, folk who do not yet know you."

Joan understood his concern and agreed to an escort at first, but if she meant to make this her home she must learn the land. Thomas said that he would relax after all had met her. Then they would know her and watch out for her.

She threw herself into planning the big feast for all who lived on the manor and in the village. Dressed elegantly, as the folk expected, yet in what would have been starkly simple at court, Joan greeted them all, asking questions made possible by extensive coaching from Besetta and Andrew. She fussed over the tenants' children, especially the babies, eliciting knowing smiles from their mothers, taught the girls a dance she'd loved as a child, and told the boys some of the stories she'd heard from soldiers in France.

"You have won their hearts," Thomas said later that night.

"And they have won mine—the dancing, the laughter. They ate everything!" She hugged him tightly.

"It was not always so. There were years of sadness during Father's troubles and after his murder. And all the households here lost at least half their number with the pestilence. They are sharing our joy in beginning again."

Their lovemaking that night was different from before — slower, dreamier, as if at last they understood that they need not hurry, they had all the time in the world. And, being together day in, day out, they knew each other as they had not before. Joan learned Thomas's moods, the languor that kept him abed many mornings, much to her delight, the single-minded con- centration with which he tackled a project, the inexplicable si- lences, the buoyant energy after a good hunt or a long ride or any physical labor.

By Candlemas, Joan knew she was with child, and the re- alization filled her with such joy that she was almost afraid to speak the words and break the magic. But Efa, too, noticed the changes, and then Helena. Joan swore them to secrecy until she told Thomas.

That very evening as they climbed into bed, Joan drew

Thomas's hand to her stomach. "Do you feel the miracle? Our child grows within. At last!"

He regarded her with wonder, then bent to kiss her bare stomach. "When?"

"At the very latest, the first frost."

He pulled her onto his lap, covering her with kisses.

Determined to do nothing to risk the child, Joan stayed behind when Thomas rode to Windsor for the second gathering of the Order of the Garter in April. In truth, it was no sacrifice—she was happy to delay a reunion with her royal kin. She wanted nothing to spoil her happiness. And, as spring took hold at Upholland, she let Efa, Helena, and Besetta fuss all they wished as she wandered the manor proper, acquainting herself with its gentler seasons.

Windsor
ST. GEORGE'S DAY, 1350

ON THE RIDE FROM LANCASHIRE TO WINDSOR, THROUGH THE TENder awakening of the earth, Thomas felt as if he were reentering the world from Eden. The months with Joan seemed as a dream in contrast to the haunted countryside. Though he, Joan, and all on the manor grieved for kinfolk and friends lost to the pestilence, the general mood had been one of hope, of looking forward and giving thanks to God. Now, to see the abandoned farms, shuttered inns, thinly populated villages, and the desperate looks on the wandering penitents and beggars, he vowed to do penance for having forgotten the misery. For the moment, he and his men were on the alcrt for the inevitable thieves. A few skirmishes had them in fighting form by the time they reached Windsor.

After the unnatural quiet of the countryside, he welcomed

the noise in the lower ward of the castle, knights and their retinues jostling to move about among the bright-colored pavilions.

"It's too crowded for the cart," Hugh said to the others.
"We'll unload here after I've found—"

"I'll show you the way." Otho appeared out of the crowd.

"That will save time." Thomas embraced his brother.

"I've watched for you up on the walls. Where is Joan?
You've not lost her?"

"She's in Upholland surrounded by people I trust. I'm to be
a father!"

"Well done, brother!" Otho nodded to Hugh. "See to all this.
I'm taking Thomas off to celebrate with a tankard or three."

Along the way to the drink, they gathered well-wishers. By
the time they arrived at the tent, they were a dozen strong. God
had spared so many of his friends. It was indeed a joyous reunion. Thomas eased down onto a bench, glad to stretch out his
legs after the long ride.

His old friend Roland brought him the first tankard. "God
grant Lady Joan is safe delivered of a male heir!" He sank down
next to Thomas, well on his way to a good drunk.

Thomas had downed two tankards by the time Prince
Edward parted the crowd to find out if it was true about his
cousin's pregnancy. His words and manner were merry, his con-
gratulations loud, but his eyes—Thomas did not like what he
saw there.

The prince took a seat and regaled the crowd with the tale
of a Christmas adventure—he, his father the king, and the Earl
of March had assembled an army to defend Calais against an intended raid by the French, and succeeded brilliantly. "I should
have summoned you, Thomas," said the prince. "You would
not have had the time to get Joan with child and we all might
have celebrated now." He laughed as if he'd said it in jest, and
departed.

But he'd not been in jest. And the devil of it was, hearing about the skirmish, Thomas regretted having missed it.

"We'll be back in the fight by summer," Otho predicted. "You'll get your chance."

"You know me so well."

"Anyone could see that you wished you'd been there." He leaned close. "I don't know what to make of the prince's remarks. Surely he does not see himself as your rival?"

"You read him well. Now come, drink up. This is no place for such talk."

In all the waiting and yearning for marriage, Thomas had never considered how it might muddle things. If he took part in the summer mission, would he be home in time for the birth? Did that matter? He shook off such thoughts. Joan was everything to him. For now, a tourney was enough. He settled in to enjoy the reunion with his comrades-in-arms.

As spring advanced Joan slowed down, napping in the afternoons, walking shorter distances with Jester and riding very little, heeding Efa's advice even when she yearned for more activity. This child growing in her womb was too precious for her to do otherwise; she had waited too long for this experience. Her senses heightened; she felt everything more keenly—emotions, beauty, wonder. For the first time since childhood, she would sit for hours in the garden listening to the insects and the wind, the animals in the distance, watching butterflies and bees sample the blossoms.

"God's wondrous world. Nothing at court equals this," she said to Besetta one afternoon as the two of them sat in the kitchen garden enjoying the natural light for their needlework. Joan was embroidering a little cap for the baby, and Besetta was darning her husband's hose.

The housekeeper smiled. "Carrying a child brings us close

to our animal companions, and all nature," she said. "Does the queen enjoy such peace when she is with child?"

Joan told her about Philippa giving birth to Lionel in Antwerp, John in Ghent, her pregnancy in Calais.

"Poor woman," said Besetta, bending to her work. "I should not like to be a queen."

"Nor would I."

JOAN CELEBRATED THOMAS'S RETURN A FORTNIGHT LATER, EAGER TO share her new experiences with him. Patiently she listened to his account of the Garter gathering, then rushed to tell him about the birth of a litter of kittens, the first wobbly steps of several lambs, how she'd helped prepare the kitchen garden for spring.

"You, my love?" Thomas took her hands, turned them over and over. "I am relieved to find them still smooth. So you jest."

"I wear gloves, you foolish man. Did you love me only for my uncalloused hands?"

"I am not so foolish as that."

"They do say that mothers-to-be are strangers even to themselves. . . . You're frowning. What is wrong?"

He told her of the summer mission. "Will you be bored? Lonely? Shall I send for Blanche? Would you prefer to go to her?"

She kissed him to silence him. "I'll send word to Aunt Blanche, but only because she made me promise to do so. I am content, my love, and have Efa, Besetta, and Helena to spoil me. Believe me, I am happier than I can ever remember."

True, she had imagined him by her side in the last months of her pregnancy, and had thought he might insist on being with her, but it had been a dream. Long ago, Thomas had pledged his life to the restoration of the honor of his house. His greatest moment had not been winning his petition but becoming a founding member of the Order of the Garter. She'd known this. Yet in no way did Thomas neglect her, and she could see in his unguarded eye how he loved her. Still, in her weaker moments she was jealous—of his armor, so lovingly tended, of his destrier, fed and exercised with such care, even of Hugh, who had served him so long, as page, then squire, and now sergeant.

Until his departure, Thomas easily fell back into the life on the land. Having lost so many tenants and servants to the pestilence, he joined in to help with much of the work in early summer. Men and women did appear seeking work, and Joan learned from Thomas's caution, as well as his trust of the judgment of Andrew and Besetta, how to choose good help. Knowing that departures and homecomings would shape their life together, Joan meant to become self-sufficient.

But when the time came for Thomas to depart, Joan thought her heart would break. He found it no easier, swearing that he could not leave after all, his place was with her and their child. And it fell to Joan to assure him that she was in the best hands and there was little he could do. "Bring honor to our family, my love."

After Thomas and Hugh departed, the summer played out in quiet days filled with dreams of motherhood, Joan lazing in the garden, talking to the grooms as she visited the horses, walking in the fields with Jester and the hunting dogs, planning a mews with Andrew and a carpenter. Lady Blanche arrived in mid-October with piles of beautiful coverlets for the cradle and gorgeous wool and silk cloths for a post-pregnancy wardrobe. Joan had feared that she might find her aunt aging and broken with grief. But mourning had given Blanche new impetus. She was at law with an abbot whose lands abutted hers, and deep in plans to revitalize several manors. She approved of Joan's adaptation to married life.

"Few women are so industrious during their first pregnancy. Good. How do you like being lady of the manor?"

"I wake every morning wondering how long this contentment can possibly last, who is about to shatter it."

Blanche kissed Joan's forehead, lifted her chin to look into her eyes. "It will last as long as you keep your head."

In short order, Blanche organized a thorough freshening of the master bedchamber in preparation for Joan's lying-in. She, Efa, and Helena would sleep with Joan as she took to her bed before birth, while Besetta ran the household.

By the time Thomas returned, Joan had withdrawn for the birth. But she insisted that he be permitted some time with her in their bedchamber. He looked frightened as he picked his way past the pallets set up for her three companions.

Joan drew him down onto the bed beside her, holding him so that he might feel their rowdy child. "This is how we continue, my love," she said. "Through mothers' pain."

She was not so philosophical when her labor began. For years she'd listened to the ladies of the queen's chamber exchange dramatic stories of their labors, particularly in the days leading up to the queen's deliveries. But nothing had prepared her for her own descent into travail. That such a miracle as a child should be born of such agony.

"Blame it on Eve's sin, my lady," said Blanche.

"I'm not Eve!"

Back and forth she walked, supported by Besetta and Efa, then Blanche and Helena, the women trading off as the hours added up to a day, and still the child tested Joan's endurance. She wept to think that her mother had endured such pain to bring her into the world.

At last, the moment. She'd been torn apart and waited for death, but instead she heard an infant's shrill cry, the sound tugging at her heart so strongly she gasped. Efa handed Joan her son, a perfectly formed child. Nothing she had ever felt, nothing she had called love, nothing came close to what welled up within her at that beholding.

"A son!" Blanche called down to all who waited. "A fine, healthy son. His dam is weary, but rest will renew her."

When Joan woke, Thomas was sitting beside her, holding her hand, gazing on her as if she were the most amazing woman in God's creation. "We have a son, my love," he whispered.

"I know." She smiled and squeezed his hand. "Have you seen him? He has ten fingers and ten toes, and I very much fear he has the long Plantagenet nose."

"Nonsense!" Blanche set the swaddled baby in Thomas's arms. "Look. It is a baby's nose like all others."

"A button," said Thomas, kissing it.

"I must have dreamed it." Joan laughed.

"He is perfect, my love." Thomas's voice was husky with emotion. "I wish our mothers had lived to see this day."

They said nothing for a while, holding hands, gazing on their son.

"We must send word to the king," Joan said. "And Ned," she added with some reluctance.

"The prince? Why?" Blanche asked sharply.

"He begged the honor of standing as godfather to our first-born son. It is an auspicious beginning for our child." It was. But already she wondered at herself for pursuing this.

"God help us," said Blanche. "Where will we put his retinue?"

"Oh, Aunt, don't worry. He'll send a messenger with gifts. He won't come all this way himself."

"At what cost to us, this honor?" Thomas asked, softly, as if uncertain he wished her to hear.

But Joan heard. "What's happened, Thomas? What's Ned done now?"

A false smile. "Nothing, my love. It's a passing mood." Now his smile became true, as the baby squirmed.

"Our little Tom," said Joan. "He's ours, Thomas—ours, not the king's or the prince's."

Joan had been wrong in her prediction. Shortly before her churching, Ned arrived carrying gifts, and stayed for two nights. She'd not had time to find the white hart bed coverings he'd given them and, when he noted their absence, lied about taking them down for the birthing. "I could not bear to stain them." She heard Thomas's intake of breath at her lie, but so be it. Ned had come all this way in honor of their son and she would be courteous, if not loving. "We haven't the room for all your retinue."

He walked her to the window to show her that his men were putting up pavilions in the far meadow. "They are accustomed to campaigning, they will be fine."

Ned did not think about the cost of feeding them all, or the work involved. Thomas and Blanche shared the honor and burden of hosting him with Besetta and Andrew. Joan preened in the attention he showered on her. And, afterward, the tenants paid in depleted stores.

"I pray you do not invite him after the next birth, Joan, or we'll starve, and all our tenants with us."

Thomas's words stung with truth, and though she had not invited Ned, she promised to be more careful in future.

But Thomas still paced, brow furrowed.

"Something more?"

"The lie about the white hart hangings."

"Diplomacy, my love. It was a generous gift—"

"An intrusive gift, Joan." He held her eyes.

"Yes it was, my love. My Plantagenet relatives have ever been a curse in my life. But they are my family and our sovereigns, and they deserve our respect, if not our affection. For our son's sake, if not for ours. Is that not so? Even Robert has been forgiven. And Blanche."

Thomas groaned and slumped down beside her, taking one of her hands and kissing it. A vein pulsed on his scarred left temple. "I hoped—you are of no use to them now, wed to someone already subject to them. I'd hoped they would leave you in peace, except for the annual St. George's Day gathering of the order. What if he follows through on what he said, taking charge of his godson's fosterage? Our son would be beholden to him. And so would we."

"I know. But he will be anyway. Ned will be his prince, and someday his king. But I do pray the war focuses my cousin's attention elsewhere."

The tension broke as baby Tom's shrieks preceded his appearance in Efa's arms. Thomas laughed, kissed Joan's hand again, and rose. "Saved by a hungry child," he said, lifting Tom from Efa's arms. Handing him to Joan, her bodice unbuttoned and ready, Thomas whispered, "How I envy you, my son."

Joan watched her beloved melt as their son's mouth closed round her nipple, sucking contentedly. She reached up to stroke his face. "I am who I am."

"And I would not have you any other way." He kissed her hand and strode out of the hall, whistling.

Peace had been restored, but a crack had appeared in paradise, and it was her doing. Joan had spent her life resenting the burden of her Plantagenet blood, and now she had brought that curse on her son. And on Thomas. God forgive her.

Upholland
FEBRUARY 1352

POOR HARVESTS, THE EXPENSE OF FIGHTING IN FRANCE, THE PAPAL petition, and then pestilence had depleted Thomas's coffers. He had never received the full payment King Edward promised him for the Count of Eu, nor would he in future, for Raoul, his dear friend, had been executed as a traitor upon his return to France. Had Thomas and Joan accompanied him, they might have met a similar fate. Thomas crossed himself. God had been good to them. But, with a fine son and another child on the way, he needed an appointment by which he might prove his worth to the king and earn an annuity. Even better if it afforded a chance for booty. Joan was a woman made for jewels and fine clothes, and he wanted to give them to her. She never complained, but he could not imagine that she would always be content to live such a simple life, so much humbler than the one she had once known.

He himself grew weary of the sameness at Upholland. He was a knight, not a farmer. He missed life in the field. So when the king appointed him captain of Calais Castle, Thomas did not know whether to express or hide his relief.

He need not have worried. Joan beamed with pride. "It is such an honor, my love." It was. The king thought Calais important enough to have interrupted his Yuletide celebrations a few years past to defend it. "I am so proud of you!" She asked him the details—when he must depart, whom he would take in his party, and, at last, with telling hesitance, she asked, "Do you want me with you?"

"You'd prefer to remain at Upholland?"

"Efa has warned me that this pregnancy will not necessarily be as easy as my first. But I will come if you need me."

"No. Stay here where you will have the best of care in the peace of the countryside. I will miss you as I would my right arm," he said, and meant it. "But in truth we can ill afford the expense of shifting the household."

He felt guilty when she hugged him hard, whispering her thanks.

She was less cheerful a week later as they lay awake the night before his departure. "Our quiet time is over, husband." She sighed. "I am grateful we had these few years of peace."

"Our quiet time is over?"

"This is only the beginning of the honors you will earn, and each will add to your burden of responsibility."

"As does each child," said Thomas. He kissed her swollen stomach. "Would you have it any other way, Joan?"

"No. It's just the morning sickness clouding my mood. It is all just as it should be."

It was harder to leave now. Much, much harder. And when, months later, the king's courier brought Thomas the news of the birth of his son John, he spent the morning in church searching his soul. For years he'd fought to claim Joan as his wife, and now he was missing this precious moment. He prayed that the prince had not been summoned.

47

Westminster
LATE JANUARY 1353

Tragedy brought Thomas back from Calais. Two days after Christmas, Joan's brother John had bled to death after a wild boar ripped his leg from knee to groin. Suddenly Joan was the heir both to the earldom of Kent and to her uncle Thomas Wake's lands. As Joan's husband, Thomas was summoned to Westminster to arrange the dower for John's thirteen-year-old widow, Elizabeth of Juliers, as well as the appropriate homage and fealty to King Edward for the estates. Admitting his profound inexperience with property lawyers, Thomas asked Blanche Wake to guide him through the legal labyrinth. That freed his mind so that he might comfort Joan in her grief over her brother's death, which was complicated by guilt that she had declined John's invitation to Woking for Christmas. *If I'd been there with Efa, he might have survived.* It was a familiar refrain among soldiers, the guilt of being the one who still lived. Thomas held her at night, listening to her, loving her, speaking softly of his affection for John, his courage in the field, his love of the hunt.

All the while Thomas wrestled with his own guilt. Little by little, he was realizing that his young family was now wealthy beyond anything he had ever imagined. Had Joan come into this inheritance just three years earlier, Thomas wondered whether the pope's decision would have been the same. He would surely have been suspected of lusting after Joan's status and wealth. In one thrust of a boar's tusks, Thomas's future, and that of his children, had been transformed from poor landholders to a great baronial family. Poring over the myriad estate documents with Blanche, he struggled to contain his profound gratitude and relief. Joan no longer need suffer for choosing him. She was restored to her high status.

So her reaction to the sudden elevation confounded him. In Westminster, Joan's grief turned to anger. She snapped at the attorneys and their clerks, railed against the conditions limiting their decisions, even berated her aunt for her attempts to smooth the feathers she'd ruffled.

"Don't you see?" she asked Thomas. "With this inheritance our paradise has been breached for good. We are far more beholden to the whims of my royal cousins than we were when we were simply Thomas and Joan Holland." When he protested that they were freer than before, that he was no longer dependent on the king's appointments to feed his servants and tenants, she looked at him as if he'd said something utterly witless.

Into this tense and contentious atmosphere strode Prince Edward, greeting Joan as Countess of Kent, as he scooped her off her feet in an overlong embrace.

"You've me to thank for the efficiency of the turnover," the prince bragged. "I'm looking after my godson's future." He patted Thomas on the back. "How fortunate that you were in Calais and my cousin in the depths of Lancashire when Earl John met his untimely end, eh? Folk might have suspected a plot to restore Joan to the status to which she was born."

The barb hit too close to the mark, and Thomas barely managed to respond with the respect and courtesy due his prince.

Joan had no such compunction. "That was unworthy of you, cousin. I would happily forgo all that has come to me in exchange for my dear brother's life. Shame on you."

Ned bowed and apologized, but Thomas saw no remorse in his clear blue eyes. How right Joan had been.

At the end of an irritating day dealing with the lawyers and Ned's caustic humor, Joan was grateful for Thomas's strong arm around her as they walked back to the house in Westminster. In the hall she knelt to her sweet two-year-old, hugging Tom while he stammered out a tale of two cats stalking a bird along the riverbank. Her wide-eyed boy steadied her, bringing her back to reality, reminding her that although her happy life with Thomas and the boys had changed, had become more challenging to protect, it had not crumbled. Thomas, too, seemed eager to touch reality, swinging the infant John out of Efa's arms and praising his chubby cheeks while the baby gurgled happily.

Joan felt an easing of the stricture that had gripped her ever since the royal courier rode into the yard at Upholland. She'd rushed out, fearing the worst about Thomas—that he had been seriously injured defending Calais Castle or, God help her, killed. For why else would a royal courier come to Lancashire? Her momentary relief had turned to grief as she took in the news of her brother's death. Sweet John—he had been their mother's comfort, an easier child than Joan, never questioning duty, but not at all self-righteous. He'd been passionate about the hunt, preferring a bestial opponent to a human one. For such pleasure to come to this. How he must have suffered.

Her duty lay at Woking, comforting her sister-in-law, Elizabeth, so briefly wed that Joan hardly knew her. Handing John to a wet nurse Efa chose with care, Joan had gone south with Helena in the company of four of her brother's retainers to find the thirteen-year-old widow already beset with messengers from her family in Juliers, as well as by her aunt the queen, bearing lists of potential suitors for her to consider. So soon! The young woman, a slender version of her aunt Philippa but with a fiery complexion and snapping dark eyes, paced the hall muttering curses. Joan had anticipated quite a different scene, more akin to her own fearful silence in Ghent.

"Do they not know I'm in mourning?" Elizabeth hissed when one of the suitors rode into the yard, begging her favor—an older man, though not displeasing to the eye and of good family. "I don't want anyone else, I want John! You must leave, sir." She ordered a servant to escort the startled man from the hall.

Seeing Elizabeth's strength, Joan had relaxed her maternal hovering, simply extending to the young widow an open invitation to escape to her household if she wished for a respite from the battle.

But Elizabeth declared herself determined to stand her ground there at Woking, even after the arrival of her brother, who was determined to remind her of her duty to the family. Elizabeth had Philippa's deep sense of her own worth and integrity. John had been most fortunate in his wife.

When Thomas arrived and asked Joan to join him in Westminster, she had packed in haste and taken her leave, sending word to Efa to bring the children and the wet nurse to meet them. She needed her family, and Efa, around her.

She took Thomas's hand now, drawing him away from the boys and up to the bedchamber. "Hold me, my love. Just hold me. And promise me that when you return to Calais you take me with you."

"I need more than that," he growled, pushing her down on the bed and covering her with kisses, laughingly spewing curses as he fumbled with her buttons.

After lovemaking, as they sat back against a mound of pillows, sharing a mazer of wine, Thomas broke the news that he would not be returning to Calais. "Otho is now acting captain. I need the next month to move to accommodations more suited to our expanded household—you saw what happened at

Upholland when Ned brought his entourage. What say you to Donington Castle?"

Joan groaned. "John chose Woking because Donington had suffered flood damage."

"His widow has chosen to keep Woking. We must honor that."

"What says the king to this plan regarding Calais?"

"It was his recommendation that I take this opportunity before we sail to Brittany in spring. Donington was also his suggestion."

"Repairing a castle. How easily he spends our newfound wealth." Already her cousin interfered. She'd been resting her head on Thomas's chest, soothed by his steady heartbeat. Now she noticed it begin to race and, glancing up, saw his disappointment. Of course Donington would appeal. "You must forgive me for railing against the inevitable, my love. You are right, Upholland is insufficient for our new responsibilities, and Donington deserves attention. We are now a baronial family, and we shall show our peers just how well suited we are to the title. It's just that we've been so happy at Upholland. Might you charm Besetta into moving with us to Donington?" She pulled his head down to kiss him, rewarded by a show of dimples. "No matter what happens, I still have the husband I chose and our two dear boys."

She resolved to put aside her resentment and set to work ensuring that Thomas was at ease in his new role, proud of her, his boys, and their household. She told herself it was gratifying that in saving her he had, in the end, saved his family's honor. And she was a woman of status now, not a vulnerable child easily manipulated by the king and queen.

In April, Thomas returned from Brittany in time to escort Joan to the St. George's Day festivities at Windsor. He reveled in being openly with Joan at such an official gathering, dancing with her, whispering in her ear at the high table, walking with her hand on his arm. They were given a comfortable chamber in the castle, his first taste of his new status. It was a heady experience to be treated as a peer by the earls, even Will Montagu, now happily married to Elizabeth de Mohun and expecting his first child. Thomas wished his father might see this, that his second son had recovered the honor of his family and raised it higher than before.

But Thomas's time at Windsor was not all play. He spent much of it talking to those who were now his peers about legal matters, inviting recommendations for household officers. He also quietly arranged for a consultation regarding a matter that he chose not to discuss with Joan, uncertain how she would react. There was a new pope in Avignon, Innocent VI, and, anxious to protect the estates for his sons, Thomas had prepared a new petition asking for validation of his marriage to Joan. It was his new status that unsettled him, a sense that he was not worthy, or might be judged so. With the pope's validation, he might rest easy.

Joan spent much time in discussion with Bella regarding a new wardrobe, and making sure Ned did not lead young Tom into games she did not wish him to play. Thomas disliked the prince's too keen interest in his godson, and his attempts to monopolize Joan on the dance floor.

So he was hesitant to trust that the prince was sincere when he took him aside and asked for his patience.

"I blunder my way toward my new role in my cousin's life. I insulted you with my clumsy attempt at humor about your good fortune. I regret that—I pray you believe me. I want only Joan's happiness, and I am stupidly proud of being godfather to your son and heir."

"Why are you telling me this now, my lord?"

"Ned. Call me Ned." The prince shone his brightest smile

on Thomas. "I have seen my mistake and mean to step back, wait for your invitation. I pray you will let me know if there is anything you desire that my influence might help bring to fruition. Anything."

There was the matter of the papal petition; the prince's support might go a long way toward its consideration. Thomas said nothing then, but it was much on his mind throughout the festivities. He did not want his pride to stand in the way of his family's welfare. After the tourney, he chose to sit down with Ned to discuss the matter. The prince was more than happy to provide all the necessary letters, and recommended the men suitable for the job of representing Thomas in Avignon. When they had settled the arrangements, Thomas asked that it be kept their secret, confiding his fear that someone might interpret his actions as affirming his right to Joan's inheritance.

"Even Joan must not know. I wish to surprise her with the pope's blessing."

Ned promised to keep it between them.

Donington Castle
SUMMER 1353

IN BETWEEN FLASHES OF LIGHTNING, JOAN WATCHED HER GUARDS open the gates to a company of men on horseback. She'd expected the carpenter and the stone mason, but not Ned, and certainly not so many in the party.

In a few long strides her cousin was in the hall, shouting for a servant to come pull off his soaked gloves while he leaned close to kiss Joan on the forehead.

"So where is my godson? And the little one, John?"

"In the nursery on such a day. Why are you here?"

"I could use your counsel. And I thought to impress upon

Master Owen and Sam Trent the personal interest I will take in their work on this leaking pile. Why did you not choose Woking?"

"Elizabeth wished to stay there."

"Ah, the wilful widow."

The timing of their arrival proved providential, for chaos ensued as the river rose with the summer storms. In no time, the carpenter and the mason understood the enormity of the work ahead.

And Joan was relieved by the brevity of Ned's stay. He did indeed ask her advice about various members of his household, but, mostly, he focused on the boys, entertaining them with his gift of mimicry and his tall tales.

He visited often thereafter, showering the boys with gifts and spending time with them, while in the evenings playing chess with Joan and discussing practical matters. She began to relax with him.

Until one visit, when he told her something that he knew would upset her, something that Thomas had told him in confidence. She sent him away without permitting him to bid farewell to the boys.

Donington Castle
SPRING 1354

THE BOYS WERE GROWING SO QUICKLY — THE BABY, JOHN, WAS already two, Tom four. Thomas had been gone so much of their young lives that it took several days for them to feel easy with him. He had good news, some he shared with Joan right away (he was now the king's lieutenant in Brittany) and some he could not yet decide how to tell her (his latest petition to the pope had been granted, and their marriage blessed twice over). He put off revealing his insecurity until he'd enjoyed some time at home.

Within a few days the boys were following him about, showing off their ponies, their dogs, their favorite climbing trees. And then, just as Thomas was ready to talk to Joan, Ned arrived.

He strode in with his entourage as if he were the lord of Donington Castle, eliciting shrieks of excitement from Tom and John as they searched his pack.

"Ned and his men are quite at home here," Thomas noted to Joan as they lay in bed that night. "His men move through the castle with easy familiarity. How frequent are the prince's visits?"

She'd been lazily drawing circles on his legs with her toes, teasing him, but stopped now, propping herself up on one elbow to see his expression. "Ned brought the mason and the carpenter, and sought my council, as he did when we were children. He said he did so with your blessing. Is that not true?"

"I recall no such thing. And I don't like his staying here when I'm away."

"Was it his suggestion that you petition the pope without my knowledge?" She nodded at his curse. "Yes, Ned told me."

"He promised to tell no one, most of all you. God's blood, how he played me."

"Thomas, this is about us, our life together. Why could you not share this with me? Do you doubt the legitimacy of our marriage? I could not believe it. I sent Ned away as punishment for bringing such disturbing news. Why did you tell him and not me?"

He bought a moment to think how best to phrase it by pouring the remainder of the brandywine they'd brought to bed. "It was the new pope. I wanted to ensure that there would be no question of our children's legitimacy. Especially Tom. Do you not want him to inherit if anything were to happen to me?"

"Of course I do, and you should have known that. Don't you trust me?"

He raked a hand through his hair. "Of course I do. God help

me, I believed all Ned said about standing back, waiting for us to come to him."

"He has a knack for overstepping." Joan sat up, taking the cup from his hand for a sip. "So we are well and truly wed." He relaxed when she took his arm and drew it round her, leaning her head against him. "No more secrets, my love," she whispered. The storm had passed.

"It is time you joined me in Brittany."

"Are you serious? Is this because of Ned?"

"I am. And so what if it is?"

She snuggled closer. "Yes. It *is* time."

On hearing the plan, Ned urged them to send young Tom to the Tower with other noble youths, to ensure his safety in case, God forbid, something should happen to them.

"My sons come with us," Thomas said.

The prince looked to Joan. "What says my sweet cousin?"

"I agree. We will go to Brittany as a family."

The prince's long fingers toyed with the hilt of his dagger, his eyes sweeping the room, pausing at the children at play with Efa in the corner. Thomas noticed her glance up, feeling the prince's gaze, then bend to the boys and suggest that they visit the mews. The prince looked again at Thomas. He bowed. "May God watch over you."

It was the customary phrase. But in Ned's rendering it sounded like a warning of trouble ahead.

Brittany
SPRING 1354–SEPTEMBER 1355

WET, WINDY, COLD, BRITTANY WAS NOTHING LIKE WHAT JOAN HAD imagined. Though, to be fair, Thomas had warned her that the terrain was rough, and the men over whom he must gain control rougher still. She'd assured him that she welcomed the challenge. But, at the moment, travel-weary and cold, with two whining boys queasy from riding in a cart with a wheel that wobbled, and frightened by Jester's barking, Joan wished she were back home in Donington—better yet, at Upholland, lying in soft grass on a warm summer day, the boys rolling about beside her. Not huddled into her fur-lined cloak, her hood drawn down over her face, pacing back and forth on a slippery rock working out a cramp from riding an unfamiliar palfrey made skittish by the high voices of the boys and the yapping terrier. Thomas had ridden on ahead to alert the servants at the citadel that they would be there by sunset, and in need of a blazing fire, hot food, and dry beds. He'd been gone far longer than she'd expected.

Well, then. If she meant to prove herself a good partner, valuable to Thomas in just such difficult circumstances, it was time to steady herself and calm the boys. She picked up John, handed Tom Jester's leash, and called to Efa and one of the men to accompany them on a walk. The boys were soon cheered by the activity, John kicking to be let down to look at the animal skull his brother had discovered beside a rock, Jester rushing about them, answering their happy shouts with raucous barking.

"They'll keep the wolves at bay with all that clatter," the guard remarked with a laugh. "You've good little travelers there, my lady. I wouldn't have thought."

The praise warmed her, and she crouched down by the boys to let them show her their precious finds—a beetle, the skull, a bird claw, a worn shoe, the leather brittle with age and moisture. Efa wove the items into a tale that enthralled them on the walk back.

Thomas's face, on his return, challenged Joan's resolve. The citadel that he'd been promised proved uninhabitable without far more work than they had either the time or the men to devote to it, having been abandoned to animals and the elements far too long. But it was what they had until his men found a more suitable abode. Joan lifted her chin and suggested that they move on so they might have it set up before nightfall.

In truth, the citadel was but a stone shell precariously perched on a rocky outcrop over a rushing stream, the forest reclaiming it from three sides. Joan hid her dismay from Thomas, calling on Efa to organize the household. The boys thought it a grand campsite, particularly when Thomas's men set up tents for them in what had been the great hall.

After the evening meal, all but those on watch lingered round the fire listening to Efa's tales from her Welsh childhood. She was a gifted storyteller, a woman of many voices, and the men listened as raptly as the boys. Joan sat with her head resting on Thomas's shoulder, John in her lap, young Tom snuggled beside her, holding Jester. A moment to cherish. But when Efa began the tale of the washer at the ford, Thomas suggested that it was time for the boys to go to sleep.

"I begin to understand why your mother sent Efa away. This is a tale presaging death. The boys will be fearful whenever your women wash at the river."

Joan thought it prudent to instill in the boys a wariness of the waterways in this rocky landscape with their swift, treacherous currents, and of strangers, no matter how innocuous their occupations. But it grew late, and she was loath to spoil the evening with an argument.

That night, the wind wailed about them, setting their tents thrumming, and Joan wished Thomas were sharing her bed instead of Helena, Efa, and the two boys. But her husband's place was with the men, ordering the night watch.

A few days later they moved to an abandoned farmhouse, small but quiet and dry, where they slept in one great room until Thomas's men found a much larger, fortified manor house that suited their purpose.

But here they discovered a different problem. The house

was said by the local people to be haunted, and they refused to work there, forcing Thomas's men far afield in their search for sufficient servants. Many of those they found did not speak French, and even those who supposedly did were difficult to understand. Efa's knowledge of Welsh helped, and young Tom and John quickly came to understand Breton and the odd mix of French and Breton the servants spoke.

The "haunts" persisted. The locals had said they were vengeful spirits conjured by the blood spilled on the land. But Joan found it curious that these spirits never manifested in human form to frighten the intruder but, rather, seemed content to help themselves to supplies and occasionally topple furniture or spook the horses. Joan alerted the household to follow any locals they found on the property, reporting petty thefts and the destruction of property. The "hauntings" soon ceased.

Thomas's greatest headaches in Brittany were his own captains. Many of them had been there long enough to take on a territorial ownership, holding the countryside ransom in order to pay for their needs and a little more. After all, the king's council expected them to survive by rents from the landowners and towns they were "protecting." It reminded Joan of the wounded soldiers waiting for passage home from Calais.

"My cousin the king plays at being King Arthur come again at tourneys, but in reality he has no chivalry, squeezing out the last bit of loyalty from his people and then discarding them."

"Do you think I don't see that, Joan?" Thomas rubbed his blind eye and reached for the brandywine.

"Forgive me. What can I do?"

"The wives are eager to meet the Countess of Kent, cousin to the king of England. It's been several months. It is time. You will do this?"

"Of course!" Anything to tease out a smile from him.

And so Joan made it her business to seek out the captains in their own fortified manors in order to meet their wives, many of whom were Breton or French. Thomas was partly right; her status proved a blessing in many instances, but a curse in others. Many of the captains and their wives warmed to her, looking on Thomas with new respect, that he should be wed to such a high-born woman. But some of the captains and their men resented any representative of the king they blamed for leaving them to fend for themselves. By extension, they blamed his man and the wife he'd brought along to impress them with a pedigree they considered poisonous.

At first, Joan was distracted by the animosity simmering beneath her hosts' showy courtesy, truncating her visits when the discomfort grew unbearable. But gradually she grew more confident and ventured longer visits, farther afield. Too confident, and too ready to flaunt it. One afternoon, she chose to move on from one manor to another nearby, which Thomas had explicitly warned her to avoid, thinking to surprise him with her diplomatic skills. Before they reached the gatehouse, her small party was surrounded by a much larger one, weapons in hand.

"Run, my lady," whispered the guard closest to her as he signaled to his men to charge their opponents.

Spurring her horse, Joan rushed into the trees, the captain's men in hot pursuit. Using a move Ned had taught her, one of his favorite tourney maneuvers, Joan slipped her feet from the stirrups, drew her cloak tight round her, and flung herself sideways into the brush, rolling, rolling, as the horsemen thundered past, still chasing her horse.

Scratched and bruised but, thankfully, able to move her limbs, Joan crawled beneath a mound of fallen logs and lay still, fighting to stay calm, pushing away thoughts of what might be her fate if found, cringing as one of the horses bolted in her direction. God watched over her, or one of Efa's charms, for the horse leaped right over her and galloped on.

The sounds of fighting faded, and still she waited, her head pounding, a scratch on her neck freely bleeding, an ankle throbbing and sending shooting pains up her leg. At last she heard a familiar voice. "Show me, lad, take me there," he said softly. It was Hugh, now Thomas's first sergeant, his voice coming from the direction in which the horse had run. He was almost upon her when she found the courage to crawl out from her hiding place. The horse shied, but Hugh steadied him. "God have mercy, my lady," Hugh whispered, dismounting, nodding his men on. "You're bleeding!"

"It's no wonder, throwing myself off my horse into these brambles. I've a sprained ankle as well."

The men who had gone on called out that it was safe.

Hugh helped Joan onto the runaway horse and led her home.

Thomas held her tight in bed that night, asking if she wished to go home. But she wanted only to learn to defend herself.

"I should have brought my bow. All that practice and it never occurred to me."

"You shouldn't need it."

"Just as you shouldn't need to placate the king's abandoned men?"

The very next day, Thomas's retainers set to teaching her to defend herself with a dagger and even to wield a modest sword. Tom and John cheered her on as she trained in the yard, her skirts tucked up in her girdle, her hair gathered in a scarf, dancing about with one of Thomas's sergeants, ducking and thrusting. She beamed with pride when the sergeant praised her skill to Thomas.

"You have the strength of kings in you, my love."

Efa also worked some charms around the property and let it be known to the countryside that she was available when the local midwife was busy. Between Joan and Efa, Thomas soon gained the trust of enough of the captains that he was confident they would rally if Joan and the children were threatened. And the captain who had set his men on her party was ousted, his citadel burned, his men scattered.

As Thomas went out on longer and longer sweeps of the area, sometimes gone for a week at a time, Joan kept the boys close, especially when the scent of burning was carried on the air. Thomas was doing His Grace's bidding, ravishing the land. He would return filthy, taciturn, far different from the man she knew at home. She learned to allow him quiet, letting the servants see to his bath, his food, until he came looking for her and the children. She lay beside him on the silent nights, if he came to bed at all, allowing him to make the first move toward her. Often he simply turned from her, and she would leave him in peace. Some nights their bodies would join in wild, wordless passion. A part of her liked this rough Thomas, with his fierce strength and hunger. But too often, as they lay together afterward, she discovered open wounds, horrific bruises that needed Efa's attention. Death had never felt so omnipresent. The life of a warrior seemed all passion and destruction.

Still, they shared tender moments, and Thomas increasingly sought Joan's opinion when his soul was quieter, respecting her powers of observation. She had no regrets about accompanying him. Young Tom was gaining a new respect for his father, and Joan, too, saw for herself why her cousin the king had long held Thomas in such high regard. She was proud to be his partner.

But in October Blanche's brother Henry of Grosmont, Earl of Lancaster, was named King's Lieutenant in Brittany, heralding an escalation, a true scourge of Brittany and Normandy, with Thomas serving as one of his captains. Now Thomas wanted Joan back in England. "This will be far bloodier, and there are certain to be attacks on our bases, particularly our families if they are here. You must remove the household to England, Joan. I want you all safe across the Channel. You've helped more than you know, but with this campaign—I can't be worrying about you."

She did not argue, having seen what it was to do what he did, how it took every shred of his being to stay alive. "I've tried to take on some of the burden, but it is your burden to bear. I'm now in the way. And we must think of the little one." She took his hand and placed it on her stomach. Though it was barely swelling, she saw his expression softened into wonder. "I would that the child I carry knows you, Thomas. I'll have Lancaster's head if he loses you."

He kissed her tenderly. "Be assured, I intend to meet this child as well."

But there was a sadness in him that he could not hide. "You would be safer under your own command," she said. "Lancaster doesn't know the men as you do, neither the allies nor the enemies. It's not his ability but his name the king wants leading the charge." She saw by his wince that she had guessed the source of his pain. "I shall pray for you every day. Keep the white hart silk on you at all times, my love." It would protect him against all enemies, even those on his own side. Whence had that thought arisen? She'd not known she distrusted Lancaster.

Woodstock
AUTUMN 1355

AFTER A FOUR-YEAR HIATUS IN WHICH QUEEN PHILIPPA wondered whether she had borne her last child (another Joan, who had lived but a few months), she had the previous January borne a healthy boy, Thomas. And now, much to her surprise, she again found herself with child. This pregnancy troubled her. From the very first, she felt that something was wrong. She wanted distraction, entertainment, but she tired of her ladies and all the fighting men were away—Edward in Scotland, her three eldest sons in France or preparing for it, Lionel and John both taking part this time. Ned had begun yet another onslaught into the south of France, stoking once again the fear he'd inspired in his last sweep of burning and pillage. They called him *l'Homme Noir*, and he was proud of it. She crossed herself, said a prayer for their safety.

She needed a spark in her coterie, a Lucienne. Bella urged her to summon her cousin Joan. "You've heard how she wooed and won some of the worst of the captains in Brittany. Imagine the stories she's collected. And she's with child. The two of you can share your misery."

"Ned says her estates have been criminally neglected. She should see to them."

"Offer her a few advisers in exchange for her company. Do try."

JOAN COULD NOT DENY HOW WELCOME SUCH HELP WOULD BE. Andrew, Thomas's longtime steward, was beside himself with remorse for the poor harvests, the uncollected rents, the run-down state of some of the manor houses. But she dreaded the thought of returning to the queen's household, and Woodstock, where Ned had drowned Bruno. She'd not been there since he confessed.

"If I may express an opinion, my lady?"

"Efa, when have I ever refused your advice?"

"Beneath her generous and timely offer is a plea for your company. She needs cheering. If you do this, you will have the queen on your side in future matters, and perhaps she will take Tom and John into the infant Thomas's household. Growing up within the household of one of the king's sons—that would please my lord, would it not?"

Joan hated the prospect of the boys' fostering. But it was inevitable, and where better? Where might they be safer? "I will do this. It will be good for Thomas and my boys." She wrinkled her nose at Efa's grin. "*And* me. But I shall put you to work. You are far more likely to cheer the queen than I am."

❖ ❖ ❖

How changed she was, Philippa thought, watching Joan with her boys. Tom, the eldest, was a dark-eyed, dark-haired charmer. He had his father's dimples and square physique, but was a momma's boy, looking to Joan for approval. The younger one troubled Philippa, so like Ned that she must needs remind herself over and over that he was not her grandson, just a male version of his mother, who had looked so like Ned as a child. He took after Ned in temperament as well, stomping and shrieking when he did not get his way. He would be a handful, and then some. Joan doted on him, just as Philippa had on Ned. He would break her heart. She shook herself. Ned was a hero and would be a worthy successor to her beloved Edward. All the same, she prayed that this war exhausted her eldest's dark humors, that the fire of combat would purge them from his system.

Meanwhile, his favorite cousin had offered the services of her nurse, Efa, and within a few days the Welsh healer had lifted the shadow on Philippa's heart, though she did wonder at the need for daily walks and such a plain diet. As for Joan, her tales of Brittany—the haunted manor house, the ruined citadel, the peculiar airs of the French whores who fancied themselves the "ladies" of the renegade captains—all the household crowded round to hear her stories, and Philippa quite forgot herself in listening. Joan inspired affection in all around her, including, to her own surprise, the queen.

Donington Castle
SPRING 1356

THE QUEEN'S PREGNANCY HAD NOT ENDED HAPPILY. SHE HAD BEEN delivered of a stillborn girl a fortnight earlier, and Bella followed Joan to Donington, wishing to escape the gloom.

They sat now in Donington's kitchen garden on a cool spring morning, lazily watching Efa patiently trying to teach the boys the names of the various herbs. But the boys fidgeted and gazed over their shoulders toward the stables. Finally, after a sudden whispered countdown, the two burst into a lively jig.

Joan laughed so hard she felt a wetness, then realized with a start that her water had broken. Efa helped her to the temporary bedchamber screened off in a sunny corner of the hall and, within a short while, before Joan could even break into a sweat, she was delivered of a baby girl. A daughter at last. Joan felt the familiar surge of love for the pink-faced, squalling child of her loins. This child, more than the boys, would be her companion and her joy.

"You must call her Joan, for my sister and your cousin," said Bella. "Let my sister's spirit live on in this sweet child."

"As her godmother, it is your privilege to name her, though I'd thought to name our first daughter Maud, for Thomas's dear mother, who risked the pestilence to help us in Avignon."

"Faith, that is the better choice. Joan shall be next."

The king's offering in honor of the birth of Maud Holland was to name Thomas Keeper of the Channel Islands. It was a thankless post, the garrisons small and vulnerable to attack from the sea. For now, Otho would go in Thomas's place while his brother was fighting with Lancaster in Normandy. Joan thought to join him once he was free to take up his new post.

"This insult," Thomas growled.

"We will make it an honor, my love," Joan assured him.

Donington Castle
NOVEMBER 1356

IN THE LATE AUTUMN THOMAS RETURNED TO ENGLAND, SUM-
moned by the king to confer on conditions in Brittany—how he
read the temper of the captains after Lancaster's autumn raids
through Normandy, what he could tell him of the renegade
companies of soldiers roaming the countryside, up to no good.
It had been a frustrating time for him, Joan knew. Lancaster's
blusterous approach undid alliances Thomas had worked hard
to form. He felt it all the more keenly in light of the glory showered on Ned and many of the Garter Knights for the great
English victory at Poitiers. They had captured both King Jean
of France and his son, Philippe. Even Will had fought in the
battle.

Joan worried about how gaunt Thomas was, the gray streaks
in his hair, the twitch on the temple near his blind eye. As she
helped him undress she grieved to see a raw, puckered scar just
above his left collarbone, his blind side, and a fresh wound that
creased the top of his right thigh.

"I lose you a little at a time." She kissed both scars.

In the morning he was most eager to spend time with Maud,
the daughter he'd only glimpsed the previous evening. Almost
six months old and thriving, she was a happy baby, her laugh
throaty, her eyes bright blue and curious, her hair brown and
curly.

"My mother's hair." Thomas held her gingerly. "A
beauty, eh?"

"She is. But she's as strong as the boys, my love. Do not be
afraid to hold her close."

Later, over a meal in the hall, she cheered him with her
news that she meant to accompany him to the Channel Islands.
"We'll bring Maud, of course."

"And the boys?" Thomas took her hands. "This would be a

good time to foster them, eh?" He squinted as if steeling himself for a protest.

"As much as I dread it, I agree, my love. And I have a plan, if it pleases you. The queen wishes them both to join the household of her youngest, Thomas. They're a little old for him, but—what do you think?"

His relief was clear. "The queen honors us. Had I been so fostered, I might have shared in the glory of Poitiers. It will be the making of them both."

Joan's heart twisted to hear the regret in him. "My love, we have so much. You were at Caen, Crécy. . . ."

"And now I am the one who clears the way for another's glory and cleans up after him while he basks in undeserved praise." He ran his hands through his hair. "Forgive me. My sour words are unbecoming, I know. But all we have is yours, Joan. It is little of my doing." He smiled as John charged into the room, lifting him and swinging him up and over his shoulder. "Save for these angels. I do proudly take credit for them."

Joan saw his wince, the pain in the shoulder. She hugged herself against a sudden chill. He was aging so quickly of a sudden, the difference in their years all too clear. *God grant me more time with him. It is far too soon to lose him.*

London
MAY 1357

JOAN AND THE CHILDREN WERE INVITED TO OBSERVE NED'S triumphal entry into London from a stand erected for the royal family along the route. Thomas would ride with his fellow Garter Knights. From the prince's palace of Kennington the men rode, King Jean by choice on a small black palfrey, Ned on a white charger, the Garter Knights and the barons of the realm spread out behind them, including all who had fought at Poitiers. The mayor and the leading citizens of London met them on the road and escorted them into the city, where the streets were hung with tapestries, bows, and armor suspended from windows, and from the rooftops gold and silver leaf showered down on Ned and King Jean. The sound was deafening, the cheers, the church bells clanging. Guilds and companies stood in their livery at the intersections—a thousand such mounted citizens lining the route. Fountains spouted wine, so the people crowding every building and alleyway along the way were merry. The boys were terribly excited to see their father in full armor, his blue and white cloak powdered with silver garters catching the light even from afar.

Joan had not seen Ned in a long while. She hardly recognized him. Where he had been lithesome and sharp-jawed he was bulky and bearded, his hair darkened, as if all the blood he'd shed . . . She shook her head to clear it of such nonsense. But at the feast afterward she was loath to approach him, remembering how he had played her and Thomas against each other. He was every inch a duke and a prince now, straight-backed, muscled, and bold, with that habit she'd first noticed in Calais of surveying a room to see that all had noticed him even more pronounced, as if insatiable in his hunger for admiration. Even her boys shied away from him. It was the gentle King Jean who drew them out, remarking that their uncle had spoken true when he'd bragged about them—they were handsome boys, and clever. Now Tom and John approached their uncle and Ned laughingly greeted them, meeting Joan's eyes with a warm smile as he exaggerated his surprise at how they had grown, challenging them to punch him in the stomach, stumbling back. They were all giggling by the time Thomas joined them, finding himself warmly welcomed by Ned and invited to a small dinner the following day to discuss the situation in northern France.

Watching how deftly Ned manipulated her sons and her husband, Joan worried that they too easily succumbed to his charm. But she hid her misgivings as Thomas told her that night how Ned had promised to speed up his elevation to the title of Earl. He'd assured Thomas that he knew it was his work and not Lancaster's that had brought a' modicum of peace to northern France.

"I was wrong about him, Joan. He does wish us well."

Joan warned him to tread with care, not to commit to anything until they saw whether Ned was true to his word. "He respects and values your service to the Crown, I've no doubt. But he's no better than his father in rewarding such loyalty."

Thomas bowed his head. "Of course. You know him better than I do."

Was that a hint of resentment in his voice? God help her, even when absent Ned cast a shadow on their happiness.

THE RHYTHM OF THE NEXT THREE YEARS WAS ONE OF ARRIVALS AND departures for Joan. They were not long in the Channel Islands when Thomas was made custodian of Cruyk Castle in Normandy, then governor of the Cotentin Peninsula, based at Saint-Sauveur-le-Vicomte. Now that they would be biding in territory devastated by the English, Joan sent Maud home, entrusting her to the care of Efa and Blanche. The land was so desolate, the people embittered, starving, with little to lose. It was no place for a child. Nor did Joan have the time to spend with her—as Thomas traveled across the peninsula, she remained at Cruyk, then at Saint-Saveur, receiving supplicants, mediating contested claims to commands, garrisons, properties, rights of way. Though she was surrounded by clerks, sergeants, and a complete administrative staff, they were all making do with minimal comforts. Their supplies ebbed and flowed. The few elegant gowns she had brought remained in locked chests, along with jewels and silver plate, except when she entertained someone of sufficient rank.

It was only when Joan was quite certain she was again with child that she reluctantly returned to England. Reluctantly, for she enjoyed the work and how Thomas appreciated it, treasuring their discussions, how he valued her opinion—but, most of all, she wished to be by his side as much as possible, jealous of what time they had left together.

The dowager queen Isabella had died while Joan was away, succumbing to a summer fever. It was whispered that she'd taken her own life with dangerously large doses of her medications, but Joan did not believe it. No one with such sins darkening her soul would welcome her reckoning. Joan felt the air a little clearer at home, her family safer.

But Otho, too, had died, mortally wounded in battle. For him, Joan mourned. Not for Isabella.

48

Donington Castle
SEPTEMBER 1360

In late summer, Thomas returned home to meet for the first time his youngest child, Jeannette, on her first birthday. Fair and blue-eyed, she looked like her mother, and Thomas yearned to hold her, but whenever he reached for her she shrieked. Efa assured him that it was Jeannette's disposition, always dissatisfied. But why should she come to him? He was a stranger with a scarred face, gray, thinning hair, and a halting gait. Even Joan had been taken aback upon his return. Though she quickly recovered and rushed into his embrace, he'd seen her shock. He was well aware that he'd aged in the year and a half since she had seen him. He felt the weight of his years, the heaviness that robbed him of speed and dulled his mind. Joan had changed as well—her figure was fuller and worry lines had worn a crease in her forehead—but to him she was more beautiful than ever.

It was a double celebration, Jeannette's birthday and Thomas's elevation, at long last, to the earldom of Kent.

But before he might settle down, become reacquainted with his family and his lands, and take his place in Parliament, he had one more mission to carry out for the king. He was to return as Edward's captain and lieutenant in Normandy to cleanse it of Bretons, Gascons, and English in preparation for handing it back to the French in the New Year. It was an honorable post, but the goal was impossible in so short a time, and it required diplomacy. Thomas's strength was strategy—for diplomacy, he needed Joan.

She was ready, though she balked at his insistence that the girls stay behind in Blanche Wake's household, under Efa's care.

"I want Efa with us. Let us not pretend you are well, Thomas. You have more need of Efa than do our girls. Jeannette's wet nurse will be more than sufficient in Blanche's household."

He tried to reason with her—Efa could not accompany him on forays—but Joan was adamant, and he backed off. It was little to ask in return.

On the crossing, Joan felt a dread deep in her bones. She told herself it was the natural after-effect of two crises that had rattled her composure on their last days at Donington. Two days before their departure, Maud had a bad fall while playing with her brother John, spraining an ankle and suffering a deep, dangerous gash in her forearm. Efa had to stay behind to nurse her, neither Joan nor Thomas trusting anyone else with such a wound. And on the eve of their journey Thomas could not find the white hart silk. He'd not worn it while at home, so it might have gone missing anytime in the month they'd been at Donington, or perhaps the week in Windsor for his investiture as earl. Yes, he remembered seeing it there, in the chamber where Hugh and his squire had helped him with his armor while Ned gave him last-minute advice. The boys had to be chased out several times. Might it have been lost in the ensuing confusion? He tried to shrug it off, a superstition his confessor often chided him for. But they were both troubled by it.

Joan stood on the deck with Thomas, his arm round her shoulders, drawing her close. All seemed peaceful, even the water, with just enough breeze for the sails. She rested her head against his chest and listened for the soothing trio of sounds—

his heartbeat, his steady breath, the wind snapping the sails. She sought to calm her own racing mind, her fear that their daughter's injuries and the loss of the silk were omens. But Thomas's heart beat irregularly, and his breathing was shallow. She hated Edward for insisting on this last mission. Why could he not have included Thomas in the company escorting King Jean to Calais for a meeting regarding his unpaid ransom? Why this final, too heavy burden?

On landfall, Joan's uneasiness grew as she crossed the dock, facing a barren, blasted landscape. Two years ago, she had thought it a wasteland. Now it seemed impossible that it had ever held life. Thomas had been right to insist that they leave the girls at home. But he was her immediate concern. All Efa's work to ease his limp had been undone by the journey, and the suffering caused by his halting gait was visible in the set of his mouth, the tension in his jaw and eye. She wished her second-born had not been so careless with his little sister, letting Maud fall, robbing his father of Efa's care.

As the men organized the company for the further journey, Joan, Helena, and the other servants sat on chests, calling out directions as needed. During a lull in the activity, Helena pointed out a solitary man leading his horse through the crowd. He was dressed more like a merchant than a soldier, and moved through the crowd as if not a part of it and quite comfortable with that. Joan watched as he strode up to Thomas, bowing, speaking to him with much gesturing. And now he approached her, escorted by Sir Hugh.

"This is Simon, my lady, apprentice to Master Adam, one of the king's physicians, sent by royal command to assist you in seeing to the welfare of my lord's company." Hugh bowed and left the stranger to her.

Joan did not like how this Simon avoided meeting her gaze, his heavy-lidded eyes regarding the ground in false humility, as if he thought she'd not seen how boldly he'd walked among the company of soldiers. "Assistant to the king's physician, yet you are not familiar to me, Simon. How can that be?"

"At court Master Adam prefers me in his workroom, my lady. On campaign, I play a more active role. My orders are to travel with Earl Thomas."

"He has never been offered your services before. Why now?"

A gesture toward the lifelessness surrounding them. "Old campaigners such as the earl know where to find healing plants and soils in the countryside. But all that has been destroyed. I was sent with supplies that I pray will be sufficient for the duration of his mission."

It seemed possible this unpleasant man was God's answer to her prayers for Thomas's well-being. Joan nodded to him and sent him back to Sir Hugh.

Through the ravished countryside they traveled in a large company—household, military and administrative staff—to Saint-Sauveur-le-Vicomte, past burned fields, homes, towns, and villages destroyed, churches fortified to protect the survivors. They were an uncharacteristically mute party, speaking only when necessary.

Thomas spent the first week settling in, waiting for his team of outriders to report the lay of the land. He laughed at Joan's continued discomfort with Simon.

"He assumes an authority he doesn't deserve," she said.

"A little power can turn the head of a little man, my love. I will relieve you of him on the morrow."

As Thomas and his company of soldiers began their journey through the towns and citadels of Normandy, Joan settled with her women and servants in the château, well protected within massive walls.

As before, word spread that an English noblewoman was at the château. Joan gave what hospitality she could to a few disenfranchised noblewomen, widowed or left unprotected by husbands taken prisoner. Ignoring the advice of her counselors, she encouraged the women to dictate their stories to the clerks, stating their needs and the condition of their properties, so that she might hand over the information to the French administrators who would follow. The women were frustrated that although Joan offered material comfort—cots, food—it was only for a few days at best. They thrust their children before them, lifting their tunics to show protruding ribs. But there was little enough for the garrison and Thomas's large company, particularly when supplies were still uncertain.

Joan did what she could. Her heart was not easy.

THOMAS AND HIS MEN SLEPT ROUGH ON THE MARCH, KNOWING better than to trust their luck to the hospitality of those King Edward had ordered out of their comfortable holdings. They spent their days riding down armed bands, surrounding the churches they'd fortified and smoking them out. Thomas was painfully aware that he was growing too old for such campaigning. The worst were the sudden attacks, when he must dismount without aid, rushing for cover. A week of it and his old thigh injury made mounting, dismounting, and any sudden movement an agony. Each morning and evening, Simon worked a soothing balm into Thomas's muscles, but he did not have Efa's touch.

Hugh urged Thomas to return to the château and use his sergeants for the forays. "Trust us. We can carry on as you would, my lord. I pray you, let us do this for you."

When he became a drag on his men, Thomas decided that Hugh was right. He would participate in one more foray from the camp, then head back to the citadel.

On that morning his party came upon a renegade band and chased after them, too late realizing their mistake. They'd been led into a trap, an abandoned village surrounded by skilled archers. Seeking cover in the burned-out shell of a house, Thomas lost his balance and fell through rotten boards, tearing a long, deep gash in his right thigh. As if that were not bad enough, the fall reopened an old wound below. He'd lost a great deal of blood before his squire, Giles, managed to stop the flow with a belt high on his thigh. Between the pain and the need to keep the belt taut, Thomas could not walk. While the battle raged he lay there, impotent, cursing himself for his stubborn pride.

Simon reached him from the camp a day later, sucking air through his teeth as he packed the wound with a foul-smelling ointment and sewed it closed.

Thomas refused milk of poppy to deaden the pain. "Not until we reach the château."

"My lord, you must rest. Your body needs all the strength left to fight against the corruption of the flesh and blood."

Had Thomas taken Hugh's advice when offered, he would be safe at the château now. He finally agreed to the milk of poppy, swimming in and out of consciousness as slowly, by litter, they made the journey back to Saint-Sauveur-le-Vicomte, his company focused on his protection.

A RUNNER HAD BROUGHT THE NEWS OF THOMAS'S INJURY TO THE château, and Joan rode out to meet him with a midwife who had come to her offering her services in exchange for food. Joan trusted Gabriella far more than she did Simon. They wore men's clothes to ride more swiftly, and she met the company before nightfall.

"*Merde!*" whispered the healer, shaking her head at the stench of the wound.

"It is my medicines," said Simon, insulted by the very presence of such a woman.

But Joan saw by Gabriella's expression that it was the wound that stank, already corrupted. The healer wanted to open the stitches and clean and repack the wound with boiled boneset and heal-all. Simon disagreed, threatening to leave the camp if she defied his authority. The men sided with him. But Joan trusted Gabriella, who had warned her privately that Simon either knew nothing of healing or purposed to kill his lord. Joan overrode the men's protests, insisting that the midwife was right; the wound needed to be opened and drained of corruption. She stayed with Thomas throughout the terrible ordeal, holding his hand, praying with him.

Afterward, he slept more peacefully. Hugh apologized for doubting Joan's judgment.

At daybreak, they discovered Simon still there, humbled, he said, by the midwife's superior skill. It took two days of slow riding to reach the château.

A few days after their return Gabriella vanished, leaving no trace.

"It is not uncommon in the field, my lady," Hugh assured her. "They come for the comfort and leave as they will. She was skilled, though. We will miss her."

For Joan it was like losing Efa again, for she had no confidence in Simon's skill. She sent out a few servants to search for the woman, but Thomas put a stop to it.

"The loss of a midwife is of little importance, Joan. We have Simon."

Reluctantly, Joan let the apprentice work on Thomas's leg. She watched him like a hawk, and Helena did as well. They relaxed a little as Thomas gained some strength, enough to order his men, then walk short distances, and finally ride, though he needed help mounting and dismounting. They were to shift their base to Rouen in December to meet with churchmen and barons. Joan was more than ready to leave. Simon put them off for a few more weeks, to give him more time to drain the pus.

"It is important that Earl Thomas regain his strength before the journey," he told Joan, "for the pestilence has returned—the winter one, the one that robs breath, the silent killer."

Joan lay awake nights, praying that God spare her family, selfishly arguing with him that she'd waited so long for joy that she deserved his protection.

Often she discovered Thomas sitting up to massage his leg, and she would take over. By an unspoken agreement, they kept their conversations in the night to their children and the plans they had for their properties—safe topics, looking forward to a future together. But one night, when Thomas's pain was grievous, he confided that he did not believe he would see his children again.

"God would not be so cruel," Joan whispered, drawing Thomas into her arms. But his constant pain worried her.

The first stage of their journey was by sea, from Barfleur to Honfleur. Then they would ride south along the Seine, their party too large to be accommodated on the river. An icy rain fell as they disembarked to continue on horseback.

THEY RODE SIDEWISE AGAINST A GALE WIND AND DRIVING RAIN, forcing Thomas to press his thighs into his mount to stay balanced, the wounded one throbbing and burning. Faith, his whole body burned, yet he shivered as the storm soaked through his heavy cloak, the heat within consuming, not warming. Broken, useless, he sat by the riverbank as his men made camp, watching the flow, wishing he might just glide in and let it take him, like the filthy cloth the current tore from the hand of the woman kneeling on the bank, washing bloody clothing.

As if hearing his thoughts, the woman turned, smiling, and whispered, "You're mine."

How could he hear her at this distance, in this storm? He called his squire, told him to bring her to him.

Giles squinted through the rain. "Who, my lord?"

"The washerwoman on the bank. With the bloody clothes."

Giles shook his head. "There is no one there, my lord."

Thomas saw that it was true. She was gone. "I must have fallen asleep." Giles looked askance, as well he should. Asleep in the icy downpour? Something flickered in memory: Efa's voice, telling the tale of the washer at the ford. *When you see her, you are about to die.* "Is that a ford, Giles?"

"They say it is in summer, my lord. But not in this season."

So this was it. Thomas forbade Giles to mention the incident to anyone. Joan must not hear of it.

EVERYONE WAS DISPIRITED BY THE TIME THEY ARRIVED IN THE CITY, Joan most of all. Thomas was slipping from her, despite Simon's constant care.

They were to bide in a town house Ned had acquired as part of a ransom, and the staff who had traveled on ahead to ensure all was ready had done their job well. The servants welcomed them with hearty food, fine wine, soft, warm, dry beds. The cellars were well stocked so Joan and Thomas might woo the French nobles and churchmen with lavish entertainment. Tempers were high, for there was much at stake, and much resentment on all sides. But clearly Thomas had not the strength for such diplomacy. Joan assured him that the king would understand that he could not fulfill this part of the mission. But Thomas insisted that she carry on, with Hugh's help.

"Wear your elegant gowns, your jewels, and fit Hugh out in my velvets and silks. Preside over a table aglitter with silver plate, Italian glass goblets and jeweled mazers. You're a better countess than I'm an earl. You're a Plantagenet. Finish this for me, my love."

"We will see."

First, she sent for the infirmarian of the Abbey of Saint-Ouen. Simon overheard and expressed outrage. Rudely, and with far too much panic in his voice. She ignored him, leaving orders that he was not to be permitted into Thomas's chamber until the infirmarian had rendered his judgment.

Brother Francis was a compact man with huge, moist eyes. He listened with bent head to Joan's account, whispering to himself and here and there asking for clarification. "I will see him now." Stepping over the threshold of Thomas's chamber, he paused, sniffing, then hurried to the bed, stopping only to bow and introduce himself. "I would see the wound, my lord." And without waiting for permission he lifted the covers. "Mon Dieu," he whispered, moving up to sniff Thomas's breath. He turned those moist eyes on Joan. "My lady, is there a urine sample?" A servant stepped forward with the flask. Francis sniffed, then shook his head, and, bowing to Thomas, took Joan aside. "I would meet this Simon, assistant to your king's physician."

But Simon was nowhere to be found. Cursing herself for not locking him up, Joan ordered Hugh to organize a search for him. "And find out whether any of our barons are in France. The archbishop will know."

When she returned to the infirmarian, Joan found Thomas sleeping naked on the bed, a novice washing him with warm cloths. His right leg was dark, angry red streaks radiating out from the putrefying flesh surrounding the wound.

"God have mercy," she sobbed.

Francis took her hands and drew her out into the corridor. "I have given him something to make him sleep while Antony bathes him and then opens the wound to drain." He kissed both her hands. "I am sorry, my lady. Earl Thomas is far too weak to survive surgery to remove the leg. The poison—it has already so weakened his heart. I am too late. There is little I can do."

For a moment, Joan forgot how to breathe. "What *can* you do for my husband?"

"Make him as comfortable as possible, that is all. It breaks my heart to tell you this, my lady, though I see that you are not entirely surprised."

"Did Simon poison him?"

"Tell me about his care. All that you know." Francis listened intently, asking here and there for clarification. At the end, he sighed. "He did not need poison. With neglect, he turned the earl's body against itself. The midwife said as much, did she not? And when he saw that she knew, he killed her, I've no doubt. May she rest in peace."

Joan crossed herself.

"Did he leave you any physic?"

"No. He kept close control. All his things are gone."

"I ordered my assistant to keep the soiled cloths with which he's cleaning the wound," said Francis. "We might learn more. But it will not save your husband. We will make him comfortable, then take the cloths away. I will return in the morning— with answers, I hope. May God watch over you."

When the monk had gone, Joan sat at the edge of the bed, smoothing the damp hair from Thomas's forehead, kissing his brow, his cheeks, his lips. Taking his hand in hers, she bowed her head and silently prayed that he suffer no more pain, prayed that her children were safe, prayed that whoever had set Simon on them died a long, painful death.

Thomas woke in a few hours, seeming more lucid. He wanted to hear all that Francis had said. When Joan hesitated, he told her about the washer at the ford.

She felt a dread chill. "Why did you keep this from me? We should have put Simon in chains there, at the ford."

"The harm, if it was done by him, is done. My love, promise me that you will not waste your life searching for my murderer."

"Thomas!"

He put a finger to her lips. "I might have died a thousand times on the battlefield, or in a raid. This is no different."

"It is, Thomas. He was an assassin. I would know who sent him."

"Promise me, Joan."

"Our fathers—"

"All the more reason to prevent our children from suffering as we did, carrying the burden of resentment for a past that cannot be undone."

He soon fell asleep, and Joan stayed beside him, holding him as if, by her will, she might draw him out of the clutch of Death.

In the early morning, Thomas cried out in his sleep that something was chasing him. When he rose to consciousness he complained of a dry mouth, a racing heart. Joan sent for the infirmarian, refusing to wait until Brother Francis saw fit to appear.

In the hall she found Sir John Chandos, one of Ned's most trusted knights.

"My messenger found you?"

He nodded. "My lord Prince Edward sent me to observe the meetings. But the news—Earl Thomas—I have sent a message to my lord at Calais. I know he holds you in the highest regard. I very much think that he would wish to know, and that you might find comfort in his knowing—and his presence, if it is possible. I will see to it that the nobles and churchmen understand the situation."

"I am grateful for your kindness, Sir John."

Despite Joan's summons, Brother Francis did not arrive until late in the afternoon. "I wanted to have an answer for you, and I have. The residue in the cloths was a grease with no healing qualities whatsoever. His poison was neglect, as I said. This Simon was no healer."

"God rot his soul."

Thomas shook his head. "Forget him, my love."

His breathy speech caused Brother Francis to lean close, smelling Thomas's mouth, then putting an ear to his chest. He shook his head as he rose. "Your chest fills with fluid." He called to the servants, "Cushions! Ensure that the earl is upright at all times."

Joan crossed herself as she witnessed how much assistance Thomas needed to sit up.

Brother Francis took her aside. "He is sinking rapidly. I would purge or bleed, but he is too weak. A sweat might help draw out the poison."

Joan sat with her beloved as he slept, watching Brother Francis's novice place hot stones wrapped in cloths soaked in a physic at Thomas's feet, all along his sides, tucked in toward his neck. As the sweat came forth, Antony bathed Thomas with fragrant water, praying all the while. She sensed Thomas relaxing under the regimen.

Yet in the morning Thomas was so weak that he could not hold a spoon. Joan fed him some broth. In halting, slurred speech, he apologized for his condition. The fear in his eye made her cold.

"My love, my love, do not agitate yourself with worry for me. I thank God that I am here with you. I love you, and I will do everything in my power to bring you back to health."

Shakily, he curled his hand round her wrist and drew her close, pressing his forehead to hers. "I have been so blessed to have your love."

She did not leave his side except to relieve herself. Sometimes she stood and walked slowly round his bed as he slept, and sometimes she slept beside him.

ONE MORNING SEVERAL DAYS AFTER HE'D TAKEN TO HIS BED, Thomas asked for a priest. "I would be shriven, in casc."

Joan was privy to his halting confession of minor ill feelings, a few politic lies, his doubts about his father's honor.

"Doubting God is a sin, my son, but doubting that you understood another's heart—there is no blame in that," said the priest.

Joan wished Thomas would save his strength. As if he'd heard her distress, the priest cut the confession short and gave Thomas absolution, then the last rites.

The following day, Thomas did not seem to know any of the old comrades who came to pay their respects, even Hugh. Joan and Hugh held each other's hands as they sat beside him after the others had filed through.

And then, a commotion at the door, a scent of myrrh and fresh air, and Ned strode into the room. He bowed to Joan, hand to heart, then dropped to one knee beside Thomas and took his hand, and with bent head remained there a long while, sometimes murmuring prayers, sometimes silent.

When at last he rose, Ned joined Joan and Hugh, taking Joan's free hand in both of his. His warmth steadied her.

At one point Thomas woke, asking for her, and Joan went to him, whispering comfort. He put a shaky finger to her lips, smoothed her hair.

"I see him there," he whispered. "He has waited for you all this time. I hated him for it. But now—"

"Hush, my beloved. You have my heart, now and forever."

"He can protect you. And the children. *Let him.*"

Joan silenced him with a kiss, then stretched out beside him as he drifted off again, whispering to him of her love, of the joy he had brought her, and speaking of their beautiful children. Now and then his eyelids flickered and his breathing changed. Once he groped for her hand. She believed he heard her endearments. She was still there beside him, in the dark of the night, when Thomas breathed his last, a much quieter exhaling than before, and then, a terrible peace.

"My lady," whispered Brother Francis, touching her shoulder. "It is over. Now you must rest."

She sat up, but only to kneel beside the bed. "I'll watch with my husband until dawn." Brother Francis bowed and stepped back, murmuring prayers behind her.

At dawn, Ned lifted her and carried her to her chamber, softly calling for Helena to prepare her for rest. He kissed Joan on the forehead, and withdrew.

She had such dreams. Riding after Thomas, whose horse was swifter, better at maneuvering between the trees of an increasingly dense forest. Floating on a lake in a mist, listening for the oars of his boat. Flying through the air toward a high tower on which he stood, watching the sunrise. Joan woke to a yawning emptiness. Her hands were so cold, her mind so blank that she thought she might have died as well.

"My lady, will you dress?" Helena asked, her face marked by grief.

"Who is still here? Brother Francis?"

"The infirmarian left his novice Antony to assist you in preparing my lord's body, if you wish his help. Prince Edward is biding nearby, awaiting your summons. Sir Hugh and the other retainers have organized watches with their lord's body. And the servants are going about their duties as silently as possible, their hearts heavy for your loss. Our loss. All the household loved my lord Thomas. He was the best of men."

He was. Of that Joan had no doubt.

"While you sat with my lord, the maid Janet and I busied ourselves, my lady." Helena held up a black wool gown. "You have another one for more elegant—"

"And you spared me the task. Bless you." Joan was a widow. As Helena dressed her, Joan called on God to help her cope with all that must be done.

"Have they found any trace of Simon?"

"No, my lady."

"Have Sir Hugh question the servants who are not of my household." Someone might have seen him depart. Someone

might have helped him. Though too late to save Thomas, Joan
meant to know who had robbed her of her beloved. "While he
does that, we shall wash Earl Thomas's body. The novice can assist. And send for my cousin the prince." He could advise her on
where to have Thomas held until she could remove him to the
Greyfriars in Stamford, according to his will. "Come, Helena, it
is time." She needed to busy herself.

Reentering the room, she was moved by the quiet presence
of Thomas's battle-scarred men, bowed in grief or sitting tall,
determined to be strong yet showing their sorrow by their very
stiffness. He had inspired devotion.

Her breath caught as she drew the cover from her beloved's
body. Already he lacked healthy color. So soon he had slipped
away from her. Emotion nearly choked her. Taking the wet
cloth from Helena, Joan bathed Thomas. Such cold flesh. She
noted the wounds marking his courage, discipline, dedication,
and prayed that God would mark them as well and keep him
close. How she wished Thomas might have lived long enough
to rest easy at last, reaping the bounty of the earldom that she
had brought him and the renown that he had earned, and to
enjoy Tom, John, Maud, and Jeannette, and they him. Their
father had been absent so much of their young lives. He might
have been so inspiring as the boys grew older. Not now. With
the help of Helena and Antony, Joan sewed Thomas into his
shroud with fine herbs. She did her best to remember the words
Efa had said over her mother.

Hugh awaited Joan outside the chamber to report what
he'd learned from the local servants. She'd forgotten that he was
questioning them.

"They swear they did not know Simon. One saw him leave,
alone, but did not know to challenge him."

"And you believe them?"

"I do, my lady."

She turned at the sound of Ned's voice in the hall beyond,

familiar, a touchstone. For a moment, she rejoiced. She might relax in his protection. But Thomas had been jealous of him. *No, my love, no. It was you from the moment you smiled at me.*

"His Grace the Prince of Wales requests your presence at dinner," said Hugh.

So formal? "How did he say that to you?"

"My lady?"

"His very words."

"He asked if you had sat down to a meal since my lord fell ill. I did not think so. He said, 'I thought not. Tell my cousin that Ned is here. Over dinner she can tell me how I can best be of service.'"

Joan felt a flutter of hope. She need not bear all this alone. "Have you told him about Simon?"

"I did, my lady. He said the man did not sound familiar, nor had he been sent by the royal party in Calais."

How bold a plan, how confident that neither she nor Thomas would question his story. He'd had no letter, no royal seal. She stood aghast at her negligence.

"My lady?"

She took Hugh's hand. "I have so many regrets. But you have been so very steadfast. Thank you. For everything."

Hand to heart, he bowed to her.

In the hall, Ned stood resplendent in velvet and silk, dark colors trimmed with silver. Regal mourning. He seemed uncertain how to greet her, starting to lift his arms to embrace her, but halting mid-gesture.

"It is so good to see you, Ned." She walked into his embrace, holding him for a moment. Then she led him to the table. "Distract me from my remorse, my grief, and my worry about my fatherless children."

"They have you, Joan, and that is far more than most children have. You are Countess of Kent, you will now be granted seisin of the estates of the earldom. You've the wealth, the lands, the power to take good care of your children, and you have your family to turn to—you are a Plantagenet."

Joan looked at the large, calloused hand he'd placed over her own cold, trembling one. His rings proclaimed his wealth and status, and reminded her that he was right; she was not one of the disenfranchised widows she had encountered in France. Soon she would return to her estates, see her children, find a life in them.

"I should be with them."

"I'll arrange your journey home."

She softly thanked him. "But Simon . . . he let Thomas die, Ned, he hastened—" She paused and breathed to clear her head. "How did he know we would accept him? Who helped him? It is as if he knew that Efa stayed behind at the last minute."

"No doubt there are spies at home. We have them here. Thomas made many enemies."

"Doing your father's bidding."

"We will find him, Joan. I swear to you, I will avenge Thomas's untimely death. But your place now is with your children. Only you can comfort them."

He had leaned close, but now sat back, quietly waiting as the servants brought the food. He looked weary, his eyes heavy-lidded, his posture not as sharp as was his custom. He looked more like the old Ned. Human. Vulnerable.

"Thomas's burial," she said. "He wished to be buried in the church of the Greyfriars in Stamford."

"I have made arrangements. The Church of the Friars Minor in Rouen will hold Thomas's coffin in a stone sarcophagus in the undercroft until the Greyfriars are ready to receive him in Stamford. I shall arrange for the journey, with several of Thomas's men accompanying him, led by Sir Hugh, and, of course, several of the friars. This is my mourning gift to you, cousin. I pray you will accept it."

"All the way to Lincolnshire?" Coffin. Sarcophagus. Mourning. She did not like those words. She drank more wine to flush away the taste, but it lingered.

"Will you accept?"

"Yes. You are most generous."

"You can return to England directly after Thomas's requiem Mass."

Leaving her beloved behind. She fought tears. She still listened for a cry of surprise and one of Thomas's men rushing in with the news that their lord yet lived.

Softly, Ned said, "Joan, your children already missed you at Christmas. You must go to them."

"Christmas?"

"It was four days ago."

She counted backward. "Thomas died on the Feast of the Holy Innocents." She lifted her hand to cross herself, but dropped it. Prayer had not saved Thomas; God was not listening. She wanted to close her eyes and join Thomas, be done with this purgatory.

"Your children are innocents, Joan. They need their mother."

Did he still know her so well that he could guess her thoughts? She nodded. Of course, he was right.

By his quietly reassuring presence, Ned supported her through the long ordeal of separation—Thomas's shrouded body lifted into a wooden casket, the slow procession through the streets of Rouen to the friary, the moment when she must walk away from her beloved, leaving him in the hands of the friars, strangers, men who'd not known Thomas's goodness. As he had when she'd run from her life and tumbled into the hole, Ned stood watch by her during those first nights when she feared sleep, feared touching Thomas's spirit and finding him changed, no longer needing her, no longer wanting her. In a chair by her bed, the hero of Poitiers slept, guarding her from the creatures of the night as he'd once guarded her from Will. This time she was grateful.

ON THE LAST DAY IN NORMANDY, JOAN WALKED IN ON HELENA AND Janet packing the chests for the journey. Thomas's favorite jacket and a worn pair of his boots lay beside an open chest. Dear God, he would never wear them again. With a sob, Joan sank to her knees, gathering Thomas's things to her. "Leave me," she whispered. Until now she had been strong, and, once home, she must be again. But here she could rock and keen her grief, giving in to her sorrow.

49

Kennington Palace
JANUARY 1361

On the eve of her departure for home, Joan received Sir John Chandos, who told her that his men had caught Simon riding west and questioned him. He'd been hired by the Breton captain who had thought to take her captive in Brittany, whose citadel Thomas's men had burned.

"Bring him to me. I want to hear his confession," she said. "I want to curse him to his face."

"My lady, he had something on him when captured, some poison. He was already slurring his words when we questioned him, and by nightfall he was dead. I am sorry."

"Then his captain."

Sir John bowed. "We will do our utmost to find him, my lady, but you yourself know all too well the chaos of the countryside."

"I do. But I pray your men do not use that as an excuse to neglect their duty." She saw that her words stung, and quickly assured him that she did not question his honor. She needed him. Ned had returned to Calais, and her own men, Thomas's men, were already across the Channel, heading for Lincolnshire.

"I am at your service, my lady." Sir John bowed again, hand to heart.

On her own crossing, Joan felt as alone and vulnerable as she had so long ago on board the ship to Ghent. Until Thomas befriended her. How warm he had been, how strong and steadfast, how safe she had felt in his presence. Even the company of Helena and all who had been so kind could not comfort her. She withdrew into silence, sunk in remorse for all the choices that had led to Thomas's death by malicious neglect, sick with the frustration of being denied a chance to confront his murderer.

Ned's steward Sir Richard Stafford met her at the dock in Portsmouth to escort her to Westminster, where she was to see to the legal matters involved in taking seisin of her estates. As they rode, he regretfully informed her of a troubling situation with her property, requiring extensive politics to undo. "My lord Prince Edward has instructed me to see to recovering all of it, which might prove a lengthy process."

"Undo what?"

He claimed that Thomas had signed over properties in a way that removed them from Joan's control in the event of his death abroad. She could not imagine Thomas being such a fool. He had been inexperienced in such matters, it was true, but he had hired good lawyers and stewards, many of them recommended by Ned and Queen Philippa.

"I am sorry to distress you so in your mourning, my lady. Rest assured, we will correct this," said Sir Richard.

She accepted his apology and suggested that they ride the rest of the way in silence. She would consult with Blanche. Together they would get to the bottom of all this and make it right.

NED HAD ARRANGED FOR HER TO BIDE IN HIS PALACE OF KENNINGton while untangling the legal mess, Westminster being a brief ferry ride across the Thames. She'd remembered it as a modest country home, but as they approached up a long drive planted with young trees, a grand palace appeared, bustling with building works—a surprising amount of activity in winter, as if Ned were preparing for a state event.

"It would seem you have sufficient work providing the funds for all this," she said to Stafford. "My cousin is spending a fortune on his grand estate."

"He will one day be king, my lady," Stafford said, as if that explained all.

"One day years from now, God willing, so why this haste? Has he a wife in mind?"

"I have heard no such rumor, my lady."

As Joan entered the yard, a small group stepped through the hall door. God in heaven, they were here—Blanche, Maud, Efa with Jeannette in her arms. She had not hoped to see them until she went north for Thomas's burial. Her heart lifted. Calling impatiently for a groom to assist her in dismounting, Joan then rushed to her daughters, gathering them in her arms, showering them with kisses. Then Blanche, and finally Efa. "If only you had been with us," she sobbed in her nurse's ear.

Her sons arrived later that day, and only then did she tell them all of their father's death. Maud's wail began the dirge, Jeannette's following hard on, though the baby was merely alarmed by her sister's emotion, could not possibly comprehend her loss. Then Tom's "No!," a shout that trembled, then collapsed in a sob. John went running, head lowered, his arms pumping, down the steps from the hall and out along the river. Joan sent two guards to follow at a discreet distance.

"He's just disappointed his uncle Ned isn't here to spoil him," Maud muttered.

"Hush, my love. It is just his way of grieving," Joan whispered, holding her daughter close.

Stamford
FEBRUARY 1361

JOAN STOOD BESIDE THOMAS'S TOMB OF ALABASTER, MARBLE, AND iron, her children clustered round her, tearfully watching as Thomas's brother Robert, Sir Hugh, Sir Roland, and Ned lifted the coffin onto the marble slab. Maud reached for Joan's hand, no doubt frightened by the grief on the men's faces. Robert and Hugh came to stand on either side of her, Ned behind, resting a hand on her shoulder. Joan shrugged it off, shaking her head. She sensed Thomas's presence expanding to surround her and the children, embracing them with love as his soul began to take its leave. This was a private, loving moment that Ned could not share.

LADY BLANCHE HAD NOTICED THAT SHRUG WITH SATISFACTION. But as soon as the ceremony ended Joan turned to the prince, seeming to welcome his arm round her as they exited the church together, and, as they paused outside, she leaned her head against her cousin's shoulder and he looked down at her with unguarded tenderness. Blanche felt the urge to warn her niece. She disliked how Joan's children clung to the prince, how they loved him. Any future stepfather must needs compete against the great hero of Poitiers, future king of the realm. That tender moment as they left the church told a troubling tale.

And there was more. Blanche's lawyers kept coming up against road blocks that only a royal seal could clear, and now the prince's seal was all over Joan's properties. By design? She'd heard, as well, of Thomas's last words, confided by Joan as an explanation for her seeming dependence on the prince and his household. All well and good if his parents agreed to the match, but, considering the queen's former fear of just such an outcome of their childhood closeness, Blanche did not see an honorable resolution. So what was the prince's game? And Joan's?

Woking
LATE WINTER 1361

WHILE BLANCHE'S LAWYERS FOUGHT ON, JOAN TOOK REFUGE NEAR Westminster at the home of her brother's widow, Elizabeth of Juliers, now remarried despite an ill-advised vow of celibacy. At the naïve age of thirteen, Elizabeth had taken the vow, then several years later fell in love with a Hainaulter in Ned's entourage, Eustache d'Auberchicourt. In retribution for the broken vow, the archbishop of Canterbury had enjoined the couple to provide charity to six poor people after carnal copulation, and to abstain from the dish of flesh or fish they most hungered for. Once a year, Elizabeth had to journey on foot to the shrine of St. Thomas of Canterbury, and once a week she was to take no food except bread and a mess of potage. She declared it all worth it. All of Woking knew when they'd coupled, and prayed they did it frequently. Elizabeth laughed to tell the tale, though Sir Eustache was notably absent, and had been for months.

Joan enjoyed her sanguine humor, and the freedom of not being beholden to Ned for all her comfort. He had steered her through a difficult time, while tactfully keeping his distance as she grieved with her children, and she was grateful. But now, though she still woke each morning with a prayer that Thomas's death had been a terrible dream, she was ready to stand on her own two feet. In truth, she missed her own household staff and planned to return to Donington as soon as she was no longer needed here.

Ned, however, was reluctant to let her go. Within a week of

Joan's move to Woking, he called on her. Elizabeth invited him to dine with them.

"He is wooing you," Elizabeth teased as they stood in the hall door after the meal, watching Ned ride from the yard. "You most fortunate of women! Prince Edward, the hero of Crécy and Poitiers, our future king. And such a man. Those eyes, those shoulders." She gave a happy shiver and hugged Joan.

"As a result of one dinner you have him crowning me? You make too much of a cousin's visit." Her own hasty denial unsettled Joan.

Elizabeth ignored it. "The way to know your heart is to lie with him. That is how I chose Eustache." She smiled at the memory. "Not so beautiful as your brother, but experienced."

Ned returned the following day, and the next, bringing presents, smoothing out the legal wrangles, leaving after dinner.

As Efa massaged her shoulders one night, Joan asked what she thought.

"That he loves you I've no doubt, my lady. Fiercely."

"Fierce love? I don't know how I like that, except in the act." Joan smiled, but looking over her shoulder she saw that Efa did not find it humorous. "I have felt so close to him since Thomas's death. He's been gentle, attentive. I almost wish— Efa, I've thought how safe my family would be if Ned were to me what Earl William was to Mother, my lover and protector."

"And you know what he wants. That you should be his queen."

"Impossible."

"Perhaps. But whatever you do, my lady, do not tease him. The prince, for all his tenderness for you, is not a man to trifle with."

Was she trifling with Ned?

To put some distance between them and have a chance to breathe, Joan accepted an invitation to spend a fortnight with

Queen Philippa at Windsor. The queen had been seriously injured a few years earlier in a fall while riding and seldom traveled about her kingdom now, so she entertained often. Joan was
shocked to see her halting gait and how carefully her clothes
were cut to compensate for her twisted posture. This cleverness
was the work of a new lady of the chamber, Alice Perrers, an
elegant young widow of whom the queen seemed very fond
despite her merchant background. The king, too. Philippa was
eager to introduce Joan to the young widow, suggesting they
might comfort each other in their mourning.

"Perhaps she would be more comfortable among her own
people while in mourning," Joan suggested to Philippa.

The queen dismissed the idea. "She is precisely where she
needs to be, my dear Joan. As are you. I understand Ned has a
small army of lawyers untangling your affairs. I am sorry that
Edward kept Thomas so often away. Of course you had no one
to oversee your stewards in your absence. You are quite alone
now. Please consider us your family, my dear."

Joan found herself enfolded in a warm embrace. She'd been
about to remind Philippa that she'd had advisors overseeing her
stewards, advisors she herself had recommended. But instead
she found herself blinking back tears. Joan had come to Windsor to cleanse her heart of Ned, but being there summoned
memories of him at every turn. And Philippa's affectionate welcome disarmed her.

On the day that Ned came to Woking to announce that all
was resolved and she might go where she pleased, instead of
relief Joan was struck by a wave of sadness. Wishing to cover
her confusion while she regained her composure, she suggested
a walk in the winter garden. It had begun to snow, fat flakes
lazily floating down.

The path led through a high hedge. Once out of sight of the

house, Ned turned to her, tipping up her chin. "Tears, cousin? Are you not pleased to be free of me?" He bent to kiss her, a long, searching kiss that left her breathless and trembling with the passion of her response. "I pray you, Joan, tell me your heart."

She'd not been sure of the wisdom of Thomas's last words until the kiss, uncertain whether she wanted Ned as a lover. But she did. She could not bear to walk away. With shaking hands she removed one of Ned's gloves and kissed his palm. "Come to me tonight."

He cupped her face. "But what do you mean by this?"

"For now, I would lie with you. What comes after I can't say."

"Just that?"

"For now, Ned." When he began to protest, she put a finger to his lips. "Come to me?"

He took her hand, kissed it, and bowed. "Look for me at midnight."

NED BROUGHT INTO HER CHAMBER THE SCENT OF SNOW. JOAN slipped from the bed, barefoot and wearing only a silk chemise.

"You are wet."

"I walked the yard a hundred times, waiting for the time to depart. I cannot believe I'm here, in your chamber."

She helped him undress, feeling shy with him, never having known him in this way, in this different intimacy. As she moved about him he stole kisses, ran his hands over her breasts, her hips, finally lifting the chemise over her head so that they stood naked, face to face. Her flesh burned under his gaze, and she saw that he, too, was aroused. But he stayed her, lifting up a mazer of spiced wine.

"Let us drink to our union, speak our intention."

"I said I want to lie with you. Then we shall see."

"I want you as my queen."

"Your parents—"

"They dare not cross me. Tomorrow I will bring a priest, and witnesses."

"Ned, you are dreaming. Come, let us first make love. Then we can talk."

"No! If I beget a child on you, I want to keep it. Our perfect child . . ."

"I am in mourning, Ned. Until Thomas's year, mind, I cannot commit to anything."

"But what if you're with child?"

She heard his determination. *Do not trifle with him,* Efa had warned. Heaven help her, she wanted him. "Say the words, then. But we tell no one until we must." And then he would see she was right, the king would find a way to nullify their vows.

Once more Ned lifted up the mazer, and now he spoke his intention. His vow curled round her, an incantatory spell, binding her to him. She heard herself answering him, her words like a gentle breeze chilling her, drawing her to him for warmth.

Waking at dawn, alone in the great bed, Joan waited for the rush of grief that had met her waking for months. But this morning her body tingled, and the memory of their lovemaking brought a smile. God help her, she actually prayed they might prevail.

"Are you awake, my lady?" Efa bent over the brazier, stirring something in a little pot. "You must drink this first thing."

The herbs to prevent conception. Joan pushed them away. "We pledged our troth. He is returning this morning with a priest."

The frown flitted across Efa's brow so quickly that Joan almost missed it. "And how long will you need to conceal your marriage, my lady? His sons' legitimacy must never be questioned."

"Swear to me that he will never know."

"Never, my lady."

Joan drank down the bitter brew.

"He pleased you?"

Joan tried a little smile. "Fiercely."

Efa relaxed. "Then it is well done."

Ned returned in the afternoon, with a priest and his brother John to join Elizabeth as witness.

As Joan waited to pledge her troth to Ned, she felt Thomas near, his warmth at her back, encouraging her to move forward into this new life. For a heartbeat she hesitated, wanted to sink backward into Thomas's arms.

"Joan?" Ned whispered.

All eyes were upon her, and Thomas's breath was on her neck, coaching her to speak the words that would ensure their children the prince's protection. She spoke the words, embraced Ned, feeling his love, his devotion. It was well done.

50

Donington Castle
LATE MARCH 1361

The pestilence was stirring again, taking in late winter Henry, Duke of Lancaster, Blanche's brother. The seemingly invincible Henry of Grosmont, King Edward's most trusted commander. Joan accompanied her aunt to Leicester for the state funeral, both of them bowed beneath memories of the summer they had lost Thomas Wake and Margaret.

Ned, accompanying the king and queen, honored Joan's wish that they give each other a wide berth. But they both found it difficult, catching glimpses, smiles, finding excuses to pass closely.

Though she was deep in mourning, Blanche noticed, and reminded Joan how closely Philippa had always watched her in the presence of her eldest son. On the journey back to Donington, Joan confessed. Blanche's exclamation set her horse dancing and she called the company to a halt, dismounting to take Joan aside.

"You are not so naïve, niece! You know how they twist our lives."

"I love him, Aunt. I want to be with him. *Thomas* wanted this, to protect our children."

"He feared for your safety, I know. But this is not the answer, Joan. Philippa and Edward will never agree. You risk all that you have fought for."

Joan was no longer so sure of that. Someone had made a casual remark at the funeral feast that now Ned's brother John, who had married Henry's daughter, was certain to be named Duke of Lancaster, enriching himself immensely. Philippa had smiled proudly. "Lionel and John married wealth and power, Ulster and Lancaster. Now my eldest must needs wed a queen to best them." She had looked straight at Joan.

"Have you someone in mind?" Bella had asked, clearly goading her mother. Philippa had waved her hand as if to say she was not ready to comment, but her smile taunted Joan, and she remembered the embrace at Windsor.

"Ned will protect us, Aunt, whether I am his wife or his mistress. And I do love him."

Blanche gave her a long, searching look. "Not as you did Thomas."

It was true. Ned did not steady her as Thomas had, nor was he as selflessly kind. "It is different. I know him better than I did Thomas. I hardly remember a time Ned was not in my life."

"And the incident with Bruno?"

That had been the most difficult part. "If God can forgive, who am I to refuse to do so?"

"Hmm . . . I see that the fire is lit within you. How will you live?"

"As Countess of Kent. Or Princess of Wales. That is up to my cousin the king. I've banned Ned from Donington for now, while the sickness threatens. I'm keeping the children close to me, in Efa's care. He has promised to tell his parents by St. George's Day."

"I shall look out for earthquakes and bloody portents in the skies. Though at least Isabella is not here to poison it." Blanche sighed. "I pray you know what you are about."

Windsor Castle
LATE APRIL 1361

Philippa chose a perfect spring morning on which to invite Joan for a conversation in the rose garden. A gauzy pavilion suggested shade, Italian glass in enchanting blues held the watered wine, the fruits and cakes. She had to admit, her daughter-in-law looked the part of a queen as she approached, softly swathed in green and blue silk, her hair catching the sunlight, the loose strands curling prettily around her pale neck, teasing the cleft between her generous breasts. She'd taken to wearing low-cut bodices, a new style for her that had men walking into servants, spilling wine, generally making fools of themselves. So many would be disappointed when they learned that she had already remarried.

"Your Grace."

Philippa averted her eyes from Joan's bosom as she bowed. "I wouldn't lean over quite so far if I were you, my dear," she said. "Come, sit down, daughter." A startled glance. How alert she was, to catch that last word. "Yes, I know all about it. I should have expected it."

"Do we have your blessing, Your Grace?"

"Does it matter?" It didn't. Edward and Ned had returned from Calais so smitten by the idea that she'd known better than to waste her breath protesting. She'd reminded herself of her affection for and gratitude toward Joan's father, Edmund of Kent, the first one to befriend her at court. And she had grown closer to the young woman in recent years. Indeed, Joan had the grace and intelligence Ned would need in a queen. She shook her head. "No, you needn't answer that. Just tell me this. Do you love him?"

"I would be a fool not to." She spoke of how kind and generous he'd been when Thomas died, how her children loved him, how particularly good he was with her son John, who reminded her of Ned as a boy, imperious, believing rules did not pertain to him. "Ned has been good for him. He understands."

It did not escape Philippa that Joan had not answered her question. "You love him for all this, of course, but what of your heart? Is he as dear to you as Thomas was?" Joan had fought for that one for nine years. Would she have done so for Ned?

"I don't understand—you have always worried about my loving Ned, Your Grace. And now that I have pledged myself to him, you doubt me?"

"I am a fond mother, worried about the happiness of my firstborn. When you face your Tom's intended, you will understand." She patted Joan's hand. "In truth, I imagine your father smiling down on you. With this marriage, you will mend the terrible rift Isabella caused in this family."

That night, Philippa confided in Edward that she believed Joan was marrying their son for the sake of the children only, that she did not particularly *like* Ned.

Edward laughed. "You often don't like me! It is the way with men and women. It's the bed sport that matters, and Ned tells me that is very good indeed. Don't worry." When she did not laugh, he said that he was certain Joan loved Ned, always had, and reminded Philippa of Joan's experience in Brittany and Normandy. "She is just the wife for him as he works to unite the Aquitaine."

That much was true, and she had noticed a change in Ned, a softening, more laughter, as if Joan brought him a confidence that allowed him to relax the heroic posture off the field. Perhaps she just had a habit of distrusting Joan. She would work on that.

ONCE THE KING AND QUEEN GAVE THEIR BLESSING, THEY INSISTED that all should be finalized as soon as the papal dispensation was received. Ned would soon take up his duties as Duke of

Aquitaine and Joan must be with him. But, more important, Philippa and Edward were anxious to legitimize the marriage bed.

"Surely it is little to ask, Joan, when we feared they would never agree?"

Joan distrusted how quickly the king and queen had agreed to their marriage. "Why such haste? We have vowed to stay apart until we wed. Do they not trust us?"

Ned promised to observe Thomas's first-year obit on the Feast of the Holy Innocents with a full service, almsgiving, and a royal feast. "His children will see with what respect we honor their father's memory."

"I will hold you to that. Every year."

"Every year, my love."

By the end of summer, Ned had cleared all foreseeable arguments against her crowning, seeing to yet another papal bull acknowledging the legitimacy of her marriage to Thomas so that no one could claim bigamy, as Will yet lived. The king had dissolved their initial marriage, and petitioned the pope for the dispensation for Ned to wed his cousin.

Windsor
OCTOBER 1361

THE FORMAL ESPOUSAL WAS CELEBRATED ON 6 OCTOBER, BOTH Joan's and Ned's households wearing his livery of green and white, with his ostrich plumes and her white hart prominent motifs in the decorations of Windsor's great hall. The celebration lasted long into the night.

For the first time, Joan and Ned shared a bedchamber in the castle. It was there she had dressed in the morning, but while they had entertained their guests the chamber had been transformed into a nighttime woodland, with the white hart the centerpiece of the great bed. She gasped at the discovery. Helena and Efa quickly prepared her to receive her prince, then departed. There was a moment, as Helena glanced back, when Joan remembered the chamber in Katarina's home, how nervous she'd been, how Thomas had reassured her.

The memory dissolved as Ned stepped through the side door, shedding his cloak, revealing his gorgeous nakedness. "Do you like the room?"

"I feel I've walked into a dream." Ned's arms encircled her from behind and he held her close, his breath stirring her hair, warming her, as Thomas might have done. "I never want to wake up. Never," she said, turning in his arms.

FOUR DAYS LATER A MUCH LARGER, MORE FORMAL GATHERING WITnessed their marriage in St. George's Chapel, at Windsor, officiated by Archbishop Islip. Joan wore a deep scarlet gown of finest silk, so heavily embroidered with gold thread and powdered with gems that it weighed her down, as did the magnitude of her decision. All her life she had run away from the royal household, and now she was joining it in a most intimate way.

Two days earlier, Ned had laughed as he recounted to Joan how Islip had originally doubted, then retreated in apologies. "Had I worn a sword when he questioned your honor, I would have drawn it and committed a grave sin. How dare he." Like quicksilver, Ned's moods, darkening like a sudden summer storm when his honor was questioned, brightening with breathtaking speed when his opponent was vanquished. "We considered every angle with great care before I ever approached you."

"We?"

He'd kissed away the question.

Now, standing beside Ned, regal in red brocade and cloth of gold, she remembered that "we" and hesitated before speaking her vows. But he looked on her with such love. Surely only good could come of this. She straightened, once more vowing to obey him unto death. When they kissed the bells rang out, and she looked up to behold a face that she loved so well, she could not see how she would ever have denied him.

51

Berkhamsted Castle
NOVEMBER 1361

Maud was like a tinderbox when her brother John was around, and he her spark. She resented him for the long scar on her arm, a reminder of the accident that had kept Efa in England, a change of plans that she blamed for her father's death. Their arguments were legion, and Joan seldom paid them any heed. But one morning she came upon them fighting over a piece of cloth, their faces red with the effort, her daughter shrieking that John was a thief, a sneak, a murderer.

"What is this?"

Startled, Maud lost her hold and John stuffed the piece behind his back.

"Give it to me, son." Joan held out her hand.

He backed away. She might have left it but for the look on his face—trapped, frightened. She lunged for him, twisting the cloth out of his grasp. God help her. It was Thomas's white hart silk. Her hands went cold. "Where did you get this?"

"I found it in his chest," said Maud. She began to cry. "It was Father's, wasn't it? His protection."

"How did you come to have it, John?" Joan demanded.

"Found it."

"When? Where?"

He shrugged, then suddenly shouted, "I hate you, both of you!" and ran out of the room.

Joan sank down on a bench, dumbstruck. Her daughter climbed up beside her, putting an arm around her. "He said Uncle Ned gave it to him and told him to keep it hidden."

Ned. Joan's mind spun as she consoled her daughter, assuring her that the prince had not meant her father harm, nor had John, and silently praying that it was true. She took her doubts to Efa, who whispered something in Welsh and bowed her head.

"I am so afraid, Efa. I don't want to know. If Ned planned it. Simon, the ambush . . . He had the power." Thomas's accused murderer had not been found.

"You must confront him with the cloth, my lady. Look in his eyes. There is every chance he is innocent. But you will never know if you don't ask."

Joan brought it out that night, as they shared a mazer of wine before sleep.

Ned sucked in his breath and looked away. "I'm sorry you've seen it."

"So am I. Now tell me why you took this."

"It's so long ago."

"Not so long you don't remember."

"It dropped as his squire was helping him with his armor on the day he was made earl. No one noticed. I'd always wanted it—you know what it meant to me. So I took it."

She slapped him. So hard her hand tingled. "What right had you?"

"Do you think I'm so callous I haven't felt a twinge of guilt? But surely a piece of silk holds little power over life and death. Thomas was frail, Joan. Fading."

"What else did you do to speed his death, Ned? What else to clear the way?"

"Joan, my love. I did nothing. Nothing. Faith, I love you, but I would not dishonor myself for you."

"But you did by taking the silk."

He hung his head. "I've done penance every day since—for my weakness, my selfishness. And when Thomas died—God help me, I knew I must make it right, I must take care of you and the children. I must do this for him."

Her head spun. He spoke from his heart, she felt that, but such an act. Such consequences. "Why give it to John? Was Maud's injury—"

"No! How could you think such a thing of your son?"

He'd responded too quickly. "Then why?"

"John is not so unfeeling as he pretends. When you and Thomas returned to Normandy, he missed you. See? I loved him even then, all four of your children. I have always wanted the best for them." Ned reached for her.

She leaned away. "I want to believe you, Ned. But this—" She held up the silk, shaking it at him.

He grasped her wrist, brought her hand to his mouth, kissed it. "You must believe me, Joan. I love you more than my life."

It was a familiar feeling, wanting to believe Ned, feeling sick that she thought him capable of such cruelty. "You would swear before a priest?"

He did not hesitate. "I would swear before the Holy Father himself. Look what I've given you, Joan. I've restored your family's honor, and Thomas's. You will be queen. *My queen*. Just as I promised so long ago, that night beneath our tree. Remember?"

Then, it had been a comfort. Now?

"Joan, please. Forgive me. Let me have the silk. I'll wear it as a penance."

She hid it behind her back. "No."

He bowed his head, pressing it into her shoulder, a gesture familiar from their childhood when she'd found him out. And, more recently, when he confessed to drowning Bruno. She felt a panic rising. What had she done?

"I would do anything for you, Joan. Anything. I will walk

barefoot to Canterbury in penance. Forgive me. It was such a little thing. Your heart was in that square. I knew what it meant to you. When I saw it there ... I am only human, Joan. I'd waited so long."

There was no going back. She had pledged him her troth, knowing he walked in darkness. She had wanted him so—it was not just for the sake of her children. Now he was hers, in all his complexity. And she was Princess of Wales, Duchess of the Aquitaine, and would someday be Queen of England. It was what he had promised her. He'd never wavered.

God forgive me.

Acknowledgments

I wish to thank Anthony Goodman for bringing Joan of Kent to life for me. Tony's notes toward a biography of Joan, his thoughtful and thorough answers to my questions by letter and e-mail, and our enthusiastic discussions about her over lunches in York, our special city, breathed life into a woman who intrigued but mystified me. How I shaped her story will undoubtedly surprise him; I foresee some lively arguments on my next visit.

I am blessed with an abundance of fine historians working in the field of fourteenth-century studies: Richard Barber, Lisa Benz St. John, Hugh Collins, Mark Ormrod, Clifford Rogers, Jonathan Sumption, Juliet Vale, and Martin Vale to name just the ones whose books and articles on the period covered in this novel spent the most time on my desk during the past several years, bristling with book darts. As always, I am grateful for the welcome I've received in the Society of the White Hart sessions at the annual Medieval Congress in Kalamazoo.

My heartfelt thanks to Laura Hodges and Joyce Gibb for thorough readings of several drafts of this book, to Lorraine Stock for hunting down a crucial article for me, and to Mary Evans for encouraging me all along the way. And to my editors Suzanne O'Neill and Anna Thompson for guiding me all along the way, Kim Silverton for shepherding the book through the final stages with such grace, Dyana Messina for painless publicity, and Sarah Pekdemir for making marketing fun.

And most of all, I am grateful to my husband, Charlie, for all his support behind the scenes. He is my anchor.

Author's Note

Small details shaped the story you have just read. (I hope you are not cheating and reading this before the novel. You'll be sorry!) The project grew out of my curiosity about Joan's wish to be buried with Thomas Holland, not Edward the Black Prince. It seemed out of place in the usually accepted story of Joan's and Edward's marriage being a romantic happily-ever-after union. I quickly realized I needed to understand how she came to wed Thomas Holland in the first place.

In spring 1340 a proposed betrothal was recorded between Margaret, "daughter of Edmund of Kent," and "Armand," the eldest son of Bernard, lord of Albret, a liaison that would benefit King Edward, creating for him a solid ally in Gascony. As there is no record of Joan having a sister, it is likely the names of Joan and her mother were confused, as they had been in another document, and it was Joan who was to be betrothed to Armand. Nothing more is ever said about this union. I was intrigued. What happened? Clearly she never married him. Why? What if she'd found someone to hand, preferably someone she already liked very much, and convinced him to rescue her? In Thomas Holland's later testimony before the papal committee investigating his claim to be Joan's rightful husband, he stated that their marriage took place in spring 1340. This was something I could work with.

I connected Joan's proposed marriage to Arnaud Amanieu (I chose to use this alternate spelling of his name in the book) to a possibility historian Anthony Goodman suggested during one of our long lunches in York, that Joan might have accompanied the royal family to the Low Countries before her betrothal to Will Montagu—"might," because we have no firm record of Joan in those years. Sending Joan to join the royal family in Antwerp and Ghent gave me the opportunity to explore the crown's financial difficulties and Joan's growing understanding of her expected role as a Plantagenet as well. On foreign soil, far from her mother's protection, Joan needed to be her own advocate. The politics became personal. Her decision to marry in secret, and so young, made far more sense to me.

Tony is also responsible for Joan's sister-in-law's appearance toward the end of the book. I wondered how Edward and Joan managed to find the privacy for their love affair and secret marriage; Tony said he liked to think Elizabeth's house in Sussex might have provided a convenient love nest, and she would be in character in encouraging their liaison—after all, she had chosen to follow her heart despite having taken a vow of celibacy. And to be honest, Elizabeth of Julier's story is one of the juiciest and most unexpected items I found in his notes toward a biography of Joan of Kent, notes he generously shared with me when I was still working on Alice Perrers. I could not resist including her.

As for the emblem of the white hart, I knew that Prince Edward was said to have had "a bed-covering that displayed the hart encircled with the arms of Kent and Wake, suggesting that the device derived from [King Richard II's] mother,

Joan of Kent," which became the inspiration for King Richard's adoption of the emblem.[1] It is said that "one of [Joan of Kent's] ancestors (according to legend) caught a white stag in Windsor Forest."[2] But I found nothing to suggest whether the ancestors were in her mother's or her father's line, so I chose her father's.

Another famous emblem of the time is of course the garter worn by King Edward's select Knights of the Order of the Garter. For more about the theories regarding its origin, see the two August 2011 posts on my blog, *A Writer's Retreat* (ecampion .wordpress.com), "The Order of Whose Garter?"

In the end, I simply could not find a happily-ever-after for Joan. But I have gained a great deal of respect for her.

A special note on clandestine marriage: The word comes from the Latin *clandestīnus,* meaning secret, hidden. In contemporary use the word implies deception or illicit purpose. But Joan's "clandestine" marriages were both quite legitimate from the moment she spoke her vows—or, more accurately, they were binding. In fourteenth-century England what constituted a valid matrimonial bond according to canon (Church) and civil law was the consent of the partners; the will of the parents, guardians, or lord was secondary. What was required was a verbal exchange of present consent, "I marry you," "I take you"; if the couple exchanged words of future consent, "I will marry you," "I will take you," it was deemed a betrothal, but if followed by intercourse it became a validly contracted marriage. Neither a priest nor a church was necessary to create a binding matrimonial union.

That does not mean such seemingly casual contracts were encouraged or condoned. Both the Church and the state pre-

---

[1] "Richard II and the Visual Arts," Eleanor Scheifele, in *Richard II: The Art of Kingship,* Anthony Goodman and James L. Gillespie, eds., Oxford 2003, p. 258.

[2] *Notes and Queries,* K.R, 29 September 1934, p. 231

ferred the posting of banns and a public ceremony before a priest and witnesses, but for pragmatic reasons: such public marriages went far in preventing bigamous unions or later claims of coercion or misunderstanding—"She heard what she wanted to hear before we lay together."

So when in writing about the Church's attitude toward clandestine marriages, James Brundage's comment about Joan's "bigamous" marriage is a tad misleading: "More prominent offenders, such as Joan Plantagenet, the Fair Maid of Kent, seem to have escaped . . . harsh treatment. Joan entered two clandestine marriages (the second one with the Prince of Wales), as well as a bigamous public marriage, which was ultimately declared invalid by the Roman Rota. While her conduct was scandalous, there is no evidence that she was ever seriously penalized for her marital adventures."[3] Joan's union with Will Montagu was never a legitimate marriage.

And her escape from punishment was not necessarily owing to her status. Consider: "Several examples illustrate ecclesiastical adherence to the standard of upholding clandestine nuptials despite parental wishes. Agnes Nakerer fell in love with a travelling minstrel, John Kent [no relation to our Joan!], and married him secretly in the early fourteenth century. Not only did her parents object, they forced her to deny that marriage and marry a more suitable son-in-law. The minstrel sued to enforce his prior marriage contract, and the Church officials at the ecclesiastical court at York decided against the parents in favor of the minstrel and the young woman's first, valid, nuptials. The record provides no indication that this couple suffered ecclesiastical punishment for the marriage."[4]

---

[3] *Law, Sex, and Christian Society in Medieval Europe,* James A Brundage, University of Chicago Press, 1987, pp. 500-501.

[4] *Stolen Women in Medieval England: Rape, Abduction, and Adultery, 1100—1500,* Caroline Dunn, Cambridge University Press, 2013, p. 109.

Other European countries rejected the legitimacy of such simple vows earlier than England. But it was not until Lord Hardwicke's Act in 1753 that English authorities criminalized clandestine marriage.[5]

Still, Joan knew the enormity of her action when she pledged her troth with Thomas Holland, and so did he. Not only was she the granddaughter of a king, but she was the present king's ward. And her father had been executed—she knew the price one paid for crossing royalty.

And yet she did. Therein lies the tale.

I've assembled an annotated bibliography as a companion to *A Triple Knot*. You can find the link on my website (emma campion.com).

---

[5] Ibid., p. 113

ALSO BY EMMA CAMPION

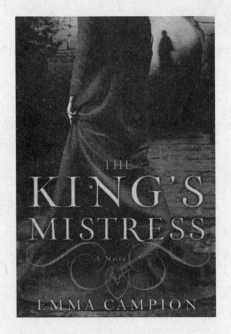

B\D\W\Y
BROADWAY BOOKS
Available wherever books are sold